THE MYSTERY OF THE SS
SOUTHERN CROSS

❧ A NOVEL ❧

Canada Council   Conseil des Arts
for the Arts   du Canada

Canada

 Newfoundland
Labrador

We gratefully acknowledge the financial support of the Canada Council for the Arts,
the Government of Canada through the Canada Book Fund (CBF),
and the Government of Newfoundland and Labrador through the Department
of Tourism, Culture and Recreation for our publishing program.

Printed on acid-free paper
Cover Design by Todd Manning
Layout by Joanne Snook-Hann

Published by
KILLICK PRESS
an imprint of CREATIVE BOOK PUBLISHING
a Transcontinental Inc. associated company
P.O. Box 8660, Stn. A
St. John's, Newfoundland and Labrador A1B 3T7

Printed in Canada

Library and Archives Canada Cataloguing in Publication

Rogers, Tim, 1942-, author
    The mystery of the SS Southern Cross / Tim Rogers.

ISBN 978-1-77103-031-1 (pbk.)

    1. Southern Cross (Ship)--Fiction. 2. Shipwrecks--
Newfoundland and Labrador--Fiction. I. Title.

PS8635.O4275M98 2014   C813'.6   C2014-901356-6

THE MYSTERY OF THE SS
SOUTHERN CROSS

⊰ A NOVEL ⊱

killick press
an imprint of Creative Publishers

St. John's, Newfoundland and Labrador
2014

To Ted and Maureen Rowe,
in thanks for their boundless encouragement, generosity and hospitality

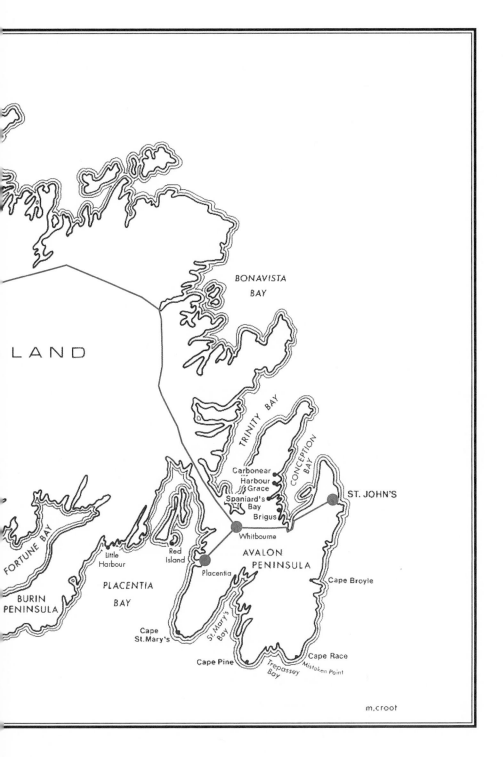

BONAVISTA
BAY

LAND

TRINITY BAY

CONCEPTION BAY

Carbonear
Harbour
Grace
Spaniard's
Bay
Brigus

ST. JOHN'S

Whitbourne

AVALON
PENINSULA

FORTUNE BAY

Little
Harbour

Red
Island

Placentia

Cape Broyle

PLACENTIA
BAY

BURIN
PENINSULA

Cape
St.Mary's

St. Mary's
Bay

Cape Pine

Trepassey
Bay

Cape Race
Mistaken Point

m,croot

ABOUT THE CD

The CD included with this book contains recordings of music related to the Newfoundland seal hunt. Most of the tracks were written during that time and they all provide a vivid window into that period in history. Detailed notes about the songs and performers can be found in the epilogue.

ONE

Abel Lundrigan was taken aback by the limpness of the mortician's hand-shake and the softness of his palm. His own great fisherman's paw, calloused from years of hauling nets, dwarfed the meagre hand offered by the sombre gentleman dressed in a black jacket and striped trousers. The two were standing on the front steps of the Seaman's Institute in St. John's that, as of yesterday, had become the temporary mortuary for corpses from the disaster of the SS *Newfoundland*. Seventy-seven sealers had perished on the ice.

The mortician motioned Abel into the entry alcove, out of the midday drizzle. "And you'd be...?" he asked in a practiced whisper.

"Lundrigan," Abel answered, pulling a crumpled copy of *The Evening Telegram* from his pocket. The paper was folded open to a page entitled 'Names of Those Who Succumbed to the Ravages of the Storm.' He pointed to the name 'Jno. Lundrigan, Red Island P.B.' "That's my son, John. He was on the *Newfoundland*. I've come to see him." Abel's voice faltered.

"Ah, yes. Please follow me." The mortician led Abel through the heavy wooden door, held open by an old-timer who refused to look at them as they passed. The pair creaked up the wooden stairs to an open lobby, Abel clinging to the sculpted wooden banister. Groups of people lingered around overstuffed chairs and sofas along the walls. Muted weeping filled the room.

The man pointed toward a double door. Abel hesitated. The mortician turned and, with a glance, urged the fisherman to proceed. "This is the mortuary," he said softly, "there's no time for delay." Abel took a deep breath and walked forward into the hall.

The smell of death assaulted him, not the raw smell of dying he had come to know in his years fishing and sealing, but the chemical odour of funerals, that timid effort to hide the realities of decomposing flesh. Formaldehyde. Row after row of coffins stood before him, each supported on chair backs and draped with white sheets. A family of four was huddled around an unsheeted coffin in the corner. Nurses in white uniforms hovered silently among the sheets.

1

Abel's escort whispered something to a nurse and she pulled out a paper stuffed in her starched apron. After reading for a moment, she pointed to the seventh coffin in the second row. Abel's heart stopped. The man went over to the designated casket and beckoned him to come. Hesitantly, Abel followed, careful not to disturb other sheets as he slipped by.

The man motioned for him to stand at the head. Then he leaned over and took the sheet corners.

Abel drew a deep breath as the sheet was pulled back to reveal a crude spruce coffin. Then he saw the corpse, face white, eyes closed, freshly combed sandy hair. The fisherman gasped. He buried his face in his hands. "Oh, my God," he moaned. "Oh, my God."

The man touched his shoulder. "I'm so sorry, Mr. Lundrigan."

"Sorry? There's no need to be sorry."

The mortician drew back.

Abel struggled to regain his composure. Then he said slowly and with conviction, "That's not my boy." He paused and looked again at the lifeless body. "That's not my son." He pointed toward the colourless face, "That's Peter Lamb, my son's best friend. That's Peter Lamb. It's not John at all. It's not John."

The man gasped.

Abel turned on his heel and left the room. The mortician scurried along behind. "It's not my fault," was the last thing Abel heard, as he turned onto Water Street and began to run.

ii

The sun broke through the clouds and glinted into the front window of a modest house up the back way in Brigus. It exploded onto a crystal vase, scattering small rainbows across the living room ceiling. No sooner had the flashes of coloured light appeared than a passing cloud extinguished them. Charles Jenkins, the Methodist preacher, was sitting in one of the rickety wicker chairs in Lucy Clarke's living room. The darkness of his clothes mirrored the mood of the room.

"Can I get you some tea?" Lucy asked.

"Oh no, my dear, thank you," the preacher said. "I'm so full of tea I couldn't stomach another drop. I've been drinking the stuff all day, working with the families of men lost on the *Newfoundland*. It's no easy job, Lucy, I've just about run out of comfort." He let out a tired groan.

She frowned. Lucy had her own need for comfort today. She was exhausted from worry because her husband's ship, the *Southern Cross*, had not been seen since that huge storm — four days now. "Biggest blizzard of the decade," the papers had said. "Would take a real sailor to get a ship through that wind," was the opinion of the local sea folk. Waiting for news of her husband's ship had been excruciating.

The captain's wife looked fragile as she fidgeted with a lace handkerchief, red eyes cast downward.

2

Jenkins sat up slowly, marshalling what little energy he had left. "My dear," he said, without a great deal of conviction, "there's nothing to fear." He forced a laugh. "Everyone is saying that your husband's ship has simply been blown out to sea, that's all. Sure as the Good Lord is watching over us, George is beating his way home this very minute." He slumped back into his chair as if all the empathy had been drained out of him.

Lucy choked back several sobs while she watched one of the fleeting rainbows come and go. "But there's no news from St. John's or Harbour Grace," she said weakly.

"Patience, my dear, patience," Jenkins said. "There's no need to fret. This delay is just God's way of testing you. It's only a matter of time before George shows up safe and sound." The minister was unwilling to meet Lucy's distraught gaze. "They've sent the *Kyle* out to find her. We'll hear back in a few days, just you watch now." A hitch in his voice betrayed his own concern for the old wooden walled sealer, last seen by the *Portia* at the height of that wild storm. He stood up and, with a very serious air, began to say something, but stopped himself.

Lucy looked at him quizzically.

"Oh, never mind," he said absently. "It wasn't important." Jenkins pulled out his pocket watch and scowled at it. "Oh dear, it's three o'clock, I must see Azariah Munden up in Bull Cove. He's terribly ill and is calling for me."

With a sigh, Lucy stood and led him silently to the front door.

"I'll let you know the minute I hear anything," he said.

She handed him his overcoat. As he slipped it on he pulled out a newspaper and, without saying a word, put it on the table. "God will be with you, my dear, never fear."

Lucy nodded and watched him plod slowly down the front walk. When he was out of sight, she went to the bedroom and picked up a framed photograph of her husband. He had given it to her before leaving for the ice. A burly man, six-foot two, stared back at the camera. He looked uncomfortable in his Sunday suit, hair freshly combed. She smiled, remembering how comical he had been when the portrait was taken. "All done up like a Christmas candy," he said, strutting around in his new brogans. "I hope the boys don't see me all gussied up like this. I'd never hear the end of it." He laughed his big, deep laugh. She looked closer at the photograph. For the first time, she noticed how awkwardly his hands were clenched. "All for the best, I suppose, my dear," he had said, trying to make light of his embarrassment. "We should have at least one good picture for posterity."

"Posterity," Lucy said out loud. "Who cares about posterity? All I want is to have you home, safe in my arms." She took the picture and held it against her breast. The captain's wife rocked back and forth slowly, cotton dress swinging, as though she was putting a baby to sleep. But try as she might, she could not put her growing fear to rest.

She returned to the front room. New clouds shrouded the sky, dousing the rainbows. The captain's wife picked up the newspaper left by the preacher. The front page listed the names of men who had been lost on the *Newfoundland*. Her heart went out to the seventy-seven souls who perished during the great storm. And their families, she could not bear to think about them. The death list was a shock, so long. She looked closer, seeing several names she recognized. Without thinking, Lucy went to the kitchen and sat down at the table. She began to leaf through the paper. When she reached the fourth page she let out a shriek. There was another list. The top name was her husband's, 'George Clarke, Brigus, Master.' With trembling hands she pulled the paper closer. Here was the crew of the *Southern Cross*, all one hundred and seventy-three men, listed in the same typeface, with the same organization, as the seventy-seven lost on the *Newfoundland*. The message of the two lists in the same paper was unmistakable. Even though the experts were holding forth that the *Southern Cross* was safe, the crew list in the paper spoke a different truth, a truth she could no longer deny. George was lost. Even the minister knew and he would not tell her. What else could it all mean? Everyone was saying what she was trying so hard to deny. The *Southern Cross* was gone.

Lucy began to weep, deep wailing sobs. Slowly, the loss of her husband became real. The thought of holding her lover once more to her bosom, hearing his boisterous laugh, slipped away. She stared blankly ahead.

iii

"We're forty-seven miles southwest of Virgin Rocks, Mr. Grieve," the captain said. "The wind is from the west-sou'west, fine weather."

"Thank you, Captain," Walter Baine Grieve said, scanning the smooth ocean from the warmth of the wheelhouse of the SS *Kyle*. No matter where he looked, he could find no sign of his ship, the *Southern Cross*. Even with the help of binoculars, all he could see was the numbing greyness of the North Atlantic.

Despite his white hair and sixty-four years, Grieve appeared energetic as he moved from side to side on the bridge, hoping to see something that would transform into the *Cross*'s familiar three masts and yellow-painted funnel. Deep creases around his eyes were the only evidence of his worry about the vessel he had been sending out on the seal hunt every spring since 1901. Grieve let the binoculars fall against the strap around his neck. "How far have we run now?"

Captain John Snow, young to be in charge of such a fine ship, consulted his notebook. He made several quick calculations. "A hundred and ten miles." He looked up at Grieve and smiled. "We'll be coming about at eleven hundred hours for the second leg of our search."

Grieve nodded. "It's a wonderful thing to have a fine ship like the *Kyle* to look for the *Cross*," he said, glassing the horizon once again. The old merchant carried himself with an aristocratic air, not the kind meant to intimidate others, but a confident manner born of years overseeing men. Success and wealth were evident in every detail of his person: the fine cut of his tweed jacket, understated but clearly elegant; his well-trimmed hair and moustache; shoes that shone like mirrors.

4

"Yes, sir," Snow said, "the *Kyle*'s a first-rate ship. She'll do thirteen and a half knots on a dead sea like this. We'll find your ship sir, never you fret."

"Yes, Captain, I certainly hope so." But Grieve had doubts about ever finding the *Southern Cross*. From all reports, the storm had been ferocious. It was hard to imagine what it would have been like, especially with the sea so calm now, but he knew it would have been terrifying. And the hours were ticking away. It was only a matter of time before they were scouring the sea for flotsam and wreckage to confirm her sinking. He handed the binoculars back to Captain Snow. "Keep up the good work," he said as he left the wheelhouse.

Grieve headed aft. That braggart Archibald Piccott, the Fisheries Minister, was holding court with his entourage of lackeys in the Smoking Room, so he passed by quietly and entered the Music Room. He loved the bird's eye maple panelling and matching grand piano. The plush furniture reminded him of his luxurious premises in St. John's. He lowered himself into in a chair in the corner.

"That you, sir?" a voice asked from behind a pillar.

Grieve startled. "Thomas?"

"Yes sir, over here by the piano." Thomas Collingwood, Grieve's longtime assistant, stood up to show himself. His thinning hair and laboured movement belied the twenty-eight year age difference between them. He appeared to be Grieve's contemporary, rather than his junior. Collingwood looked small in the oversized wool turtleneck sweater he was wearing.

"Don't you look like the common deckhand in that sweater," Grieve said. "Where did you get that outfit?"

"One of the sailors lent it to me, keeps the chill at bay."

"I see, but isn't it beneath you to wear one of those?"

"Can't say as I care, sir. I've been cold ever since we came on board. Better warm than proper."

"I suppose," Grieve said, settling into his neatly upholstered chair.

"May I join you?"

"Certainly."

Collingwood came over and slipped into the chair beside his employer. Several minutes passed before he spoke. "It's a hard wait sir, a hard wait." He paused, looking at Grieve. "I feel so helpless. There's nothing to do."

Grieve nodded. "I'm sorry you had to come along, Thomas. I would have brought Joshua, but I couldn't find him anywhere — very unlike him."

"No matter," Collingwood said with a shrug.

The two looked off toward the empty window.

"You know, Thomas, this whole business about the *Southern Cross* is a real mystery. Why would Clarke head into that storm? Why didn't he shelter up when he saw the weather coming?" Grieve resettled himself in the big chair. "And what happened in the end?"

TWO

In the spring of 1909, Newfoundlanders were enjoying their first hot spell of the year. Placentia, the largest of the island's south-facing bays, was strangely calm in the heat. The sea was at peace, no ground swell, no wind lop. The water was a mirror, stretching out into the North Atlantic as far as the eye could see, reflecting the steel blue sky back on itself. Off the shore of Red Island, which sits mid-bay, the air hung hot around two figures in a small boat. Towering terra cotta cliffs shimmering in the early summer sun loomed over the rodney. Four small cod lay on the floor, eyes gazing blankly upwards, a poor catch for three hours of handlining. The smell of fish, almost sweet in the hot air, hung over the old boat.

Abel Lundrigan sat in the stern. He squinted up at the sheer cliffs and then looked down at John, his eleven-year-old son, seated at the oars. "So still, my son," he said, "it looks like the new ice on a cold morning. Too hot for that though," he added with a lopsided grin. "Don't see it like this too often." Abel stripped off his jacket and stuffed it under his seat. "A real tar-melting day."

The boy nodded and then smiled, brushing away a lock of black hair that had fallen across his face. He was slotting the oars between the two wooden tole pins, proud that his father had asked him to row to a new fishing spot. He was happy to be asked to do a share of the unending work of the sea. He fiddled with the sweeps to get them proper in the pins. Too far out and he could not get a good pull, too far in and they would hit each other ruining the rhythm and bruising his thumbs. Finally, he got them just right and heaved back with all his might. The force against the paddles pulled him clear off the seat. He almost toppled over but kept his balance, eventually levering his ninety-pound frame against the weight of the boat. The rodney lugged forward reluctantly, paddles sending ripples across the yellow-orange reflection of the sun. The second stroke also lifted him off the seat, but this time John anticipated it and managed to keep going. Stroke by awkward stroke he managed a rhythmic squeak, oar binding on tole pin, and felt the boat begin to lumber forward.

"Harder than my row punt," John said, puffing. "These oars are long for me."

"Best thing for you," his father said, "put some beef on those spindly arms of yours. Watch your wake now and keep her straight. "

John inspected the riffle behind the boat and gave the starboard oar a heavier tug to make the right course. He plodded on, each stroke more confident than the last. The boy worked the boat parallel to the watchful terra cotta cliffs shrouded in heat haze.

Abel's old rodney was a perfect reflection of her owner. She was built in the tradition of Red Island's 'western boats' with thick risers that gave her a strong look, squat, but powerful. "Built like a tree trunk," old Daniel Payne said. "She'll take anything the sea throws at her and more." Abel didn't waste any paint on her, but worked to keep her drop dry. "Good at all points," he would say.

Now the father watched his young son trying his best to do a man's job. To Abel, the child looked weak, like a girl, barely a muscle on him; hardly a figure cut out for the tough life that lay ahead. "Row her dry," Abel ordered. "If there's a wind, any splash will end up in your face. Keep her quiet. Come on son, pull strong."

John responded by doing his best to keep the boat moving smartly. Slowly his rowing settled into a cadence and Abel began to relax. The older man rocked back and forth with his son's earnest efforts to pilot the old boat. The strokes and creaks of the paddles in the pins, along with the warmth, lulled Abel's eyes closed.

The boy felt energized as the rhythm of rowing slowly took over. He was surprised when a vague sense of foreboding began to spread through him. It grew and soon he was overwhelmed by a deep fear telling him that something important was about to happen…

He sees a small black spot over the water, just above his father's slumped shoulder. It starts to grow, getting bigger, until he makes out two yellow eyes in the middle, ferocious and treacherous. In slow motion, the black spot transforms into a hideous monster with horns and huge, lumbering wings. Bat-like in its movement, the body is covered with black scales as it zooms toward the boy. The creature's eyes are fastened on him as it sweeps up toward the stern of the old boat. Before John realizes what happens, the monster engulfs him and everything turns black, as though he is inside it. His heart begins to race. Then there is a small white speck in the gloom. It too begins to grow and John sees another creature, like none he has ever seen before. It is a beautiful white bird that feels safe and warm. The bird flies right past the boat and heads straight toward home. He did not know why, but he knew they must get back to the harbour, and quickly. Something terrible was about to happen.

His father jolted him out of his spell when he moved quickly to catch one of the oars before it slipped over the gunwale. John rubbed his eyes. Trembles spread through his small body.

"You've got to row!" he screamed at his father. "I'm too slow. You've got to do it, now, now."

Abel looked surprised and then anger began to well up. "Lord God, can't you do anything right? Is it too much to ask you to do a share of work?" He squared himself in his seat and loomed up before the boy. John cowered. More than a few times he'd felt the force of his old man's violent temper, but knew he must hold fast this time.

"No, it's not that. We've got to get home. Something bad is going to happen. We have to get back, now. We have to. I can't row fast enough." The boy was frantic.

"Lord Jesus, you're more stubborn than your mother. If she was alive now she'd teach you a thing or two about getting work done." The old man stopped, red-faced. He threw his hands up in disgust. "How do you know we should go?"

"I can't say. I just know. Please, please, you row, now."

Abel was about to reply when he was interrupted by the screech of a seagull. He looked up and saw a large flock flying low, directly south. He watched them for a moment. "That's not right," he said under his breath. Abel watched the birds for a moment longer. "Well…" He paused. "Maybe we should head back." He cast a last worried glance over his shoulder, then motioned for John to change places with him. The fisherman raised his hand to cuff the young boy as they slipped past each other, but stopped himself. He settled into his seat. In addition to the extra hundred pounds of weight Abel had to put behind the oars, he now had the energy of his anxiety. Soon the tole pins creaked with sounds that made the boy's efforts sound like timid mice. The boat surged forward, pushing an aggressive bow wave.

John sat in the stern seat facing backwards. He could feel his father's rage burn a hole in the back of his neck. After ten minutes, his father settled into a rhythm. Only then did the boy notice the strange wrinkle on the water. At first he thought it was his father rowing, but soon it was everywhere, a nondescript riffle that crept over the mirrored surface. It was not the cat's paws of coming wind, but a pattern on the water he had never seen before. The wind was dead, but the water was changing.

Out of the corner of his eye he caught a glimmer of movement in the south, over the open ocean. When he looked, all he could see was blue sky over flat water. He noticed a smell that was somehow familiar, but he could not put a name to it. Then he saw a thin line on the sea. It was hard to tell from the horizon at first. Slowly the line rose, as if coming out of the ocean itself. Within minutes the rodney was rolling on a low, lazy swell. John watched the apparition rise, fascinated by how it was going straight up. But then he saw that it was not going upwards at all. It was coming right at them. A great grey cloudbank rushed forward with alarming speed. He then recognized the unmistakable smell of a summer squall, the familiar odour he had sensed before, only now ten times stronger. Such storms from the south were rare this time of year. But when they did come, they packed more fury than he cared to think about.

John felt his father put his back into the oars. He had seen it too. The boy glanced over his shoulder to see how long it would take them to clear Red Head and then run for the shelter of the harbour. On a good day, he reckoned, it would take thirty minutes. He started to doubt they could make it as the swell grew to three-foot waves, now whipped by a brisk wind. They would have to make good headway east before the real seas came. Once the great waves arrived, the boat would not be able to ride broadside. Then they would have no choice but to ride north with the wind and waves. The danger lay in not going far enough east and being crushed on the rocks at Cochrane Cove. Or they could go too far and be swept right past the harbour entrance onto the waiting rocks of Herring Point. Because the gap was so narrow, less than one hundred feet wide, their timing had to be perfect.

Abel pulled the old boat across the swell. John felt the dory begin to heave in the growing waves as she drove broadside to the wind and swell, up and down, combined with a side-to-side twist that grew more intense as the fury of the waves grew. Sea caps began to explode on the peaks. The howling wind threw brine into the air and drenched them. Water, now sheer black in the squall, came dangerously close to the gunwales as the boat slid down crosswise to the ever-growing waves. The scud closed in and Red Head disappeared. All they could do now was locate the harbour from the crash of the seas breaking on the rocks. They were rowing blind.

A cold wave overran the gunwales, dumping water into the boat and sending the fish on the floor slithering to the lee. She could not handle any more crosswaves. Abel turned the boat and began to run with the swell. Only by the grace of God would they find the harbour entrance now.

The squall intensified. Cold rain lashed their faces. Fog blinded them. Brutal gusts whisked water off the tops of the giant waves now driving the small boat downwind. The world closed in.

John was not sure at first, but soon he heard the unmistakable sound of seas breaking. He peered into the gloom for any sign that would tell when they should turn and run for the gap. The crashing grew so loud he was certain they were going to be crushed on the rocks. But the scud opened up to show they were clearing the rocks by two oar lengths. The seas booming on the rocks dwarfed the boat as she flew by, driven by the gale force winds.

"Now," Abel said out loud as the last of the white breakers disappeared into the abyss. He pulled the old rodney across the wind and rowed hard, raising himself off the seat with the effort. The sweeps bowed under the strain. Two desperate strokes, and the swell caught them broadside. Water gushed over the gunwale. Two more frantic pulls, another wave, more sea into the boat. Two more. Water halfway up the risings. The old boat became cranky and heavy. She could not take any more. The next one would finish her. Two more desperate strokes, but no new water came aboard. Two more strokes, another smaller wave. Two more and they found the lee. Abel stopped rowing for a moment to catch his breath and then began to pull again, this time toward safe home.

The rusty old bailing can floated at Abel's feet. He kicked it over toward John, who had been holding onto the gunwales for dear life. "Get her dry, boy. You should have it done by the time we get to the stage."

John jumped to it, happy to have a way to avoid his father's glare.

ii

The wind was gone by the time they made the wharf. All that remained of the squall was a mizzle that felt more like fog. Abel gutted the fish, tossing the innards in a lazy arc toward the bay. No sooner had they splashed than four gulls descended, each screeching for their share. John and his father trudged home side by side, working their way around the puddles in the muddy track.

"Why did you stop rowing out there?" Abel asked.

John looked down, expecting another outburst.

"No, no," Abel said. "I'm not mad. You knew the storm was coming before I did. How come?"

They had reached the wooden footbridge that crossed a creek tumbling down into the harbour. John stomped his feet to get the mud off his boots, all the while trying to avoid his father's question.

"Come now, son."

"Well," he said, bringing his dark eyes into contact with his father's for the first time since the outburst, "I had a kind of dream."

Abel stopped and looked down at his son.

Reluctantly, John told him about the black monster and how the white bird had told him to head back. "It flew right past me and went straight toward home. I just knew we had to get back, and fast." He stopped and looked away. "I was so scared I thought I'd die, right then and there." A tear ran down his cheek. "I've never had anything like it before."

Abel reached over and squeezed the boy's shoulder.

"What was it?" John said. "Couldn't have been a dream because I was awake."

Abel started walking again. "Can't say as I know, son." He looked down at the boy. "I've heard lots of stories about women having visions that tell the future. But yes, by Jesus, you did stop rowing at the right time, and you did have that dream, or whatever it was. There's something strange about this." The fisherman looked confused. He lapsed into silence. Abel shoved his son forward so he would keep up with his quickened pace as they headed uphill toward their two-storey clapboard house at the back of the village.

iii

Abel's kitchen was remarkably similar to his rodney. Both were more practical than they were polished. The old stove showed more signs of wear than it did efforts to keep it sparkling. But the chimney drew and it worked well enough to cook the rough-and-tumble meals they had become used to. Since his mother's death, just after his fifth birthday, John had been toughing it out with his father. The boy was slowly taking over more of the household chores as he became able.

When they finished supper, sitting at the old table by the stove, talk turned to fishing. "Never seen the likes before," Abel said. "Haven't had a good catch all year. Young Cecil had a water haul the other day, not a single fish. Maybe this storm will stir things up and get them moving." Abel grew silent, furrowing his brow. After several minutes he said, "I'm still bothered by your dream. It's different from our stories about faeries and devils." He screwed up his face. While Abel was never much for words, stories were another matter. Here, with what he called his cuffers, the fisherman was in his element. Words flowed as freely as the brooks tumbling down from the Pinnacle. He smiled. "You ever see the hoof-print in the rock up at South Head?"

"No," John said, sitting forward in his chair.

"I'll show you where it's at some time. The print is so clear you'd think it was made in new mud, a cloven hoof mark, plain as the nose on your face." Abel paused. "I hear it got put there years ago, when the harbour was full of banking schooners. Lots of strangers back in those days. There was a game of six-handed Auction going on in McCarthy's store. One of the players got called away for some reason, left his partners high and dry. 'Lord,' this one old-timer says, 'I'd take the Devil for a partner if I could keep winning like this.'" Abel stopped, looking carefully at John to be sure he was listening.

The boy nodded. He treasured these times when his father's temper was at bay and they could enjoy each other's company.

"Well, everybody laughs and gets ready to quit," Abel said, shifting in his chair. He leaned toward his son and lowered his voice. "Then there was this knock at the door." Abel rapped under the table.

John jumped in surprise.

"McCarthy opens the door and finds this stranger standing there, a tall hand who says he hopes they're having luck with their game. 'We were,' the old-timer says. 'But our partner left and now we're scuppered. Don't suppose you play Auction?' 'Indeed I do,' the stranger says. 'Well, pull up a seat then.' The stranger hesitates, so McCarthy leads him by the arm to his place."

Abel stretched back in his chair, lit a pipe, and looked at his son who was sitting forward in his chair, wide eyed.

"Then what happened?"

"Patience, boy," Abel said as he drew a long puff and sent a plume of smoke toward the stove. After a time he continued. "It turns out the stranger and the old-timer couldn't lose. Every time they bid, twenty, thirty for sixty, slam-bang, they got the right cards, every time." He took a deep puff of his pipe and sent a stream of smoke across the table. "This one time, the old-timer drops a card. When he leans over to get it, he gets the shock of his life. Under the table he sees the stranger's foot, but it isn't a foot at all, it's a hoof!" Abel whistled a low, mysterious whistle. "I'll tell you the old-timer's heart sunk when he remembered saying he'd take the Devil for a partner. Lord have mercy, he'd conjured up Satan himself. And now here he was, playing Auction with him."

John took a deep breath.

"Then this old-timer makes some feeble excuse to leave and runs straight over to the priest. He confesses right there and the good Father puts on his stole, grabs some holy water, his cross, and the two of them go back to McCarthy's. When they come in, the stranger smiles, bows, and takes off his hat. The card players gasp when they spy the two pointed horns atop his head. 'I see you are here and up to no good,' the priest says. 'I was invited,' the dark angel answers. 'They even helped me to my seat.'" Abel gave the Devil a low, raspy voice.

"'Time you left then,' says the priest, and he starts into his ritual. He lights a candle, says all manner of prayers, the whole deal. The Devil just sits there, amused like. But then a drop of holy water hits him. Satan screams and utters a string of black oaths that would make Skipper Joe blush. In a burst of fire and brimstone he blows up through the roof, leaving a huge hole. They all run outside just in time to see him land on South Head." Abel sat back and, with an air of finality, said, "And that's how the hoofprint got up there." He struck a match, all the while looking into his son's enraptured eyes. The kitchen was silent save for the suck of Abel's pipe.

The boy was quiet for several minutes. Then he said, "So was my dream like that, the Devil's work?"

Abel shook his head. "Can't say, son. All I know is that it doesn't feel right for a boy like you to have such things. They're for women. It's a bad sign, even though it might have saved us." Once again he was searching for words that were as hard to catch as the cod this season. Silence filled the old kitchen. Then the father's eyes brightened. "Let's talk about better things," he said. "It's time for you to come out to the trap with me. Skipper Joe can't go anymore, says his rheumatism ties him down. I need another hand, even if it is a green youngster like you."

John could scarcely contain his excitement. "I'm ready. I'll do my best."

"You'll have to work with a will every minute you're out on the water, none of this taking spells. This is serious business, man's work. I've got no time for your fancies or visions." He sat forward, looming in front of the boy, "You've got to apply yourself double tides and learn to be a man out there." He pointed a finger at John and wagged it up and down. "Any of this dreaming and you'll be back on shore faster than you can open your eyes. You hear me?"

"Yes, sir."

"I don't want to hear any more about this queer faerie stuff. That's for women and girls. You're small enough already without having to worry about the spirits, too. Understand?"

"Yes, sir."

"Well, off to bed then. We'll be up early to the trap to see how much linnet made it through the storm. Get a good night's sleep now."

"Yes, sir."

THREE

June 21, 1909
St. John's, Newfoundland

Walter Baine Grieve sat behind the huge oak desk in his opulent premises on Water Street. The fine woodwork gleamed. Knick-knacks from all corners of the British Empire, displayed in cases and on shelves, complemented the evident luxury and wealth of the successful owner. With his sleeves rolled up and tweed jacket hung over the back of his chair, Grieve was hunched over a newspaper spread across the invoices strewn on the desk. 'People Indignant,' read the editorial in *The Evening Telegram*. "People indignant," Grieve said out loud. "Indeed." The indignation in the paper involved the people in Torbay who were angry because roadwork was being doled out to Tories. The government had replaced the inspector with one of their lackeys and only Conservative supporters were being hired. According to the editorial, this was just another example of the lying and corruption under the Edward Morris regime. "No news there," Grieve said.

Grieve's indignation, however, was different from the editor's, but no less intense. Two months earlier he had been arrested by Morris's men and charged with criminal libel for saying the premier favoured confederation with Canada. Grieve was fuming because he had been treated so badly and muzzled by the legal action. Anger simmered just below his usually genial surface. He could not bear feeling so helpless. The merchant rankled at being gagged by Morris and his gang of power mongers.

Grieve stood up and walked over to the window. Sun sparkled off a light riffle on the harbour. He watched a steamer work toward the Narrows. "Probably got some of my fish aboard," he said absently. His firm was a leader in the export of salt fish, keeping a small army of men in work. He was also involved in many good deeds. Yet, all he got in return was to be treated like a common criminal. "Indignant," Grieve said looking back at *The Telegram* on his desk, "Indignant to be sure."

Thomas Collingwood burst into the office, not even bothering to knock. His thinning hair was askew and several rivers of sweat ran down his face, disappearing into his well-trimmed goatee. "Good news, sir," he said excitedly, "good news. Morris has dropped the lawsuit against you." He stopped to catch his breath.

"What?"

"Yes, sir. He's filed to have the whole affair quashed. Harvey Morine told me. That's good news, isn't it, sir?"

"Yes, Thomas, that it is," Grieve said. A self-satisfied smile spread across his face. "I guess that buffoon has finally admitted I was right." He went to the window and watched a banking schooner pass by his wharf, sails luffing in an uncertain breeze. "I knew all along Morris was scheming to sell us out to Canada. Now I know I was right."

"I don't think that's what he had in mind dropping the case," Collingwood said tentatively. "According to Harvey, you're not to speak any more about this rumour or he'll refile."

Grieve glared over at him. "So he's still trying to legislate what I can say." His face reddened. "Morris certainly has his bloody nerve."

"I couldn't believe it, sir, when the Constabulary barged in here and arrested you, like a scene out of some play. Anything to quiet the opposition, I suppose."

"Aye, Thomas. Morris will do anything to get his way." He pulled his gold pocket watch out of his vest fob and checked the time. "I certainly didn't enjoy being treated like that, something I'd just as soon avoid in the future." He went over and sat behind his desk, absently fondling the watch. A twinkle came into his eyes. "You know, Thomas, I saw an empty carriage pull up in front of Government House yesterday." He stopped, then chuckled, "And Morris got out of it."

"Oh, sir." Collingwood laughed. "It's certainly a relief knowing that Morris's men won't be crashing down our door any time soon."

The snap of Grieve's watch shutting announced the return to business matters. He slipped the timepiece into his vest. "Is there anything new?"

"There's only one thing out of the ordinary, sir; a letter from David Cheeseman in Edinburgh. He says you were friends at university in Glasgow." Collingwood pulled the letter out of his case.

"Yes, yes, I remember him. What does he want?"

"He's asking if you might find a position for his son, Joshua. Evidently, the boy is very ambitious and wants to come to the Colonies to make his fortune. Let's see now, how did he phrase it?" Collingwood looked through the letter. "Ah, yes, here it is. 'Joshua is an ambitious young man with a clear vision of what he wants to achieve. I have no doubt he would do well in your establishment and become a credit to its enterprise.'" Collingwood stopped and looked up.

"Hmm. Must be David's third or fourth son. He'd never send his first-born. Did he mention a remittance?"

"Not exactly. He said he wouldn't expect you to pay full salary for a year, until the boy had proven himself."

"That's strange, the usual offer is to pay full salary for at least two years, sometimes more." He stopped, deep in thought. "But I do owe David a huge favour. Can we use the boy?"

"No, sir, there's nothing available."

Grieve shook his head. "There's always work at the rendering plant in Harbour Grace. We could use another set of eyes and ears over there."

"I don't think so," Collingwood said firmly.

"Yes, Thomas," Grieve said, making certain Collingwood understood this was not a suggestion. "Please make the arrangements."

"Yes, sir," Collingwood said as he left the room.

Grieve looked around his waterfront office. The oak panelling, the gargantuan desk and the view of the harbour from the six-windowed tower, created a space worthy of his wealth and influence. He was comfortable standing in his turret, watching the commerce of the Island pass by. Shipping, selling salt fish, representing Newport and Cunard, selling ships, sealing, and more fed into the financial empire that he managed from his waterfront command post.

The *Neptune*, one of the Job Brothers' wooden steamers, chugged past the end of his wharf. The sun bounced off the old ship making her look almost majestic as she steamed toward the Narrows. "Probably off to Harbour Grace to wait for next year's seal hunt," Grieve said absently. He watched the old sealer and saw how she reflected the old ways: dirty, rotten, more of a historical antiquity than a safe home for two hundred men on the brutal ice fields surrounding springtime Newfoundland. The steel steamers, like the *Florizel* and the *Beothic*, modern through and through, were the future. But still, he was drawn toward the old ships, the wooden walls. Despite being decrepit, they echoed the glory days of the seal hunt. Grieve knew these times were disappearing, but still, he longed for the way things had been.

FOUR

George Clarke's deep, resonant laugh filled his small house in Brigus. He had just seen Lucy's face after she finally figured out his latest prank. Earlier, he had set some boots and a pair of his pants in the outhouse so that when she peeked under the door she thought he was inside. He'd also managed to lock the door by squeezing his ponderous frame through the space beneath the door. Once the scene was set, Lucy had waited patiently for over two hours. She came out every five minutes to see if it was vacant. Finally, she began to shout at the outhouse, demanding that the occupant hurry up. George emerged from the woodshed, tears of laughter streaming down his cheeks.

"You and your darn fool pranks," she said. "You'll be the death of me." All the time it took him to unlatch the door he was laughing. He finally ushered in his miffed wife with a mock bow.

Lucy shook her head in mild reproach as she came back into the kitchen. While these pranks made her life difficult, she much preferred them to the despondency that would sometimes overtake her husband, leaving him morose and distant.

George started laughing again, a big, deep laugh that made the windows shake.

"I don't understand why you have to do those things," she said, making no effort to hide her exasperation.

"Aw, come on Lucy, it's just a bit of fun. You know how a good laugh always makes things go better — humour is the grease that keeps everything running smooth." He laughed again, eyes sparkling, trying to show her how it worked.

"You mark my words," she said, "one of these days that legendary charm of yours won't work. Then you'll be in trouble." She glanced back toward the outhouse. The room grew quiet. George let out a short, infectious giggle. Despite herself, a forgiving smile flooded across her face. "Oh, what's the use? I give up." Her smile grew into a breathy laugh.

"See how it works," he said. Then he patted the breast pocket of his jacket. By the time he pulled out a letter all signs of mirth had vanished. "I'm not so sure I can laugh this off though." He handed the paper over to his wife.

She took the letter and began to read.

St. John's
June 15, 1909

Dear George,

I'm sure you'll be happy to join in my happiness that I've just been made captain of the Southern Cross for the seal hunt this coming spring. At last, I have my own ship.

As you know only too well, our family has been hoping for an opportunity like this for years, so we can join the Bartletts and Keans as top captains. At last we're on our way.

I'm writing to ask if you will join me as my second hand. Together I'm sure we'll be able to put a fine rout on those harp seals in the Gulf. Please think this over and we can work out the details when I get back to Brigus next week.

Your devoted older brother,
John

Lucy looked up at her husband, now seated at the table, eyebrows knitted in a scowl.

"Surely this is good news," she said.

"Well, it is and it isn't," he said hesitantly. "Sure I'm happy for John. It's a good break for him. And it reflects well on the family. But..."

Lucy looked directly at her husband.

"But," he said, taking a deep breath, "I think there are times when my brother has got it all wrong." He looked away. After a moment, he continued. "You know, when we go sealing John's a real soft touch on the men. 'How you feeling?' 'How's the missus?' he's always asking. Says he wants to be their friend. He doesn't understand that the only way to get those Catholic louts to work is to make them afraid to do anything but their jobs." He began to fidget with a napkin. "You don't go sealing to make friends, you go sealing to make money. John just doesn't get it." George looked up at Lucy. "And now they give him the jeezly job." His voice trailed off into silence.

Lucy came over and brushed the hair out of his eyes.

"I was sure Mr. Grieve would skip over John and pick me for the Southern Cross. I was sure he would. He's no fool, or at least I thought he wasn't." George frowned as he looked out the window. "How long am I going to be a captain-in-waiting?" he continued, beginning to sound more like a little boy than a seasoned sealer. "I've done everything they asked of me, nineteen years now." There was a catch in his voice. "Nineteen years. And now they give the Cross to that brother of mine. That was my post." George stopped, struggling to regain his composure. "It's like when they made Moses Bartlett captain of the Cross last year and he took John as second hand. I'd have done ten times the job, you know. I said then that Bartlett made a mistake picking him, and I was right." He thumped the table. "Moses never found the patch, not one whitecoat, just a few old seals. He only brought home twelve hundred, just two thousand dollars worth. What a disaster that was." He paused to catch his breath. "It didn't help my brother's reputation to be second hand on that trip, I'll tell you." He stood up and went over to the kitchen window, bracing his hands against the casement. "When I heard Moses was released, I was sure Mr. Grieve would choose me. I've got the knack for finding the seals. But oh no, he goes and gives the ship to John. However much my brother knows about sealing, the left cheek of me arse knows more. Mr. Grieve should have figured that out by now." He turned around and glared at his wife.

She smiled warmly. "Yes, dear."

"John'll do such a bad job. It'll poison my chances too. I'm crushed Lucy, crushed." He left the kitchen and went into the front room where he sat in one of the wicker chairs reserved for visitors. Lucy trailed behind. "It's so bloody unfair." He grew silent for a moment, deep in thought. "And John is so useless at the Lodge, too. You know how I put my heart and soul into the chapter, and he just goes along for the ride." He looked out the window in the direction of the Lodge hall. "Yet he's the one who gets the rewards. That brother of mine won't do anything to keep those goddamned Papists in line. All he wants is a good time. Not a true Orangeman." He stopped, and then whispered, "Between you and me, Lucy, I'm ashamed he's one of us Methodist Clarkes." He stared past his wife. Slowly his anger ebbed and he looked at her. "Did you see what those Catholic bastards did to our sign on the door of the Landwash House?"

She shook her head.

"Under our sign that says 'All but Papists enter here,' one of those low-minded Micks scrawled, 'Whoever wrote this wrote it well, the same thing is written on the gates of Hell.' Can you imagine it?"

Lucy looked away.

"What a smack in the face that was," he said, tension clear on every crease of his weather-worn face. "I can't see how anyone would wreck private property like that. Just goes to show what animals those Cat-licks are. We've got to work to keep them in their place."

George got up and went over to the mantel. He began to rearrange the knick-knacks, finally picking up an intricately carved star with five arms. "I wish my brother would honour the five points of Orangeman fellowship," he said under his breath. George held the star up and rotated it in his huge hands. He touched each point in succession, silently repeating a Lodge oath. Gradually he began to relax. The lines in his face returned to normal and he began to emerge from his reverie. "Did you hear about that drunk Catholic staggering home last night?"

"No."

"Well, he falls down and finds this golden lantern see, just like Aladdin. He picks it up and rubs it and, lo and behold, out pops this genie — offers him three wishes."

Lucy smiled, watching George return to his element.

"The Mick looks at his empty rum flask and says he'd like one that never got empty. Wouldn't you know it, the flask fills up right there in front of his eyes. He drains it and, saints be praised, it was full again. The drunk smiles and staggers off." George paused, a big grin on his face. "'You've got two more wishes,' the genie says. The Papist fool almost trips, holds up his flask and says, 'Give me two more of these.'" George began to howl with laughter. He could not stop laughing, despite Lucy's unamused gaze.

She waited for him to settle down, then held up the letter. "Are you going to sail with John, as his second hand?"

George did not answer for the longest time. "I suppose I might," he said with an air of defeat. "Shipping with him would be better than any of those others. At least I know what to expect from him." He frowned, but then his face brightened. "Maybe I can get him into the main patch this year and we'll bring home some real money. That'd be a change, wouldn't it?" Again his raucous laugh echoed through the small Brigus house.

ii

The next spring, 1910, George Clarke came home from the seal hunt triumphant and full of himself. Jokes and pranks filled the Brigus house. "I talked John into heading deeper west into the ice and we found the seals," he told Lucy. "More seals than I've ever seen in one place, unbelievable. They were small, but we brought back over twenty-three thousand. More than the *Southern Cross* ever fetched. Our load was worth thirty-eight thousand dollars, a bloody fortune." He could not stop laughing. "We're on the move now, my dear." He pranced around their little house like a circus bear. "We were the third ship in, hit the narrows on March 28th, just behind Old Bartlett. Damned near won the silk flag. Just wait until next year. We'll be the first home, with the biggest load ever. I can feel it in my bones. That'll be something, won't it? Then no one will doubt us Clarkes are the best. They won't call us 'rough around the edges' behind our backs anymore. We'll get the respect we deserve." He roared with laughter.

iii

The next year, 1911, the Brigus house was relatively laughless. George and his brother did not fare well. The seals were scarce. Despite Herculean efforts that kept them out until mid-April, the *Southern Cross* fetched only thirteen thousand pelts. George, as second hand, had to assert himself to keep the *Cross*'s crew at their posts through weeks of spotty hunting. "If it hadn't been for me bullying those lazy Catholic boys, we'd have come home empty," he told Lucy. "It's a good thing John had me to keep things running." He stopped to catch his breath. "When all was tallied up the crew took home forty-one dollars, not as good as last year, but still a decent payout, especially since they weren't the hardest working crowd I've ever seen. Too many lazy, bloody Papists."

He paused, sat down at the table, pulled off his boot, and began to massage his left foot through the grey wool sock. "And to make matters worse, my gout started acting up. Nearly couldn't walk for a few days."

Lucy nodded sympathetically. "Was Mr. Grieve happy?"

"Not really," George said, darkness spreading over his face. "Disappointed, I'd say. He expected us to do as well as last year, but what can you do if the seals aren't there? There's no pleasing that man." He shrugged and looked down at the floor. "If the *Viking* hadn't got five thousand more than us, I figure he'd have been happy. But Mr. Grieve was upset those others beat him."

iv

Early in January 1912, George Clarke was invited to join Walter Baine Grieve in Harbour Grace. He was puzzled that the old merchant wanted to meet him at the quay of his rendering plant there, not in St. John's where Grieve did most of his work. Clarke arrived to find one of Baine, Johnston's sealers, the *Bloodhound*, tied up at the wharf. She was a finer ship than the *Southern Cross*, more sleek looking and better appointed. A pang of jealousy shot through him as he looked at her more modern and sheltered bridge. "Officers' quarters are probably better too," he thought as he approached the vessel. He was interrupted when two people came out of the office. One was Grieve, looking quite dapper in a heavy tweed overcoat. The other was a smallish young man dressed in foreign clothes who looked British — maybe sixteen years old. His hair was cut strangely and he had his arms wrapped around his body trying to fend off the cold.

Grieve greeted Clarke warmly and then introduced him to the stranger. "George, this is Joshua Cheeseman, my new junior assistant. He's just arrived from Scotland and will be helping me with the sealing operation."

Clarke shook the boy's hand, surprised at the weakness of his grip. "Pleased to meet you, Joshua," he said with a smile. "Are you enjoying our lovely weather?"

Cheeseman looked around, shivered, and shook his head. "A wee bit cold and damp for me," he said in an accent that Clarke recognized from some of the Glasgow engineers aboard the *Southern Cross*.

"Never mind, me b'y," Clarke said, giving the boy a playful pat on the shoulder "you'll get used to it after a while."

Cheeseman recoiled from Clarke's touch. "I doubt it," he said pulling up his collar against a gust of wind. He stomped his feet.

Grieve began to walk toward the gangway leading to the *Bloodhound*. The other two followed. Over his shoulder, Grieve said, "I thought you two should get to know each other, since you'll be working together over the next while."

Clarke was puzzled.

"After all," Grieve continued, "our captains should get to know the staff who outfit their ships. Don't you think, George?" The old man smiled as he held open the door to the officers' quarters.

Cheeseman barged through the door ahead of Clarke. When the big man entered he was surprised to find that he did not have to hunch down to prevent cracking his head on the massive ceiling beams. Grieve went to the captain's cabin and sat down at the table. "Well, what do you think of her, George?"

"Looks fine enough to me," he said rather nonchalantly.

Grieve laughed quietly. "Perhaps you didn't hear me. I said, 'our captains should get to know the staff.'" He looked over at Cheeseman who sat down on the bunk.

"Our captains?" Clarke said.

"Yes, George. I'm offering you the captaincy of this lovely ship." He slapped the table.

"Me?"

"Yes, you, Captain Clarke. Sounds good, doesn't it? Captain Clarke."

The big man's head began to swim. "Me?"

"Yes, George."

"I don't believe it."

Cheeseman laughed in a way that made Clarke feel like he was being mocked. The big man shot a cold look at the boy and returned his attention to Grieve. "Is this true?"

Grieve nodded.

Clarke shook his head in disbelief. "Me, captain of the *Bloodhound*? Just wait 'til John hears about this." A broad smile erupted across his face.

"As you know, Captain Clarke, I usually send the *Bloodhound* up north to the Front. But this year I want to try something different. I'm going to send both of my wooden ships south, to the Gulf. The *Hound* is better in the ice and my hope is she'll pay dividends in the St. Lawrence. You're just the man to take her there and bring home the log-load."

Slowly, Clarke began to appreciate his changed fortunes. "Yes, sir. I am, sir." He looked around at the cabin, this time with new appreciation. This was going to be his home, his realm. His grin widened. "She certainly is well-appointed," he said, running his hand along the carved pillar that stood mid-cabin. "Yes, indeed, she's some fine. Much nicer than the *Southern Cross*." His deep laugh filled the room.

Cheeseman shuffled uncomfortably.

"I'm putting a lot of faith in you, George," Grieve said. "Don't disappoint me. We must have a good hunt to keep our enterprise afloat." He pointed toward the rendering plant. "It's up to you. Do you understand?"

"Yes, sir, I do. You can count on me, sir."

Grieve smiled at his newest captain.

Clarke went over to the map cabinet and pulled out a chart. As he unfurled it, he asked, "if you don't mind me asking, sir, what's to become of Skipper Jacob now that he's no longer master of the *Bloodhound*?"

"Ah, yes," Grieve replied. "I've purchased another ship, the *Erna*. She's a steel steamer, bigger than the *Bloodhound*. I'm giving her to Jacob for the Front.

Right now, he's on his way to Glasgow to sail her home. If you do well, we'll retire the *Hound* to the Gulf, and she'll be yours for the future."

Clarke nodded, faintly aware that getting the *Bloodhound* was not exactly the plum promotion he had thought — he was not chosen ahead of Jacob or his brother. Nonetheless, he recognized this was a great step forward, no doubt a turning point in his career. He was now a captain. Clarke laughed again, causing the boy sitting on the bunk to stir once more. The big man glared at him.

"Now, George," Grieve said, "you'll be working closely with Joshua, not only here at the plant, but also in St. John's when we outfit the ship. It's important that you two get along and work together."

Clarke smiled as he nodded agreement. "To be sure," he said, softening his tone. "We can do that."

Cheeseman looked down. There was an embarrassing silence.

"Joshua," Grieve said.

The boy finally looked up. "Yes, sir," he said.

Clarke stood back and examined the youthful Scot who was still sitting on the bunk. "So what do we do next, young man?" he asked, doing his best to be cordial.

Cheeseman looked over at Grieve, then back at the captain. "Well," he said uncertainly, "I guess I'll have to learn how to get the ship supplied and then we'll get it ready for the voyage."

Clarke was struck by the boy's lack of confidence and his ignorance of the sealing operation. "Yes, boy," he said, "let's the two of us work together on this. We'll make you a top hand in the sealing business before you know what hit you." Clarke smiled, doing his best to draw the boy out.

Cheeseman looked away.

Clarke shook his head and then looked over at Grieve. "This is a great opportunity, sir," he said. "Thank you for giving me the chance to prove myself. You'll not regret your choice. I'll bring home the log-load, just you watch."

Grieve smiled. "I certainly hope so."

The new captain had forgotten about Cheeseman by the time he got back to Brigus. George's trademark joviality returned as he laughed his way around the cottage, talking up his inevitable success. His brother John was particularly happy for him. "John didn't even care I passed him by," George said to Lucy afterwards. "I'll never understand him. He doesn't want to get ahead, always happy to come in second. Not me! I don't understand why he doesn't mind that I got the better ship and I'll fetch the top load this year."

v

George Clarke stood on the wharf at the rendering plant in Harbour Grace, having just returned from his first outing as captain in late April 1912. The winches barely groaned as a paltry cargo of seven hundred seals was unloaded. He stood with his second hand, James Kelly, a small man, never without a pipe clenched between his teeth. The two were a study in contrasts with Clarke's ponderous bearing and reputation as a jowler on the ice offset by Kelly's perpetual calm and diminutive stature. This unlikely pair worked well together. Kelly was the better seaman of the two, but once on the ice, Clarke was the undisputed master. The second hand respected his captain and had the knack of gently persuading him to take the right action, without getting the big man's back up. For his part, Clarke's only reservation about Kelly was his Catholic-sounding name. He always went out his way to tell everyone that his second hand was one of the 'Protestant Kellys from Bull Cove,' lest he be accused of having a Papist friend.

"I've never seen such a bad hunt," Clarke said when they finished unloading. A frigid wind whistled through his jacket like it was made of chintz, leaving him to shiver in the cold. "The only good thing is that we're done unloading in jig time."

"Aye, George, but only because we had such a bad catch," Kelly said, searching his pockets for a tobacco pouch.

"Yes, my son," Clarke replied with a hiss, "this spring has been the worst of the worst." He paused. "You're a religious man, James, why do you think the good Lord did this to us?"

The second hand found his flap of tobacco, loaded his pipe. "Can't say as I know."

Clarke started to pace along the wharf, a noticeable limp in his agitated gait.

"That's some go you've had with the gout," Kelly said as he walked along beside his captain.

"The worst I can remember. Some painful at the big toe." He stopped walking and lifted his left foot, shaking it to try and make the pain go away. "Can you imagine, killing only seven hundred?" Clarke said. "It's a good thing none of the other ships took any whitecoats either. Young Bartlett on the *Neptune* got none, not a single pup. Hard to believe after all the time he spent out there. The young harps have disappeared off the face of the Earth. Never seen it this bad before."

"Maybe all this talk about the seal herd being on the decline is right after all," Kelly said. "Sure seems like it right now. Maybe we killed them all."

Clarke frowned and shook his head dismissively. "Isn't it just my luck, the first chance to show them how good I am, and the seals decide to disappear." He limped toward the rendering plant.

"Aye," Kelly said, following along.

"I thought for sure we'd have a bumper trip and I'd be the top captain." He sighed as a great sadness passed across his face. "But not this year. And Mr. Grieve put so much faith in me. I've let him down." He stomped his feet against the cold, causing a painful wince. "But it's not my fault — an act of God. I did the best any man could. It's a good thing my brother on the *Cross* didn't do well either. Maybe Mr. Grieve and his lapdog Cheeseman will understand." He stopped and looked nervously across the harbour. "Still, I'm not looking forward to seeing the old man. Lord, James, my gut aches. I have this feeling I'm as good as replaced."

FIVE

APRIL 14, 1912
RED ISLAND, NEWFOUNDLAND

On a warm Sunday afternoon John Lundrigan and his two closest friends ventured out toward Johnny's Pond on the north end of Red Island. Getting out in the bush was an antidote to the boring Mass they had just sat through. The first hint of true spring was in the air. Sun bounced off the snow, the heat sculpting large crystals that yielded readily under foot. Meltwater ran down the ruts on the pathways and the breeze had an unaccustomed softness.

"Warm enough for you two?" Tommy Dunphy said, as he struck off through the scrub spruce along a walking trail. He crunched along, big-soled boots breaking through the crust, sometimes over the tops. The other two followed, stepping carefully into the impressions made by their friend. Tommy, the tallest and oldest of the three, was the designated trailbreaker. When he moved, the fifteen-year-old flailed, all elbows and knees. The times he recognized how gawky he looked, he would make fun of himself. This gave him the reputation as a comical hand. The shock of red hair atop a face spattered with freckles only added to this impression.

Tommy turned around and watched the two younger boys picking their way along in his tracks. He sang out:

Mark my footsteps my good page…

Then the redhead stopped and laughed. "Look at you two. Here I'm doing all the work and all you can do is lag behind with nothing to say for yourselves."

"Shut up," Peter Lamb said, "can we help it if you got legs like stilts?"

"Yeah?"

"Yeah."

Peter reached Tommy and the two began to push each other out of their footholds.

Peter was halfway between Tommy and John in age, height and strength. He had a round face under a mop of sandy hair. A gentleness in his blue eyes belied his willingness to stand up to Tommy.

By the time John reached his friends, Peter lay on his back, face reddened from a fresh wash in the snow.

"Finally decided to join us, eh," Tommy said, standing triumphantly over Peter, hands on hips. He wiped a lamb's leg from his nose on the back of his mitt.

"Could use some snowshoes up here," John said, stopping before he came within reach of the Tommy's long arms.

"No wonder your father's always at you to 'be a man,'" Tommy said. "Why don't you just get down to work instead of always trying to find shortcuts? Snowshoes, my arse." He shook his head.

John ignored the taunt and looked down at Peter, who was getting up and brushing the snow off his jacket. "Leave him be," Peter said.

"Well, I'm thinking he deserves it. He's slower than cold molasses."

Peter's eyes narrowed. "Tell me that the next time John whips you in a race. He runs circles around you. Remember?"

Tommy scowled. He turned around and resumed his trailbreaking. "Good King Wenceslas" sounded out as he crunched away.

Peter looked at John, "Your old man gave you a real tongue banging yesterday."

John nodded. "He's getting worse all the time. I deserved it though. I wasn't paying attention and knit up some net wrong. I ended up with a real mess when I tried to take it apart. Had to toss it all out. The old man got pretty mad."

"He's sure getting to be a tough bugger."

"Yep. Always says it's for my own good." John looked out across the hills.

"Sure it is."

"Come on," Tommy hollered from the top of the next hill. "Not that much sun left."

John followed as they began tracing Tommy's steps. Even though he had just passed his fourteenth birthday, and gone through two growth spurts, he was still small for his age. He had trouble keeping up, continually having to jump to reach the next footprint. Unable to establish a good rhythm for walking, he soon lagged behind.

John found himself alone in a small valley, the other two out of sight over the hill. A familiar feeling began to well up. He shuddered…

He looks down the valley and sees the speck. The monster comes at him from behind a grove of scrub trees and soon the black presence engulfs him once again. This time, the white bird comes from the northeast and flies directly over him, toward Sand Pond.

Then it was gone. John began to tremble. Peter and Tommy came back toward him.

"You all right?" Peter asked.

"I think so," John said, shaking as if to wake himself up. He paused to collect himself and then said, "There's something to see over at Sand Pond," he said, pointing in the direction the bird had just flown.

"How do you know that?" Tommy said.

"Can't say. Just seems like a good idea to head over there."

"And we're supposed to jump up and charge over that Jesus hill just because you tell us to?"

"Why not?" Peter said. "Got nothing else to do."

"Sweet Jesus," Tommy said, seeing he was outnumbered.

They struck off southwest through the woods. John took the lead, blazing a trail through the unmarked snow. He had such energy now that the other two had trouble keeping up. Soon they found an icy slide path, rutted by runners of sleds that had hauled wood back to town.

"Just over the next hill," John said as he skidded on the ice, catching a small tree to stop himself from tumbling headlong into the scrub brush. They slipped and slid up to crest the ridge.

"Lord Jesus," Tommy said, pointing toward the ice-covered lake, "there's old Daniel up to his neck in the middle of the pond. What's he doing in there?"

"Looks like he fell through the ice hauling his logs," John shouted, running down the hill toward the old man. "He's not moving. Let's pray he's still alive."

"Look at his horse there, old Jonas, he's still hitched to the sled," Peter said, doing his best to keep up.

John threw off his jacket and ran across the ice but he broke through into two feet of water. Tommy and Peter helped him back to shore.

"We need help," John said through his shivers. He stamped his doused feet. "Tommy, you're the fastest, you run back to town and bring some men. Peter and I will try to get Daniel out. Hurry now."

Tommy nodded and struck off, slip-sliding up the hill.

ii

An hour later Tommy came back over the rise with twelve men, including Abel Lundrigan. John and Daniel were hunkered down at the edge of a roaring fire, both stark naked. Peter was stoking the blaze. The wrinkly old man rubbed his hands, trying to get warmth back into them. Steam rose from the clothes laid out over nearby bushes.

"My son, the things you see when you haven't got your gun," one of the men said as they approached.

"Hey, Daniel, a bit early for your bath this year, isn't it?"

The men donated jackets and the fire was stoked higher, bringing it to a six-foot blaze.

The men unhitched Jonas and coaxed him to shore. The old horse stood on the bank, shaggy hair dripping, head down in a sulk. Then they fastened a rope to the sled and pulled it to shore. Soon they had the runners fitted into the ruts, ready for the pull home.

The rescuers then turned their attention to the fire, crowding in to hear Daniel's story. The old man was shy at first but after some prodding he loosened up and began.

"Well boys, serves me right for working on Sunday but I had to get this last load in before the ice gave out. She'd be stuck in the woods all summer if I didn't get her done now." He looked away to show his shame for having broken the Sunday rule.

"Yes, Daniel," said Uncle Joe Skinner, "you shouldn't have been hauling on the Lord's Day. Serves you right, sure."

"Yes," Daniel said, contrition clear in his voice. "But the ice looked good when I started out. But when I get to the middle I hear this noise like a shot from a sealer's gun." He pointed to the opening on the ice. "The whole lot cracks open and before I know it, I'm up to my neck. That water near took the breath clean out of me." He stopped to hold a shiver. The crowd drew closer.

"I try to get out, but every time I pull myself up, the ice breaks and I fall back in. Soon got right played out. Figured I was done." Another dramatic pause. "I open my eyes this one time, and what do I see but an angel coming right for me. Glowing white, she was. Scared me some, I'll tell you. 'Saints be praised,' I said, 'here's Gabriel coming for my soul.' 'Daniel,' the angel says, 'take a hold of this and I'll pull you out.' She tosses me this strange rope, thick and knotty, like nothing I ever saw before." The old man stopped to cough. He pulled the jacket closer to his frail body. "Then I see it is the boy here." Daniel said, pointing at John. "Buff naked he was, stretched out on the ice. The rope was his pants, jacket, and shirt all tied together. I got my hands on it. He pulls and I thrashes until we get to shore. By the time we make it, I can hardly breathe. Then the two of us look at each other and start laughing, me wetter than a drowned hen, him buff white, rolling in the snow." Smiles spread through the group.

"Then we start to shiver. My teeth chattered so loud I figure you'd be able to hear them down by the landwash. The boy here was shaking like a mouse on a skillet. This other lad," he said, pointing to Peter, "made up the fire."

A nod circulated through the crowd.

"Saints be praised, saved from the lion's den again," Joe Skinner said. "Not bad for a couple of young fellers." He put his hand on Abel's shoulder, showing approval of his son's bravery and quick wit.

Despite the praise being heaped on him, John did not enjoy the attention. The lingering fear from his vision left him disconsolate, as did being frozen to the bone. But more than anything he feared someone might ask why they came to the pond in the first place. He was not sure he could lie his way out if he was asked.

"Some lucky the boys came over this way," young Cecil said.

"Must have been the hand of God sent them my way," Daniel replied. This answer seemed to satisfy the crowd, all except one person. John saw a steely look come over his father's face. His old man knew what had happened. Without doubt, more of the dreaded 'be a mans' would be on their way as soon as he got home. Meanwhile, John gained some comfort in seeing how Daniel had come back to life, as though from the dead, eyes alive, gap-toothed grin from ear to ear.

iii

On the way home the three boys yammered away, drawn together by their newfound glory. "That was some strange how you took us over to Sand Pond," Tommy said. "How'd you know to go over there?"

John did not answer. But Tommy would not leave it alone. After more cajoling, John relented and told the story.

"Name o' God, that's something," Tommy said after John finished. "Wouldn't have thought it true, but I saw it with my own eyes. Amazing. There's more to this boy than meets the eye. It's not enough that the girls fall over themselves to be with you, but now you can see the future. That's really something."

John was pleased that Tommy accepted his story, so he recounted the first vision.

"Lord lifting Jesus," the older boy said, shaking his head.

In the silence that followed, John said, "Now, Tommy, don't you go spreading this around. Can't have people thinking I'm sensitive. It's hard enough being small." He paused, looking into the distance. "I just want to be one of the boys. Promise you'll keep quiet."

"Sure," the older boy said.

SIX

The City Club of St. John's was abuzz with talk about the RMS *Titanic*. The Library was alive with animated debate about the report that the largest ship in the world, unsinkable they said, had struck some ice and foundered. Every one of the library's leather chairs was occupied by a portly merchant, each with a different opinion about what the papers called 'the worst ocean tragedy ever recorded.' The smell of leather and tobacco filled the room.

"Yes, sir," one of the merchants said, eyes darting excitedly above a pointed beard. "The first distress calls were picked up in Cape Race. And she hit the 'berg just three hundred miles from here."

"Lots of survivors in boats on the water, I hear," another said.

The main point of contention was how the ship, said to be unsinkable, could possibly have gone down. Opinions varied from design flaws to the captain being incompetent.

Grieve was in a chair by the window, discussing the matter with Henry Youmans. "What do you think, Walter? You know more about this kind of thing than I do."

Grieve sat forward in his chair. "To my mind," he said slowly, "we don't have enough good information to say anything definite yet. What we read is changing every minute, just rumours." He paused and took a puff of his pipe. "But there is one thing I can say for sure," he added. "There's a lot more happens when a ship goes down than we think. Whether it's a monster like the *Titanic* or the smallest banking schooner, it's always a lot more complicated than we realize." He paused to consider his words. "Sure people make mistakes, like Captain Smith of the *Titanic* might have. But there has to be more, a lot more."

Youmans sat forward, eager to hear more.

Grieve stopped, reamed out his pipe, and restuffed it from a leather flap he drew from his breast pocket. "There have to be design flaws." He lit his pipe. "And there are other things too: being in a hurry, blinded by routine, distracted, not knowing the water or the ship, a whole raft of things." His pipe had not taken, so he paused to relight it. "And, of course, there's the one thing you just can't control, the big unknown, luck, or more properly the lack of it." He stopped to be sure Youmans was listening. "All of these have to be woven into each other, intertwined like a braid, for a ship to sink. They all have to work together. You can't just consider them one at a time." Grieve paused and sat forward. "Anybody who tries to blame one person or a single thing when a ship goes down is a fool. There's always more than that, much more."

"It sounds like you've been thinking a lot about this," Youmans said.

"Yes, it's been on my mind a lot lately," Grieve said slowly. "Right now, I have a ship overdue and I'm racking my brain trying to figure out what happened."

"Which ship is that?"

"The *Erna*. I paid over fourteen thousand pounds for her, and that much again refitting her for the seal hunt. She would have been my first steelhulled sealer. The ship left Glasgow a month ago with a fine captain and a top crew, thirty-five hands. I'm beside myself trying to figure out what happened." Grieve grew silent, looking down. He fidgeted with his watch chain.

"She insured?"

Grieve looked up and nodded.

"Well, that's one good thing at least."

"I suppose," Grieve said. "But now with the *Titanic*, Lloyds's shares will no doubt take a tumble. Their brokers will probably squeeze me on the *Erna*. Could be a serious loss." He paused and settled back into his chair. After a time he sat forward. "You know, there are two kinds of shipwrecks. There are ones like the *Titanic*, with survivors. When they come back everyone will be reminded of what happened."

"Yes."

"And then there's wrecks like the *Erna* that disappear without a trace. Nobody remembers these because there are no tales to tell. Everybody forgets this kind." He furrowed his brow. "Hardly seems right. The men in both kinds of wrecks are just as drowned." Grieve looked away toward the window overlooking Water Street.

ii

Three weeks after the *Titanic* disaster, Grieve summoned George Clarke to his office. When ushered into the inner sanctum of Baine, Johnston and Co., the captain was already in a dither, positive he was going to be dismissed. The lavishness of Grieve's office — a carpet that it seemed a shame to walk on, electricity, a telephone — only added to his distress. "No amount of joking will save me now," he said to himself as he entered hesitantly, eyes to the floor.

When Clarke came in, Grieve was hunkered behind his huge desk, jacket off, sleeves rolled up. Joshua Cheeseman sat by his side. The big man was amazed at the transformation of the young Scot from the awkward boy he had first met in Harbour Grace to a confident, if not cocky, clerk. He had become a bit of a dandy, resplendent in new Scottish tweed with a fine silk tie, hair trimmed and slicked down in the latest fashion. In a very short time Cheeseman had insinuated himself into Grieve's inner circle, becoming the old man's favoured helper. As well, he had perfected a perpetual sneer that gave the impression he thought everyone else a fool.

A third person sat off to Cheeseman's side. Like Clarke, he was dressed in city clothes that did not sit quite right on him; a bayman, probably from up north. Long and lanky, he had the look of a sealing captain. Clarke grimaced when he saw him in the room. He knew for certain now that he had lost the *Bloodhound*. To make matters worse, the third man would not meet Clarke's eyes. He just stared at the floor.

"Welcome, Captain Clarke," Grieve said, "have a chair." The old man motioned to the seat in front of his desk.

"This gentleman," Grieve said, pointing to the stranger, "Is Captain Jessie Winsor. You've heard about the Winsors haven't you, those fine sealers from Wesleyville?"

George nodded and slouched into the chair.

"Captain Winsor had a wonderful year on the *Fagota* this year. He came home with seventeen thousand dollars' worth, a bumper trip for that small ship. And he won the silk flag, first one in. An amazing feat." Grieve beamed like he was praising his own son. "Captain Winsor's the real highliner."

Clarke shuffled uneasily in his chair.

"You know, Captain Clarke," Grieve went on, talking as though he was scolding a schoolboy, "you had a very bad trip last year. Can't say as I remember a total catch under fourteen hundred dollars. You didn't even cover the cost of stores. I'm very disappointed, particularly after all the trust I put in you."

Clarke grimaced. "But no one did well in the Gulf, sir. Martin on the *Labrador* only earned his crew a five-dollar payout, and I did better than young Bill Bartlett on the *Viking*."

Grieve nodded dismissively. "Baine, Johnston can't afford another bad season."

"But…"

"No buts, Captain Clarke."

The captain prepared to defend himself again, but Grieve silenced him with a raised hand.

"Captain Clarke," the old man said, "I'd rather not waste our time here." A frown came across his face. "I'm giving the *Bloodhound* to Captain Winsor."

Clarke's face fell.

Cheeseman looked directly at Clarke and began wagging his head the way a mother might scold a disobedient child. To compound the rebuke, he made an annoying "tcch" sound, by clicking his tongue behind his teeth. Clarke's face began to turn red as he squirmed in his chair.

Winsor kept staring at the floor.

"As you know," Grieve continued, "the *Bloodhound* is better suited for the Front, and Captain Winsor knows that area. It only makes sense that I give him the ship. Don't you agree?"

Clarke stared at his hands clasped in his lap.

"You may have heard that my third ship, the one I'd intended to send up North to the Front, has been lost. She never made it here from Glasgow."

Clarke looked up.

"Yes, the *Erna* has been declared lost, officially now. What a terrible waste," he said, looking right past Clarke. "I lost Linklater, our ship inspector, and thirty of my best men." The room grew so silent that Clarke's laboured breathing was all that could be heard. After a moment, Grieve regrouped. "This leaves me with only the *Bloodhound* for the Front. We'll have to make do with her for now. We're lucky to have Captain Winsor to take her up there."

Clarke shot a desperate look at Grieve, then at Winsor, and finally settled on Cheeseman, who returned his stare with a smug grin. After an embarrassing silence Clarke said, "Well, I guess that's that." He heaved a sigh and got up to leave.

"Don't go yet, Captain, there's more to talk about," Grieve said.

Clarke sat back down. "I won't serve under him," he said, pointing a shaking finger at Winsor.

"No, Captain Clarke, that's not it."

Clarke looked confused. "So I'm going to be demoted back to second hand with my brother John on the *Southern Cross* then. I won't go back to him hat in hand." He was almost shouting.

"Not that either," Grieve said.

Clarke looked even more confused.

Cheeseman continued to wag his head. "Tcch, tcch."

"I've decided to give you captaincy of the *Southern Cross*," Grieve said with a smile.

"What?"

"Yes, Captain Clarke, I think you're the better man for the whitecoats in the Gulf."

Clarke remained expressionless for a long time. "Really?"

Grieve smiled as he nodded.

Finally a huge grin exploded across Clarke's face. "Thank you, sir. I can't believe it," he gushed. "Thank you for promoting me ahead of my brother, you won't regret it."

Grieve shook his head. "That's not it."

Confusion returned to Clarke's face.

"The fact is," Grieve said, "just today, your brother got on full-time with one of Reid's supply boats, the *Ethie*. No more sealing for him." There was hint of sadness in his voice.

Clarke's smile disappeared as fast as it had come.

"You don't look pleased," Grieve said.

"Oh, no," Clarke said, doing his best to recover. "I'm overjoyed. She's a fine ship, the *Southern Cross*. I'm just surprised John would quit before I had a chance to pass him, that's all." He paused to think. "But now, I'm thinking about how I can do better than him and bring the *Cross* home full to the gunwales."

"That's the spirit," Grieve said with a grin.

"Congratulations, George," Winsor said, coming over to Clarke. "I guess we're mates now." He offered his hand, which Clarke shook carefully. The other captain did not give the Lodge handshake, so Clarke just smiled politely.

Then Grieve launched into a long rant about how both captains must have bumper years this coming spring. All the while, though, he kept looking at Clarke. Once again he mentioned the *Erna* and how he had lost money on the insurance. That, combined with last year's dreadful hunt, put the sealing operation in desperate shape. "This coming season will make or break us," the old man said. "Our rendering plant in Harbour Grace is a strain and if we don't have boatloads, we're done. Your job hangs in the balance," he said. "Don't disappoint me, Captain Clarke."

"No, sir, I won't, sir. Thank you for giving me a another chance."

Cheeseman wagged his head. "Tcch, tcch."

Grieve nodded. "One other thing. I've promoted Mr. Cheeseman. He'll be managing the day-to-day affairs of the sealing operation, so Thomas can concentrate on the fish. You'll be working even closer with Joshua from now on." Clarke shot an uneasy glare at Cheeseman, and then at Grieve.

SEVEN

After Old Christmas Day, with the mummering finally dying off, talk among the men of Red Island turned to sealing. Daylight had forsaken the island. Two thirds of the day was stolen by gloomy nights and the remainder obscured by unending banks of fog and low grey clouds. Wind howled incessantly and the damp cold seeped into every corner. The men, huddled around the stove in McCarthy's store, began to talk sealing and its promise of adventure, perhaps even some cash. A fever mounted as the talk grew. The promise of the seal hunt gave the younger men patience to wait for the grudging wheel of the seasons to begin turning.

Uncle Joe Skinner spoke. "It's going to be hard to get a ticket this year, too many sealers, not enough ships. Three swilers for every berth, I hear." Some of the men shuffled in their chairs, while others shook their heads. "Last year was good for the crew share," Skinner continued. "Billy Winsor on the *Beothic* earned his boys over seventy dollars. And his brother, Jessie, on the *Fagota*, won the silk flag, the first ship in. Those boys from Wesleyville finally beat the famous Keans at their own game." He lit his pipe.

"How much did the *Fagota* pay?"

"Over sixty dollars," Skinner replied.

"How did the ships in the Gulf do?"

"It was a terrible year for them," Skinner said. "All the ships in the St. Lawrence did poorly. George Clarke on the *Bloodhound* came home almost empty." The men shuffled uncomfortably. "I hear tell Clarke pushed his men some hard. He left them out on the ice too log — some had to overnight. There'd have been trouble if any weather had blown in, I'll tell you. Most of them said he was reckless." He paused to relight his pipe. "Still, Clarke has a good nose for the seals, I'll give him that. Even so, I reckon his older brother on the *Southern Cross* is a better bet."

The men around the table nodded their heads in agreement.

Skinner paused to be sure everyone was listening. "One thing I can tell you," he said, "if you're thinking about sealing this spring, you better get yourself to St. John's early. That crowd from Conception Bay has got all the berths tied up, makes it harder for us. We have to work extra hard to get a ticket now." He scratched his chin and then swept the end of his pipe in a wide circle around the room, stopping for a moment at each of the younger men. "Best you jump on the train and get down there quick, just to be sure." Each man nodded when Joe's pipe pointed to him, acknowledging the wisdom in the old man's words.

"It isn't fair," young Cecil said. He was standing with his arms crossed, outside of the circle of chairs. "It was better in the old days. We could take a schooner to the ice and everything stayed in the family." His voice rose. "Those St. John's merchants wouldn't be involved at all. But now, with those big steamers, swiling is too rich for us baymen. We have to work for the Water Street princes, got no choice." His anger subsided into resignation. "It's the captains who have the power now, you have to know one of them to get a ticket." Silence overtook the circle.

"All the same," Dennis Reddy said. "Swiling's the great game. Something to get worked up about." Nods spread around the room. "Yes, my son, even though I know it sounds better in the stories than when you're doing it, I still get this fever burning in my blood come February, this itch what needs scratching. I have to go out on the ice for the hunt. A chance to prove I'm still alive. And I might even come home with a bundle of cash. No small thing, that."

ii

John Lundrigan, fourteen years old, never paid much attention to this chatter about sealing, even though he heard enough of it. Swiling talk was for the older folks. But this year was different. His friend, Tommy Dunphy, who just turned sixteen, was now of age so he could go out on the hunt.

"Yes, boys," Tommy said to John and Peter as they huddled against the cold in Charlie Lamb's stage, "got me a berth on the *Bloodhound* this spring. I'm going to be a top hand in the sealing game. No more of this child's play. This is the real thing." His bravado worked. The two younger lads were awestruck that one of them was going out to the floes. What had been talk of the old folks suddenly became part of their young lives.

The younger boys buzzed with excitement as they hunkered against the lee wall of the net loft. "How'd you get a ticket?" Peter asked. "My dad says they're scarcer than hen's teeth this year."

"Your old man doesn't know anything. It's not half as hard as everyone says. You just have to know someone, that's all." The older boy beamed, enjoying his moment of triumph. Then he dropped his voice to share a deep secret. "My Uncle Jessie is the skipper of the *Bloodhound*. He put aside a berth for me."

"You arse," Peter said.

Tommy smirked and continued, condescension dripping from every word. "Uncle Jessie won the silk flag last year. He did so well, they gave him a bigger ship. He'll make a real killing this year. When I come back, you two will be nothing but little grannies. I'll have a good junk of money, too. Don't expect me to waste any of it on you."

Peter whistled. "Boy, Tommy, you're the luckiest guy on Earth."

"Lady luck is sitting on your shoulder, sure," John said, slapping Tommy on the back. After an awkward pause, he asked, "What's it going to be like?"

Tommy smiled. "They tell me it's a grand time. I take the train from Placentia to Whitbourne, then to St. John's. Uncle Jessie says there's lots of yarning and singing. Then, when I get to St. John's I help load the ship. I head for the ice around the middle of March. We'll be going up to the Front, that's where the biggest patch of seals is at." He paused to build excitement. "They birth them on the ice and the hunting is easy. You go out on the floes and the mothers bugger off. They just leave the young ones right there, waiting to be bashed on the head."

"That'll be no problem for you," Peter said. "That cockeyed face of yours is enough to scare the poor little buggers to death."

Tommy glared. "Watch your mouth."

Peter carried on. "That'll be something to see. Tommy, the biggest screw-up on the ice, trying to keep himself dry on the pans." He laughed. "You better take a twenty-foot gaff so they can haul you out."

"What do you boys know? The pans are bigger out there. It'll be a snap."

"Sure thing," Peter said, laughing.

Tommy scowled and then rallied. "When we get the holds full to the jeezly rails we'll come home. There'll be this great party at the wharf in St. John's. Then I'll get my share. A few years back they paid a hundred and forty-eight dollars." He stopped and whistled. "You two don't even know what that amount of cash looks like. More money than your whole family has ever seen, a frigging fortune."

Despite efforts to bring Tommy down a peg or two, the boys were impressed. They huddled around, joking, trying to find out as much as they could, celebrating his good luck. The more they talked, the more going off to the floes became their shared passion. Soon sealing was all the boys talked about. Legendary sealing captains — Arthur Jackman, Charles Dawe, Samuel Blandford, Abram Kean — became their heroes, soon elevated to the status of minor gods. Stories of spectacular success on the floes were told over and over. The fortunes earned by sealers grew with each retelling. The boys argued back and forth about who was the top captain. They knew which ones were cautious and which ones took risks for the big payout. "I hear that George Clarke is a real jowler," Tommy said, "he'll do anything to find the log-load."

"That's the kind of skipper I'd like to be with," Peter said.

Throughout the late winter the swiling game consumed the boys. Going to the ice became their dream.

iii

John and his father had spent a hard day cutting wood. They found some good long lumber for the wharf out by Big Pond as well as a load of shorts for

43

firewood. Father and son sat down together on a rock, taking a spell before the hard chore of hauling the load home.

"Tommy's going to the ice this spring," John said. "He sure is lucky."

Abel shook his head slowly from side to side. In a low voice he said, "No son, that's not good luck at all, it's bad. That'll be the end of him. Swiling is too dangerous these days."

John looked puzzled.

"It's not safe for man nor beast out there these days." After several moments of silence, Abel asked, "How'd Tommy get a ticket?"

"His uncle is the skipper of one of the boats."

"Who's that?"

"Winsor, Jessie Winsor, on the *Bloodhound*."

"Can't say as I've heard of him, but there's a whole clan of Winsors in the trade. You'd think he'd have more sense than to take kin to the ice."

"Tommy says his uncle won the silk flag last year and paid out nearly seventy dollars."

"I suppose you could say Tommy was lucky. Henry Locke and old James from up the harbour couldn't get on with anyone last year, not even the rotten wooden walls going to the Gulf. They were some angry, I'll tell you. Got to St. John's too late. As far as I'm concerned, they were the lucky ones — lucky they didn't get on." Abel stopped and looked off into the distance. "I used to think a man wasn't a man until he had a couple of seasons on the ice. That's where you found out who you were, what you were made of."

"You went sealing, didn't you?"

"Yep. Last time was in '89, just before you were born."

"How come you stopped?"

"Things changed, more of a young man's game. And once you quit going out, it's hard to get back on."

"Who did you sail with?"

"George Barbour, a good man on the ice. Went with him for six springs, a couple of good payouts, too. Baine, Johnstons ran that ship. They're good people, care about sealers. But now, with the big steel ships, things are different." Darkness came over Abel's face. "These new captains are a different lot. They don't give a goddamn about their men, so long as there are seals on the ice." He stood up and walked over to the sled, absently rearranging several logs.

"What ship did you go on?"

"That's not important," Abel said gruffly, "best leave that alone. I came home that year, married your mother, and said goodbye to my gaff and hauling rope. That's that."

Abel spoke with such finality that John was silent for several minutes. Then he stood up and came over to his father. "Boy, I can't wait to get my chance on the ice."

Abel's eyes widened as an angry "no" exploded from deep within him. "No, you won't," he growled. "You'll never go sealing, never."

John stepped back.

Abel went on, shouting. "Sealing's a bad game now, too dangerous. Too many trying for too few whitecoats." He slammed his clenched fist down on the logs, sending loose snow flying. "They've all gone crazy with the greed. These days, a sealskin is worth more than a man's life." He looked straight into John's eyes, wagging his finger in his face. "You put any thought of swiling out of your head, boy. You hear me?" Abel's face turned hard with resolve. "There's no chance you'll ever go sealing, no chance. You're not cut out for it. You're too small, too weak, too much a woman. I'll hear no more of this swiling talk, no more. You hear me?" Abel turned his back and began preparations for hauling their load home.

John knew only too well when a conversation with his father had ended: the anger etched on the old man's face, the way he turned his back, the dark cloud that came out of nowhere. The two worked on in silence, but John did not abandon his dream of going to the ice.

EIGHT

APRIL 16, 1913
HARBOUR GRACE

George Clarke, returning from the Gulf aboard his ship the *Southern Cross*, sailed into Harbour Grace. The stench of rendering seal fat met his nose the moment they steamed by Feather Point. "Already fired up the plant," he said to James Kelly standing by his side. "Must be expecting us." He grinned.

Joshua J. Cheeseman, in his tweed suit and bowler hat, stood on the wharf. He looked minute in comparison to the huge ship and quay. "He's the last person I want to see," Clarke said to Kelly, as his men threw the lines ashore. "Apart from being a royal pain, that idiot is probably a Mason too. I can't abide him."

Cheeseman rushed on board, the first to cross the gangway. He looked disdainfully around at the filth and squalor, careful not to rub against any part of the fat-encrusted deck works as he came to the bridge. He started to talk as soon as he reached the bridge, but the captain barged in. "Yes, boy," he said, his voice booming above the racket, "we had the good hunt. More pans than you can shake a stick at."

Cheeseman looked perplexed. "Pans?"

Clarke shook his head in disgust.

"Pans are what we sealers calls piles of pelts set on the ice, ready to be picked up by the ship," Kelly said quietly. "We call the pelts 'sculps.'"

Clarke forged ahead. "Yes, Joshua, my boy, we fished sixteen thousand, better than all the other captains on the *Southern Cross* since Blandford, back a decade ago. Mr. Grieve should be happy now."

Again Cheeseman looked puzzled. "Why do you say 'fished,' surely you don't fish for seals with a hook and line." He smirked as if to say he had caught Clarke in a mistake.

Clarke stepped closer to Cheeseman, his voice rising. "His lordship the Pope has declared that seals are fish, so's those bloody Catholics can eat flippers on Friday. Can you imagine? We talk about fishing for seals just to keep them happy. You should know that."

Cheeseman shook his head.

Clarke continued. "My gout even left me alone this year," he said with a smile. "I reckon a crew share of sixty dollars. Not bad for a month's work. Certainly better than last year." He chuckled. "Yes, Joshua, my boy, we're loaded down all right." He slapped Cheeseman on the shoulder and let go a booming laugh.

Cheeseman recoiled from Clarke's touch. "If you say so." A look of contempt spread across his face as he looked at the ship. He ran a finger across the rail, picking up some soot-infested grease. When he rubbed it with his thumb, it turned a slimy grey. "I don't see how you can live in all this filth," he said. He put his finger to his nose and sniffed. Then he gagged. "And among these wretches." He pointed toward several sealers tussling and laughing atop the sculps in the hold as they waited for the winch line. "This place is my idea of hell," he said, trying to wipe his hands clean with a silk handkerchief.

"You don't seem to be suffering from it," Clarke said, "with all your fancy clothes and that high talk of yours."

Cheeseman's eyes narrowed. He clenched his jaws, making the lines on his temples pulse. "I must warn you, Captain Clarke, that Mr. Grieve is not impressed with your performance. Compared to the other ships in the Gulf, you haven't fared that well. Bartlett senior brought in over forty-one thousand dollars on the *Viking*, while young Bob fetched over forty-six thousand dollars." He refused to meet Clarke's eyes, looking nervously at Kelly and then down at the deck. "Your thirty thousand dollars doesn't stand up. Not enough to make any of us rich." He stood before the hulking captain, hands on his hips. "Mr. Grieve is upset he's been bested by those other firms. Seems your reputation as a top hand on the ice is overrated." He paused long enough to revel in Clarke's clear discomfort. "By the way, Jessie Winsor is doing very well on the *Bloodhound*."

The captain scowled.

"Grieve has ordered you back to St. John's as soon as you're done here. He wants to talk to you; something very serious, he said. Probably going to dismiss you." Cheeseman grinned.

ii

Inside Baine, Johnston's main office, Grieve huddled with Thomas Collingwood. "So, what else do we have on the calendar?" he asked.

Collingwood consulted the notes scrawled on his pad. "There's a wireless message from the *Bonaventure* saying the *Bloodhound* has been jammed in the ice for over a week now. She's going to head home as soon as she can break free. Evidently Jessie hasn't lived up to his early success. It says he's got a poor cargo, maybe fourteen thousand dollars."

"That's disappointing. I had higher hopes for him." Grieve's face saddened.

"I guess that makes the *Southern Cross*'s thirty thousand dollars look better now."

"Aye," Grieve said, searching for something buried beneath his newspaper. He retrieved a legal document, a summons. 'Robert Bartlett *vs*. George Clarke' was written in legal script at the top. 'In the matter of 8,000 seals claimed to

48

have been stolen by the *Southern Cross* from the pans of the *Neptune*.' Holding it up he said, "But the costs of this will no doubt cut into whatever profit we'll make from that ship."

"Ah, yes," Collingwood said, looking at the paper.

"You know, Thomas, sometimes I think these sealing captains were born a hundred years too late." He looked at the summons. "They all should have been pirates." He sighed. "I swear I'm getting too old for this foolishness."

"George Clarke is waiting outside," Collingwood said. "Do you want to see him now?"

"I suppose so. We have to do something about this quickly. Go fetch him."

When Collingwood ushered Clarke into the room, the captain looked even more awkward than Grieve remembered. He entered slowly, with deference. Grieve did not stand up or offer his hand. He simply motioned Clarke to take the chair in front of the desk.

"See if you can find Joshua, will you Thomas? I want him to hear this."

Clarke grimaced.

Collingwood threw a quick "Yes, sir" back over his shoulder as he scurried out of the office.

Clarke wrung his hands with an unfortunate handkerchief, wet with perspiration, the victim of his worry about losing his position. The white cloth, trapped within huge fists, tumbled over and over. Clarke kept his eyes down.

"Good to see you, George."

"Yes, sir."

"How were the stores on your trip? Did you have enough food?" Grieve asked.

"Yes, sir. We were well fitted out. Not a single complaint from the men."

"Joshua did a good job getting you set up then, did he?"

After a long silence Clarke said, "I suppose."

"That's good news," Grieve said with forced joviality. "I'll be sure to tell him how happy you are with his work." Then he grew serious. "A lot has happened in the last few days and I wanted to talk to you face to face. That's why I summoned you here."

"Yes, sir," Clarke said.

"For one thing, I've just heard that Captain Winsor has run into a patch of bad luck and won't be coming home loaded like we thought."

Clarke looked up at Grieve. "That's bad news, sir," he said, his voice rising to make it more a question than a comment.

Grieve nodded. "Looks like he'll bring home about half of what you did."

"I heard the other sealers did well," Clarke said. "What happened?"

"We don't know for sure, but he was jammed in the ice for at least a week."

Clarke began to fidget again, uncertain about how to react. Finally he said, "A rough go, that. I can feel for Jessie being so helpless." He could not suppress a slight smile.

Grieve went on. "Just so you know, before we proceed, I will be offering you the *Southern Cross* next year."

A befuddled expression flooded across Clarke's face. He furrowed his brow, seemingly unable to understand what Grieve had said.

"Do you hear me, man? I said I'm giving you the *Southern Cross* again."

Clarke snapped to attention, struggling to recover himself. "Yes, sir. I hear you, but I can't believe it." He stared at Grieve, looking more like a small boy than a gruff sealing captain. "I was sure you were going to dis—." He stopped himself mid-word and sat forward.

"I'm not that happy with your performance this year, but you're improving. I'll expect better next year," Grieve said.

Clarke began to sputter. Finally a big grin erupted across his face. He began to squirm in his chair, making no effort to hide his glee. "Oh, sir. Thank you, sir."

"Never mind that," Grieve said, flipping his hand to stop the captain's gushing. "There are more important matters before us."

He was interrupted by a quiet knock at the door.

"Come."

Cheeseman entered, sporting his perpetual smug smile, which turned to a frown upon seeing Clarke.

"Please, Joshua, sit," Grieve said, motioning to Cheeseman's usual chair beside the desk. The young man turned to Grieve, all smiles again, and went to his place. "Now to the important matters," Grieve said, picking up the legal document from his desk. "Captain Clarke," he said slowly, "Robert Bartlett has filed a lawsuit against you."

"What?"

"Tcch, tcch," said Joshua.

"Yes, he's alleging you stole over eight thousand seals from his pans. He's suing you for ten thousand dollars."

Clarke drew a deep breath. His face reddened. "I don't believe it."

"Believe it. Here are the papers."

Grieve passed the summons over to Clarke. The captain cradled the paper in both hands as though it would break. When he finished reading it, he slumped down in his chair, deflated. "I don't believe it."

"This is serious, George," Grieve said. "We must take immediate steps to minimize the costs of this. The last thing I want is to lose what little profit we make this year to the Job Brothers and their pack of lawyers. We've got to handle this very carefully."

"Yes, b'y," Clarke said, inadvertently lapsing into sealer talk.

Grieve frowned and then continued. "I've always held that the best defense is a good offense in these matters."

Clarke looked mystified.

"But before we make any plans, I have to know your side of the story."

Clarke looked at his owner, uncertain of what to say.

"Now, now Captain Clarke, we're going to handle this together, but I need to know what happened so we can plan our strategy."

"But I've never been sued before."

"Well I have, too many times to count. You'll have to trust me. I've hired Harvey Morine for your defense. So what happened out there?"

Clarke sat up and gathered himself. He began tentatively. "Bartlett, that's Young Bill, got lucky and hit the main patch off Cape St. George. More seals in one place than you can imagine. He must have lost control of his men 'cause they killed over forty thousand, left most of them on the ice. The *Neptune* can only hold twenty thousand packed to the gunwales." Clarke paused, deep in thought. "That left twenty thousand panned and on the ice, twenty thousand. Can you imagine how many that was?"

"Yes, Clarke, that's how many you should bring home every year," Cheeseman said.

"Enough, Joshua," Grieve said.

Clarke continued. "Both myself and Farquhar on the *Seal* came onto Bartlett just as he was done loading. He got twenty-four thousand aboard her, practically no freeboard showing." Clarke put the summons back on the desk and began, again, to wring his hands. "I saw Farquhar take some of the sculps on board. Bartlett couldn't take on any more and the leftovers were just lying there on the ice. He had to leave the pelts where they were at, or perhaps he was planning to drown them, I don't know." He sat forward on his chair. "I didn't want the *Seal* grabbing them all, so I sent my men to bring in as many as they could."

"How many?"

"Oh, maybe a thousand or so. We'd been doing well ourselves over toward Byron Island."

"You sure about that number? It sounds as though there were a lot more than that on the ice."

"Well, maybe two thousand. Maybe a few more." Clarke reddened. He looked to his left, trying to avoid Cheeseman's gaze.

"So Bartlett left thousands on the ice?"

"Yes, sir."

"And he couldn't take any more on board?"

"No sir, he couldn't."

Grieve paused, deep in thought. His face lightened and he sat up. "Well that's how we'll proceed then," he said. A look of firm resolve come over his face. "We'll launch a counter-suit against Bartlett for leaving so many on the ice. Yes, that's it." He slapped his hand down on the papers on his desk. "The crowd who are so concerned about overhunting, like that Lady Davidson, should like that." He stopped to think through his argument. "Totally unreasonable to leave those pelts out there. The only crime here was Bartlett killing too many. Captain Clarke, you were only doing what was proper." The old man paused, fiddling with the papers on his desk. "And we'll throw in a libel action to boot, because your good name has been slandered."

Clarke looked stunned. "Are you sure, sir?"

"Yes, Captain Clarke. We can hardly sit idly by and let someone else pick our pocket, can we? We'll launch a countersuit against Bartlett and his firm. Sixteen thousand dollars should be enough. That ought to slow them down." Grieve smiled. "You can trust me, I know what I'm doing. This could turn out to be fun."

"Fun?" Clarke said with incredulity, "I hardly think so."

Grieve nodded. "Joshua, you run over and fetch Morine so we can begin."

Cheeseman stood up, pulled down his sleeves, and slicked his hair. "As you wish, sir." He left the room.

After a moment Grieve continued. "We'll have to hold back a portion of your crew's payout as insurance against the possibility of losing the case."

"Can we do that?"

"Yes, we can. I've already instructed my agent withhold twenty-five dollars from each hand."

"Will the boys get it back?"

"Yes, when we win the case."

"That seems harsh on the men, sir."

Grieve paused for a while, looking intently at his captain. "Well, we do have a choice," he said.

"We do?"

A sly grin came over the merchant's face. "Yes, we do." He paused again. "We could withhold the insurance from your pay."

Clarke looked shocked. After a moment he nodded and said, "I see, sir." There was another long silence while he stared out the window. Finally, he looked back at Grieve. "I see you have great wisdom dealing with these kinds of things, sir. Of course, I'll accept your wise counsel in this matter."

"Never you fret about this, Captain Clarke. Nothing will come of it. Job Brothers will be begging to settle out of court at a fraction of the value of the pelts you rescued from Davy Jones' locker." A warm smile came over his face. "I can even see us making a bit of money out of this."

Grieve was more lively as he ushered Clarke out. The competitive juices were flowing. He was back into the thick of it. "Yes sir, this could be fun," the old man said as he closed the door behind his captain.

NINE

As the days lengthened and spring began to nibble at the edges of Red Island's winter, Peter and John awaited the return of their friend Tommy from his adventures sealing aboard the SS *Bloodhound*. Two men from other ships straggled back home and the boys were quick to ask about Tommy's ship. "Stayed out after we left the ice," one said. "Heard they were fixing to go after some bluebacks."

One early May morning, when the work of getting ready for the herring was done, the boys sat atop the hill overlooking Jimmy's Cove. They scanned the ocean, hoping to see a boat with Tommy aboard. "Hope the silly bugger didn't pass through the ice and drown," Peter said. "He's sure taking his time about getting home."

"Just to worry us, I suspect," John added.

"My dad says it was a bad year for the sealing ships."

"Yeah?"

"Yep, three sealers wrecked on their way to the floes," Peter said.

"Three? Go away, not that many."

"God's truth," Peter said, lying back on the emerging grass and propping himself up on one elbow. "Dad says the *Labrador* sprung a leak and doused her engine. The skipper ran her aground before she sunk." He paused. "Then the *Lloydson* hit a shoal coming out of Channel. She had to go back to St. John's to get fixed up."

"You sure about this?" John said, bringing his knees up and wrapping his arms around his shins.

"Yep." Peter paused. "But the worst was in St. John's. The big steel steamers were racing through the Narrows. The *Bonaventure* beat the *Beothic* through, but then she slowed down." He sat up and moved his hands in the air to sketch out the naval drama he was describing. "The *Beothic* tried to get by her and crossed the *Bon's* bow." He showed this with his hands, the left coming atop the right. "Seems the skipper figured wrong and got rammed on the port side, aft." Peter clapped his hands together to make the collision. "The smack was so hard the *Beothic* swung around and ended up on the rocks." He crumpled his hand into a fist to show the ship crash. "There was a fire and she shipped big water, almost didn't made it back to the wharf." He looked at his left hand as if seeing it for the first time. "Dad says some of her plates were stove right in."

"Go on," John said, "they must go crazy for the hunt."

"The shore's lined with folks waving and shouting. Makes them push harder. Seems the *Beothic* pushed too hard."

"Was anybody hurt?"

"No, that's the miracle of it. Not a single bruise in any of the three wrecks. The *Labrador*'s crew even got berths on the steel ships."

"Some lucky. Perhaps that was a warning."

"Perhaps."

ii

The boys' concerns about Tommy mounted when Dennis Reddy came back several days later saying that the *Bloodhound* had arrived in Harbour Grace and was unloaded. But Tommy had not arrived home yet. Dennis told the boys not to worry. "The *Hound*'s flag was flying full staff when she steamed through the Narrows — nobody died."

"Well, at least he wasn't drowned," Peter said as they walked away.

A serious look came over John's face. "You know, if there's one thing that worries me even more than my visions, it's drowning. I can't think of anything worse." A violent shiver caught hold of him. "You see," he said, "if you drown, you've been beaten by the sea. She's won." He pointed at the breakers crashing on the rocks at the gap.

"Yes, drowning would be the worst."

Peter punched his friend on the arm and began running toward his Uncle Charlie's stage. "Enough of this talk, catch me if you can."

The two sprinted off down the pathway.

iii

Two weeks passed before old Daniel came up to the boys and said, "Your buddy Tommy's just come home."

"Great," John said, starting up the path toward Tommy's house.

"No," Daniel said, "you can't go up there."

John stopped, "How come?"

"The boy's not well," the old man said. "He cut himself up bad."

Both boys looked shocked.

"They say it would have been real bad if his uncle hadn't got it treated proper."

"Yeah."

"His father says they're not sure if he'll get the full cure."

The boys turned and walked away, stunned at the news.

iv

Tommy emerged from seclusion a week later.

"My Lord," Peter said on first seeing him, "you shrunk." The redhead's gaunt face, with eyes surrounded by grey shadows, left him looking feeble and sickly. His clothes hung loosely about his frame and there was an unaccustomed stiffness to his walk.

"You look ten years older," John said, smiling. "Right grown up, I'd say, a real man now."

Tommy looked down. "Don't feel grown up," he said, holding up his left hand, completely wrapped in cloth.

"Jesus," Peter said with a good-hearted laugh, "a boxing glove." He threw a few mock punches, but Tommy ignored him. "You're the grump."

"You'd be too."

Unaccustomed silence overtook the trio. They walked along the path, heads down.

"Does it hurt much?" John asked.

"Didn't feel a thing when I first cut it. Then it really began to sting. Got right swollen up. Started throbbing, just like the luffs in the sails you two set." He smiled briefly. "It's steady now though, as long as I don't move it too much."

"How long until your get your flipper back?"

"They won't say, just that it'll take time."

"So what was it like, the hunt, before you got hurt?"

For the first time Tommy's eyes brightened, old vitality returned. "Well, I'll tell you, it was some good."

The younger boys smiled.

"Never heard such singing and yarning as up at Whitbourne and on the train. More songs than I knew there was, even learned a couple of new dance steps." He began a step shuffle but stopped, pain etched on his face. "Lord have mercy," he said under his breath, pulling his injured hand into his stomach.

"How was it when you got to St. John's?"

"They drove us some hard getting the ship loaded. 'Show a leg, you abbey-lubbers' they'd holler at us. Worked us heavy, they did. We'd be right jiggered up by nighttime." Tommy paused, lost in memory. "She's some beauty, that *Bloodhound*. Bigger than any ship you've ever seen. You'd get dizzy just walking up her gangway. I walked it a hundred times, carrying stores into her, barrels of pork, beef, flour, sacks of potatoes, tubs of butter, tea chests. What a pile of grub." He paused, and then his eyes began to twinkle. "But at night, we'd get down to some serious yarning and singing. There was this accordion player from Keels who could play the notes off a banker. Knew every tune there is and then some. Yes, boys, it was some good." He smiled.

The trio reached the Lookout and sat down on the warm rocks.

Tommy continued. "The yarns they told come nighttime were enough to send you two sissies scampering home." He looked at John. "But you'd be right at home out there with your visions. You'd be one of the boys, right quick."

John flushed.

"One cuffer," Tommy said, "told of a young lad I figure must be like our John here. This one night he was on his way to bed, see, and his older brother stops him on the stairs. He asks to borrow his cap. 'Nick off' the boy says. The queer thing was, the older brother wasn't home at the time. He was out on the floes! This was a vision." Tommy reached over with his good hand and tousled John's hair. "Lord dyin' Jesus," he said, "then the brother vanishes right before the boy's eyes." Tommy paused long enough to be sure this sank in. "And then it turns out the older brother was lost that very night on the floes, bare headed, frozen clear through on the ice. Some queer, that."

The two younger boys looked at each other.

"Every night they told these stories, lots of them," Tommy said. "After a time, when we heard about the auld witch and Boo Darby and the banshee, us boys were afraid to go on deck after dark. We huddled together below just to be safe."

"You maid," Peter said, "all scared up by these stories. You're worse than my little sister. Jesus, they're just yarns."

"No, sir. Those tales tell it like it is out on the floes — they're how it is. You have to be out there, on the ice, to understand. They're the God's truth."

"You cockeyed ninny, they've got you all worked up about nothing."

"You'll have to see for yourself, go to the ice. Then you'll know," Tommy said, mustering all the authority he could.

John kept silent, identifying with Tommy's stories. "So what was it like when you finally set out?"

"When time came to leave St. John's, everybody got serious and quiet, kind of sad. Then this one hand starts singing, and the whole lot of us join in, everybody. Made me heart stop." Tentative at first, Tommy began to sing, his voice wobbling.

> *With bat and gaff and panning staff*
> *Surmounted with a flag, sir*
> *Away we go on the great ice floe*
> *And we never care to lag, sir*

As he sang the chorus, Tommy looked right through the other boys, caught up in his own world.

> *For we are swoilers, toilers bold*
> *And we copy from pan to pan, sir*
> *With pelts astern we shipward go*
> *Nor yield to any man, sir*

A grin came over his face as he looked out over the blue ocean.

Old bedlamers we often take
Their pelts being quite as good, sir
As any swile in yield of oil
Be he dog harp or hood, sir

Tommy's voice strengthened as the song came to life. He swung with the rhythm, eyes closed.

And when we're loaded, hold and deck
With pelts and flippers fine, sir
We leave the floe and homeward go
To hug those girls sublime, sir

A mischievous grin came over Tommy's face. He repeated the chorus, his voice ringing in the soft spring air. "Yes, boys," he said. "That was a time."

There was a long pause, each boy deep in thought.

Finally, John broke the silence. "How was the grub?"

Tommy snapped out of his reverie. "Good. Enough to feed an army. Never hungry one time." He lapsed briefly into thought. "You know," he said seriously, "the grub tastes really good out there. Once you're away from the land, there's nothing to smell. So when it comes time to eat, you're not only starved for grub, but for smells too." Tommy paused, sniffing the air. "And you know boys, when you finally do come home, you smell things you never smelled before, stuff you thought had no smell, like rocks."

"You're full of it."

"No, you can tell you're close to land with your nose. You can even taste it, like metal. I never knew that before."

John and Peter grew silent, caught up in the moment. The bandaged hand, held so stiffly across the older boy's stomach, seemed a small price to pay to be part of this wondrous world.

Tommy went on. "Boys, I'll tell you, it was some cold out there. Like as not freeze the kerosene in a lit lamp. Never shivered so much in my life, frost Devil-deep on the rigging, ice in the piss pots come morning."

John shuddered.

"One thing I learned though." He paused to make certain his friends were listening. "There's no such thing as bad weather out there."

The younger boys looked puzzled. "Go on."

"Yep," Tommy said, pausing to draw the moment out. "Only bad clothes." He smiled.

John and Peter nodded their understanding.

"But a few days after we left," Tommy said, the look of pain returning to his face, "That's when things turned bad. Took us forever to get up to Twillingate to pick up the rest of the crew. Then we almost couldn't get out of the harbour for the ice. The new boys didn't want to join in, so the fun went out of it." He paused. "After a couple of days skirting the ice, we found the seals. Funny, if the wind's right, you hear them first, barking and yakking from miles away. Then other times you can smell them before you see the little buggers. The men got some worked up when we finally saw the mothers on the ice with their pups. Some cute, those whitecoats." A strange grin crept over his face. "There were hundreds of them," he said, sweeping his hand in an arc.

"Once we were on the ice, it took me a while to get the knack of killing them. Old Jimmie Trask took me under his wing and showed me how to do it. 'Get that gaff moving smart,' he said, 'so you can hear the wind in her. Then she'll work.' Soon I was a regular hand out there." The old Tommy boomed through now, cockiness and confidence returning to his pale face. "Hard days, though; daylight to dark on the floes, packing the pelts away at night, shifting coal to make room for the seals. No end to the work. Not much time for singing or cuffing either, except Sundays. I just fell into my berth at night. Times I figured the morning call came before I closed my eyes."

"Sounds hard," Peter said, making no effort to hide his growing respect.

"Yes, but good work, you know. A man can really see what he gets done when the holds start to fill up."

The younger boys nodded.

"Skinning them, sculping they call it, was what did me in. Harder than it looks. You start the same as a fish, on the cutthroat, and then slice the full length." He made the incision in the air with his unbandaged hand, kneeling down as though he were actually doing it. "Then you carve away the fur and the fat, slicing as close to the carcass as you can. 'Work in circles,' Trask said." Tommy demonstrated. "When it's working good it's like cutting butter with a hot knife. There's a way it sounds when you get it going right." He smiled. "Still you have to be careful not to hit a bone or nick the hide. Bone dulls the knife, so you waste time sharpening your blade back up." He stopped to catch his breath. "The flippers are tricky, especially the shoulder bone, because it's buried in fat."

"Must be tough," Peter said.

Tommy nodded. "I had trouble getting it right at first, but I kept at it, getting better every time." He smiled proudly. "Didn't take me too long before I got into the rhythm of it." Then his manner became grave. "But this one time I saw my blood was going on the ice too, not just the seal's. Cut my palm right deep." He held up his bandaged hand. "But I wrapped it up and kept going. Would have been fine if it didn't swell up. After three days, old Trask says to me, 'Your uncle wants to see you topside.' 'How's she going?' Captain Jessie asks. 'Good,' I say. 'Let's see that hand there,' he orders." Tommy stopped to catch his breath. "Well you should have seen the look on Jessie's face. He started swearing up and down,

'Goddamn seal finger!' he hollered. Then he tells me I'm finished for the trip. 'You do exactly what Trask tells you,' he said, wagging his finger in my face. After that, all I did was sit around doing nothing. They made me drink this vile stuff that tasted like Wilson's Bog." He paused. "Felt a proper Jesus fool, and lonely, boys, never felt anything like it before." Tommy's eyes clouded over. "And to make matters worse, Uncle Jessie wouldn't let me come home until they were sure I was on the mend. He made me stay at his boarding house in St. John's. The landlady, Elsie, fussed over me like an old mother hen." He wiped his eyes on the back of his shirtsleeve.

"Boys, oh boys," Peter said.

Tommy looked away. But then his face brightened and he sat up. "Still, I'd go back in a heartbeat, already thinking about next year. It's worth the pain. I'll get in a full hunt next time. Even with my seal finger, Uncle Jessie paid me a full share, twenty-six dollars and eighty-six cents. They kept a few dollars for supplies and medicine, the crop they call it, but I brought home over fifteen dollars. Not bad, eh?"

As the days passed, Tommy told and retold his story, with more detail and exaggeration in each round. As John listened, the seal hunt became an adventure where he would finally prove to his father that he was a man, worthy of this greatest of all challenges. He began to dream about going to the ice next year, even though he would be would not be sixteen, the required age, by several weeks. Peter got excited, too, and they all began to plan for next spring.

vi

Three weeks after Tommy emerged from seclusion, John was working alone in his father's stage. Heavy rain pelted the old roof. The sound of individual drops slowly merged into a steady drone that soon became a humdrum accompaniment to John's solitary presence in the loft. He had finished the net repairs ordered by his father and decided to stay in the netloft rather than return home to yet another chore.

Idly, he eyed the trusses along the roof. The collar ties were four feet long, nailed like cross strokes of a capital letter "A" between each pair of rafters. A few old boards had been laid across the ties to create a shelf that ran the full length of the stage. John had never noticed this before. He pushed up on one of the boards and found it was loose. He pushed up on the next one and found moved as well. The third one, though, did not lift. He heaved up harder and a long pole tumbled off the plank, clattering onto the uncovered portion of the collar ties.

The pole looked like a boat hook, seven feet long. John manoeuvred it down through the cross ties and brushed off the dust. The metal spike at the end was heavy and finely cast, twice the size and weight of a boat hook. The wood handle felt smooth to the touch, almost soft. He marvelled at the care that had gone into fashioning it. The gentle flex from whipping the pole in his hands made it feel alive. This was no ordinary boat hook.

59

"Ahoy, there," someone shouted from below.

John startled and began to replace the pole.

"Hey, John, you hiding up here?"

He recognized Tommy's voice. "I'm in the loft. Come on up. I found something."

Tommy, along with Peter, scrambled up. John showed them his new find.

"Lord above," Tommy said grabbing the pole. "Where'd you steal this?"

John pointed.

"Holy Mother of God," Tommy said, flexing it in his hands. "This is the finest gaff I ever saw." He flexed it in his hands. "What a trim whip, just enough to do a whitecoat without busting your wrists. Could work all day with this." He ran his hand the length of the gaff with an air of reverence. "Most times a gaff is just a plain stick with a rough spike. This one is special. A man would have to be pretty high up to earn a gaff as good as this. Look at the metal there." He lovingly caressed the blunt hook and made a low, respectful whistle.

Peter touched the gaff. "Is it your father's?"

"I guess so," John said.

"Is there anything else up there?" Tommy asked.

John shrugged.

"I see something," Peter said, looking along the shelf on his tiptoes. "Looks like a box." He went over and pulled it down. The chest was just short of one foot high, one by two feet on the bottom, cornered with metal strips. Like the gaff, it showed considerable care in its building. Peter set the box on the floor. In the light, the boys could see that it was painted a faded blue.

John knelt down and ran his fingers across the smooth wood and metal surface. "Any idea what it is?"

"Sealer's chest, I reckon," Tommy said. "For keeping all your gear together."

John reached for the lid hoping to find it full of treasures from his father's adventures on the floes. To his disappointment, there were only two things inside. First was a knife in a wooden case that he recognized as a sculping blade. There was also a strange-shaped piece of wood, twelve inches long, made up of three separate parts joined to each other. Beautifully carved, it lay akimbo on the bottom of the box. John picked up the middle part. On lifting, it fell into shape to reveal a miniature water hoop with two buckets attached. The middle yoke was shaped like a regular hoop with a crook for the neck of the water hauler. The buckets were crafted in painstaking detail, attached by a wooden handle to each end of the yoke. A fine hand had carved this curious thing. John held it up. The old loft grew silent as the boys looked at it, wondering why, of all things, this was in Abel's old sealing chest.

"Never seen anything like it," John said, now sitting on the floor in front of the chest.

"Me neither," Peter said.

"Some of the hands on the *Bloodhound* carved things when they had time," Tommy said. "They'd use pieces from broken gaffs. Can't say as I ever saw anything this fine though. Must've taken a lot of time. Good skill, too."

John held the wooden buckets up, rolling the yoke in his fingers so the pails swung back and forth. "There must be a fine yarn that goes with this," he said, gesturing to include the chest and gaff.

Peter nodded. "You'd better ask your old man about it."

"Not on your life," John said decisively. "Every time I mention swiling he gets all wound up and preaches to me about what a bad game it is. There are times when I figure he's fixing to whip me even more. He says I won't ever be going to the ice, never."

"Jesus," Peter said. "He's always saying 'be a man' and then he won't let you do it. What an arse."

"Just afraid for me, I reckon."

"Yeah, but you've got to get away some time."

John paused, lost in thought. "We'd best put this stuff back where we found it. I don't want him to know we been poking around in his secret life." They put everything back and left the loft.

TEN

"Where is that Cheeseman?" Grieve said to Collingwood as he stubbed out his cigar in the ashtray of the first class rail coach. The old merchant took out his pocket watch and flipped it open, agitation clear in his abrupt movements. "We're about to pull out and there's no sign of him." He drummed his fingers on the arm of his seat. "I was hoping we could get him interested in the rendering operation at Harbour Grace, and here he decides not to show up." He looked anxiously toward the back of the coach.

Collingwood sat in the chair beside his longtime employer. "I'm sure he'll be here. Joshua always cuts it close."

Grieve turned. "Tell me, Thomas, how is Joshua doing?"

Collingwood looked away, reluctant to speak.

"Well?"

"There are problems, sir. I don't think he's doing that well. Poorly, in fact."

"I'm surprised to hear you say that," Grieve said. "The boy certainly works hard. Yesterday morning I came in early and found he'd worked all night."

"Yes," Collingwood said, "but even with Clarke's decent performance last spring, our profits for the sealing operation are lower than last year." He shuffled uneasily in his chair and looked down at the floor. "I think it may be the boy's doing."

"Do you think so?" Grieve said, with a hard edge to his voice.

"I do. I think it's his fault. The boy's a problem all around."

"You should cut him some slack, Thomas," Grieve said, looking out the window. "There's more to Joshua than meets the eye. He was a great help with Christmas at the orphanage last year, a real trooper. The boy delivered turkeys and geese all over the city, went well into the night. Then he came back and worked like a slave on the feast we put up for the children. Couldn't have managed without him." Grieve sighed. "The boy seemed to enjoy himself, too, one of the few times I've seen him really laugh. He wants to help again this year."

Collingwood nodded.

"Tell me, Thomas, what's really bothering you?

"Well, sir," Collingwood said hesitantly, "I wish you hadn't promoted him. I had everything in order, and Joshua has just made things more difficult." He looked away, slouching down in his chair.

After a long pause, Grieve said, "I see." He furrowed his brow. "A little competition never hurt anyone, did it?"

"I suppose not, sir. But it seems so unnecessary."

Grieve continued. "I think Joshua's doing a good job. He pestered the *Lloydson's* captain mercilessly and landed us his cargo for the rendering plant last year, a huge catch of old hoods and bedlamers. But I see you're not satisfied."

"Well, sir," Collingwood said, looking right past Grieve's probing eyes. "He's a hard case. Everything has to be done his way." He stopped, reluctant to proceed.

"And?" Grieve said, impatience welling in his voice.

"The boy gets put out if I question him on details. Very touchy."

"That's a problem?"

"Yes, sir, I can't trust him because he's so secretive, makes me uncomfortable."

"He's getting the job done, isn't he?"

"So it seems, sir." Collingwood shuffled uneasily in his chair. "You must have concerns about Joshua, too. Why else would you be taking this trip to Harbour Grace?"

"You're right, Thomas. The boy seems to spend too much time trying to get on my good side. He rankles me at times. I feel he may put his personal ambitions ahead of the firm's."

"There's no doubt he wants to get rich, very rich," Collingwood said. "I suspect he has his heart set on a partnership with you."

Grieve nodded. "Nothing wrong with a little ambition, probably got it from his father. But too much can be trouble." He stopped and began drumming his fingers on the chair arm. "I find the boy to be a cold fish; never been able to warm up to him."

"Joshua told me once he hates it here," Collingwood said. "He talked about how he couldn't stand the coarseness of the people and the language, the cold, the greyness. No wonder he's so lonely. He's got no friends, you know, none at all."

Their conversation was interrupted by a loud "all aboard" shouted from the back of the car. The train jerked forward.

Collingwood shrugged. "Looks like Joshua cut it too close, this time."

"I'm getting too old for this," Grieve said.

The carriage door slammed behind them and the sound of a breathless man came up from behind. Grieve turned around to see a red-faced Cheeseman approaching. His tweed suit was ruffled, tie askew. Sweat ran down his face. The young Scot had trouble keeping his balance against the pitching railroad car, having to steady himself on the backs of the seats as he approached. When he reached the front of the coach he settled into the seat facing Collingwood.

"Ach, sir," Cheeseman said, "the streetcar was shut down by a wee accident. One of those automobiles crashed into a tram." He laughed in the way a child does when he wants adults to agree. "I had to run all the way here. Good thing I did the harrier at Abbey School. I won the half marathon, you know," he said in a forced Edinburgh accent.

"Yes, b'y, we's some glad you joined us," Grieve said, putting on a mock bayman's dialect to challenge the put-on, high-tone accent of his young assistant.

"Sorry, sir."

The men grew quiet as the Waterford River clicked by. The pitching of the car settled down to a rhythmic sway as the train reached cruising speed. All three men watched out the window, heads bobbing in unison, each lost in thought. The city began to thin out.

"Well, Joshua," Grieve said finally. "The profits for the sealing operation are lower that I expected. Tell me, what do you have in mind to improve things?"

Cheeseman came alert. "Well, sir," he said in his usual Glasgow accent, "I've had a long look at the figures and it seems clear we can't count on a steady income from our sealers. You can never be sure if that Clarke will come home loaded or empty. His brother was more predictable." Cheeseman sat forward, eager to press his point. "All this means that we have only one choice — spend less money."

"I agree," Grieve said.

Cheeseman paused to be certain both of his listeners were with him. "The biggest problem I see is that troublemaker William Coaker and his confounded Fishermen's Protective Union. I swear they're out to bankrupt us. Who does this Coaker think he is, anyway? He'll be the death of the sealing operation. Too much luxury will spoil the men." He waved a finger like a preacher delivering a sermon.

"Easy now, laddie," Grieve said. "Coaker's not to be taken lightly. He's part of a long tradition hereabouts, and an important one."

"Such as?"

"Back in 1902, the sealers went on strike. There were thousands of angry men wandering the streets of St. John's — frightened everyone. After that, we learned to be careful how we treated the men. We signed an agreement in 1905."

"We?"

"Yes, me and the other owners."

"What's in this agreement?"

"Oh, most of what we take for granted now. Berths had to be free. We used to charge a coaling fee so they could ship with us." Grieve paused. "Oh, yes, and all this business about advertising the dates for sealers to sign on came from that agreement, too."

"I see. All that seems to favour the sealers, sir," Cheeseman said with a nasty grin.

Grieve frowned. "I suppose you could see it that way. But the fact is, if the sealers did band together and get organized, we couldn't stop them. We're too badly outnumbered. So we have to do everything we can to keep them quiet. Understand?"

Cheeseman shook his head.

The old man continued. "And now Coaker, with his Fishermen's Protective Union, has taken up the sealers' cause. He's given them political clout. We have to tread even more carefully now."

"That's a problem, sir," Cheeseman said. "Everything Coaker does makes it harder for us to make money."

Grieve looked unconvinced.

"Come on, sir, you've seen the wretched poverty of these people, their clothes, their houses. Isn't it up to us to do everything we can to improve the economy so they can have a better life? Maybe we can get things as good as they are back home." He smiled, looking wistfully at the passing Barrens. "We have to do everything in our power to make this sealing business work. Otherwise we're letting them down." Cheeseman paused, searching his superiors' faces. "But Coaker's demands will make beggars of us all. If he has his way, he'll turn our gallies into restaurants. He's got the menu all laid out, you know. We can't afford that, meat three times a week, really now." The young Scot scoffed. "He even wants us to have a bakery on board. And all the renovations he expects, it's ridiculous." Cheeseman raised his eyebrows and looked toward the ceiling. "Every single thing those Unionists want takes dollars out of our pockets." He paused. "And, of course, out of the men's pockets, too."

Collingwood looked uneasily at Grieve and then asked, "Do you propose we ignore Coaker?"

"Yes, as much as we can get away with. It's the only way we can make ourselves rich." He sat forward. "We can go through the motions of living up to these silly demands, but cut back when the ship gets out to the ice."

"That won't do, Joshua," Grieve said angrily. "So far, we've done a good job keeping Coaker away from important things, like our setting the price for seal fat and keeping the crew share down to one third. If he went after these, we'd be in real trouble." He shifted in his chair to get closer to his junior assistant. "So far, we've kept the FPU at bay by giving in on smaller issues like the menu and more comfortable quarters for the men." He looked intently at Cheeseman. "We have to pay more than handwaving attention to Coaker's demands if we want to keep control. Do you understand?"

Cheeseman shook his head. "As far as I can see, the best way to keep those illiterate sealers in their place is to be firm with them, show them who's got the power. Good Lord, what's the point of having power if you don't use it?"

Grieve looked at his assistant, eyebrows raised.

"Yes, sir, that's how to deal with these half-witted straumels. Keep them in their place."

Grieve said nothing for a long time. Slowly he puffed himself up, mustering all the authority he could. "I see you have a lot more growing up to do than I thought."

Collingwood nodded his agreement.

"Perhaps I was hasty giving you more responsibility."

Cheeseman's eyes darted back and forth between the two men in front of him. There was a moment of indecision, followed by an embarrassing silence. Finally, the young Scot said, "I see the wisdom of your words. Of course, you're right. We should do our best to accommodate the little things so we can keep control of the big ones. Brilliant, sir." He let go a timid laugh.

Grieve smiled.

"It's best to work with the men, especially Coaker, to keep things in order. Yes sir, that's the best way, sir. Absolutely." After a time, Cheeseman added, "You know, sir, this will reduce our profits."

"Yes, Joshua, that's the challenge of your job. You have to find a way to keep Coaker and his friends happy, but at the same time make the operation more profitable."

Cheeseman sat back in his chair, an agitated look on his face.

"Here's what I propose," Grieve said, taking charge. "I want you to prepare a list of costs just after the New Year. Choose all items to keep them as low as possible."

Cheeseman nodded. "I understand, sir."

"You be sure to do your best, Joshua, but not at the expense of our men's safety or their full bellies. We can't get Coaker's back up either, no matter what."

"Yes, sir. Exactly as you say."

Grieve looked out the window. The grey roofs and clapboard houses of Topsail bumped by. He started to fidget with his watch chain. "Yes, Joshua," he said, "you be sure to submit all your figures to me as soon as you can."

"Aye, aye sir."

ELEVEN

McCarthy's Store, a one-room affair with a flat roof, sat beside the owner's house up from Red Island's main wharf. Despite being the hub of social life, the store never held much interest for John Lundrigan. Mostly the boy thought it was a place for idle gossip and woman talk. A display of jackknives in one of the front windows had tempted him last summer. However, his father's account was already so much in McCarthy's favour the young Lundrigan knew the best thing was to ignore these trinkets dangling so seductively behind the glass. He entered the store reluctantly, and only at the bidding of his father.

On a day in late September, Abel sent him to McCarthy's to pick up some molasses. The boy slipped in quietly and moved behind the high shelf in the middle of the store so the women gathered around the old stove would not notice him. Their jabbering reminded him of the nuns at school, whispering among each other when they thought the children could not hear. He was startled when he heard his name cascade out of the gossipy babble.

"That John Lundrigan," he heard Cecil's wife, Margaret, say, "he's not what you'd expect. He's been touched by the spirits you know."

John froze.

"Just the other day, I heard that young Tommy Dunphy telling how John led them to Daniel on Sand Pond. Says he had a vision. This big white bird took him there."

"Imagine that? Such a young snip of a lad."

"Yep," she continued, "I hear he's had other messages too, lots of them. A regular wireless to the other side."

"You'd never figure that skinny boy for a sensitive," old man McCarthy said from behind his counter. "Doesn't seem the right type."

"So just what is the right type?" Margaret asked, a tinge of annoyance in her voice.

"I've never heard of young boys having those kinds of visits. It's not right, I say. That John Lundrigan is trouble, a real jinker."

John's ears burned but he remained frozen, hidden behind the shelves stacked with boxes and bags.

"If it's true," Margaret continued, "Abel must be some poisoned. He's dead set against the spirits, you know. Never heard anybody talk so strong against them — particularly after the accident." There was a pause. "Can you imagine how tortured he must be if his son's got the touch?"

The group became silent just long enough for John to realize he was breathing so loudly he could be heard. He held his breath to recover the silence. The grown-up talk retreated to background as questions swirled around the boy: 'What accident?' 'A jinker?' He reeled from the onslaught, head swimming, face reddening, near tears. The molasses crock he had been carrying crashed to the floor, shards scattering every which way. John turned and made for the door, slamming it as he bolted out. The women around the stove sat in embarrassed silence as they watched the boy run down the road.

ii

"So where's the 'lassy?" Abel said when John burst into the kitchen. The boy looked down at his empty hands, then up at his father, tears cascading down his cheeks. Anger rose up in the old man, capturing his whole body. Abel stood up and came toward the boy. He raised a huge hand and brought it down backhand onto the boy's face, sending him staggering backwards, once, twice, three times. John fell against the door and raised his hands over his head, half pleading, half trying to protect himself.

Abel caught himself before launching the next blow. Unable to speak, he motioned for the boy to go upstairs. John obeyed almost crawling. He wiped the blood from his nose on the back of his hand as he slithered past his father's monstrous back. After a few minutes, Abel growled, "Don't you leave that room until I say you can."

iii

After three days, life in the Lundrigan house had evolved into a silent truce. Grunts and "yeps" became the mainstay of conversation. John tried to spend as much of his spare time as he could away from home. Long walks became his favouite pastime. On one unusually warm day he was out by Margery Cove when the now-familiar feeling of dread began to well up. Another vision was coming.

He sees a speck in the distance out over the Cove. The monster, black and menacing as ever, comes at him and everything goes black. After what feels like an eternity the white bird appears in the distance and flies directly toward the town.

John knew what this meant and began to sprint down the trail. He was surprised when he arrived at the dock to find nothing unusual — everything appeared normal. Peter's Uncle Charlie and Oliver Ryan were getting ready to go out fishing, but that was all. The boy looked everywhere trying to find out what was wrong, but to no avail. He could not understand why his vision had been so wrong this time.

It was not until three days later, when the two men who had been on the dock were lost at sea, that John began to understand. They had disappeared without a trace after leaving the harbour. Now John knew that he was supposed to have warned them, but he had failed. The more he thought about it the more he blamed himself for the tragedy — it was all his fault. If only he had understood. He became despondent, filled with guilt.

iv

John's only respite was exploring the island with Tommy and Peter. On a crisp October day the three boys walked toward Long Point on the back part of the island. The gloom that had spread over his life began to lift the deeper they got into the woods. The bush was one place where his father and the other grownups could not get at him. He had forgiven Tommy for blathering about his visions, knowing the island would find out sooner or later. The talk at the store still troubled him, but time had changed all that woman talk into idle prattle. Here, with his friends, he was safe. Fluffy clouds sped by, sending shadows dancing along the path as they picked their way toward the western shore.

"Yes, boys," Tommy said. "Now that I'm none the worse for me seal finger, I'll write Uncle Jessie and get us tickets on the *Bloodhound* for next spring. It'll be some time having the three of us together on the ice."

The younger boys nodded.

Tommy said, "And you, young Johnny, you be sure to bring along your visions when we go to the ice. You can be our insurance policy." He gave the youngest a condescending pat on the head.

John fired back a dirty look.

"What's the matter, afraid of your visions?" Tommy said. "You're bloody lucky to have them, you dummy. They'll make you a top hand on the ice. You ought to be proud."

John stopped walking, head down, staring at the ground. "Don't feel proud at all. I hate these things. They're a curse. I wish I never had them. They make me so scared I can hardly stand it." He scuffed a rock on the trail with his boot. "People treat me so strange, like I'm a witch or something. Nobody around here understands. Nobody knows how awful it is." He did his best to quell the rising tears.

After a long silence, Peter put his hand on his friend's shoulder. "You know, John, my father mentioned an old man in Little Harbour who knows all about these kinds of things. Jacob Newtry, they call him. I've heard my dad call him Doc."

John looked up, rubbing his eyes. "Really?"

"Yeah, they say he knows everything. Maybe you could talk to him. Might help."

"Newtry you said?"

"Yep, Jacob."

"That's queer. Newtry was my mother's name before she got married. Maybe he's kin."

"Merciful God," Tommy said, "don't tell me it runs in the family. That'd be too much." He let out a cackle intended to sound like a witch.

V

As the days passed, the coming winter mirrored John's world. By late November everything had become cold and closed in. Lengthening nights reflected the darkness that had become his constant companion since his third vision. The relentless sameness of the snow-covered land, the ice, the continual grey fog, weighed heavily on his soul. John had no words for how he felt, only deep abiding pain, like a toothache, gnawing, ever-present.

Abel began to heap more and more work onto the boy. "Best thing for you, son." As soon as John finished one backbreaking chore, Abel would pile on another.

John's days blurred into constant drudgery. As he stumbled along, mechanically doing his father's bidding, the need to talk to old Jacob Newtry in Little Harbour grew greater and greater. He had to know if the visions were the Devil's work. He had to learn how to break out of the terrible numbness trapping him since his third vision. Jacob became a beacon of hope, the one thing that offered a way ahead. As the days shortened and melded into December, he dreamed of making the long trip to Little Harbour to talk with the wise old man.

"I hear Cecil's going over to Fox Harbour tomorrow," Tommy said one cold afternoon as they walked home from the waterfront.

"Can you get to Little Harbour from there?" John asked.

"Not sure. Cecil would know. He's got family across the bay. You planning on making a run for it?"

John did not answer. He was already galloping toward Cecil's stage. The boy arrived, puffing, to find Cecil moving some wood upland.

"Cecil, I hear you're going to Fox Harbour," John said, pitching in to help.

"Yep. Want to get over and back in case some shore ice forms up."

John looked out into the bay, seeing a smattering of pancake ice moving up and down in the swell. "Could happen this year," he said.

"Yep."

"Tell me, Cecil, can you get to Little Harbour from there?"

"I suppose. You could take the train up to Whitbourne, then catch the westbound. They'd let you off at the path to Little Harbour." He paused. "Wouldn't take half a day if the schedule was right."

"Could a boy walk?"

"Yes, I suppose, but it'd be a long trek. Wouldn't think of trying it this time of year. She's a lot colder upland."

They moved more wood in silence.

"When you leaving for Fox Harbour?" John asked.

"First light tomorrow, so long as the wind isn't up."

The boy smiled for the first time since his third vision.

vi

"You're more lively today," Abel said as they finished supper that night. John nodded, looking out the darkened window to avoid his father's probing gaze. "Glad to see it. Always said the best cure for the glums was good hard work. That's what will make a real man out of you. No more of this woman stuff, visions and all that." John got up from the table and went over to the stove, turning his back to his father. Abel continued. "Tomorrow we'll start knitting the new trap, lots of work. I want you to go out in the bush and gather a good load of wood for the barking kettle. Cut it into long junks and split the bigger pieces for a good hot fire." He paused. "You listening, boy?"

"Yes, sir."

"I'll ready the twine," Abel said. "We'll get started soon as you have the wood down to the stage."

After a moment John replied, "I'll get out in the woods at first light, before you're up. Should be back before breakfast with my first load."

"Proper thing," Abel said, smiling to see his son brighten up.

Before going to bed John gathered the clothes he would need for his journey to Little Harbour: his trigger mitts, fur-lined cap, a heavy scarf, wool pullover and his old greatcoat. He piled these neatly at the foot of his bed.

vii

Sleep did not come easily. He tossed and turned, rehearsing his early morning escape plan, replaying the guilt and worry from his third vision and dreaming about talking to Jacob. He had no difficulty rising before the grey fog lightened outside his east-facing window. He dressed, slipped downstairs and stuffed a small bag of oatmeal into his pocket. The boy paused as he closed the door. He breathed deeply, turned his back on the house and walked away. His breath surged out in front of him in the cold, pre-dawn air, drawing him forward, toward the unknown.

Cecil's stage was abandoned when he arrived, but the boat was tied wharfside. John sat down and waited in a world closed in by darkness and fog. Before long he heard the crunch of footsteps and Cecil loomed out of the early morning fog, flailing his arms back and forth.

"That you, Johnny?" he said as he arrived on the stage head. "Up some early, aren't you?"

"Yes, Cecil. We're starting on a new trap and father wants me to get some good twine in Fox Harbour. He doesn't like the kind McCarthy has, can't abide that two-strand."

"It's true. McCarthy's is more thread than twine. I double it up myself." Cecil jumped down into the boat and began preparations for leaving. "You sure this is what Abel wants?" he said, looking up at John.

The boy drew in his breath. "Yes, sir. He couldn't believe his luck when I told him you were heading over today. He's going in the woods this morning. Figured he could get a better load than me and I should do the easy job of going across for the twine."

"Sounds like Abel." Cecil paused. "Well, don't just stand there. Throw in the lines. We've got places to go and work to do."

John jumped to it and before long sat in the bow, guiding Cecil around the chunks of ice in the harbour.

The calmness of the open water made for a quick trip. John watched over the bow as the sun rose behind the mainland. Early winter warmth embraced him through the grey fog.

viii

"There's no three strand in Fox Harbour," John said to Cecil. "I hear they've got some good twine up at Ship Harbour."

"Lord, John, I don't have time to go up there," Cecil said.

"That's all right. I'll walk up."

"You expect me to wait for you?"

"No, Cecil. There are several boats going over tomorrow. I'll ship with one of them. Josiah Groves says I can stay the night with him."

"Maybe you should come back with me and forget the twine."

"Jeez, no. The old man would whip me silly if I showed up empty-handed."

"Well you take care, son. We'll see you tomorrow then."

John began to run along the well-worn pathway that led from Fox Harbour, sprinting between the two snow-covered hills. Once out of sight, he settled into a brisk walk. The trees were taller, compared to the island, different shapes, too. Waving in the light breeze, they seemed alive, moving in and out, threatening. John steeled himself against looming fear, pushing forward despite his uneasiness. "What have I got myself into?" he said out loud. Then he took a deep breath and forged ahead.

When he crested a hill and looked ahead he began to understand the huge distances on the mainland. Again a wave of fear passed over him. But he pushed on, gaining confidence as he conquered this new land with his footsteps. The trail led along the crest of a high hill and then dropped into a valley where he found the rail line. The hard permanence of the shiny steel, its brute strength, was an antidote to his fear.

John marvelled at the amount of work that had gone into building the railway: clearing, levelling, laying the gravel, building bridges, setting sleepers, spiking tracks. For the first time he began to understand the colossal size of this great iron trail. He had only heard talk of it before, never been up close to see the results of the backbreaking work that went into it. The size and length were almost beyond comprehension. Two parallel tracks ran as far as he could see, all the way from shore to shore they said.

He came to a place where stones were lined up beside the track to mark where the train would stop to pick up Fox Harbour passengers.

The boy followed the track, walking along the sleepers. After a time he found a comfortable stride and nameless ponds and creeks loomed up, only to disappear at his back. His fear returned momentarily as the snow in the woods grew deeper. However, the track bed remained clear, affording an easy walk. The fresh smell of evergreens swept over him. Occasional chickadee calls and crow caws punctuated the silence. Soon, he began to feel a sense of peace.

After an hour, passing by bogs and treed hills, he came to a lone shack at the side of the line. It was one-storey, clapboard, with a flat roof, sitting on posts, like the tilts back home. The roof gleamed with fresh black tar. Shutters were set on hinges beside the windows and it had a strong storm door. The east side of the cabin was braced with stout poles as though someone had tried to push it over. A clothesline, with shirts fluttering like flags in the soft winter breeze, linked the shack to the outhouse. John passed by quietly, happy to know he was not totally alone.

Occasionally the trees would open up and provide a grand vista of a rocky, tree-covered landscape. John looked forward to these openings because most of the time he walked in a treed canyon that hemmed him in. In these valleys all he could do was trust the rails to guide him to Little Harbour.

An hour later, a second shack turned up on the other side of the tracks. John waved at children watching him through the window. He began to use the shacks to measure his progress, one an hour. "These tilts must be for the men who look after the track," he mused.

As the miles fell behind, John began to feel happiness, long forgotten. The words of an old song began to run through his mind. The tune was "The Girl I Left Behind Me," but he preferred the words Tommy had taught him. Almost inaudibly at first, John began to sing:

Ooooo, the Block House flag is up today
To welcome home the stranger
Annnnnd Stewart's House is looking out
For Barbour in the Ranger

Louder singing filled the empty landscape.

But Job's are wishing Blandford first
Who never missed the patches
He struck them on the twenty-third
And filled her to the hatches

Arms swung in rhythm. His stride gained gusto with each bar, matching the song's cadence. Snow slithered off a tall spruce up ahead, showering a thin veil that remained suspended in the still air.

> *And Bowring too will bet a few*
> *On Jackman in the* Howler
> *The little* Kite *she bore in sight*
> *With Billy Knee the jowler*

John broke through the curtain of suspended snow, enjoying the cold wisps on his face.

> *Though short of grog still lots of prog*
> *To bring us home quite hearty*
> *Each Trinity Dove fell wild in love*
> *With Walsh and Luke McCarthy*

He laughed out loud thinking on the words. Old Simon Walsh and pock-faced Luke McCarthy being courted by some Trinity Dove… "Not likely," he said, and then continued on his way.

> *Though some may sing of lords or kings*
> *Brave heroes in each battle*
> *Our boys for fat, would gaff and bat*
> *And make the whitecoats rattle*

His pace quickened. John's young voice blossomed in the crisp winter air.

> *They kill their foe at every blow*
> *Was Waterloo more grander?*
> *To face, who could, an old dog hood*
> *Like a plucky Newfoundlander*

There was a trestle in the distance. As he sprung toward it, glee surged through him.

> *We danced on shore in McCarthy's Store*
> *The darling girls were dancers*
> *Jemima Snooks …*

A whoosh up from behind him almost knocked John off the sleepers, leaving his interrupted song dangling in the cold air. A strange-looking machine sped by on the tracks. It looked like somebody had stolen the two-man bilge pump from Frank Ryan's schooner and put it on a platform with wheels. One man, now facing John, worked the up-and-down handle to make the contraption move along the tracks. The man at the pump trolley waved as he disappeared into a fog of loose snow blown up by his passage.

The boy stopped to wait for the snow to settle. He watched the machine cross the trestle and vanish around the bend. Then John resumed his journey; soon back in his newfound walker's world. The song returned:

We dance on shore in McCarthy's Store
The darling girls were dancers
Jemima Snooks our boys would hook
At every set of lancers

He sang as loudly as he could, shouting really:

Don't talk to me of balls or sprees
You never saw such a party
That time on shore in McCarthy's store
Made all feel good and hearty

"Yes boy," he said out loud, "made all feel good and hearty."

The further he got from Red Island the lighter his spirit became and the more his fear subsided. It was all measured by the near-predictable passage of small shacks on the hour. He crossed a wooden bridge over another large creek. He looked up and down the stream to see how it carved its way through the rugged landscape.

In the early afternoon, expecting his next shack, he came instead to a collection of five buildings; a small community that seemed to be the middle of nowhere. Three huge wooden boxes with wheels sat on a run of track beside the one he walked on. The size of this railroad equipment impressed the young Red Islander. "So tall," he mused, "they had to put a ladder up the side to reach the top." The boxes were painted with the same red ochre as the stages back home. He wondered why they covered the cars with names and numbers, painted in white on the sides. "Are they afraid someone is going to steal them?" The bilge pump trolley that had passed him sat, unmanned, on two pieces of track set at right angles to the main line. John returned the waves of several people as he walked through the small settlement.

ix

The sun had almost dropped behind the trees by the time he reached Placentia Junction, a cluster of ten shacks, one bigger house and two large buildings. Everything was ochre. Railway tracks ran every which way. John saw how trains could be turned by the tracks to go either back to Placentia or pass straight through. More of the big boxes on wheels rested on extra tracks, including one with windows. "Must be for people," John mused. Following Cecil's instructions, he turned left and followed the tracks away from the junction, heading north.

The shacks started to come much sooner than he expected. "Must be walking faster." In time, though, he realized he was not moving more quickly. Rather, the tilts were simply closer together on the main line. Signposts told him the little shacks were a mile apart, a twenty-minute walk between each one. As he moved north, the trees became shorter and more sparse. More bare rock showed through the snow. The view opened out before him, revealing a panorama of a hard, rocky land. Yet the tilts, passing at a rate of three per hour, gave him a foothold, an anchor, in this otherwise barren place.

The temperature dropped along with the sun. Soon the warm orange lights in the windows of the line shacks began to beckon. He could feel the warmth and wondered about the lives of the people inside, so far away from others, so cut off.

Full darkness had fallen when he rounded a corner and came to a group of people. Two grown-ups and three children, along with a big black dog, stood on the track. A lantern, which threw dancing light along the shiny steel rails, dangled in the man's hand.

"Ahoy there, time for a spell from your long walk." The man came forward, extended his hand, and said, "Sebastian Roberts, section man on this piece of the main line. They call me Seb."

John shook the outstretched hand. He felt the strength of years of hard work in the man's grip. Up close, he could see a weatherworn face under a scruffy beard. The man's eyes twinkled as they smiled a warm welcome.

"This is my family." Pride was evident as he introduced the others. "And our dog, St. Thomas." The huge black beast came up and nuzzled John's leg. "We'd be honoured if you'd take supper with us and, if it suits your purpose, spend the night in our home."

John could not find the strength to refuse and soon found himself surrounded by children, being herded toward the small shack. When he entered, he saw a table set for six. The plates were a raggle-taggle collection of different sizes and colours, all chipped. The table, covered with a clean piece of sailcloth, was an old door sitting on two sawhorses. Chairs were crates. Roughly carved wood cutlery, mixed with occasional metal forks and knives, sat neatly arranged beside the plates.

He barely had his greatcoat off before Seb motioned him to a seat at the table. Mrs. Roberts served freshly cooked trout and boiled potatoes. "There you go, John," she said. "This will put some meat on your bones." The room fell silent, save for the clinking of wood and metal on porcelain.

Before they finished, everyone jumped up in answer to some unheard signal. They headed for the door, with Seb motioning John to follow. Everyone gathered and peered up the track in the direction from which John had come. There was a pale yellow shadow in the sky, and then he heard a deep rumble. Soon the shadow transformed to a bright orange light coming out of the black. For a brief moment John recalled his visions, but the shaking ground and a near-deafening noise soon snapped him out of it. The children began to wave. The dog barked. A mammoth black machine on huge wheels flew by, steam hissing from numerous vents, smoke rising from an orange flume atop the chimney. Sparks flew. The engine, with its huge side pistons and rods clanking and hissing in time with the wheels, passed, followed by a car full of coal. John caught a glimpse of a man shovelling into a flame-filled box in the cab. Then four boxcars clicked by followed by three with windows, from which a gentle orange light shimmered. He could see people in the windows, some asleep, some with heads down. And then it was gone, vanishing as quickly as it had come. Silence recaptured the cold night.

Again in answer to an unseen signal, the family headed back into the cabin. John followed, lost in awe at the sheer size of the beast that had just sped by. Everyone returned to the table as if nothing had happened.

When the meal was finished John said, "Can't remember trout tasting that good, Mrs. Roberts. Must have been hungrier than I thought." He smiled. "Thank you kindly." The woman blushed and looked over at her husband. The oldest child, perhaps eight, looked down and giggled. Only then did John notice the threadbare overalls, patch upon patch in many places.

"How did you know I was coming?" he asked. "You were waiting for me on the tracks out there and had the table set. Seems you can see into the future."

"No, son, it's nothing that fancy," Seb said with a grin. "We're well-connected along the line here. There's always section men come by on hand cars and tell us the news. We knew you were coming before you made the Junction, although we weren't sure you were coming this way, until you went through." Seb stopped and smiled. "Yes, we hear about everything here. Jees, b'y, if a rabbit farts up in Clarenville we hear about it before the stink clears."

All three children began laughing. Their mother tried to shush them with embarrassed whispers.

Talk turned to the weather and how easy winter had been so far. "Hear there's a blizzard around Corner Brook, but they say we'll be fine for a few days yet."

John marvelled at how much information these people had and how willingly they shared it, same as back home. The distances were greater but that didn't matter.

Seb did not push for details about John's trip except to ask his name and a few questions regarding the track he had just walked. John was impressed by how easy these folks were to talk to, not like his father where you had to be careful with every word you said. "I'm headed for Little Harbour to visit," he volunteered. "Do I have far to go?"

"No, son," Seb said. "The path to Little Harbour is just after mile eighty-seven. It's about an hour walk from there. We're at mile seventy-three here."

John calculated there would be fourteen section man shacks left to walk plus the hour to Little Harbour, maybe five hours altogether. He smiled when he realized he would be in Little Harbour by noon the next day.

After more chat, Mrs. Roberts began herding the children to bed. By the time the children settled down, Seb made it clear that everyone should turn in. They offered John a big bed with spanking clean sheets and a tattered comforter. He had displaced the children, consigning the whole family to the other bed. After a period of tossing and turning, St. Thomas joined him. The weary traveller dropped into an unaccustomed deep sleep.

x

John awoke to a whistling kettle. Light rain spattered on the windows in front of a grey fog.

"Getting thick out there," Seb said. "Just got tea and a bit of soft Tommy for breakfast."

The boy nodded as he slipped on his boots. He went over to his coat and retrieved the bag of oatmeal out of his pocket. Without saying anything he handed it to Seb's wife who was fussing by the stove. He raised his hand before she had a chance to protest and said, "Got no use for this today. I'll be in Little Harbour by midday. A good hot breakfast for us all would be the best thing."

She looked over at Seb and, without words, they debated and came to an agreement. She accepted the gift with a gracious smile. A chorus of cheers came from the children.

"Haven't had porridge for a month," Seb said. "Hard to come by out here."

The Roberts surprised John with their thankfulness for his small gesture. "Thank yous" and "hurrahs" filled the time it took to boil up and serve the porridge. Even St. Thomas showed his gratitude, getting underfoot every time John tried to move.

The hot porridge and the gratefulness of his hosts filled John with warmth. Before long he stood at the door saying goodbye. Mrs. Roberts handed him a bag full of leftover porridge, still warm. "I mixed some raisins and 'lassy in it. If you don't wait too long it will be a nice lunch. But if it gets too cold it'll turn into a cannonball," she said, a gentle smile in her eyes.

"Thank you," he said. "And thank you all for your kindness." They waved as he struck out. St. Thomas followed for a while, but John finally sent him home. Peacefulness returned as he moved ahead, only vaguely noticing that the spitting rain blew directly into his face and the air was colder.

Try as he might, John could not recover the easy walking stride of the day before. The gusting wind and rain in his face made each step a chore, unlike yesterday. He felt tired within minutes. Soon a bone-numbing chill replaced the warmth of his big breakfast and the Roberts' company.

After he laboured past three section man shacks, the weather began to worsen. The clouds dropped, deeply threatening. The wind began to bluster with occasional gusts that nearly blew him off the sleepers. The rain, now heavy, pelted unforgivingly into his face, forcing him to walk with his head down. His collar and the neck of his pullover got soaked.

The blow steadied and turned into what Skipper Joe called a two-reef wind. The shutters were closed over the windows of the line shacks and the storm doors drawn shut.

At the seventh shack he looked up and the prickling on his face told him the rain was turning to sleet. Within minutes the sleet turned to snow. The wind-blown flakes became white lines as they flew through his small downward-looking tunnel of vision.

After an hour of fighting the headwind, John scrambled down the track bed into a grove of scruffy trees. He sat down in the lee and unwrapped the hardened porridge that weighed so heavily in his pocket. He nibbled at the solid mass for a while and finally threw it toward the track. It vanished into the blizzard as if by magic.

He resumed his walk, the snow now accumulating behind the sleepers and on the track bed itself. The relentless whiteness, the unforgiving cold radiating from his neck and feet, the work of bucking the wind, melded into a travel trance. He plodded along, any sense of progress obliterated by the horizontal shards of snow. The blizzard was so thick he thought he might have passed by a number of section shacks without seeing them. Walking grew harder when he had to break trail in the snow, now up to the tops of the rails, even heavier in places where gnarly trees afforded windbreaks.

Suddenly, the track stopped at the edge of a cliff. John looked over the brink in shock to see a creek running below. The line had ended in the middle of nowhere. Confusion reigned until he realized he had wandered off the snow-covered track, fooled by the snow, now completely covering the line. He retraced his footprints and recovered the rail line, resuming his trek into the teeth of the growing storm.

Numbness crept in from his feet and hands. He flailed his arms. An urge to curl up and let fatigue luxuriate over him began to fill his thoughts. The more he plodded along, the more reasonable lying down seemed to be. "Just a short nap," he said. Then he snapped out of it, recognizing that lying down would be fatal. "But it would feel so nice." Onward he trekked, numbness gaining a stronger hold with each step. Alertness and caution waned. More than once, he resisted the urge to throw off his hat and mitts. Only the thought of seeing Jacob drove him forward.

His pace slowed as he pushed harder against the growing gale. He staggered with the effort. Without warning the wind stopped, flinging him forward. John tumbled down into knee-deep snow, losing his cap. He found himself lying face down in a deep drift. He lay there for a moment, feeling the warmth, almost giving in to the urge to close his eyes. After a spell, he looked up and saw he had fallen over an embankment, again having wandered off the track. By the time he scrambled back to the top, his footprints had been erased by the wind. The flat whiteness left no clue where the track might be. He walked criss-cross, dragging his feet through the snow, hoping to trip over the rail. At one point he felt something beneath the snow but was distracted by hearing what sounded like a bell far in the gloom. He continued searching for the track. Coldness, fatigue and the sickening fear that he had lost connection with his steel lifeline finally won out. John staggered and dropped to his knees. He hollered out "Jacob" as loudly as he could, but the sound was whisked away by the wind. He rocked back and forth and then fell face first into the snow. Within minutes, only the black of John's greatcoat and the scroll of his scarf were visible on the solid white canvas of the Avalon Isthmus.

TWELVE

An official letter arrived for George Clarke in Brigus just before Christmas, 1913. It announced the settlement of the lawsuit against him. While the details had been worked out in May, it took until then to get it finalized. "It sure took those lawyers long enough to make it official," George said to Lucy.

She nodded.

"I haven't wanted to burden you with the details, my dear, but Mr. Grieve was a genius handling the whole matter. On the day before the court date, Bartlett's lawyers asked for a postponement. Then they approached the old man with an offer."

"Mr. Grieve certainly knows how to deal with these things, doesn't he?" Lucy said, as she sat down at the kitchen table.

"Yes, my dear, he does." He waved the letter in the air. "It says here that Grieve agreed to four thousand dollars damages which includes the legal fees. That's a whole lot less money than the six thousand sculps I salvaged from the *Neptune*'s pans." George laughed. "I hear Mr. Grieve is pleased. He was right when he said we'd make money on the deal — quite a bit, actually." Clarke beamed. "He's covered the legal fees from the firm's share." He sat down opposite his wife. "That ought to show that little bugger Cheeseman how things are done."

Lucy nodded.

"The men got their twenty-five dollars back, too," George said. He frowned and began to fidget, fingers tapping on the red-checkered tablecloth. "But I've heard that some of the older hands are in a tizzy about the holdback and won't sign on with me next season. I suppose I'll have an even greener crew this year. I'll say one thing about my brother John, he was always better than me with the older men. He knew how to handle them." He looked away, deep in thought. "It's not all bad, though. The younger boys work harder, they've got more respect." He stopped fidgeting.

"It's all for the best then," Lucy said with a smile. "It saddens me to see those old sealers give up on you, George. After all, it wasn't your fault. I can't fathom why anyone wouldn't want to work with you."

George shrugged and resumed drumming his fingers on the tablecloth.

"The Bartletts haven't been too sporting about this," Lucy said. "Emily crossed over to the other side of the road yesterday so that she wouldn't have to talk to me. I guess we'll have to do without their friendship until things heal over. We haven't been that close, anyway." She smiled warmly, reached over, and took her husband's fidgeting hands into hers.

George smiled. "Mr. Grieve was a pillar of strength through all of this, a saint. I wouldn't have made it through without him standing up for me like he did. He's a good man. He may not belong to the Lodge, but he's an Orangeman at heart. Yes, my dear, a true Orangeman. His kindness has me feeling beholden to him." He put his other huge hand on top of Lucy's. "The best way I can repay his faith in me is to do well, really well, this spring, and I'll do exactly that. Yes, the important thing now is that I have my finest year on the *Cross*."

He picked up the lawyer's letter and looked carefully at it, running his fingers over the embossed letterhead. "These lawyers sure have the money," he said absently, "but usually at the cost of someone's suffering." He began to smile. "You know, Lucy, I heard this story about Grieve who's always having a terrible time with lawyers. This time it was something about owing money for a shipment he never received. One day he wanders into a store on Water Street. He finds this beautiful, life-sized sculpture of a rat, made out of gold." George began to laugh. "He asks how much it costs. 'Four dollars for the rat, sir, and a hundred dollars for the story behind it.' Being a resourceful sort, Grieve says, 'You can keep the story, old man, but I'll take the rat.'"

Lucy watched him intently as his energy grew and his eyes began to sparkle.

"Rat in hand, he heads down toward the harbour. When he crosses the street, two large rats — the real thing — come out of the alley and fall into step behind him. The merchant begins to walk a bit faster when the two rats are joined by five or six more. Soon there's over a hundred of them trailing on behind. People begin to point and shout." George paused to catch his breath and chuckle. "Soon he's running full speed with thousands of rats chasing him. In a panic he looks behind and sees millions of rats, stretched out the length of Water Street — like a carpet. He bolts onto Bowring's quay, jumps up onto a wharf grump, and heaves the statue as far as he can." George demonstrated the throw. "And wouldn't you know it, the tide of rats surges over the dock, right into the water. All of them drown, every single one of them."

Lucy began to shake her head, a bemused grin on her face.

George continued. "Mumbling to himself, Grieve goes back to the shop. 'So you've come back for the story,' the shopkeeper says. Grieve shakes his head, all sullen like. 'No, boy,' he says, 'I've come back to see if you've got a gold lawyer.'" George was quiet for a moment and then let out a booming laugh. He held up the letter. "Have you got a gold lawyer?" he said, barely able to get the words out between cackles.

Lucy smiled.

ii

George Clarke attended a Lodge meeting later that week. During a break in the proceedings, he was admiring his Lodge's banner, proudly on display behind the Worshipful Grand Master's chair. Beautifully crafted on lush scarlet silk, the only writing on it was the embossed "L.O.L. 59: Brigus." Otherwise the flag was surrounded by a carefully embroidered border that encircled a large number of symbols, each beautifully stitched. To an outsider, these designs would appear to be a hodgepodge jumble, but to Clarke each one held a special place, documenting his rise from the menial Orange Degree to his current position as Deputy Master. He smiled as he remembered how, through the Lodge and his brothers, he had found a home for the desire that burned within him. This was a place of friends who were willing to take a stand against the Papist tyranny.

"Thinking back on the rituals, are you?" a gentle voice said from behind him. Clarke turned around to see William Norman, the eldest of the active Lodge brothers, standing beside him. His grey hair glistened in the light, above bright blue eyes that belied his frail appearance.

"Aye," George said. "I am. I love how these signs make everything so clear and so easy. Out there," he said, pointing toward the frost-covered window, "everything is so complicated. All those Catholics trying to take over and put us down." He shuddered. "But here it's different. Everything is as it should be, everything is right."

The old man nodded and put his hand on George's arm. "I remember when we started this Lodge back in '67. Your father, God rest his soul, was one of the founders, as was I." He chuckled. "We had our first meeting in Caleb's house and your Aunt Louisa wouldn't leave her kitchen. 'I'll not leave my home just so's you can gabble with your friends,' she said. We eventually had to initiate her and appoint her to make sure only brothers came into the kitchen during meetings, you know, as Lodge Tyler." The old man laughed. "Probably the first woman Orangeman in the Colony."

"My father was a hard man, strict as the Bible. I'm surprised he would have put up with that from a woman."

"We had to work on him, I remember, but in the end he saw the wisdom of it. That's why we built this hall so quickly."

Clarke nodded. "Yes, sir. Father was some iron-fisted. He'd put a licking on me if he fancied I was even having a bad thought. He taught me the importance of obedience and respect."

"Yes," Norman said, "he was a fine man."

Clarke smiled.

Norman stroked the scarlet banner. "What part of the rituals do you remember the best?"

Without hesitation, Clarke answered, "The Oath, I can still recite it. 'I will have such a sense of my duty as a Protestant that I will not marry a member of the Romanish Church, nor stand sponsor for the child of a Roman Catholic when receiving baptism by a Priest of Rome, nor permit a Papist to stand sponsor for my child at its baptism.'" He looked upwards. "And, so help me God, I've upheld my obligation to the letter of the law and will continue to do so."

"Yes, George, you are certainly a dedicated brother," Norman said, a shadow of worry flashing across his face. He paused, hesitant to proceed. "You know, George," he said in a near whisper, "there are times when you take this Papist business a bit too far."

Clarke's eyes widened. He stepped back.

The old man stepped forward so he could still whisper. "Yes, George, it's hard enough to keep things running smoothly in Brigus without adding all this anger. I think it's better to keep to ourselves and let those Catholics be."

Clarke began to shake his head. "No," he said, anger rising, "not you too. You haven't gone soft like those others." He stopped. "Have you?"

"I still believe in the Lodge, George," Norman replied firmly, "but feel we should be helping to keep things on an even keel, not getting everyone's back up."

"But—"

The voice of the Worshipful Grand Master brought conversation to a halt. In regal tones, he announced, "To your seats, brethern, young Spracklin is ready for his initiation." Each brother scurried to his chair and the hall became silent.

Three sharp knocks rattled the old wooden door. The Grand Master stood up, majestically dominating the room. His voice boomed out: "What profane or unworthy person is this, coming here to disturb the peace and harmony of this, our Royal Scarlet Chapter meeting, dedicated by us unto God and brother Joshua?"

The door opened and Brother Whelan conducted the blindfolded candidate into the room. "He is not profane, nor unworthy at all, but a friend with a brother, and a brother with a friend, seeking admission into this, your Royal Scarlet Chapter meeting, dedicated by you unto God and Brother Joshua."

Clarke looked at young Spracklin, recalling how he too had been divested of his coat, collar and tie, trouser legs rolled up, and shirt open to expose his left breast. He had forgotten about the bare left foot. There was a brashness to this young initiate that reminded him of Cheeseman and his perpetual sneer.

"Password," the Tyler demanded, standing to block Spracklin's way.

"Shib-Bo-Leth," the candidate said timidly.

"Say again," the Tyler bellowed, "so we can all hear."

"Shib-Bo-Leth," Spracklin responded loudly, with a hint of impertinence.

"You may pass."

Clarke leaned over to the brother beside him. "A bit too proud, I'd say."

"I suppose."

"I'll take him down a peg or two before this is over," Clarke said. He reached down and picked up the alder switch under his chair and rolled it between his fingers. "Yes, sir," he said under his breath, "he won't wonder about death's sting by the time I'm done with him. These youngsters need to learn respect."

The initiation proceeded through the usual rituals that Clarke knew by heart. The circumambulation, said to represent Moses's journey through the wilderness, was the part he was waiting for. When it came, Clarke lined up with several of his brothers along the path the barelegged and blindfolded Spracklin would be led. The captain got down on his knees in readiness. The other brothers rubbed their alder switches on the passing bare legs, one or two giving playful swats as the young man went by. Clarke reared back and laid a hard blow on Spracklin's left shin. A whack resounded through the hall. The young man stepped back in surprise. Another whack, this time on the calf. The neophyte brother bit his lip and stepped away. Clarke crawled over and caught Spraklin's calf with one last blow that drew blood. The sealing captain rocked back on his knees, rolling the alder whip between his fingers. He smiled.

Knowing looks among the elder brothers resulted in George not being able to find a place at the blanket for the toss, known as 'riding the goat.' Clarke sat down to watch the goat and sulked all through the redressing period and lecture. Young Spracklin showed considerable wit and understanding in his answers to the questions during the lecture. With each clever response, Clarke settled deeper into his chair, his frown growing. The lecture lasted forever, going over old ground that Clarke found boring. At last, the end.

The Worshipful Grand Master stood up and raised his arms, a sign for the members to crowd around their new brother and congratulate him with handshakes and shoulder slaps. All the members came over except one. George Clarke drifted into the darkness at the back of the hall and slipped out, unnoticed.

On his way home, caught in a swirl of confusion, Clarke moaned out loud, "They've all gone soft. That boy needed upbraiding and they let him go. They've lost their way. What's the point of having the Lodge if we don't make a difference?" He limped on toward home, head bowed, hands in his pockets. He looked skyward. "Lord, I feel like I've been abandoned."

THIRTEEN

John Lundrigan found himself in a strange new world.

One minute he is laughing face to face with Tommy and Peter, exploring the back part of Red Island. Then, in a blink, he is floating above the harbour, looking down. The white bird from his visions comes. He is out on the water off Stoney with his father, then on the deck of a steelhulled sealing ship. Seconds later he finds himself struggling under the weight of a giant version of the carved water hoop on his shoulders, buckets full to overflowing with black tar. All of these images stream into one another, seamlessly, making sense, tumbling into a montage. The smell of sap in the barking kettle, the odour on humid days at the stage, fresh spruce, the pong of early season dandelions, all braid into this hurly burly world. The fearful monster from his visions comes back, a sneer from the Devil on South Head.

The face of an old man begins to appear, rarely at first, then more often. Even though the skin is stretched so tightly over the stranger's cheeks it seems to be cracking, the visage draws the boy toward it. Bushy eyebrows and a scruffy white beard encircle the face. Crowsfeet lead John's gaze directly into the eyes, which remain unfathomable black patches. Tousled white hair and a gimpy walk are woven into the impression of this spirit, which soon becomes the most frequent vision. Images, smells, sounds continue to swirl and tumble. He drifts off into a black void, only to return to this wild world again.

A second scene begins to appear more frequently. At first, he sees the loft in his father's stage, rafters with roof boards attached from above. Then it changes, somehow different, yet familiar.

The two images, the old man and the ceiling, begin to dominate. They reappear so often that the other scenes begin to disappear. Before long, the old man and the ceiling are the only images he sees.

Trembles spread through John's body as a massive struggle takes place.

Then it ended. John woke up.

He found himself in a bed with the ceiling rafters above him. The white-haired man, now real, sat on the bed beside him stroking his hair. "So you finally decided to come back," he said.

John blinked, confused and disoriented. He began to speak but only an incoherent jibberish came out.

"Take her slow, lad," the white-haired man said, kindness and understanding clear in his voice. "You've been away for nearly two days now. You need time to get your bearings. Keep a berth, now." John closed his eyes and drifted into a black void.

ii

Slowly, over the next day, John regained his strength. His mind swam with questions. The sound of an uneven walk preceded the door opening.

"What happened?" he asked, as the old man entered. "Where am I? Where is this section shack?"

"Easy now. Take it slow." He sat down on the bed and began to spoon hot broth into John's mouth. The soup tasted so good that the boy put his questions on hold for the sheer luxury of feeling warmth and strength flow back into his body.

"That's more like it," the old man said as he put the empty bowl and spoon down on the floor. "Now, to why you're here." He paused, looking carefully at the boy. "Moses Green, a track man, heard his snow bell in the middle of the storm. He ties a rope to the track that rings the bell on his shack, see?" The old man paused and looked intently at John. "He found you face down in the snow twenty yards off the main line, nearly finished. You were so badly frozen he took you for dead. But you fooled him. When he got you back to his shack, you began to toss and turn and shout all kinds of curses. You didn't cheat the Devil one bit."

John blushed.

"Moses says he never saw a boy with such a will to live. 'Couldn't kill him with an axe,' he said." The old man grinned showing chipped and discoloured teeth behind his scraggly beard. "So he called me up the line. I'm the local healer, see."

John tried to speak but his voice deserted him. He struggled against exhaustion.

"You're right played out. I'll leave you to rest."

John nodded as he drifted off.

iii

Long afternoon shadows flickered through the window when John awoke. He swung his feet over the bed and sat up. Blood rushed from his head, making him light-headed. After a minute, steadiness returned. The boy swung his bare feet back and forth over the bed edge, creating a welcome rush of movement.

He noticed several black blotches on his toes. John eased himself off the bed and stood up. Pain stabbed through his feet and he fell, barely able to catch the bed as he went down. Soon he heard the old man's awkward gait, followed by soothing words as he was helped back onto the bed.

"Not ready for that yet," the old man said. "Steady as she goes now."

When John's head hit the pillow he exhaled a deep sigh. After catching his breath, he raised himself on his elbows and asked, "What's your name? Where am I?"

The old man, now standing beside the bed, looked down at him. "Most people around here call me Doc." He paused, scratching his cheek. "But my real name's Newtry, Jacob Newtry."

John's eyes opened wide. Again his voice abandoned him. He stammered, making no sense.

The old man walked over to the window and pulled back the curtain. "See there," he said pointing to a run of water in the distance. "That's Little Harbour. That's where you're at." Jacob grinned.

"I'm not on the railroad line?"

"No. Moses and me brought you over here so I could watch you close."

"But how did you know?"

Jacob said nothing.

"How did you know I was coming to see you? Yes you, Jacob Newtry. That's why I came. How did you know?"

The old man smiled. "Well, I could say I had a vision that told me you were coming, but it's easier than that. Between the curses you shouted at Moses, the only other thing he could make out was my name. 'Jacob, Jacob, Jacob Newtry,' over and over. Only proper we bring you here." The old man's eyes narrowed as he came over to the bed. "And I nearly gave up the ghost when I came into Moses' shack and saw your face. You're the spitting image of my nephew, Alfred. Just as handsome, dark hair, same eyes." The old man sighed. "Alfred's long gone now. But for a minute I thought he'd risen from the dead. Jesus Christ." He let go a deep chuckle.

John smiled, but could not hide his bewilderment. "How could that be?"

"Well, son, the more I looked at you lying there and the more I reckoned your age, the more I knew you had to be my niece Mildred's boy. She married a top hand and went off to Red Island." Jacob's face darkened. "But sadly, she passed after having a son. That boy would be fifteen now. Lundrigan, Abel Lundrigan, that was her man's name."

Even though he had had a slight inkling that this might be the case, John could not take it in. "But my name's Lundrigan," he said. "John Lundrigan, and I come from Red Island."

"I know," the old man said with a serene smile.

iv

As the days passed, John and Jacob had longer and longer talks, John came to love the old man's stories. He learned how, as a young woman, his mother had defied her parents by marrying a Catholic from away. How her parents, John's grandparents, both died of consumption the next year. And he heard how Mildred's brother, Alfred, had been lost in the *Greenland* sealing disaster. As John's strength returned, he learned about his lost family, the uncles and aunts he never knew he had, the cousins from away and, of course, his new great-uncle.

"So, I look like Alfred?" John said.

"You're his spit, same hair, same eyes." Jacob looked away, reliving some distant memory. "You don't whittle sticks do you, carve things out of wood?"

"No, I never had a good knife."

"Your father never gave you one?"

"Nope. 'No way for a boy to waste time,' he said."

Jacob nodded.

"Why do you ask?"

"Alfred had the knack for carving, could make the most beautiful things with his old knife and a junk of wood, uncanny. Just thought you might have the gift, too."

John shook his head and stared out the window, watching the breeze nudge the fog above the harbour. "Tell me about my father."

"Folks hereabouts didn't take too kindly to him," Jacob said. "He blew in from away and stole one of Little Harbour's finest. And he was a Catholic to boot. The boys didn't like that too much." The old man shook his head sadly, and then brightened up. "Your father tried to join in, mind you, but people hereabouts can be pretty stubborn. They never accepted him." He paused and looked away from John. "I, for one, saw a hard streak in him that made me fear for Millie. Still, I took Abel to be a good man at heart. But the others weren't so soft. He was an outsider, and a Papist too."

Jacob paused in reflection, then continued. "Abel and Alfred got on good though — took to each other like brothers. Alfred followed Abel around like a lost crackie. Your father arranged a sealing ticket for Albert on the *Greenland*. He was a top hand in the swiling game, an ice master on his third hunt. Got to be a second master watch by '89, what they call a deck router."

John smiled.

"When he got the ticket for Alfred, Abel promised to look after the boy. But, for some reason, he didn't take Alfred on his watch, probably figured he wasn't strong enough." A frown came over the old man's face. "When this storm came up, Abel's watch was called off the ice to repack the sculps because a change in the wind made the cargo shift. By the time Abel's watch got the ship back level, the weather had changed and the ship was frozen fast. Two watches were caught on the ice, including Alfred's. After a day and a half they brought him back, frozen dead solid, kneeling as if he'd been praying. Forty-eight hands were lost." The old man's eyes darkened and he looked away. "After that, there was no place for Abel Lundrigan in Little Harbour. He'd broken his word, see."

"What did my mother do?"

Jacob looked over at the boy. "They were already married." The old man faltered, losing his train of thought. After a time, with John peering at him intently, he said, "Millie knew it wasn't Abel's fault, so they went off to Red Island. Her parents were pretty upset, I'll tell you. Your mother prayed she'd be able to come back, especially after you were born, but it was never to be." Jacob looked wistfully out the window.

"How come my father never told me this?"

"I can't speak for the man, John. You'll have to ask him that yourself. Losing Alfred and Millie near did him in though. I know he gave up swiling."

John nodded. "And he's dead set against me taking it up, too."

"Can't say as I blame him," Jacob said.

v

John could walk now, albeit with a limp. He hobbled around Jacob's old house wrapped in a blanket, staring longingly out the window toward the open water. "I'd love to get out for a walk and feel the sun on my face," he said.

"Perhaps tomorrow," Jacob said.

John smiled at the old man who sat at the table, gnarled hands wrapped around a steaming cup of tea. In just a few days he had developed a deep love for Jacob. He enjoyed his company and relished the talks that flowed so effortlessly between them. The old man's stories were magic, taking John back to times only vaguely sensed, opening doors to age old secrets and understandings. With Jacob, his kind eyes, his gentle ways, John could be himself. There was no need to think about what he should or should not say, like it was with his father. This small orange house on the hill, overlooking Little Harbour, had become home.

Despite being so comfortable, John resisted mentioning his visions. Nobody understood what he went through when the black monster swept down on him. Nobody could grasp the paralyzing fear that lingered for days after. Nobody could comprehend the responsibility that weighed on his shoulders. Yet he knew he had to tell Jacob. Still, he hesitated, looking out the window for a reason to stop himself. But there was no excuse. The time had come.

"Jacob," he said.

"Yes."

"I have to tell you why I came to see you."

The old man turned in his chair and looked at John, ready to listen. Haltingly at first, the young man recounted his first two visions. Jacob encouraged him, offering the strength to proceed. A nod or a smile from the old man made it possible to share his deepest terrors. By the time he had finished, the boy was crying.

"That takes me back more than a few years," Jacob said after John had composed himself. He took a swig of his tea and wiped his mouth on a ragged sleeve.

93

"A young girl once told me a story just like that, maybe thirty years ago."

"You mean I'm not the only one?"

"Far from it, son. Far from it." Jacob looked over at John, warmth and understanding in every crease of his weatherworn face. "This girl, I recall, had the knack of seeing what was going to happen to her family."

"Like me?"

"Aye. She saved her little brother from more than one fix, I'll tell you." He laughed to himself, a deep vibrant chuckle. "She feared her dreams too, just like you, frightened to death when she came to me."

"Did you help her?"

"I believe so. The first thing I did was show her the visions weren't the Devil's work. They were all for the good. 'Just look at the lives you've made better by having these dreams,' I said."

A puzzled look came over John's face. "Like the way my vision saved old Daniel in Sand Pond?"

"That's it. Why be afraid of something that can do so much good?"

"I suppose," John said, doubt lingering in his voice.

"When you sit back and look at it, these dreams are a gift, something special, just like Alfred's knack with the whittling blade. They're no curse, my boy. They're a blessing. It'd be a shame to waste them."

"So how come I'm so afraid when they come?"

"That's exactly what she asked, too."

"Did you find an answer?"

"Yes. Her fear came because she didn't understand them. Her visions had so much force; she didn't know what to do. That's all."

John grew silent. He looked down at his hands and began to fidget.

Jacob continued. "After a time, her fear got less and less. She conquered it."

John nodded. "What happened then?"

"When she was eighteen she had an important dream. No monsters anymore, just a feeling she knew what would happen. This one involved her brother." He paused to drain his tea. "Everybody was amazed when it came true. You see, the boy got himself killed in an accident. The worst part was all the townsfolk wanted to blame the girl's man for the accident, but her dream told her he had nothing to do with it. She knew her brother would have died, no matter what. See?"

John waited a long time before he spoke. "What did you say the girl's name was?"

Jacob nodded. "I didn't."

John sat forward. "Was it my mother?"

He looked deeply into John's eyes. "Yes."

"And the brother was Alfred?"

"Aye."

"Holy Mother of God," John said as he sat back in his chair. "It is true." The kitchen grew silent, save for an old man's laboured breathing and a boy's fidgeting with a spoon on his lap. "That's why she stayed with my father," he said almost under his breath. "My mother had visions, too. I can't believe it." John felt a tremendous release as he looked at the old man. Years of pent up fear loosened and began to tumble out. He smiled and then started to laugh.

"Time for that walk now," Jacob said with a smile.

The two limped down the road, around to the south side of the harbour. "Don't we make the funny couple?" Jacob laughed. "It's foggy around here most of the time. This sun feels good." They shuffled toward the waterfront, continuing down to a freshly painted stage. The odd pair sat on the wharf, recruiting nearby crates for stools. A small run of shore ice, ten feet wide in places, intervened between the rocks and the sparkling blue water. A few chunks bobbed in the lop. Bright light bounced off the waves.

"Still an easy winter, I see," Jacob said.

John nodded as he shaded his eyes to peer further out. "You can't see full into Placentia Bay from here, can you?"

"No, Long Island there gets in the way," Jacob said, pointing to a black form in the distance. "She's a fine sight."

"Yes," John said, gazing out toward the sea. The two sat in silence.

After a while John said, "I had a third vision, Jacob, one that I didn't heed, and two men died. The bird came and swooped past me toward town." John paused. "I got to town as soon as I could, but nothing was wrong. I didn't know what to do." He paused.

Jacob reached over and took the boy's hand. "Go on," the old man said, "there's nothing to fear."

Finally John was able to continue. "When I got back to town I heard that Peter's Uncle Charlie and Oliver Ryan had gone out to Ragged Point. The weather turned and they never came back. They were swallowed up like a stone — never found a single sign to tell what happened."

"Don't naggle now, my son. It's all right," Jacob said, stroking the boy's hair. "Just tell me what you remember."

John struggled to recover his composure. "All I know Jacob is that I didn't heed my vision. If I had, I would have saved them. Two men died because of me. I'm to blame, me and me alone. It's all my fault."

"There, there, now, be still. You got nothing to be ashamed of." He pulled John to him and embraced the boy.

"Now you listen to me, John Lundrigan, and you listen good," Jacob said, with a seriousness that startled the boy. "There's no way in creation those deaths are your fault." He grabbed the boy by his shoulders and peered deeply into his eyes. "You know as well as I do that they wouldn't have listened to you." He laughed deeply. "Can you imagine a young snip of a lad running down to some seasoned old hand saying he shouldn't go fishing because of a dream?" He laughed again. "No boy, it was nothing to do with you. God intended it, nothing to do with you."

John drew a deep breath and exhaled. His guilt about the two lost fishermen begin to evaporate. The boy and the old man sat side by side for a long time. The only sound was the slip of Jacob's knife along his carving stick. John watched the curly shavings tumble off and fall to the wharf.

"I think you know now," Jacob said squinting out toward the bay. "Your dreams aren't bad. Just don't dwell on them, keep the distance. Let them happen, just accept them." He looked at John and then back out to the harbour. "As you get older, the bird and monsters will go away. You'll just get these feelings that tell you what's going to happen. Just heed them the best you can." He paused. "Whatever you do, don't ignore them or try to make them go away. They're your special gift." He held up his carving stick, scowled at it, and tossed it into the water.

John peered out over the water. While still confused, he was beginning to understand the strange things that had been happening to him. He began to sense how extraordinary his dreams were and how lucky he was to have them.

vi

The next day John took a solitary walk up the hill to the rail line. When he came back into Jacob's kitchen, the old man was sewing the greatcoat he had worn on his journey from Red Island. "Don't remember ripping my coat," the boy said.

"No, son, there's no tear. I'm sewing a few dollars into your collar here. You never know when you might need a little bit of cash." He pointed to where he had stowed the money.

"You don't have to do that," John said.

"I know, just wanted to give you a little gift. Maybe you can use it to come back and visit."

"Come back and visit?"

"Yes, you're well enough to go home now. The time's come."

"But I don't want to leave. I want to stay here with you."

"No, John," Jacob said, sadness in his eyes. "There's no work for you here. Nobody needs a young hand like yourself. And you have to make things right with your father."

John had too much respect for Jacob to argue. In his heart, he knew he had to go back. Maybe now that he understood his visions, he could start over, and knowing about his mother and Alfred, perhaps he could do a better job of getting along with his father.

"I'll always be here," Jacob said.

John's eyes began to tear over. Jacob came over to the boy, embraced him, and said, "Everything will be all right, John. We'll see each other soon enough."

vii

"Look over there," Peter Lamb said from the lookout on Red Island. "There's a steamer coming around Long Island, heading right toward us."

"Where?" Tommy asked. Peter pointed. "That's a queer thing, they usually hug the shore against the mainland. They never come over here from there."

The two boys watched as the ship came directly toward them, smoke trailing out behind.

"Don't recognize her," Peter said, "looks bigger than the regular steamers."

"Appears to be brand new. Maybe she's the *Kyle*. Must have a green skipper, though, to be coming over here."

"I hope she doesn't try to come into the harbour. She'll rip that brand new hull of hers all to hell on the sunkers." But the ship kept coming. Her shiny new paint and impressive bulk headed straight at them.

"Lord sufferin' Jesus, she really is coming here," Peter said. "Maybe the Governor is coming to visit, or the King."

"Sure, the King wants to see us."

The ship stopped a safe distance outside the harbour entrance. The two boys watched her anchors splash. They heard the rhodes whir as the lines payed out. Then small men who looked like ants swarmed on the decks. A boat went over the side on a davit and was lowered into the water. A rope ladder unrolled down the side. Three figures scrambled into the boat.

"Come on," Tommy yelled over his shoulder, "we've got to see who this royal visitor is." The boys flew down the hill, sprinting across hay fields, hurdling rail fences.

A crowd had gathered by the time the boys reached the wharf. They elbowed their way to the front to see the gig from the ship was a hundred yards out. Two of the visitors wore hats — crewmembers. The third person, obviously the royal visitor, sat hatless in the bow, back to the wharf. "Must be somebody important," echoed through the crowd.

The gig turned and came toward the wharf.

Peter, looking at the royal back, said, "No, it can't be."

"What are you on about?"

"Sure looks like John's head there."

"Don't be so stunned."

One of the sailors threw a line ashore. Young Cecil caught it and pulled the boat in. Then the sailor tended the dory with a boathook and hauled it even with the wharf. The royal visitor stood up and turned. A gasp ricocheted through the crowd as they recognized their own John Lundrigan. A wave of excited talk followed as the young man climbed ashore. He turned and waved thank you to the sailors as they pushed off and headed back out the bay.

Tommy and Peter ran toward their long-lost friend. They embraced and danced around on the wharf like mad men.

"Mother of Christ," Tommy said, "how did you do that?"

"You're not the only one with friends in high places," John said to Tommy. "Old Jacob's got more friends than the King's got subjects."

"Lord, it's good to see you," Peter said. "You've been to Little Harbour?"

"Yep."

"You saw Skipper Jacob?"

"Yep."

"Jees, you look good," Tommy said, "more colour in your face since I can remember. That place must agree with you."

"It does." John radiated a deep smile.

"Tell us everything," Peter said.

"Not now, later. There are too many folks around."

Everything went black as a blinding pain exploded in John's head. He opened his eyes to find he was on his knees, looking at the wharf boards. Then he felt himself being hauled along by the back of the collar. He could not get to his feet as some great force yarded on his shoulders and dragged him away. From up ahead, he heard a voice rasp, "I'll teach you little pisswig not to fool with me."

"Easy, Abel," somebody said.

"Mind your own goddamned business."

Still dazed, John did not realize what was happening until he was thrown onto the floor of Abel's back kitchen. The door slammed shut and his father loomed over him. Blackness once again descended on John's world. He was unconscious by the time the *Kyle*'s whistle blew a long, solitary farewell.

FOURTEEN

Just before Christmas 1913, Baine, Johnston and Company had begun preparations for the coming spring seal hunt. Grieve and Collingwood sat opposite each other across the merchant's desk, going over the preliminary budget submitted by Joshua Cheeseman.

"I can't believe he'd do this," Collingwood said. He got up and paced back and forth.

"Easy now, Thomas, you'll wear a hole in the carpet if you keep that up. This is just a draft," Grieve said, tapping the leather-bound ledger that contained Cheeseman's figures. "Nothing's written in stone yet. We can still make changes."

"I certainly hope so." Collingwood came over and thumped the book. "Hell, you'd be sending our men to their graves, starving to death if we followed this." He threw his hands in the air and looked at the ceiling. "And Coaker would be at our throats like a raving banshee." He stopped to catch his breath and began to pace again. "I can't believe he'd do this." Finally he flopped back into his chair. "How can we make sure he doesn't go ahead with this?"

"Joshua is only doing what he thinks best," Grieve said.

"Hardly," Collingwood scoffed.

"He's in a tough position, you know. The sealing revenues are uncertain, at best. Seems none of our captains live up to expectation, especially Clarke. That makes it a hard job." Grieve paused, deep in thought. "We both know we're gambling with Clarke. He's such a jowler, that man. He's going to bring home a huge load one of these springs and make us all rich. Until that happens though, we have to be as frugal as we can." He looked intently at his assistant. "So I think Joshua's right, it is time to tighten up."

Collingwood sat forward. "You can't be serious, sir. If we followed Joshua's advice we'd have no income at all because none of our ships would come back." He shot a hostile look at the ledger.

"Yes, Thomas. I believe Joshua's gone too far, but he's definitely on the right track." Grieve selected a cigar out of the beautifully finished box on his desk, smelled the length of it, and began the ritual of clipping and lighting. "Would you like one?" he said, turning the box toward his assistant.

"No, thank you." Anger lingered in Collingwood's voice.

"I guess what we have to do now is go through this budget item by item and decide what we can live with," Grieve said.

"Yes, sir. We'll probably reject every single one of his suggestions," Collingwood said through a clenched jaw.

"We don't want to reject it all," Grieve said. "Can't be too generous. Let's find that fine balance between too much and too little."

"Joshua certainly didn't come close to that," Collingwood said with a scoff. "Do we have to go through every item?"

"Yes."

"That'll take a lot of time." Collingwood stood up and removed his jacket, draping it carefully over the back of the chair.

"I suppose. I'm glad Joshua gave us this well in advance. That's one good thing at least," Grieve said as he turned to the first page of the book.

Collingwood looked closely at the open page. "I'll say one thing for him. He has fine handwriting, almost like a woman's. Too bad the figures are so badly chosen." He frowned and then read for a moment. "Look here, he's decided we shouldn't recopper the hull of the *Southern Cross*. We've already put it off for two years, and now he wants to postpone again." He shook his head and pursed his lips. "We can't do that. James Black, you know, that Lloyd's inspector, told me he wouldn't approve her going to the ice without new copper."

"He did?"

"Yes, sir, when I walked him through the ship last spring."

"Do you think he was serious?"

"Yes, sir, I do. Even if he wasn't, can we risk it? Joshua was there too. He heard Black as clearly as I did." Collingwood looked out the window, and then back at Grieve. "I can't believe he'd cross this off."

"Well, I guess we'll just have to uncross it then," Grieve said with a grin.

"I don't find it amusing, sir."

"Never you mind, Thomas, we'll manage this."

Collingwood made a notation on the page. He turned to the next sheet. "And here," he said, "he's crossed off the work party you promised Clarke to clean up the *Cross*. Remember?"

"Can't say as I do."

"You must remember. Captain Clarke complained she was so dirty he could barely manage. 'Nothing shortens the life of a vessel like dirt,' he said. Remember? So you promised a crew to spruce her up this spring."

"Ah, yes, now I remember. That won't cost much. There are lots of boys around who'll work for free in the hope of getting a ticket. I guess we can uncross that one, too."

Another notation.

After half an hour of Collingwood's constant notations, Grieve looked up with a perplexed look on his face. "Is there anywhere we can agree with Joshua? We have to give in somewhere. We simply can't cross off everything he's recommended."

"Why not?" Collingwood asked.

"There, there now, Thomas, give the lad a chance."

Collingwood shook his head and began to riffle through the pages. "Not there," he said, "they'll need more tea that that. Not there. Not there." Exasperation grew with each flipped page and carefully noted change. Finally, after twelve pages, he said, "Ah, here's one, the wireless."

"What?"

"Last year you thought it might be time to put a Marconi on the *Bloodhound*."

"Well, that was when I thought Jessie was having a banner trip," Grieve said. "We can't afford a wireless now. Let alone to pay an operator to work the contraption."

"At least that's one place we agree with Joshua." Collingwood lowered his voice to a near whisper. "I hear they're pulling the wireless off the *Newfoundland* this year, say it doesn't pay on the wooden ships."

Grieve shrugged. "So Joshua was smart enough to cross off the wireless was he?"

"Yes."

"Good for him." The old merchant smiled. "At last, one place where we agree."

Collingwood flipped to the next page. "He's crossed off the new paint, too, sir."

Grieve looked absently out the window. "Maybe we can go along with that. Another year of dull yellow on our funnels won't hurt. Didn't we repaint the *Bloodhound* last year?"

"Yes, sir, and we had enough paint left over to touch up some of the metal on the *Southern Cross*."

"Good for Joshua then, he's saved us more money. We'll be the dull yellow fleet this year. I'm sure the seals won't mind." He laughed at his own joke.

Collingwood continued to leaf through the ledger, unamused. Finally Grieve said, "Thomas, we haven't even come close to the five thousand dollars Joshua claims he saved. Are there any other big items like the copper?"

"That's what I'm looking for, sir," Collingwood said, leafing through Cheeseman's meticulously inscribed pages. "As far as I can see, he's made small reductions in everything. See here," he said pointing to a page, "he's listed twenty barrels of salt beef, compared to twenty-five last year."

"I see."

"Clarke and Winsor both asked we fit them out with exactly the same as last year. And Joshua was with me when they said that. But now he's gone ahead and reduced everything by a fifth. It's like he didn't hear us. What's that boy up to?"

Grieve shook his head. "I don't know, Thomas. He should know we can always auction off any leftovers, you know, O'Driscoll and that crowd." Grieve stopped and rubbed his chin. "We'll have to tell Joshua to use last year's supply lists. Yes, that's what we'll do. We'll load them up the same as we did last year. Never mind this twenty percent reduction."

"Joshua won't be pleased."

"I can handle him. After all, he does work for me."

"I get the impression he forgets that a lot of the time. He's a bit of a Napoleon when it comes to his part of the business."

"Aye, perhaps the time has come for a strong reminder. Cheeseman's Waterloo, we'll call it."

After three hours, Grieve said, "I'm exhausted, Thomas. Can you finish things up?"

"Yes, sir," Collingwood said. "I'll have it for Monday." He picked up the book and closed it with a loud, disgruntled thump.

"Good, Thomas, I can always count on you. Once you have it done, please arrange for Joshua and me to have lunch at Woods. I'll treat him like royalty and then rein him in."

"Good idea, sir," Collingwood said with a grin.

ii

The shiny gold sign, "Woods West End Candy Store," marked Grieve's destination. At the corner of Holdsworth and Water Street, the building's turret gave the impression of a castle. A feeling of warmth, the smell of chocolate and the buzz of shoppers talking to black-skirted sales clerks greeted him as he entered. A small group sang Christmas carols in the corner. He worked his way through the crowd to the stairs and began to climb, ledger in one hand, oak banister in the other. When he entered the restaurant Cheeseman was sitting at a table overlooking Water Street. It was set out with the finest silver, porcelain and glass. Linen napkins, carefully folded to look like bishop's mitres, sat atop pristine plates. A red carnation, surrounded by feathery green fern leaves, occupied a vase mid-table.

Cheeseman and Grieve made small talk while they went through the formalities of lunch. The young man constantly glanced at the ledger the old merchant had placed on the windowsill. Despite the Christmas cheer and thronging crowds, the atmosphere at their table was strained.

"Warms my heart to see so many people in the stores," Grieve said when they were finished.

"Yes, sir. There's no better time. Many of those people are having a good Christmas because of you." The young assistant paused. "That's one benefit of running our business well. We keep the money pouring into their pockets." He grinned.

Grieve nodded. "Yes, Joshua, if we do things right, everyone benefits, even us." The old merchant smiled and motioned toward the book on the windowsill. "I must admit that I'm impressed with the work you've done here." He moved the remaining cutlery, glasses and his napkin to the side of the table. "You're definitely correct in suggesting we need to spend less money."

Cheeseman beamed like a small boy being praised in school.

"Yes, there's lots of room for improvement." Grieve reached over and picked up the book, placing it, unopened, on the table in front of him. "I agree with some of the work you've done here." He spoke slowly, with great seriousness.

"Some? Only some?" Cheeseman said, clearly concerned. "I thought you'd be enthusiastic about the completeness of my recommendations. Time for a major change, I say. Our profits will skyrocket."

Grieve pressed on. "Yes, you're right about the wireless, the paint, the pound boards. You've got these right. Good work, lad."

The young Scot smiled.

"But..."

Cheeseman's face fell.

"...you've gone too far with most of this." Grieve paused to look across the table at his assistant, who now looked shaken.

Slowly, with a hint of anger, the young Scotsman said, "For instance?"

"For instance, we've been told that the inspectors will not approve the *Southern Cross* going to the ice this year unless she has new copper plating. We simply can't cut that cost. You were told," he said sternly.

"I did know that, and I still believe we can eliminate it," Joshua replied. "They wouldn't dare stop us going to the ice if we signed on a crew, not in a million years." He sat upright. "We've got them over a barrel."

"No, Joshua," Grieve said looking intently into the young man's eyes. "I won't do business that way. There's no honour to it, and I will not compromise the safety of our men."

"Why should that concern you? Lord knows there are enough ignorant baymen just itching to sign on, more than enough. Why reduce into our profit for a bunch of illiterate fishermen who don't know any better?"

Grieve stiffened.

Cheeseman continued. "You know those men are tougher than last year's hard tack. Why should we give them any quarter, especially if it cuts into our margin?"

"Joshua," Grieve said with unaccustomed force, "how can you say that? These men are as hard-working, loyal and reliable as you'll find anywhere, not fuel for your money machine."

The young man paused for a moment and then continued. "It's the wave of the future, sir, to think of men like the coal on one of your ships. Expendable. Replaceable."

Grieve's mouth fell open. He looked at Cheeseman as if he did not know him. Then he gazed down at the crowds on Water Street, then back again.

Cheeseman continued. "You're always saying we should modernize the business, sir, adopt the new practices. So here's your chance to show you're a member of the new generation, not stuck back in some old Victorian world. Time to join the march of progress." Cheeseman leaned forward.

"Yes, Joshua," Grieve said with quiet deliberation, "there's need for change, lots of change. God knows, Morris is doing his best to bankrupt the Colony. But risking lives and treating men like coal is not the way. We've got to take small steps, work with them."

Cheeseman scowled. "You're still stuck in the old ways. No wonder we're not making any money."

Grieve pushed back in his chair to put as much distance between them as he could. "Don't you try to wrap your greed in the shroud of being modern, young man." His voice rose. His face reddened. "I've heard that speech about men being disposable more times than I can count. And I've rejected it. Do you hear me? Rejected it outright." His face turned crimson as his voice became even louder. "These are good men," he said, motioning to the throng below, "not faceless slaves that you can use up at will." Patrons from nearby tables began to look over. "Listen to me, Joshua J. Cheeseman. You work for me and I'll have no more of this talk while you're in my employ. Do you hear me? Do you understand?"

The young man pulled forward, leaning across the table to regain privacy. "I'm only trying to help, sir," he whispered. "I'm doing the best I can for you and for the men. More than anyone, you know the sealing operation is nearly bankrupt. I'm only trying to help." He looked away.

"But never at the cost of men's lives," Grieve said.

Cheeseman looked away, refusing to meet Grieve's eyes. Slowly, with a tone bordering on sarcastic, he said. "No, sir. Never."

Grieve pulled his chair closer to the table. "Good. I want you to manage the hunt using this revised plan."

He passed the ledger over to Cheeseman who opened it and began to read. He turned over a page, then another and another, anger rising with each flip. "You've rejected nearly every one of my suggestions. Look here, you even want to go back to last year's oversupply of stores." He slammed the book shut. "What's the point?" He looked up at the ceiling.

"Joshua," Grieve said, his voice steady and unwavering, "you have a choice here."

"I do?"

Grieve paused and nodded slowly. "Yes. Either you manage things according to this plan or you find work elsewhere."

A look of alarm came across Cheeseman's face. "But, sir."

Grieve stared steadfastly into his junior assistant's eyes.

"Oh, no," the young man said, "I can't go back now. I have to make it work here, even if I do hate the place." He sat back and looked out the window, trying to avoid Grieve's glare. Cheeseman began to fidget as he stared down at the street, deep in thought. After a long time he said, "I see," almost inaudibly. "I see."

"See what?" Grieve asked gently, drawing Cheeseman out of his reverie.

The young man sat forward and looked directly at the old merchant. He closed the ledger and replaced it on the windowsill. "I see my prospects here are not as promising as I'd been led to believe." Again he lapsed into silence for several moments. "If I can't earn any money with sealing, how can I expect to make my fortune?" He looked straight ahead as though Grieve was not there. "And the economy here is so bad, no money around. What's the use?" His voice trailed off as he looked down and began to fiddle with his cutlery. Darkness passed over his countenance as he grew deep in thought.

"Buck up, laddie," Grieve said, his voice much more encouraging than before. "There are opportunities here for anyone who has the sense to take hold of them. All you need is a little more time and a bit more experience. That's all."

Methodically Cheeseman arranged a new place setting in front of him, folding his napkin exactly as it had been when he arrived. Carefully, he placed it atop his dirty dessert plate. Then he shuffled the cutlery so the setting was as much like the original as possible. He placed the water glass just so. Then he looked up at Grieve. "Perhaps," he said quietly, motioning to his reconstructed place setting, "we can start all over again."

The young Scot's manner had changed. Now he refused to meet Grieve's eye. While he had managed to control his anger, he could not hide his increased hostility.

Grieve shifted uneasily in his chair as he watched his assistant. "Aye laddie, that we can."

The two settled into a detailed discussion of the revised plan. "Yes, Mr. Grieve, I'll make this work."

FIFTEEN

Lucy Clarke smiled. "George, do you remember how irritated I used to get when you'd pull your darn fool pranks?"

The captain grinned as he helped his wife over a snowbank hardened from a run of cold weather. This Sunday, though, the sun was out, offering a respite from deep winter. The blue sky and sparkling light was a welcome antidote to the perpetual grey that had shrouded their world since mid-November. Lucy and George walked arm-in-arm, on their way home from church.

"Yes, George, you certainly had the knack for getting under my skin with your antics." Lucy paused as they crossed the bridge over Harbour Pond. Then she grew serious. "As much as it pains me to say, I miss your attempts to be funny. You seem to have lost your way, no jokes, no tricks. Out of sorts, I'd say." She stopped walking and pulled on his arm, forcing him to stop. "What's bothering you, George?"

The big man shrugged and refused to meet her gaze.

"George."

Finally he looked at her. "I don't know," he said. "I just don't feel like myself, that's all." He shrugged again and began to walk on. Lucy held fast to his arm.

"George," she said, this time more firmly.

He shuffled his feet, eyes down. "I don't know, Lucy," he said in a near whisper. "I'm just finding that everything is so hard these days. Nothing comes easy, like it used to." He forced a smile. "It seems the higher up I get in this sealing business the harder it gets — no room for clowning around anymore. Too many worries."

Lucy looked at him as if to say, "Like what?"

"Well, for one," he replied slowly, "I'm concerned that I'm not a good enough seaman to be in charge of so many men." His eyes glistened over. "I'm nowhere near as good as my brother."

"Oh, come, come George. You've been running big ships for years now with no problems. And there's always James Kelly. I hear he's as good a man with the compass and dividers as there is."

Clarke began to walk again. Lucy followed, gripping his arm. "That's just it," he said, "it's never me that's got it right, it's always somebody else." He looked off into the distance as they kept walking. "I always thought that when I became captain I'd be in charge — the top hand." He sighed. "But it seems I'm beholden to more people now than ever — Grieve, Cheeseman, even Bob Bartlett is trying to run my life." He shuddered. "And now you tell me I'm obliged to Kelly, too. This isn't how was supposed to be." He stopped and looked down at his wife. "I feel like a puppet, everyone else is pulling my strings. It's as though my life isn't my own anymore." The big man sighed and began to walk again, Lucy hanging on. "No wonder I don't feel like fooling around. I wish it was like the old days when things were easier."

"It's not that bad, George. You're doing really well — one of the best known sealing captains there is. You should be proud."

Clarke quickened his pace, looking straight ahead. "You're wrong, Lucy. I've never had any success, never won the silk flag, never brought home the log-load, always coming in behind. I'm sure they're joking about me behind my back."

"Who?" Lucy said sternly. She tried again to stop him but he barged on, nearly pulling her off her feet. "Who's saying these things?"

"Everybody," he replied, "particularly that crowd at the Crosbie Hotel in St. John's, and probably my brother too."

She finally was able to stop the big man and get him to look at her. "Now you listen to me, George Clarke, and you listen good. What those people say is of no matter. You're as fine a master as there is. You hear?"

George nodded, but without conviction.

"All those waggle tongues in St. John's have nothing to do but talk about what others are up to. You're out there doing things, actually getting something done. You don't have to bother with their prattle, you're much better than they are." Her voice had risen to a near shout.

Clarke looked down at his wife. He closed his eyes for a moment, then turned on his heel and began walking again, this time so fast that she had to run to catch up. "It doesn't matter what you say Lucy, I feel like everything is closing in on me. Nothing seems right anymore. Hell, even my Lodge brothers have abandoned me."

"George," she said finally catching up, "you know that's not true."

He stopped, planted his feet, hands on hips, and glared at his wife. "And now, even you are bothering me." His face grew red. "Damn it, Lucy, why don't you just leave me alone. Christ knows, I've got enough worries without adding you to the list." His voice boomed across the wintry landscape.

Lucy stepped back.

For several moments Clarke stared away, clenching his jaw. Then he turned back and looked at her. In a low whisper he said, "I'm sorry, dear. I shouldn't be getting mad at you — of all people. You're only trying to help." He paused, working to regain his composure. "But it's still the same. I'm trapped. I have no control anymore, no control." He turned and began to plod toward home, head down.

They walked along in silence for a while, the crunch of their footsteps the only sound.

George began to slow down and he stood more upright. "You know," he finally said with just the hint of a grin, "I was talking to Mary Watts the other day. She tells me she goes to our church and the Anglican services as well." He stopped walking and looked directly at his wife.

"Really," Lucy said.

"Yep. When our Reverend Jenkins asks her why, she says she figures the more churches she goes to the better her chances of getting into Heaven." George looked over at his wife with a broad grin. "She says she even goes to those Salvation Army meetings. You know, those upstarts who are trying to steal us Methodists. 'Anything to help my chances for glory,' she says." George's speech was more animated now. "Then the Reverend asks her if she'd gone to any Catholic masses." He paused. "Mary tells me she shakes her head, looks straight at the preacher and says 'Oh no, my dear, I don't want to get to Heaven that bad.'" George let loose a deep, resonant laugh and began to walk again.

Lucy laughed as well, perhaps a bit too loudly. "It's good to have you back," she said under her breath.

SIXTEEN

"Lord God, stop scratching. Leave it alone, it'll grow," Tommy said. He and Peter wrestled through the door of a deserted tilt in Margery Cove, which had become the boys' secret meeting place. They almost knocked the door off its precarious perch on one hinge as they blustered their way through. "Whoa," Tommy said, pointing to John, who had been waiting at the cabin for an hour, "looks like Mother John's got everything ready for us, even got the fire going. What's for supper, dearie?" He stepped over the one surviving chair and sat down facing the table. "We should send you out with the women to pick berries on Goat Island — you're such a maid." He paused to sniff the musky, smoky air, and then looked over at John. "Speaking of women, I saw that Jennie Carroll staring at you yesterday. You reckon she's wild about you?" There was more than a hint of jealousy in his tone.

John, who was standing beside the stove, pretended not to hear.

"Boys, that's some warm," Peter said, throwing off his coat and retreating to his usual crate at the rickety table.

"That stove may be rusty, but she draws good enough to suck the milk out of your tea," Tommy said with a grin. Then his face darkened. "I got news from Uncle Jessie."

"Good," John said, "I want to get this sealing trip set up before my old man finds out I'm leaving."

"Yes, sir," Peter said.

"Did I say good news?" Tommy said in an ominous tone.

Peter looked anxiously at John.

Tommy pulled a letter out of his pants pocket and waved it at the other two. "Came on the steamer this morning." He paused and put on a serious face. "He tells me he can't get berths for you two on the *Bloodhound*."

"Oh, no," John said, drawing in a sharp breath. He began to pace back and forth.

Tommy continued. "He says the owners weren't happy with the number of seals he brought in last spring." With a flourish, he pulled the letter from its envelope and read. "'Mr. Grieve says he wants me to have the hunt of my career this year. He told me I can only take experienced hands. I'm afraid there's no place for your friends.'"

John grew more agitated. "Goddamn it. Goddamn it to hell. I've got to get away from this place before my father kills me." His voice cracked as he tried to control himself.

"Those owners are tighter than a muskrat's arsehole," Peter said. "What are we going to do now?"

"It's not all bad," Tommy said. "Uncle Jessie has some advice." He scanned through the letter. "Ah, yes, here it is. 'Tell your friends there's a chance of getting tickets on the wooden walls, especially the ones going to the Gulf.'"

"So does this mean we can leave this godforsaken island?" John said hopefully.

"Yep," Tommy said. He looked at the letter in his hand. "Now, where was I? Oh, yeah. Uncle Jessie says our best bet is to go to St. John's in mid-February. Here it is." He pointed to a spot on the letter. "'Sign on with a work crew loading a sealer. If you work like a horse, they might give you a ticket.'" Tommy stopped and scratched his chin. "It's hard for us bay boys to get berths because that Conception Bay crowd knows all the right people."

John stopped pacing. He came over to the table and sat on the remaining crate. "That's more like it," he said, with a faint smile.

"Now, here's how it'll work," Tommy said. "Uncle Jessie wants me in St. John's to help get the *Hound* ready. I'm going over to Placentia with Frank Ryan on Wednesday. Going to take the train from there."

The two younger boys grew restless, shifting uncomfortably on their crates.

Tommy put on a sad face to create as much suspense as he could. Then he laughed and slapped his hand on the table. "And you two can come with me."

"We can?"

"For sure. We'll show those townies how to have a good time."

"That's it," John said as a huge smile spread across his face. "Then we'll work the docks and get us a ticket."

"It gets better," Tommy said, excitement growing. "Jessie says you two can stay with me at Elsie's boarding house. We'll have a grand time, go to the flickers, look in the stores, raise all kinds of hell." He laughed. "They even have free entertainments for us sealers at the Seaman's Institute, moving pictures, concerts. Boys," Tommy said, puffing himself up, "we'll be treated like jeezly kings."

"Sounds perfect," Peter said with a wide grin.

"Perfect." John sighed. "Then we can leave this place behind and go see the world."

Tommy's face darkened. "Going early means we won't be meeting the other swilers though, none of that great singing or yarning, at least until the others arrive." He looked out the window, lost in thought. "We'll be on our own, just us to look out for each other." A worried look passed across his face and then he laughed. "Maybe John here can find us some women."

The youngest boy looked down at the floor.

"Will your old man let you go?" Peter asked John.

"Never." He paused, looking out the window. "So I'm not going to tell him. I'm just going to leave." He stood up and faced his two friends. "Now this is really important, you two. Don't tell a soul I'm going with you. Please. The old man will kill me if he finds out. Promise you won't tell?"

"Promise," Peter said.

"Sure," Tommy replied.

"Sure isn't good enough," John said, in a near shout.

Tommy startled.

"You have to promise not to tell anyone, not a soul. You promise?"

"Yeah, sure, don't I always keep my word?"

"Like the time you blathered about John's dreams to everyone on the island," Peter said.

Tommy blushed.

John continued. "Tommy, if anyone finds out I'm leaving, I won't be able to go. Please, promise."

The older boy looked flustered and finally said, "All right, not a soul. Cross my heart and hope to die." He crossed himself.

"Good." John pulled a fresh pack of cigarettes from his trouser pocket and tossed it across the table. "Let's celebrate then."

"Whoa," Peter said. "Where'd you get these?"

"McCarthy's," John said with a smile. "Bought them with some money I earned hauling wood for Cecil. This is just a sign of things to come."

Peter struck a match across the table with a flourish and lit the cigarettes. Smoke crept across the dingy room.

"By the Lord Jesus," Tommy said, blowing smoke out through his nose, "that St. John's is some kind of place. More queer stuff goes on there than you can believe."

"So tell us," Peter said, crossing his arms and stretching out his legs in anticipation of a good cuffer.

Tommy began slowly. "You ever see a Chinaman?"

Both boys shook their heads.

"They're these people in St. John's, small, with funny-shaped eyes, never look you in the face. They always watch the floor. Run most of the laundries for washing clothes and sheets and all that."

"Those townies have people to wash clothes for them?"

"The rich ones do."

"Talk about lazy."

"It was some queer, I tell you, when we came back from the hunt last year. These Chinamen shuffled around the dock where the boys were selling their extra flippers, asking if they had any seal cocks for sale."

"Seal cocks?"

"Yes, you idiot, that thing you pisses with, and, you know, that other stuff." Tommy grabbed his crotch to be sure his younger friends knew what he was talking about.

"What do they want them for? Don't tell me they eat them," John said, screwing up his face.

"Nobody knows for sure, it's a secret. But they get so excited some of the boys bring home a good collection." Tommy paused and lowered his voice. "Elsie told me they dry the cocks out and grind them into powder."

"What for?"

"She says they use the powder for making the shirt collars stiff like the rich folk want. Can't think of anything better to make something stiff than essence of cock." Tommy said with a grin.

The boys giggled.

"Anyways, Elsie tells me that her friend, Florence, grinds up some cocks and tries the powder on her husband's shirts. Well, my boys, she says, it was some sad. Those collars were limper than a new-killed tom cod. No hard-ons for her old man's collars, I'll tell you." Tommy smirked.

The boys were as puzzled as they were amused. "You're right, Tommy, that St. John's is a queer place."

"That's not the half of it. You should see the stuff in the store windows. They got gadgets for everything: machines to peel potatoes, racks to dry your socks, more stuff than you can think of. They probably got a gizmo to wipe your ass." He laughed at his own joke and then became serious. "I'm telling you bay boys, you'll get your eyes opened in the big city. You can count on that."

ii

Almost as if he knew, Abel was more talkative than usual the evening before John's planned getaway. He prattled on about the coming codfishing season, much more animated than he had been the last month.

"And maybe this year, if we talk to old Maurice, he'll give us the north trap berth on Stoney, the one he's been hogging for the past ten years. Young Mulrooney isn't with him anymore, so he can't manage alone. It's our turn." The old man grinned.

John, as had become his habit, tuned out Abel's blather. He had lost interest. The old man never wanted to talk about important things like his mother or sealing. The boy had brought these up a number of times since his return from Little Harbour, but his father always changed the subject or grew deathly silent. Now, Abel's talk was the backdrop for John's dreams about escaping to St. John's and the ice fields.

Abel's monotone changed. "You paying attention, boy, or are you being ticklesome again?" John started and looked at his father across the table. Abel continued. "I just want you to know I'm being hard on you for your own good."

John rolled his eyes. "Yeah, I suppose."

"You're not the biggest boy around and you've got to be stronger."

John nodded, eyes drifting toward the window.

"I'm doing all of this," Abel said, gesturing toward the house and pointing at the stage down the harbour, "so you can have the good life. You're too young to understand this now, but you'll thank me someday."

John nodded again.

"Damn it, boy, listen to me. I've got something important to say. You know I don't find words easy, give me a chance to say my piece."

John feigned interest.

"I do the things I do," Abel said leaning over toward John, "because, " ... he paused, almost stuttering ... "because I care for you." He blushed, his hands fidgeting on the tabletop.

John continued to stare out the window.

"You hear me, son? You understand?"

"Yes, sir," John said curtly.

Abel's face turned red as his frustration mounted. "Oh, what's the use?" He stood up, knocking his chair over backwards and stormed out.

John watched him leave. Under his breath he said, "I'll never forgive you, you bastard. I don't care how hard you try."

iii

Next morning, John retrieved the sealer's chest and gaff from the stage loft. He opened the box and picked up the water hoop, looking once again at its fineness. "Probably carved by my Uncle Alfred," he said to himself, placing it on the shelf. Then he put his things in the chest: oil clothes, an extra sweater, mitts, a cap, paper and a pencil. The lid came down with a thump and he sat down on it. He picked up his greatcoat and began to feel along the collar, locating a bulge beneath the left lapel, halfway down. Abel's old sealer's knife, still surprisingly sharp, cut the thread and John removed what Jacob had stowed there. "Ten dollars," John said, clearly awestruck, "a frigging fortune." He looked skyward. The dust motes he had stirred up danced in the morning sun streaming through the window. "Thank you, Jacob, thank you."

Minutes later he was walking with Peter toward the wharf where Frank Ryan kept his tender. "Peter," he asked tentatively, "can you carry the chest and gaff? Tell Frank they're yours. He doesn't know I'm going to the ice and might get suspicious if I'm all rigged up." He threw a worried look over his shoulder.

"Sure. You carry my duffel."

"Lord, John," Peter said after his friend nearly tripped while glancing backwards, "you're some spooked today, worse than a cat in a house full of rocking chairs. What's wrong?"

"It's my old man," John said, walking even faster. "He's still in the house, decided not to go out today, too hungover. I'm afraid he might see me." John threw another worried look over his shoulder, then ran and ducked in behind

Ryan's stage. When they walked out on the wharf, he was careful to keep his back to the village.

"It's about time you two showed up. I've been waiting here for hours," Tommy said. He was sitting at the oars of Ryan's tender, ready to heave off. "Frank's already out at the schooner. We better hurry or he'll leave without us."

Peter scrambled aboard. John untied the painter and hopped in. Tommy began rowing before they were settled, nearly capsizing the little boat.

John sat in the stern and pulled up the collar of his greatcoat. He peeked up briefly to watch the wharf recede. Then he hunched down, doing his best to be invisible from shore. When they arrived at Ryan's two-masted schooner, the boys scrambled on board.

"What are you doing here?" Frank said to John when he saw a third boy.

John took a deep breath. "I'm going to town to babysit these two. I've got to make sure they don't get in any trouble."

Frank smiled. "Good plan," he said, "they need it. You boys haul the anchor, will you?" They jumped to it, Peter and Tommy laughing and jostling, John hanging back trying to make himself as small as possible.

"Crank her up," Frank hollered toward the engine bay. The old engine erupted into action and the ship began to nudge forward. Soon she moved smartly, setting a fine wake in the calm bay. They met a mild swell as they passed Herring Point and moved into the open water. With a flourish, Frank spun the old wooden wheel clockwise to steer the ship on a course southeast, tracing the line toward Placentia.

The boys huddled at the bow, watching the prow cut through the waves. A winged escort of gulls accompanied them, but soon they broke off, leaving the schooner on its own.

As they moved away, the Pinnacle looked to be directly behind the harbour, but as they worked southeast, the hill shifted to the left, soon shrinking in the distance. The rock cliffs, a gentle red with ragged cracks running up and down the face, reached downward into the sea like giant hands. Red Head, the biggest, was crested on top with trees. As the details of the cliffs ebbed in the distance, John noticed that the island, barely four miles long, looked like a giant monster lying in the water looking south. It reminded him of the picture of an alligator he had seen in his school primer. The hills above Stony Point were the eyes and the Pinnacle the highest of the numerous spines along its back. "Only right," he said under his breath. "A monster does live there. Abel is its name." He gave a deep sigh as the buildings transformed into a smattering of white specks against a grey backdrop.

The clouds over the island were low, obscuring the tops of the mountains. "Boys," Peter said, pointing, "she's wearing her hood this morning. Means fine weather's on the way."

Tommy nodded. "A good omen."

The three young men fell silent, each in their own way anticipating the journey.

"Hey, you ladies," Tommy said, unable to bear the quiet. "You ever see a ship's deck melt?"

The other two boys looked over at their friend, uncertain of what to expect.

"Now you do exactly as I say," Tommy said with a grin. "You won't believe it. Put your hands on your face like this." He placed his open hands beside his eyes, like blinders on a horse. "Then watch the water out there, nothing else, just the water."

The younger boys complied.

"Takes a few minutes, just watch the water."

"This is dumb," Peter said, obeying nonetheless.

"Just you wait. You'll be bloody amazed." All three boys watched the sea intently through their blinkered windows. After several minutes Tommy said, "Now boys, look at the deck."

John looked down and had to grab the rail to steady himself. The boards looked like they were dissolving, dripping like hot butter toward the water. The deck was all wiggly and seemed to be alive.

"Saints be praised," Peter said. "Look at that. It is melting!"

"See. I told you so," Tommy said, with a deep laugh.

"That's something," John said. He shook his head to recover his normal vision.

"You can make it happen easy now," Tommy said. "It only takes a minute or two once you get it started."

For the next fifteen minutes the boys experimented with this new game, exclamations getting louder with each round. By the time the novelty wore off, they could see the islands off Argentia. Frank tilted the schooner's nose toward Placentia Harbour.

"Look over there," Tommy said, pointing toward two sugar loaf mountains to the north. "Don't they remind you of Laura Corrigan?"

Peter looked blankly at Tommy. John smiled.

"You know, you idiot, her..." Tommy opened his hands and gestured under his breasts with an uplifting motion.

"Oh, yeah," Peter said, eyes brightening. "I suppose they do. Trust you to notice that."

Tommy smirked.

A steel ship came into view as they rounded the point. "That's funny," Peter said, "there's no smoke coming out of her." They waited to get closer. "That's one of the mail steamers. I wonder why she's just sitting there?"

As they got closer, John said, "Boys, that ice is raftered up right against shore. The ship is jammed solid. Looks like the *Clyde*. She was home just last week."

Ryan came up behind them. "Yep, she's the *Clyde* all right. Tried to run for the wharf but got pinched, right out there in the middle. That skipper must be some fresh water jack to get nipped like that."

"Does the harbour ice over very often?" John asked.

"Not usually. This is the first time in fifteen years. Most times it's wide open."

John nodded.

"What about the steamer service to home?" Peter asked,

"I hear they're going to bring the *Ethie* down."

"So how in hell do we get to the train if the bay is full of ice?" Tommy said.

"Shank's mare," Ryan replied. "I'll snug you up to the ice and you can tramp ashore. The ice is like cement, you'll have no problem."

"Jesus, Mary and Joseph," Tommy said. "Some holiday this is."

"Holiday?" Ryan said. "I thought you were going to the ice. If you want to get to the train, you walk. It's that simple."

"Lord Jesus," Tommy said. "Nothing around here is as easy as they say it is. Something always comes up to make life hard. It's the way of this place. Nothing's easy. Nothing."

iv

After they found the pathway that led from the *Clyde*, walking the Bay became easy, but not before Tommy slipped several times, turning the air as blue as the frozen chunks aggregated into the ice underfoot. The sun shone, making for a pleasant amble toward the wharf. They walked up onto the land ice, and then along the siding that led up the hill to the Jerseyside station.

The train was waiting when they reached the depot. A huge black engine panted steam. Two boxcars sat behind the coal car, followed by one windowed carriage. The trio scrambled aboard, their noise and laughter drawing looks from the passengers already seated. Duffels, the chest and gaff rattled onto the overhead shelf. The boys claimed a double wooden bench on the port side, aft, with seats facing each other. John got the forward-looking window seat, Peter the opposite, and Tommy sat beside John. He had his long legs stretched out across the bench before the other two settled in. The pot-bellied stoves were doing their jobs of keeping the car warm.

"This is the life," Tommy said.

John offered a cigarette from a fresh pack. He was not quick enough to stop Tommy from grabbing a second cigarette that he quickly stowed behind his ear. Peter struck a match and before long, the bench was wreathed in smoke.

The boys talked for a while before the conductor hollered "All aboard!" The car lurched forward. The sounds of carriage windows rattling soon filled the passenger car. John watched the backs of passengers' heads start to bob and roll with the rocking motion of the car. He looked out the window as Larkin Pond, frozen solid, and several bleak houses passed by. Within minutes the train had run deep into the bush, surrounded by the bigger and differently shaped trees John remembered from his walk to Little Harbour. The peace he felt during that trek, long forgotten since his return home, began to steal back. He leaned his head against the glass and smiled. Much sooner than expected, he saw the path from

Fox Harbour where he had begun his trek to see Jacob. Once on familiar ground, he began to anticipate the coming of the section shacks, reliving his journey. They passed through Placentia Junction, and soon the train sat in Whitbourne. After fifteen minutes the car jerked and another passenger car was added behind. The train resumed its eastward journey. They picked up another passenger car at Brigus Junction and soon steamed toward St. John's.

v

All three boys watched as the houses and buildings got bigger and closer to each other, until there were no laneways between them at all, only the streets in front. A sooty blackness blanketed everything, residue from countless chimneys now spewing smoke to mask the afternoon sun.

Walking from the train at Riverhead Station, John and Peter got their first close look at the city. Tommy was the guide.

"Look how they fitted all those rocks together to make the station," John said as he gawked at the three-storey building. They craned their necks upwards to see the complex roofing on the station, dipping erratically between the various gables and chimneys. "Fine work, that."

"Never seen the likes," Peter said in awe.

"Come on, there's lots better stuff than this." Tommy said, directing them down Water Street toward the harbour.

The younger boys followed, jumping on the cobblestones to test how strong they were. "Jesus, they even fitted rocks to the road. You think they'd have better things to do with their time."

They laughed at the fancy clothes in Chaplin's window, oohed and ahed at the motors and engines in the Reid-Newfoundland store, pressed their noses to the window of Wood's Candy Store. "More stuff here than the whole world could use," John said.

On passing the open door of a tavern and hearing the racket from inside, Tommy said, "That's where they bet on the sealers. A man who knows the swiling game can make good money if he picks the winner. Everybody makes money off the seals around here."

John kicked one of the many pieces of horse manure strewn along the street. As soon as it came to rest a bird landed on it and began pecking. Noticing John's fascination, Tommy said, "The pigeons pick up the big parts." Then, pointing upwards, he added, "they fly up and shit all over the buildings, see that dirty grey stuff up there that looks like Gull Rock."

John looked up and nodded his head. Then he noticed the street lamps were lit, despite the lingering afternoon light. "They sure waste a lot of oil lighting up the place," he said.

"Jesus," the older boy said. "They use electricity for those lights, e-lect-tri-city, not oil."

"How's that work?"

Tommy paused, bravado deflated. "Damned if I know," he confessed. "When you turn the button up at Elsie's, this bulb thing gets all bright and you can see, even when it's pitch black outside — a miracle."

John shook his head in wonderment.

Peter sniffed the air. "Boys, there's enough stinks around here. I can tell the smoke and the crap, but there's a lot more I never smelt before. Jesus, this place is ripe."

"Never you fret, young Peter, after you've been here a day or two you won't even notice. You get used to it."

"Now there's a strange train," John said excitedly, pointing to a streetcar wobbling down Water Street toward them. "What's that stick out the back for?"

"That's how she gets her power. See how the rod runs along that wire over the street? More of that electricity stuff." As if listening, the rod sputtered and showered sparks onto the street behind the tram.

John flinched. "That must be dangerous."

"Nope," Tommy laughed. "Those flankers aren't even hot. I felt them once."

"More around here than you can believe," John said.

They turned and headed away from the harbour up toward Elsie's boarding house on Carter's Hill. Once they left Water Street, the boys had to highstep around the huge puddles and carefully pick their way uphill.

The more they climbed, the more John began to feel a sense of familiarity. Even though the city was overwhelming, he realized that, like Red Island, St. John's had begun at the waterfront, and then grown up the hill away from the harbour, just like home. This gave him a rough way to locate himself in the hurly burly of the city, something to hold onto to make this unfamiliar place less overwhelming.

They puffed up Carter's Hill and Tommy led them to the door of a row house that looked the same as all of the others on the block. John could not figure out how he knew the right one. Tommy opened the door and hollered, "Elsie, my dear, we're here."

In a whirl of skirts and lace, a middle-aged woman flew out from the back of the house. Her hair, done up in a bun, gave her face a roundish look, complementing her plump build. "Well, look at you," she said to Tommy. "All healed up and even handsomer than I remember. Here, give us a hug." She smiled and Tommy reached down in an awkward embrace, rolling his eyes toward his friends. He managed to dodge a fat kiss aimed at his cheek. "Your Uncle Jessie should be here on tomorrow's Express. Did you know he had to walk thirty miles to Gambo just to get on the train? What a man he is." She paused and looked at John. "So these are your two friends."

"This here's Peter Lamb," Tommy said. "And the small one there is John Lundrigan." Both boys smiled.

"Welcome," she said, "I hope you're comfortable here."

"Yes, ma'am, I'm sure we'll be," John said. "Thank you for taking us in."

Elsie blushed and said, "Think nothing of it."

She looked at John, smiled, and said, "Aren't you the good looking one? I'm sure the girls come after you all the time. You look too much a gaffer for the ice, though. How old are you?"

He blushed. "I turned sixteen over Christmas."

"Well, don't that beat all?" she said. "Never would have guessed it. Lundrigan, did you say?"

"Yes, ma'am," John replied with an uneasy glance at Peter.

"That's something, there's a man with the same name staying here in the front room. He belongs to Salmonier, early in town to help outfit the *Newfoundland* for the ice. He's an ice-master on her. You two kin?"

"What's his name?"

"William, we call him Will."

"Can't say as I know, but no doubt we're kin somewhere."

"Sure thing. I'll show you to your room now. While you're settling, I'll put out a mug up, and we can catch up on all the news. It's grand to see you, Tommy," she said, poking him the ribs and leading the boys upstairs.

They entered a small room with one large bed and extra blankets laid out on the floor. "One of you'll have to sleep on the floor, but there's lots of covers to make it soft. Come down to the kitchen soon as you're ready." Elsie turned and whirled down the stairs.

"Look at this," Tommy said. He turned the rotary knob by the door and the room went dark. "Bloody magic." With a click the room lit up again. Tommy did it again, this time gesturing like a magician at the light switch. Peter reached for the shining bulb. "Don't touch it, you arse. It gets hotter than a release valve."

They stowed their gear, assigning John to the floor pallet. They lounged around smoking a cigarette and then thumped downstairs to the kitchen with its waiting tea and biscuits.

SEVENTEEN

Four days before his departure for Harbour Grace to begin preparations for the hunt, George Clarke answered a summons from his brother John. "Important I talk to you, stop" the telegram read. "Must see you when I get home, stop." Once his brother returned to Brigus, George obeyed, not so much because he wanted to see him, but more out of a sense of obligation. He paused at the gate of his brother's home, hesitant to enter. He had found the big house at the foot of Noel's Hill a hard place. The location, looking up the bay directly at Molly's Island, had always struck him as pretentious. It was better than his brother deserved. And now, since John had abandoned the seal hunt, George found it even more difficult to be in his brother's house. He drew a deep breath and moved forward. In earlier days, he would just walk in the back entrance. But now, he chose the more formal entryway, knocking at the front door.

John answered. He was poured from the same mold as his brother, a tall and ponderous presence who filled the portal. He motioned George into the living room, usually reserved for formal occasions. The royal red upholstered chairs and the fine cherrywood tables, while speaking to John's new-found prosperity, annoyed George. He would have preferred to sit in the kitchen.

With an air of forced joviality John tried to recreate the old easiness the brothers had shared when they were boys. But now, despite his best efforts, an icy tension lingered.

"George," John said, adopting the tone he had used when about to share a childhood secret, "I want you to give up this swiling business and join me working with Reid. I've found a place for you as second mate on the *Ethie*. The pay's good and it's steady work. Reid's ships are a whole lot safer than those rotten wooden walls."

George thought for a moment. "The pay may be steady," he said tentatively, "but there's no chance to earn the big fortune at Reids, like there is on the floes. It just takes one bumper season. God knows I need a huge payout now if I'm going to build my captain's house." He looked around the living room as if to say "like this one."

John looked directly at his younger brother. "You know as well as I do that the *Southern Cross* is a bad ship," he said. "She's a slug in a wind, and she lists in heavy seas. Her pumps are worse than useless." He paused to be certain his brother was listening. "I hear they're not keeping her up properly now that Linklater was lost on the *Erna*. Grieve never hired a replacement inspector." John went over and sat down in one of the chairs. "The talk around town is that the old ship is cursed. Yes, sir, cursed. George, you shouldn't take her to the ice. She's too dangerous."

George scowled. "The only thing cursed at Baine, Johnstons is that damned Cheeseman. There's nothing wrong with my ship."

"Oh, come on little brother, you know as well as I do that the *Cross* is on her last legs."

George erupted. "Stop it, John. Stop running down my ship." His face reddened. "There's nothing wrong with her. They hired James Black for an inspection and Mr. Grieve is spending all kinds of money to refit her. He's had her recoppered this year." He paused, and then said, "And it's none of your business anyway. The ship is my concern, not yours."

John gathered himself. "I'm sorry, George, I didn't mean to offend you. I was only trying to say that taking the job with Reid would be better for you and Lucy. I'm only trying to help."

George looked thoughtfully at his brother and settled back into his chair. "Second mate on the *Ethie*, eh?"

"Yep, I can arrange it tomorrow. All you have to do is say the word."

"How is it you have so much pull at Reids?" George said with a hint of suspicion. "You've hardly been with them a year."

"I sat the examinations," John said. "I got my master's certificate last month." He beamed with pride. "Uncle Azariah taught us well. The exams were easy. Now they've promoted me, I'm first mate on the *Ethie*. They say it's just a matter of time before I get my own steamer." A self-satisfied smile passed across his face. "And those are the finest ships we've got."

"Do you need your papers to advance at Reids?"

"Yes."

George scowled. "I'll never be able to do that. All that theory and those imaginary lines don't sit well with me." He stared off through the window. "I'd never be able to rise at Reids."

"Oh, come now George, of course you could. You're a fine hand with the navigating. You'd just have to sharpen up what you already know, that's all. It would be easy."

"No, it wouldn't. I'd never be able to get my papers, too namby-pamby for me. I've never taken to book learning, you know that. I have to see everything as it is. It's got to be black and white." His face began to redden. "And I couldn't abandon Grieve. I owe him too much." He paused for a moment, deep in thought. His face tensed up as he sat forward in his chair. "So you want me to tag along behind you, just like I did with sealing, always a step back?"

John looked surprised.

"Now I see what you're up to," George said, standing up. He went over to the window, turning his back to his brother. "I should have known. All you want is to keep me down, like always." He put his hands on the windowsill and began to rock back and forth. "Now that I've passed you at Baine, Johnstons, you want to hold me back. You can't stand being passed by me, like in the Lodge. You can't stand it."

"No, George, no."

"Yes, John, yes. You've always needed to be ahead of me." He turned and glared at his brother. "Well, it's not going to work this time. You can forget about me coming to work under you again. I've got my own path now and it doesn't involve tagging along behind you like a lost puppy." He came forward, hulking over his older brother.

John hunkered down in his chair.

George continued, his voice quivering. "Just to show you, John, I'll go to the ice this year and come home with the biggest load of seals you ever saw. That's what I'll do." He pointed a shaking finger directly at his brother. "And I'll come home early too, just to show you how wrong you are."

John began to shake his head.

"Don't you dare treat me like a little boy," George shouted. "You're not our father. I've got my own life now."

John stood up, forcing George to step back. "It appears this conversation is over."

"You're damned right it is."

"Well," John said curtly, "if you've still got a home to go to, you'd best get back to it. I'll be putting no more coal on the fire to keep that ungrateful soul of yours warm." He turned and headed for the kitchen. When he reached the door he spun around. "People are saying you're reckless and foolhardy on the ice. You'd do well to prove them wrong."

George's face hardened. He grabbed his coat and stomped out the door, disappearing into the fog.

ii

Several days later, George Clarke stormed around the house in Brigus, searching for odds and ends to take on the seal hunt. "Where'd you hide that new house flag?" he shouted at Lucy as he rifled through a steamer trunk in the bedroom. "And have you seen those snow goggles James gave me?"

"My Lord, George," Lucy said from the kitchen, "you get some stomachy when it comes time to leave. I reckon you could do with a pork tit to settle you down."

"Where'd you put my binoculars?"

After several minutes Lucy came into the bedroom carrying a flag, neatly folded, with a pair of wooden goggles resting on top. "Your binoculars are in the china cabinet where you left them," she said quietly.

George looked up and saw her just in time to stop barking another order. "Yes, girl, I do get into a terrible Irish sulk when I have to leave. I can't help it, just comes out of me."

Lucy nodded.

He came over to her, took the flag, and placed it on the bureau. The captain drew his wife to him and they embraced, George resting his chin atop her head. After a moment he stood back and looked into her eyes. "I will miss you, my dear," he said, brushing several loose strands of hair from her face. They kissed with the casual familiarity of old lovers. "When I come back Lucy, we'll have enough money to build that captain's house you've always wanted." He looked off through the window. "For every hundred dollars of cargo I fetch, Grieve gives me four. That'll be lot of money. This year, it'll be enough to build us the grandest house, my dear, the grandest." He released Lucy. "Yes, ma'am, that's the first thing I'll do when I get back. I'll build the finest house this old town has ever seen." He laughed. "Then we'll have a piano and all kinds of fine things. That's the way it will be." George and Lucy came back into an embrace.

Lucy looked dreamily out the window, her head against George's chest. "I don't care if we get a new house, just as long as you have your laugh back."

"No, my dear," he said with a chuckle. "We need a big house to show everyone we've made it, that we deserve respect. This little cottage," he said stomping on the floor, "always reminds me of my failures. We need a big house to prove our success." He looked out the window and smiled.

Lucy snuggled up to her husband. "When do you expect you'll be home this year?"

"If all goes well, I'll walk through that door the middle of April. That'll be grand, just two months from now." He grew silent for a moment and released her, walking over to the window. His voice hardened. "And that's when I'll take care of that business about the cross. Can you imagine those friggin' Micks putting up that big white cross on the hill? Hell's flames, it's the first thing you see when you enter the harbour. What an insult, a Catholic cross right there for everyone to see. It's a call to arms for us Protestants and the Lodge." He turned around to face his wife. "I vow, Lucy, that as soon as I get home, I'm going to knock down that bloody Papist cross. Yes, my dear, I'll make things right."

"My Lord, George, you get some fussed about these things," Lucy said, moving to the other side of the room.

"Only proper," George said. "God knows there's few enough brothers willing to do anything. All talk and no action, most of them. But I'll do something about it. Just wait until I come back."

He began to rifle through the old steamer trunk again. "Oh," he said standing up, "I nearly forgot. I've got a Valentine's Day present for you." He broke off and went to the hallway closet where he pulled down a package wrapped in brown paper, tied with blue string.

"Oh, George, I don't want anything. I've got all I need, and it's only the thirteenth."

"Here," he said, handing the parcel to her, unaccustomed shyness in his movement.

"I shouldn't open it until tomorrow."

"Nonsense, I'll already be in Harbour Grace. Open it now, while I'm here to watch."

She undid the string, carefully rolling it up in a ball and slipping it into her apron pocket. She unwrapped the package and found a framed photograph of her husband. "Oh, George," she said gushing with pleasure. "It turned out well, didn't it?"

He blushed and shrugged his shoulders.

The photograph was mounted in an oval frame, ten inches tall by five across. The black border made George's figure stand out through the protective glass. Lucy held her gift at arm's length and smiled. "My, but you carry yourself well, dear. I'll put it on the bureau, so I can see you every day when you're away." She placed it on the dresser and stepped back. "I just love to see you all dressed up in your Sunday best. And don't you cut the fine figure? Look," she said, pointing, "you can see your father's watch chain all tucked neatly into your vest. And the silk tie John gave you. Doesn't it look handsome?" She picked up the picture and began to dance with it. "Thank you, George," she said, "this is the nicest gift you've ever given me. It means so much." She embraced the photograph. "Thank you, thank you, this'll make things so much easier while you're away."

EIGHTEEN

The sky was grey, dreary to the bone, when Grieve visited the Forest Road Cemetery. Autumn had been particularly damp, so much so that his joints had creaked and his back ached. Winter had been mercilessly long. The merchant reached over and touched the granite tombstone of his infant daughter. Coldness numbed his fingertips as he felt along the stippled edge of the marker. He shivered as he stepped back to look at the carved inscription.

> *Helen Curling Grieve*
> *1885-1887*
> *Our beloved Nellie will live in our hearts forever*

Grieve bowed his head, fidgeting with his hat held awkwardly in his hands. Eyes closed, he recalled how Nellie had died, followed by his wife and, most recently, his first daughter. A tear fell down his cheek as he knelt down and repositioned the vase of cut flowers he had just placed by the grave, obeying some unwritten code about the order of such things. He stood up and looked at the ghostly trees creaking in the cold wind. A fallen leaf, hardened and golden brown, blew against the vase, trapped by a cold breeze. The leaf fluttered and flipped away, dancing toward Quidi Vidi in the embrace of a winter gust.

A younger man, dressed in black, came up behind Grieve and watched the old merchant. A look of concern came over his grey eyes as he straightened his clergyman's collar. "I see you're remembering things past," he said with a south country British accent.

Grieve turned around to find Edward Brooks, a curate at the Anglican Cathedral. "Aye, Reverend," he said with a sigh, "I'm reflecting on the tragedy that has dogged my family."

The minister's eyes, all the while looking into Grieve's, worked to communicate an understanding to comfort the old merchant. He nodded. "Do you feel like walking?" Brooks said.

Grieve hesitated and then looked back at the gravestone. "I suppose," he said, pausing a moment before breaking off.

As they turned toward Bannerman Park, the minister touched Grieve's shoulder.

"Many is the day I wish my wife was resting here," Grieve said. "I'd love to visit with her."

"Where is she?" the minister asked.

"Buried in our family plot in Greenock, along with Nan, my oldest daughter. I sent Ellen home to Scotland to recuperate from her decline. But it wasn't to be." Grieve sighed as he looked off toward the park ahead of them. "I think she was always happier there, never took to this place."

"And what of your son, Robert?"

"He's in Scotland now, seems to like it over there."

"I always thought Robert had great potential. He'd be a good fit with your business, wouldn't he?"

"That he would be," Grieve said. "But I'm not sure he wants to come back to work in the firm."

Brooks looked surprised. "Do you know why?"

The old merchant shook his head. "I have no idea, but I certainly could use him. Good help is hard to find these days, and I don't have as much energy as I used to." He paused and looked up at the trees waving in the cold breeze. "I took on the son of an old acquaintance from university a few years back. I thought he might help, but he's gotten all angry and doesn't seem to be working out. Too bad, I had hope for him." Grieve signed.

"You've created a fine legacy for Robert here," Brooks said as they came over a hill to a snow covered athletic pitch.

"Yes, I have."

They walked on, Brooks subtly directing them through the warren of pathways in the Park.

Grieve continued. "There are times when I wonder if coming to St. John's would be best for him, anyway."

"How so?"

"Everything here is changing. That gang of thieves in the House of Assembly is doing its best to bankrupt us."

"Do you really think so?"

"I do. They went and appointed two new members to the House to shore up their majority, not even elected by the people — appointed by Morris, they were. It's an outrage, a flagrant attack on the Constitution." Grieve was nearly shouting. "'The public be damned,' Morris is saying."

Brooks flinched.

"Oh, I'm so sorry, Reverend. Please forgive me. I get so riled up when I see Morris flout the people like he does."

"You're forgiven," Brooks said. "I envy you your passion. I'm sure the Lord will excuse your occasional indiscretion."

Silently the two walked, side by side, hands behind their backs, heads down.

"And the business goes well?" Brooks finally asked.

"For the most part," Grieve said, "the fish look strong this year. The seals weren't too good in the spring, but at least we broke even. The cod business is steady but it's the seal hunt that tells how things are really going."

"The hunt's good for the men," Brooks said, "the one chance they have to earn some real money."

"Aye. I'm pleased to give them that chance."

"Tell me, what's left for you to accomplish now? What is it that you want?"

Grieve stopped. After a long pause, he said, "I suppose I would like some public recognition for my good works. The lawsuits and the squabbling drag me down so much. People don't really understand the things I do." He resumed walking. "Most of them see me as a moneygrubber. 'A fisherman is one thief,' they say, 'a merchant is many.' But I do give back."

"That you do."

"Just one acknowledgement, one public honour, would be nice. All I want is some respect."

The minister nodded. "I'm sure honours will come your way, just be patient." Brooks came to a halt, causing Grieve to stop as well. He lowered his voice. "I'm not sure how to say this, Walter." He paused.

"Go on."

"Well, some of the parishioners are suggesting we refuse your charity."

A look of surprise came over the merchant's face.

"They say too many men have died working for you."

Grieve's face turned red and he began to shake his head. "Well, if that's how you feel—"

"No, no," Brooks said, interrupting. "That's not how the Church feels. I just wanted to tell you what I've heard others say. Of course, they're wrong. They don't know what they're talking about." He paused to regain his composure. "We are most gratified by your generosity, sir, most gratified; always have been."

Grieve hesitated for a moment, uncertain. Then he smiled warmly. "Thank you, Reverend," he said calmly, "you've not told me anything I didn't already know."

There was an awkward pause.

"I must take my leave now," Brooks said, looking at his pocket watch.

Grieve nodded. "If the fish stay strong, I may be able to increase my donation to the Cathedral this year."

"That would be wonderful, sir, wonderful. I should tell you that your generosity to the orphanage has made a tremendous difference."

"Good."

Brooks walked off toward his church. Grieve turned and headed toward Water Street.

131

NINETEEN

When John, Peter and Tommy thundered down the stairs at Elsie's the morning after they arrived in St. John's, they found a man sitting by the stove. He balanced a mug of tea on his knee while he ate from a bowlful of steaming oatmeal laced with molasses.

"This is the other Lundrigan," Elsie said to no one in particular. She poured tea into three waiting mugs.

Tommy and Peter headed for the table, while John went over to the stranger. William Lundrigan was tall and wiry with curly brown hair. He looked to be in his mid-thirties, clearly experienced of the sea. "A top hand," John thought. "I'm John," the boy said and he approached, "John Lundrigan, from Red Island."

"Red Island?" Will said, moving his bowl and cup to the stove.

"Yes, sir, just off Argentia in Placentia Bay."

"I know where it's at. Been there a few times when I shipped on a banking schooner." The man smiled and shook John's outstretched hand. "There's two families of Lundrigans in Salmonier, where I belong. They're related from a way back, but keep to themselves these days. I remember one from the other side went to Placentia Bay, some fifteen years ago."

"Do you recall his name?"

Will looked toward the ceiling, trying to dredge up some distant memory. "Can't remember, a Bible name though, Noah or Moses, something like that."

"Abel?"

"Yes, that's it, Abel, Abel Lundrigan. A fine sealer, he was. He left just after he came back from that terrible disaster on the *Greenland*. I think he married a girl from up the bay."

John drew in his breath, shocked yet again to find he had family outside of his small world on Red Island. "Abel's my father."

"Well, doesn't that beat all? Small world, isn't it?"

John nodded and paused to think for a moment. "Why did my father leave?"

"Not sure. It was a few years back. I do remember hearing that his father was pretty hard on him. Could be something to do with it."

John nodded.

"What brings you to St. John's?" Will asked.

"Peter and I are looking for tickets to go sealing. Tommy there, the tall one, has a berth on the *Bloodhound*."

"He's Jessie's nephew?"

"Yep."

"He's some lucky. Every man jack is saying tickets will be scarce this year, harder to find than an eel in a bucket of snot." He chuckled.

John laughed, but then his face fell as the likelihood of earning a ticket became less real. "Is it really that hard?"

"Yep, you pretty well have to know someone, like your friend there."

John looked down at the floor, shuffling his feet. "We're going out today to see if we can get work loading a sealer. Tommy's uncle says there's a chance of getting a ticket if we work hard."

"That might work, but I doubt it," Will said. "It's still a matter of who you know these days. Perhaps you'll get lucky and meet someone." He paused and then put his hand on John's shoulder. "Buck up, now, lad. It's not that bad. You'll find something, sure. I hear the *Bloodhound* and *Southern Cross* are starting to load today over at Baine, Johnstons. That would be a good place to start."

"Thank you," John said, looking up at Will. "Tommy's on the way over there today, so we'll go with him. His Uncle Jessie won't take raw hands on the *Hound*, but perhaps there's a chance on the *Southern Cross*." He smiled, straightening his back to stand taller.

"Maybe. I hear George Clarke is having trouble finding old hands. I suspect he's on the lookout for good youngsters."

John nodded in agreement.

"I'll ask around at Harvey Brothers to see if there are any spare tickets."

John's eyes widened. "Really, you'd do that?"

"Sure, got to keep it in the family," Will said with wink. "There's no harm in asking. I suspect nothing will come of it, though."

"Oh, thank you, Will."

ii

After a hearty breakfast the boys headed down to Baine, Johnston's wharf with Tommy leading the way. "You two ninnies would be lost without me," he said, as they turned at corners that all looked the same to John. "Stick with me and we'll be fine." The younger boys tagged along behind.

But there were no ships at the Baine, Johnston wharf when they arrived. "I thought Will said they were loading today."

"Yeah, that's what Jessie said, too."

"They're ready to go," Peter said, pointing at the loaded wagons on the wharf. "But where are the ships?"

A well-dressed man in a tweed suit and a tie wound with a flourish around a stiff collar came up to them. He sported a bowler hat that looked out of place on the rough wharf. He had an edgy look to him, unwilling to look the boys in the eye.

"You laddies are late," he said in a clipped Scots accent. "The crew's already left." The boys looked at him, too dumfounded to speak. "Come, come now," he said pointing out toward the ice-covered harbour. "With a wee bit of hurry, you can catch them. See over there, the *Bloodhound* is caught in the ice out by the stream. You've got to get out there and help pull her around. Shake a leg now and you won't be late."

The boys looked out toward the Narrows and saw a three-masted ship lodged crosswise in the lane of open water that ran from the gap. Her yellow funnel belched smoke, while her wooden sides and masts recalled some long lost golden age of sailing ships. A crowd of men, maybe fifty, were walking across the ice toward the steamer. Without a word the trio struck out.

"I wonder who that weasel was?" Peter asked, once they were out of earshot.

"His name is Joshua J. Cheeseman," Tommy said, emphasizing the "J" in a way that mocked the use of a middle initial. "His highness, some call him. He's the big shot in charge of the stores — tough bugger too — harder than a box of nails. Watch your back around him." John turned around to see Cheeseman sitting on the seat with the teamster of a loaded wagon leaving the quay.

"That's my ship," Tommy said with pride as they walked over the ice. "She looks smaller than last year." The boys grew quiet as they approached the old sealer. By the time they reached the others, a thick line had been run off the bow of the ship. The men on the ice had taken this towrope onto their shoulders and, with their backs to the *Bloodhound*, begun to try to haul her around into the open channel. The trio slipped into open spaces on the line and added their weight to the human chain.

A deep voice hollered, "All together now boys, pull." A collective groan of exertion escaped from the line, but nothing happened. Several of the men, including Tommy, slipped and would have fallen without the rope to hold onto.

From up the line a single voice sang out:

Come get your duds in order

Through his shoulder, John felt the hawser tighten on the word "get."

For we're bound across the water

Another tug in time with the song.

Heave away me jollies heave away

The rope began to pulse to the rhythm of the song. A single voice, loud and crisp, came from up front.

Come get your duds together for we're bound to leave tomorrow
Heave away me jolly boys we're all bound away

The whole line began to throb in unison with each beat of the song. John felt the power surge through the rope as every man fell into the rhythm. By the second chorus over half of them were singing.

Sometimes we're bound for Liverpool more times we're bound for Spain
Heave away me jollies heave away

They began to make progress, each hand able to take a small step forward. The line hummed with power as the group began to trudge ahead in lockstep with the song. A strong voice rang out from behind.

But now we're bound to St John's town to watch the girls a-dancing
Heave away me jolly boys we're all bound away

Men laughed. As lustily as he could, John joined into the chorus, bending his back to the towrope.

I wrote me love a letter and I signed it with a ring
Heave away me jollies heave away

Everyone sang now. Behind them the *Bloodhound* creaked against the ice and started to swing.

I wrote me love a letter I was on the Jenny Ling
Heave away me jolly boys we're all bound away

The *Bloodhound*'s whistle shattered the air as she broke free of the ice. The men dropped the rope as the song transformed to a loud "hurrah." The hawser flopped into the water when the ship began to lug toward shore along the open channel. Deckhands recovered the line, waving at the men on the ice as they passed. The ship let out a long, low whistle.

The men watched, still standing in a line, as the stern of the ship slipped by them on her way to the wharf. A gentle gurgling sounded from the wash of her propellers.

"What do we do now?" John asked his linemate.

"I hear the *Southern Cross* is on her way just behind," he said squinting out toward the Notch. "We'd best wait here. I suspect we'll be singing more than one song for George Clarke. He's a hell of a sealer, but probably the worst sailor of the bunch."

A whistle, more shrill than the *Bloodhound*'s, split the winter air. John looked up to see another steamer coming along the channel. This one was roughly the same size and had the same yellow funnel and three masts as the first ship, but she looked more rounded, less sleek on the bow.

"The *Southern Cross* there is not half the ship the *Bloodhound* is," John's line-mate said.

The boy watched the sealer approach. She looked cumbersome in the water. Her fat prow pushed a large bow wave, much bigger than the *Bloodhound*'s. "How come she's more rounded like that?" John asked.

"She was built in Norway for whaling," his linemate said. "Over there they want ships that ride up on the ice if they get pinched. That's why she's so fat." He paused, sizing up the approaching vessel. "Can you believe it? That one ex-plored the Antarctic. She sailed down there twice. The first ship ever to enter the Ross Sea."

"What's her name mean?" John asked.

"Aren't you the curious one," he said. "The 'Southern Cross' is the name of a big bunch of stars in the southern hemisphere, you know, in Australia and down there. Just like the Big Dipper up here."

John nodded as he watched the ship lumber up the channel straight toward them. He could see now that the *Southern Cross* was not as fine a ship as the *Bloodhound*. She looked fat in the water and had a dowdy look. John craned his neck upwards as she loomed closer.

"Look at that," he said excitedly. "She's got carved seals on her bow, see, one on each side. Even painted them white. Must be for good luck."

"No doubt she'll need it."

They waited for the ship to turn and follow the open water in the channel. But the *Cross* did not veer off, she just kept coming straight at the men standing on the ice. They hesitated at first and then everyone turned tail and began to run. The ship hit the ice with a loud thud. The bow wave continued, now on top of the ice, chasing the men who began to run at full gallop. The miniature tsunami was six inches high when it caught up to the fleeing men, filling low boots and shoes with water. John saw Tommy slip and fall to his hands and knees as the wave rushed under his feet. Men stood shaking fists at the ship now nestled to amidships in a fresh crack in the ice.

John went back to his linemate who was high stepping like a nesting gannet trying to expel the freezing water from his shoes. "That's George Clarke all over," he said. "Probably laughing his head off to see us scatter like that."

They spent the rest of the day getting the *Southern Cross* through the chan-nel to the wharf. One problem followed another and John got to sing three more heave-up shanties while they pulled Clarke from one crisis after another. The sun had set before the crew returned to the wharf. Joshua J. Cheeseman thanked them all and told them that anyone who came back by 8:00 the next morning could be part of the work crew. "Just so you know," the Scots manager said, looking directly at the younger boys, "working on the crew won't help you get a ticket. No laddies, berths are only for seasoned hands this year. You may as well go home now if you're looking to go sealing." He turned abruptly and walked away.

John looked over at Peter and shook his head. Both boys turned and began to trudge along behind Tommy.

"Looks bleak, doesn't it," Peter said.

"Sure does," John replied, not bothering to look up at his friend.

iii

The boys returned the next morning at 7:30 to claim spots on the work crew. They were nervously quiet as they approached Baine, Johnston's wharf. Peter broke the silence as the *Southern Cross* came into view. "Lord Jesus in heaven, look at that man on the ladder. He's some high up there." John pointed to a form halfway up the ropes on the tall foremast.

"That's no ladder," Tommy said, slapping his friend on the shoulder. "It's a ratline. See how it's made up from three shrouds going up from the gunwale to the mast. Those are the ratlines, there, those smaller ropes going crosswise on the shrouds. They're the steps you use."

"Looks hard," Peter said craning his neck to look up at the man who was pulling himself up into the lookout barrel.

"No, it's easy," Tommy said. "Just remember to hold onto the shrouds, not the ratlines, and never look down — just like climbing stairs."

Peter looked over at his tall friend in disbelief. He shuddered.

"The lads who go up there to be on the lookout for seals are called 'scunners,'" Tommy said.

"I've heard them called 'barrelmen,'" John said.

Tommy shot an annoyed glance at his friend. "Same thing," he said, as he sped up his pace.

"Jesus," John said, excitement building in his voice. "There's more ropes than you can count up there, going everywhere. They all got names?"

"Yes, sir," Tommy said. "Can't say as I know them all yet, but the old hands will tell you what every single one is called and what it's used for."

Reverent silence returned as they approached the old sealing ship. Finally Tommy spoke. "See how she carries sail," he said, pointing to the canvas wrapped along the lower spar of the gaff rig aft. "Just like the old days."

"And she's got a jib sail too," John added, motioning toward the bowsprit.

The breeze shifted, sending black smoke billowing from her yellow funnel toward the boys. "But she doesn't need her sails anymore," Tommy said, trying to quell a cough. "They keep them, just in case."

"Looks about the same length as the *Bloodhound*," John said.

"Aye," Tommy replied, "a hundred and fifty feet along her decks. The *Cross's* beam is wider, though."

"What are these holes for?" Peter asked pointing to one of several oval openings in the ship's side.

"Those are the scuppers," Tommy said. "They drain off the water that gets trapped on her main deck."

"That main deck is sure big," John said. "Runs half the length of the whole ship, and those high decks fore and aft make it so she'd hold a lot of water in a heavy sea."

"She would," Tommy said.

The boys ran their hands along the ship's outer furring. "Hasn't been cared for too well," John said pulling a loose splinter off her side. He rolled the splinter in his fingers. "She may be a bit worse for wear, but she's lovely nonetheless — fetched a sixty-dollar crew share last year."

"A hell of a lot more than the *Bloodhound's* twenty-six dollars," Tommy said, making no effort to hide his jealousy. "Hard to see how this old biddy outfished the *Hound*, but she did." Tommy paused. "Maybe this George Clarke isn't a bad master after all. He sure looked like a chowderhead bouncing all over the channel yesterday."

"This old beauty," John said, stroking her wooden side, "just isn't good in tight places, that's all. She'll show how good she is in the open water. You watch."

A shout from the warehouse interrupted them. "Over here, laddies. Let's get in the collar."

The boys were assigned to different chores around the Baine, Johnston wharf. John worked in the forepeak of the *Southern Cross*, cleaning her up in preparation for the voyage to the Gulf. Tommy helped to load both ships. After that, he joined a rope crew on the *Bloodhound*. Peter got a good job, sanding and varnishing the officers' quarters on the *Cross*. "Sure needed sprucing up," he said. "She hasn't seen a lick of varnish in years." The best thing about Peter's duties was that he got to know the officers as they came and went.

iv

"So what are the officers like?" John asked Peter as they walked home after a week of work.

"They seem a good lot. Clarke is a moody bugger, but the others are fine." He smiled. "There's one, though, that's really number one. His name is Herb Butler, always smiling, always has a good word. He seems to really care." Peter paused and then looked over at John. "He tells me he went to school at Dalhousie over in Canada. Sure reads a lot, I'll tell you."

"What's he do?" John asked.

"He's a master watch, one of the four officers who look after the men out on the ice. He's the boss out there. I'd sure love to go hunting with him, wouldn't have any trouble following that man."

"Some people who read a lot who have their heads in the clouds. You know, out of touch, like McCarthy back home," John said. "Is this Butler anything like that?"

"Oh, no, not at all. He's down to earth, knows where it's at. Smarter than a top." Peter stopped walking and looked up dreamily toward the Cathedral. "Yes, boy, being on his watch would be the best."

"Sounds like a good man," John said.

"To be sure."

John walked along beside his friend, sharing his dreams of being out on the ice with the likes of Herb Butler. He prayed that by dedicating himself to his janitorial duties he would earn a ticket. He pictured himself moving easily through the clumpers and hummocks in search of whitecoats, returning triumphantly with a tow of seals over his shoulder, getting approving grins from his shipmates.

TWENTY

George Clarke's days grew busier as the date for the *Cross*'s departure approached. Loading stores had gone well, quite fast, in fact. According to Joseph Youdon, the trusted hand who Clarke appointed as quartermaster, the ship had been stocked exactly the same as last year. "It's all there," he said. "They must've stowed it better this year because I'm not tripping over as many barrels. But the lists tally up, just perfect."

Repairs had gone slowly. On the trip from Harbour Grace they discovered problems with the rudder works. The channels carrying the cables from the wheel to the rudder were so badly caked with soot and grease the ropes could barely travel. The cables had frayed, too. Clarke had to puff up his chest and get quite angry before Cheeseman would approve new ropes and cable mounts. "You'd think it was his money," Clarke said in exasperation. "That Cheeseman is some goddamned tight. I finally got him to order the cables, and now we have a crew reaming out the channels. Looks like we'll have her ready on time."

David Parsons, the first engineer, informed Clarke that the engines needed a lot of work. He set his crew working double shifts to be sure they were shipshape by departure. Clarke found these Scottish engineers to be a dour lot. Every time he tried to joke with them he was met with a stern look, bordering on rebuff, suggesting he was wasting their time. For a while the captain thought that he had lost his touch with the humour but, after several failed attempts, decided it was these Presbyterian souls who lacked any sense of fun.

As for crew, Clarke knew that he would have many younger sealers. "Judging from the boys I see working around the ship, we'll have more children than men this year," he said to James Kelly. "Green as spruce trees in June, but they put in the good effort. What they lack in experience, they make up in energy."

"How do the officers look?" Kelly asked.

"Pretty good," Clarke replied. "We lost two of last year's master watches because of the holdback last season. Sparkes looks like a good replacement. He shipped with young Bartlett last year." The captain smiled. "I'm not so sure about Butler, though."

"How so?"

"I can't put my finger on it, but there's something about him that bothers me. He brought this whole trunkload of books on board, what a waste of space that is. The man talks too much about going to school at Dalhousie, too. A hell of a lot of good that'll do him out swiling." Clarke paused to collect his thoughts. "Can't say as I like those fancy words he's always using either." Clarke shook his head.

"He's a good hand with the accordion," Kelly said. "Knows all the songs too. I heard him at the Crosbie — a fine singer."

"A lot of good that'll do us on the ice," Clarke said. "The man may have all that book knowledge, but he's only been to the ice four times. Not enough for a master watch." The captain looked away. "You know if he comes from a Catholic family?"

Kelly shook his head.

Clarke continued. "He told me he wasn't religious at all. Blathered on about not needing a god." Clarke paused. "I'm not sure what's worse, being a Mick or having no religion. No matter what, he bothers me."

"Why did you hire him?" Kelly asked, as he began reloading his pipe.

"He was the best I could find."

"Hmmm."

Clarke continued. "I can't stomach these know-it-alls who figure they know better than you just because they've read a bunch of books. It's like our years of going to the ice aren't worth anything. As far as I'm concerned, all that wordy claptrap isn't worth a penny when it comes to sealing. He's like that Cheeseman, green as grass."

"Never you mind, George. I'm sure this Butler will be fine once he gets the hang of things."

"We'll have to be sure to keep an eye on him though."

Kelly nodded.

ii

As March 5, their departure date, approached, the *Southern Cross* buzzed with activity. Men swarmed all over her. Being so busy kept Clarke's apprehensions at bay. Every now and then, though, the old feelings of being overwhelmed would close in on him, causing a pain in the pit of his stomach. When these moments came, Clarke would launch himself into another task and soon his worries would subside.

The nights before they were to leave Clarke chose to sleep on board rather than at the Crosbie with the other officers. The first night on board, his foot began to throb announcing another attack of gout. When he finally got to sleep he had a dream. It began, simply enough, with him and his brother John, as boys, getting into their usual mischief. They fixed the outhouse so it would leak onto the shoes of the hand using it. But then his brother's face turned white and began to get older and older. John's whole body began to float. His clothes turned to wispy shreds that followed him like ribbons in a breeze. The whole visage became white as it drifted up and down, slowly moaning something George could not make out. The apparition's eyes changed and soon became black circles in a ghostly face. But it was still John. The image was so real, Clarke felt he could reach out and touch the flowing robes. Then the phantom zoomed in. The moaning grew stronger and louder. Clarke began to shake. Slowly, the moaning changed and began to sound familiar. He recognized the sounds, but they were still incomprehensible, like hearing another language. The spirit floated back and forth in front of him, haunting, frightening. He was pinned down, like when the old hag comes. The sound clarified and took shape. "Don't go. Don't go," it moaned. Then the spirit turned to exactly the same expression on his brother's face that night when he had ranted about the *Southern Cross* being cursed. "Don't go," now sounding more like John's voice. All the while the spirit moved back and forth, in and out. "Don't go." Clarke began to feel funny and started to float in lockstep with the vision. He tried to resist but was not able stop himself. Back and forth they floated, a ghostly dance to the droning song, "Don't go." All of a sudden the face disappeared and Clarke fell, tumbling head over heels, into a black abyss, detached from everything. After an eternity a dim light appeared in the distance. He tried to reach it but could not, still falling out of control. But the brightness remained steady and, if he watched it, he stopped falling. He thrashed out and felt the bed covers wrapped around him. Clarke struggled to get free. Finally he woke up.

Night sweats soaked his shirt. He pulled himself up and sat on the bunk, trembling like a child who had just been beaten by his father. The captain sat for half an hour trying to shake off the spell. A dram of cognac finally brought him back to his senses.

Twelve hours later, the dream still lingered. Clearly, he was being warned.

Then he realized the silliness of it all. "Those dreams and spirits are just ignorance and fear," he said out loud. "Most of them are just tales, like how the bully bagger keeps young children in bed. I'd be an idiot to mind such silliness. They're made to prey on the stupidity of ordinary people. I can rise above them." He stopped, deep in thought. "Enough of this foolishness. It's just Catholic claptrap, that's all. Besides, the *Cross* is trim as a well-reefed topsail. Her rudder's fixed. Her pumps tested out. She's drip-dry in her bilges. Alexander MacLaughlin found the boilers were in top shape. No, sir, there's no need to fret, none at all. God knows I have enough worries without being concerned about a silly nightmare."

In the cold light of day, sitting in his cabin on the *Southern Cross*, the dream struck him as absurd, just his overactive imagination playing tricks; a sham warning brought on by all those people who constantly wanted a piece of him. What he needed to do now was to steel himself against any weaknesses these folks, and the apparitions they caused, might contrive. The dream increased his resolve to forge ahead, no matter what the others said. He would prove to everyone that he was the best of the bunch, the top swiler.

TWENTY-ONE

MARCH 2, 1914
ST. JOHN'S

The boys had just finished their second week working for Baine, Johnston. "I'm beat right out," Tommy said to John, as they waited for Peter to join them for the hike back to Elsie's. "God, I'm looking forward to my Sunday rest. I'm going to sleep all day."

"Me too."

They chatted for a while before they were distracted by a commotion at the warehouse. "Sweet roary-eyed Jesus," Tommy said, "look at that." He pointed toward Peter who was running wildly toward them, waving a piece of paper over his head. "What's gotten into him? Looks like he's being chased by the bully bagger."

"I got it! I got it!" Peter shouted.

"Got what, you idiot?"

He nearly crashed into his friends when he reached them. "I got my ticket on the *Southern Cross*." With a huge smile he showed them the paper. Barely able to stand still, he said, "James says he'll get me on with Herb Butler. Won't that be great?"

"James who?"

"James Kelly, the second hand."

John looked at the paper. 'Baine, Johnston and Company' was embossed across the top. He read out loud:

Jack,
This young man has proven to me he has the makings of a fine sealer. Please sign him on to the Southern Cross.

John looked up at Peter. "Who's this Jack?"

"He's the agent I sign on with. That'll be on Tuesday." Peter began to pace back and forth, trying to contain his energy.

John turned the paper over and then back again. "Is this all? Is this what we've been working so hard for?"

145

"I guess so," Peter said. "The signature on the bottom is what counts."

John looked at the paper again and saw "Jas. Kelly" signed with a flourish, along with the date, 'Feb. 28, 1914.'

"You're some lucky. You're all set now." He said as he handed the paper back to his friend.

Peter kept on grinning, still revelling in his good fortune. "I tried to get one for you John, but Mr. Kelly said he's only taking hands he knows. Have you gotten to know any of the officers?"

"Naw," John replied, looking away, "I haven't met anyone important."

"Too bad," Peter said as he turned to tag along with Tommy. He motioned for John to follow. But John lagged behind, no longer interested in his friends' talk as they jostled each other, laughing and joking. Peter finally looked back to see John trudging along, head down. He came back to his friend. "What's wrong?"

"Oh, hell," John said, wiping his eyes, "there's no chance for me now. I'll never get a ticket."

"Don't give up. There's still time."

"Hardly," John said, turning away.

There was nothing Peter could say. The two walked along slowly.

"Lord, I can't go back to Red Island with nothing to show for my time here," John said with a hitch in his voice. "All I can see is the look on the old man's face when he gets ready to beat the shit out of me." He shuddered.

Peter reached over and touched his friend's arm.

"Goddamn it," John said looking skyward. "I'll never break out of this prison, never. I'm trapped, Peter, like a lobster in a pot. Oh, what's the use?"

ii

They arrived at Elsie's to find the house jammed full of people. Loud talk and laughter greeted them. Most of the visitors had glasses in their hands, setting up a commotion that spilled out onto the street. The boys pushed their way in through the throng. Some were townsfolk, while others were from around the bay.

"Oh, there you are," Elsie shouted from across the crowded front room. "Wait there." She pushed her way through the crowd, leading with a nearly full glass held above her head. "Jessie is having a party. You boys are welcome to join in. There's something to drink in the kitchen. Help yourself, so long as you promise not to overdo it." She winked.

"Elsie," someone hollered. She looked around. "Have to go." She smiled over her shoulder as she disappeared into the mass of people. Joshua J. Cheeseman chatted with Tommy's uncle in the corner. George Clarke's loud laugh dominated the front of the house.

"See over there," Peter said, pointing to a group of officers chatting the a corner, "the one with the Protestant whisker and the pipe. That's James Kelly. He's the one gave me my ticket."

"No flies on him," Tommy said.

"Yes, my son. They say he's real religious, lives by the word."

"But he looks tough, too."

"Aye," Peter said. "I saw him give Clarke what for one time, stood up to the old man like a dockyard dog. The captain didn't seem to mind though. Kelly's a good man."

"Boys," Tommy said, "I wouldn't mind working for a man like that."

Peter smiled.

They reached the kitchen and found the table strewn with liquor bottles and glasses. Tommy poured them ample portions of Hudson Bay rum. "To a good spring on the floes," he said. The other two responded by clicking their glasses and taking tentative sips of the full strength rum. Tommy and Peter began to laugh and talk.

Will Lundrigan came in carrying a duffel. John poured another rum and followed Will to his usual chair by the stove. "You're not joining the party?" John said, pointing toward the front of the house.

"No, I'm a fish out of water in there," Will replied, accepting the glass from John. "That's the who's who of Baine, Johnston. I'm with Harvey Brothers."

"Don't they get on with each other?"

"They'll help each other out in a pinch, but other than that they're at each other's throats. I'm not sure I'd be welcome out there."

John pulled up a chair and sat beside the older Lundrigan. "It's too bad the folks don't get on better. Don't know why they have to try to outdo each other all the time. I've been talking to some of the boys and they say that working together makes us all stronger. That's what the FPU is saying."

"They're right, but rich folks, like Grieve, don't see it that way. They live in a different world, all dollars for them. When you've got money you don't have to get along with anybody else. That's the way of it. Only us working stiffs have to fret about sticking together."

John nodded his understanding.

Will took a hefty swig of his rum. "Oh, by the way, I've got something for you." He reached into his jacket. Out came a tattered piece of paper, folded over on itself several times. He handed it to John, who opened it and read.

"Oh, my God," the boy said, eyes widening in excitement. "Is this real?"

"Yes, John, it's your ticket to sail on the *Newfoundland*. Look at the top, your name is on it." John nodded. "And it's signed by the second hand, see." Will pointed to a signature at the bottom, "Geo. Tuff, Second Hand." The note was dated Feb. 26, 1914.

"I can't believe it. How'd you get this?"

"I asked around. Not as many men as they'd hoped will be joining the crew up north, so Tuff gave me this after I told him how good a worker you are. I suppose you still want it?" he said with a twinkle in his eye.

"Want it?" John stammered. "This is all I've been dreaming about for the last year." His shaking hands caused the paper to rustle. The boy read and reread, the grin on his face getting wider each time. "I can't believe my eyes. Lord above, it's even got my name on it." He pointed to the paper. "Oh thank you, Will, thank you."

The older Lundrigan smiled. "All you have to do now is show up at Harvey Brothers on Tuesday and sign on. Just be sure to take this with you," he said, motioning toward the paper, "and it'll be done. It's that easy."

John could not speak.

Will continued, "We were going to sail for Poole's Island on Wednesday, but we've been delayed."

Finally John found his tongue, "Who's her master?" he blurted out.

"Wes Kean, Abe's son." Reverence and respect were clear in how he said the second name. "Young Wes is a fair man on the sail, and good on the ice."

"Is she a good ship?"

"Not too bad. She's big, twice the size of the *Bloodhound*, a wooden wall like her though. Built in Québec in '72. She carries more men, too." He leaned over toward John and said in a whisper, "Sometimes she's a slug in the ice, but a great boat when she gets beside the patch."

"She paid fifty dollars last year, didn't she?"

Will nodded. After a pause, he said, "Well, I guess I'd better say goodbye now." He drained his glass and put it on the table.

"Goodbye?"

"Yes, I've got to look after a work crew on the *Newfoundland*, a few last-minute repairs. That's why she's not leaving on Wednesday."

"When will you have her ready?"

"Can't be sure, but they say we have to get underway by the weekend. You'll find out the exact time when you sign on. I'm heading down to her now," Will said, pointing to his duffel.

"So I'll see you on board the *Newfoundland* then?" John said with a wide grin.

Will nodded. "You'd better go over and tell the boys." He stood up, grabbed his bag, and headed for the back door. "See you in a couple of days."

"Thanks, Will. Thank you so much."

"Sure thing."

John clutched the paper to his chest and began to dance a jig. He bounced over to Tommy and Peter who were jostling in the corner. "Look at this, boys," he said with a laugh.

A grin broke across Peter's face. "Hurrah!"

"Good for you," Tommy said. "Always knew you had it in you."

"Well, we've done it," John said, still brimming with excitement. "We came to go swiling, and now we're all fixed up, all three of us."

"Too bad we're not on the same ship, but this is almost as good."

John continued. "Everything is as it should be." He grabbed the rum bottle and refilled their glasses. Then, with ceremony, he raised his tumbler. "To us," he said. "This is the finest kind of spring, the finest kind."

"Yes, boys, the finest kind of spring."

Glasses clinked.

iii

John scanned the ceiling of the auditorium in the new Seaman's Institute. Carefully finished wood beams criss-crossed the plaster giving the room a sense of formality, like he imagined he would find in Government House. Framed pictures of dignitaries added to the sombreness of the place.

The date was Monday, March 2, and the boys were at the Institute to attend the first in the series of entertainments for swilers. 'Admission free to all sealers, fishermen and seamen,' the announcement said. The formality of the auditorium belied the ruckus put up by the three hundred sealers assembled in the hall. Their ragged clothes combined with jolly laughter, loud "how you gettin' ons?" and the hubbub of animated conversation, overwhelmed the hall. The aroma of wet overcoats wafted through the room.

"See, I told you so," Tommy said to his two friends. "They treat us sealers like jeezly kings. Imagine them letting us in here for free." He paused to look around. "We're real sealers now," he said with an explosive laugh. And you, Peter, you're the luckiest because you're leaving first — the day after tomorrow." Tommy slapped his friend on the shoulder. "Yes, boy, the luckiest." He looked up at the stage. "And they're even going to play some music for us." He motioned toward the group of uniformed musicians sitting on the stage, thumping drums and playing notes in preparation for performing.

"They look like sailors," Peter said.

"Yes, boy, they're from the *Calypso*, that Naval Reserve ship. I hear they're a wonderful grand band."

A smallish man, well dressed, with a bearing that made him look important, scrambled up on stage. The hubbub subsided.

"He's all dressed up like a skip jack," Tommy said.

A loud "shhh" came from behind.

The man gave a speech telling how wonderful the merchants of St. John's had been to donate money for the new Institute and the evening's festivities. He droned on listing the names of people who had helped. "Jesus, boys," Tommy said, "everybody in St. John's must have built this place. Is he ever going to stop?"

"Shhh."

John could not be sure if the snores he began to hear were for real or if they were commentary on the speech. Finally the long awaited "without further ado" came, and the chorus of snores ceased.

A smart-looking man wearing the same uniform as the band, but with more ribbons and piping, came up. He carried a short stick, maybe a foot long. "Not

149

much of a gaff on that one," Tommy said. He smiled to hear snickers behind him.

The leader raised his mini-gaff and the band played a single note that filled the room with a brassy din. The gaff descended and the band started into a lively tune that sounded like rich folks strutting behind lighted windows in big houses. "Those are polkas," an old-timer said as the tunes ricocheted around the auditorium.

Soon the novelty of the band wore off and John felt himself surrendering to the heat of the room. His eyes grew heavy. He yawned as his head bobbed onto his chest.

A poke in the ribs, with someone saying, "This'll be more fun," woke him up. He saw the band had cleared off. A bunch of men, some dressed like women, scurried around on the stage. "Nice of you to join us," Tommy said to John. "You slept through the two-step. Wouldn't have missed it for the world." He rolled his eyes.

"I'm sure," John said. "Some of that music finishes too long after the end." Peter laughed.

"And now," one of the gussied-up men on stage shouted, "a short play called 'He Got the Job.'" The man ran off and an actor with a painted face came on stage. He began to speak in a funny accent.

"His clothes aren't right," John said.

"Shhh, he's supposed to be one of us. It's just make-believe," a large man sitting in front of John whispered. "It's all pretend."

Soon John was caught up in the story, slowly abandoning his disbelief. The play was surprisingly close to what he had just been through: a young boy coming to the city to find work, suffering embarrassment and hard luck, only to triumph in the end by landing the job of his dreams. The audience roared with laughter as the boy went from one ridiculous situation to another. The house almost came down when he finally outsmarted the city dandy who Peter said reminded him of Joshua J. Cheeseman.

At the end, the audience rose to its feet in uproarious applause, calling the actors back for three bows. The hall finally settled down enough for the man who gave the speech to announce the intermission would last for a quarter hour, after which the band would return. The furor receded to a dull roar as the men filed out to smoke, take the night air, or gabble with friends.

iv

The boys were huddled in a corner of the foyer during the intermission when a tall man with black hair came up to them, slapping Tommy on the back. "Well, look at this," the man said, "the Red Island boys."

Tommy turned around. "Jesus in the Garden," he said, "Dennis Reddy. What are you doing here? Don't you have things to do back home?"

"I've got a ticket on the *Erik*. We're leaving for Channel on Thursday."

"We're all swilers, too," Tommy said with a boastful smile. "Peter's on the *Southern Cross*, John's on the *Newfoundland*, and I'm on the *Bloodhound*."

"Good for you." Then he looked directly at John. "It's a good thing I ran into you. Your father's coming to St. John's to find you. You know, boy, he's got the canvas clear worn off the floor for missing you. From what I hear, he wants to find you really bad."

John's heart sank. "When's he coming?"

"He was supposed to arrive on tomorrow's train, but the line is closed. I was lucky and caught the last train to make it through the big snowstorm at Whitbourne. He should be here in a few days, probably Thursday."

John turned and left the Institute, walking alone through a light drizzle. At first he was full of resentment that his father would come to St. John's to stop him. But before long he began to plan how he could avoid his old man. He shivered, reliving the greeting he received on his return from Little Harbour. The joy of his newfound independence collapsed as he desperately tried to figure out how he could hide from his father until the *Newfoundland* sailed, six days from now. He knew his chances of avoiding him for that long were slim, even in a city as big as St. John's.

A hand touched his shoulder. He turned around to see Peter's smiling face. "I thought we had the good luck," he said, "but this is a bad turn."

"I don't know what to do," John said. The two began to walk together in silence, as the rain increased to a steady downpour.

After two blocks, Peter said, "You know John, I've got this urge to buy a pair of those sealer's boots from Smallwoods. 'Crome Tanned Wellies' they call them. 'Light as a feather; tight as a cup; fit like a glove,'" he said, quoting the newspaper advert from memory. "Yes, John, it'd be grand to have a pair of them." He brushed the rain out of his hair with his fingers. "They're costly though. I'm fifty cents shy on having the right amount."

John was not paying attention. He was too busy trying to figure out where he could hide. "Yeah, that'd be nice," he said absently.

"If I could get my hands on fifty cents, it'd make a big difference," Peter said, loudly enough to make John stop walking. "Just fifty cents."

"What?" John said. Peter had never asked to borrow anything. "Are you saying you want a loan?"

"No, not on your life. We're too good of friends for that. But perhaps we've got something to trade that'd put an extra fifty cents in my pocket."

"What are you on about?"

Peter reached into his jacket and pulled out his ticket for the *Southern Cross*. A sly smile came over his face. "The *Cross* is leaving before your father could find you."

Slowly, John realized Peter was offering a way out. "You mean you'd sell your berth on the *Cross* for fifty cents?"

"No, no. But I'd consider a trade, your note for the *Newfoundland* for mine on the *Cross*, plus fifty cents. You'd be long gone before your father gets here, nothing he could do then. Right? And I'd get my boots. Not bad for half a dollar. Sounds good to me." He smiled.

"But my ticket for the *Newfoundland* has my name on it."

"Never you mind. I'll sign on as you. Nobody'll know the difference."

"You'd do this for me?"

"What are friends for? And I get my boots. How about it?"

"I don't know. James Kelly might catch me."

"No, he won't. He's busy at sign-up tomorrow. That's why he gave me the note in the first place."

John looked at his friend. "You know this would mean you wouldn't be able to go onto the ice with Herb Butler."

Peter nodded. "I thought of that, but I figure the master watches on the *Newfoundland* are just as fine a lot. Look at your kin, Will."

"Are you sure about this?"

"Yes, boy. It's a good thing all around." He stopped, deep in thought, and then nodded sagely. "Maybe you should sign on under another name, just in case your father still knows somebody at Baine, Johnstons."

"Good idea," John said.

"You'd best use a good Protestant name. I hear Clarke can't abide Catholics, even though he spells his name like one."

John nodded, deep in thought. "But you're not supposed to swap berths."

"And since when did you worry about breaking the rules? When is your sixteenth birthday anyway?"

John blushed. "It's only two weeks away. I'll be old enough by the time we get back." His voice trailed off into silence. After a time he said, "But what about Will, when he finds it's you on the *Newfoundland,* and not me?"

"He'll never know. Don't you worry. I'll take care of that."

John grew silent, turning over the details of the plan in his mind. He plumbed the scheme for problems. He still had some of Jacob's ten dollars left. He would be gone before his father arrived. And, if he signed on as someone else, the old man would never be able to track him down. Peter would get his boots. The plan could work. John smiled. "Are you sure you want to do this?"

"Yep," Peter said. "I'd rather go to the Front, better chance of a good payout. And anyway, I always wanted to be you so I could have all the girls chasing me." They both laughed. The moon broke through the scudding clouds to announce the end of the rain.

TWENTY-TWO

On his way to a meeting called by Grieve, George Clarke passed a line of sealers waiting to sign on to the *Southern Cross*. Queued up for two blocks along Water Street, they were surprisingly orderly despite the excitement evident in the clamour of youthful enthusiasm.

"Morning, sir," one of the older boys said.

Clarke smiled and nodded as he passed.

"Fine day for swiling," another said.

Most, however, stood quietly, with some of the newcomers being told in whispers, "That's the skipper, Captain Clarke."

By the time Clarke entered the building, he could feel excitement welling up inside of him. That old urge to be underway, the creeping sense of agitation that he had been waiting for too long, was upon him. "I'm ready to go," he said to himself as he walked down the hall toward Grieve's office. "Can hardly wait until tomorrow afternoon, when we throw off the lines."

A crowd of officers and old hands had already assembled by the time he entered Grieve's office. Jessie Winsor was there, along with his officers and the *Bloodhound*'s engineers. Clarke's second hand, James Kelly, was standing at the back of the room, as always fiddling with his pipe. David Parsons and his three Scots engineers were present, still covered in grease from their recently interrupted repair work on the engines of the *Southern Cross*. Herb Butler, dressed in a fine jacket, was the centre of attention off to the right. He cut a fine figure as he told a story that had the officers huddled around him laughing. Joseph Youdon, Clarke's quartermaster, stooped and wearing his threadbare sealer's coat, was in the group around Butler. He looked out of place in the grand room with its showy hardwood and brass. Cheeseman was sitting a distance away from the old merchant with a noticeably disinterested look. Grieve, seated at his desk, was pale and appeared less energetic than usual. Everywhere the captain looked — Winsor, Kelly, Butler, Grieve, Cheeseman — he was reminded of how much he was under the control of others. His stomach began to ache.

The room grew strangely quiet. "Gentlemen," Grieve finally said, his voice firm despite his fragile appearance. "Thank you for taking the time out of your busy schedules to come to this meeting. I know how hectic things have been, but feel I have to tell you about some very important developments." He paused to look at the men. "You see here," Grieve said, putting his hand on a stack of papers easily four inches high. "Every single one of these is an order for seal oil or pelts." He took off the top sheet and read it. "This one is from G. S. Reid in Aberdeen." Grieve held it up so everyone could see. "He wants a hundred weight of seal oil and will pay a handsome price for it. They're all like this," he said, motioning toward the pile of papers. "We wouldn't be able to fill half of them if we had four ships. You men will have to work double tides if we hope to put a dent in this mountain of orders." He placed Reid's order back on the stack.

"Why are there so many more orders this year?" Herb Butler asked.

"Good question," Grieve said. "I can't really put my finger on it, but it seems everyone in Britain wants to have a good number of our seals in their stores this year. They're all acting like squirrels in the fall." He paused. "Maybe it's because of the uneasy times they're having over there." The merchant went on, making a strong plea for the men to do their absolute best to bring the ships home loaded to the gunwales. "This is a special year and, with demand so high, we have to put out a special effort." Then he went on about how a good hunt would help the Colony's flagging economy. "God knows that Morris is making such a mess of things that we must do our best to help out." His voice grew stronger and his manner more forceful as he went on citing reason after reason why this year's hunt was so important. Then he talked about how poorly they had done recently. "We haven't had as many seals as we could have over the last few seasons. This year things must change." Again he patted the stack of orders on his desk. "We'll need every ounce we can ship. It's our duty to bring home as much as possible. I'll accept no excuses," he said, looking directly at Clarke. "You must put out the top effort this year. We can't afford to falter this time, the need is too great. Gentlemen," Grieve slammed his fist onto the desk, "never has it been so important for you to bring your ships home full." The room was totally silent. "And I want you to get home as soon as you possibly can. The sooner we deliver, the better."

The room came alive with excited talk.

Grieve stood up and raised his hand for silence. "Home from the floes as fast as you can, with as many seals as possible, is what we need. We can accept nothing less."

The pain in Clarke's stomach began to subside as he started to understand the renewed importance of the upcoming hunt. Now he knew he must bring home the log-load, no matter what the costs. Now the hunt seemed to be more than a moneymaking venture — Grieve and the Colony needed it. He wished his brother was here so he could see how important going to the ice had become. And he knew he could deliver. Although he had not mentioned it to anyone, he had a pretty good idea that the seals would assemble near Byron Island this spring. There was something in the way the harps were acting last year and how this winter had played out that told him they would be further south and west this season. "We'll find the main patch this time," Clarke said to himself. "We'll be the heroes of the hour, without doubt."

The excitement in the room mounted as the men began to understand the importance of this year's mission to the ice. Grieve had inspired them to go forth onto the floes with vigour, rekindling the spirit for the hunt they had inherited from their fathers and grandfathers.

Grieve's speech stayed with Clarke as he returned to the *Southern Cross* and began final arrangements for departure the next afternoon. There was a spring to his step as he launched himself into the unending work of getting ready. The same held for his officers. They now shared a common purpose that steeled their passion to have a bumper hunt. "Yes, my son," Clarke said to Kelly, "we can't fail now."

TWENTY-THREE

John was so nervous on Tuesday morning he could hardly stand still. No matter how hard he tried, he could not help but envision being caught when he tried to sign on to the *Southern Cross* under a false name. He kept patting Peter's note from James Kelly in his pocket. He had joined a long line of sealers, mostly young men, which snaked out of the door of Baine, Johnstons, through the narrow entrance lane, onto Water Street.

"Pretty young crowd," the boy behind him said. "They all look raw to me."

John turned to see a tall, thin youth who looked to be even younger than he was. His eyes twinkled beneath bushy, blond eyebrows. "Yes," John replied, "don't see anyone who's weathered the Cape in this lot."

The tall boy smiled and extended his hand. "Noah Rowe. I belong to Chance Cove in Trinity Bay."

"Jo...," he stopped himself. "James Walsh, yes, James Walsh," John said. "My home is in St. Vincent's." They shook hands. "Chance Cove? That's not far from Little Harbour is it?"

"That's right. Just a couple of miles across land."

"You ever hear of my great-uncle, Jacob Newtry, over there?"

"You're old Doc Newtry's kin?" Noah exclaimed. "Lord love me, he's a legend up our way. He knows all there is to know about everything. I spent hours listening to his stories. I just love how he tells a tale."

John nodded.

"A gift he has," Noah continued. "So you're his nephew. That's something." He gave John a friendly swat on the shoulder. Then he turned around and poked the man behind him who was chatting with another sealer. An older, larger, version of Noah tuned around and faced John. "This here's my brother Jacob," Noah said. After a pause, he added. "He's named after your uncle."

"No."

"Yep, your uncle helped bring this big lug into this world. Jacob, this is James. Doc Newtry is his uncle."

"Go on. That right?"

John nodded.

"An honour," the older Rowe said, extending his hand to John. "Any kin of Jacob Newtry is a friend of mine." His wide grin showed two missing front teeth.

The three boys settled down to chat about Jacob and sealing, with John trying to keep his lies as simple as possible.

Not all the boys were as amiable as the Rowes. Many refused to return John's efforts to be friendly. The Conception Bayman in front of him was flat out rude. "Never you mind trying to shine up to us," he said. "Wait 'til you've been to the ice and can grow a whisker before talking to me. Can't see a scrod like you being any use on the ice anyways." At that, he turned his back.

As the line inched forward, John and the Rowes struck up a friendship. They decided to be mates on the coming adventure. "We can watch each other's backs," Jacob said.

"With men like him," John said, pointing to the back of the Conception Bayman in front of him, "we'll need to stick together."

They kept chatting as the line moved.

"Next," the clerk finally said, motioning John to sit in the chair across a table. "I'm Jack Mills, signing agent for Baine, Johnston. Who are you?" The agent had a glint in his eye that made John certain he must know a lie was coming.

The boy hesitated and then took a deep breath. "James Walsh, sir, from St. Vincent's, sir."

"Never heard of you," Mills said with alarming finality. "What makes you think I should give a young pup like you a ticket?"

John got flustered and muttered something incoherent.

"Well?"

He pulled the paper out of his pocket and handed it to the clerk. Mills took the note, suspicion written on every wrinkle of his sea-worn face. He opened it slowly. When he finished reading it, he smiled. "That's more like it. You couldn't have a better sponsor than James Kelly. That man's a real Christian, if ever there ever was one. He must've taken a real shine to you if he wrote this," Mills said, waving the note in the air.

John nodded.

"Let's get this done," Mills said, slapping a large yellow cardboard sheet on the table in front of him. It was entitled 'Agreement and Account of Crew.' "You sign here if you know how." He pointed to the first of a series of boxes on the form. John picked up the pen and prompted himself to write 'James Walsh,' rather than his real name.

Mills pulled the paper back toward himself. Poised to write, he asked, "Age?"

"Sixteen."

Mills looked up and cocked his brow. John stared down at the Crew Agreement. The agent shrugged and wrote '16' in the proper column. "Home town?"

"St. Vincent's, Placentia Bay," John said, staring at Mills' hand as he wrote out the name. Then he watched the agent write 'St. John's' under a column labelled 'Port of Engagement.'

"You sailed before?"

"No, sir."

Mills wrote 'nil' in the next column and dashes across the next six boxes on the form. Mills met John's curious stare. "That's where I'd put details of your last voyage, if you had one."

John nodded.

"I'm putting March 5, that's Thursday, under 'Date of Boarding.' Muster on the dock out there at one o'clock." He motioned toward the waterfront. "Should be underway by three. Don't be late now, Captain Clarke won't be waiting on a single soul." Mills moved his finger over to the next column. "I'm putting you down for a full crew share," he said, making a notation. He went on to fill in some more boxes. Toward the end Mills asked, "Do you want to sign on for the crop?"

"What's that?"

A weary look came over Mills' face. "We advance you nine dollars for the supplies you'll need for the trip, a gaff, a hauling rope, all that kind of gear. When we get back we'll take twelve dollars off your share. It's a good deal, because you don't have to pay us back if there's a poor crew share."

John frowned. "That's a lot to pay for a loan, isn't it?"

"I suppose, but if you need the supplies, I don't see you've got a choice."

John paused. He had already collected everything he needed, including two bottles of Radway's Ready Relief, said to cure every ailment a sealer might encounter. "I've got my gear already. Guess I'll pass on that," he said.

Mills looked surprised and then shrugged his shoulders. He wrote 'nil' in the column headed 'Amount of Wages Advanced.' "Well, that's it then. You're a member of the crew of the *Southern Cross*."

John stood up.

"Next," the agent said loudly, as if John were not there. The newest member of the crew of the *Southern Cross* turned and waved at the Rowes as he left. "See you tomorrow."

"For sure."

John stepped outside, past the line of sealers, into the brisk winter air. The cold on his face coincided with the release of worry that had been pent up since he had heard his father was coming. But now he had done it. John raised his hands in the air and shouted to the sky. "She's done, we're there now."

The sealers in the line outside watched in amusement as this strange boy skipped down Water Street. "He feeble-minded, or what?" one said.

TWENTY-FOUR

On the afternoon of March 5, George Clarke stood on the bridge of the *Southern Cross*, an elevated platform that straddled the afterdeck just forward of the funnel. Surrounded by a solid, three-foot high rail, the forward-facing panel was bedecked with four life buoys. Amid an air of excited anticipation, his crew of young sealers waited on the wharf, gaffs raised, duffels and sealers' chests at their feet.

Clarke braced his hands on the bridge rail and surveyed his kingdom. The ropes were taut, the deck well scrubbed. Everything was shipshape, ready to receive her crew whose impatience to be underway was evident in the growing din wharfside.

At 2:30 Clarke gave the order for the men to board. Then he climbed down the bridge ladder and retired to his cabin. He was finding, more and more, that he wanted to be by himself rather than dealing with the constant demands of his crew. As well, the captain wanted to avoid the clamour of one hundred and sixty men, shouting and jostling, claiming living and sleeping space. Alone in his cabin, Clarke began to fret about the upcoming journey. He knew that everyone shared a vision of the *Southern Cross* as an opportunity for wealth. But for the young sealers, the ship also represented an adventure, a lark, a chance to take home stories and tales of manliness. For him, though, the *Cross* was a place of awesome responsibility and weighty decisions. He begrudged the boys their easy lives, wishing he, too, could share their enthusiasm and return to those care-free days.

He tried to study the charts spread out across his table but could not concentrate. A welling sense of agitation overcame him, a combination of apprehension and excitement. His stomach ached. His gout throbbed. "Never mind," he said out loud, "it'll pass as soon as we get going." He picked up an old astrolabe and began to fiddle with the brass knobs, trying his best to remember how to use it. After sighting along the ancient instrument a few times, he put it down and stared toward the wall. He could hear the bedlam of the men moving throughout

161

the ship, looking for bunk spots and exploring the vessel that would be their home for the next six weeks. Once more, he went through his mental list of things he was supposed to do. Even though he had done everything humanly possible to get the ship ready he continued to feel that deep sense of worry as he thought about the long list of people he had to satisfy. And now all the newcomers milling about the innards of the ship were another concern.

After half an hour his agitation became unbearable. Clarke put on his jacket and went topside. He looked up at the turret on Grieve's office as he came on deck. No one was visible behind the glinting windows, but he was certain the old man and Cheeseman were watching. A sense of gratitude flooded over him as he remembered how strongly the old merchant had supported him over the last year. "Yes, sir," he said out loud, "I'll reward your trust this year. We'll be back here in record time with the log-load. I give you my word." He stared up at the turret for several moments.

A relative calm had descended upon the ship. Save for a few men topside chatting quietly at the rail, things had grown quiet. Clarke scrambled up to the bridge.

"All hands present and accounted for, Captain," James Kelly said through the pipe clenched between his teeth. "One hundred and sixty-three fine young sealers and ten officers, including you and I." The second hand smiled and offered a casual salute.

"Aye, James," Clarke said. "I see they've begun to settle in."

"They have. A good lot, I'd say. Are we ready to throw off the lines?"

Clarke scanned the ship. He took out his pocket watch. It said 3:17. The sun had begun its descent behind the steeples and buildings of St. John's. "Yes, James. Take her out."

Once again, Clarke retreated to his cabin. The pain in his stomach began to subside as he felt the old ship's steam-driven heart begin to thump.

ii

John Lundrigan, along with the Rowe brothers and some of their friends, had joined the surge of men boarding the *Southern Cross*. On John's advice, they made a beeline for the forepeak, which, he knew from his time working on the ship, was the best place on the ship. By carefully arranging their things beside a forward port stanchion, they were able to claim a small alcove as their own private quarters.

John noticed Noah eyeing his gaff. He handed it over to the younger Rowe who received it with great care. "Never seen one this fine." He flexed it in his hands and then passed it on to his brother.

"It's my father's," John said. "He used to go sealing in the old days."

Jacob touched the hook reverently and whistled his approval. "Yes, sir," he said. "Your father must've been quite the swiler."

"I suppose," John said as he received the gaff back from Jacob and stowed it in the corner.

"Thanks to our friend here," Jacob said pointing to John, "we've got the best spot."

Everyone nodded in agreement.

"We'll be right tidy here," Noah said.

John smiled and busied himself arranging his belongings.

iii

Grieve stood in the turret of his office, watching the *Southern Cross* prepare to push off from the quay. Cheeseman stood by his side.

"I always get this nervous feeling when one of my sealers leaves," Grieve said. "Never sure what's going to happen."

"Not me," Cheeseman replied, "it's just the end of a big job, as far as I'm concerned. Now, I can get some sleep."

"At least until the ships come back." Grieve laughed.

Cheeseman avoided his employer's eye. Saying nothing, the young man turned and gazed up the harbour.

The old merchant watched as dockworkers ran over to the lines holding the *Southern Cross* and untied them from the wooden pilings. They threw the fat ropes to waiting hands on the boat. Black smoke billowed from the funnel. The engines lugged and caught as the ship began to move backwards. "There she goes," Grieve said.

Cheeseman and Grieve watched her back out from the wharf.

"Let's celebrate," the old man said with a smile. He went over to a cabinet and pulled out a bottle of sherry along with three crystal glasses. "This should do the trick." He filled each glass to within a half inch of the top, stoppered the bottle, and left it atop the cabinet.

"He's turning into the stream," Cheeseman said.

Grieve returned with two glasses, handing one to his assistant. "To a prosperous voyage," he said, raising his glass in anticipation of a return toast. But Cheeseman just took a big gulp of the sherry. He almost choked.

"You seem on edge today, Joshua. Is there anything wrong?"

"No, sir, I'm just tired. There was so much last minute business, I'm exhausted, that's all. And I've got so many arrangements to make."

"Arrangements?"

Cheeseman fumbled for words. "Y-y-yes sir, getting ready for when the ships return." His voice was clipped, his manner abrupt.

A skeptical look came over the old merchant.

"Yes, sir. I want to have everything perfect, sir, for when the ships come back."

"Is everything all right, Joshua?"

"Oh, yes sir, I just want to do a good job." His eyes darted back and forth between his glass and the view outside.

"Are you happy here, Joshua?" Grieve asked gently.

"Yes, sir. I'm most grateful for the opportunity you've given me." He stopped. "And the experience has been invaluable. I'm most beholden to you, sir." Still, he avoided looking at Grieve. "I only —" Cheeseman stopped in mid-sentence.

"Yes."

"Oh, nothing, sir, nothing you would want to know." Cheeseman turned to look out the window. He took another gulp of sherry. "I'm just a wee bit tired. That's all."

"Well, maybe this will pick you up then," Grieve said, taking a sip.

The young assistant grew silent, staring into the glass cradled awkwardly in his hands.

iv

John Lundrigan stood by himself on the afterdeck as the *Southern Cross* began to work toward the Narrows. He leaned against the rail that was already showing rust through the sloppily applied yellow paint. His mood was sombre. No one took the lead to sing a hearty parting song like in Tommy's stories. There was no excitement; no well-wishing crowds massed on the hills around the harbour; no one waving farewell from the quay. The old ship was leaving on her own, uncelebrated, skulking off toward the open sea. For John, the worry remained that his father might somehow appear, grab him by the scruff of the neck and drag him away. No matter how hard he tried he could not let himself enjoy the beginning of his adventure. He shoved his hands into his pockets and leaned against the railing. Even as the dock grew smaller, his apprehension lingered. His stomach turned. He retched.

"Planning on feeding the gulls?" a soft voice asked. John turned to see Noah Rowe standing behind him, grinning.

"Yes, Noah, my stomach is fierce today. Must be something I ate."

"Probably," the younger Rowe replied, moving to John's side at the rail. He craned his neck trying to see what occupied so much of John's attention. "You expecting someone to see you off?"

"No, the opposite. My father is poisoned about my going on the hunt. I'm afraid he might turn up and try to stop me." John turned to face Noah. "I signed on under a false name, just in case the old man tries to track me down."

"You're not really James Walsh?"

"No."

"Are you Jacob's nephew?"

"Yes, that part's true. But my real name is John, John Lundrigan. I come from Red Island."

"Well I'll be. You look more like a John anyway," he said. "Pleased to meet you, John Lundrigan."

v

A knock at the door interrupted the awkward silence that had consumed Grieve's office.

"Come in."

Thomas Collingwood entered, cheeks rosy, slightly out of breath. "Sorry I'm late, sir. Something came up with O'Driscoll, you know, the auctioneer."

"There's a glass for you," Grieve said, motioning toward the cabinet. "Come over and join us. The *Southern Cross* just entered the stream."

"Thank you, sir." Collingwood's energy refreshed the room, bringing to life the festive mood that Grieve had attempted to create earlier. The three stood in the turret and watched the ship wend its way along the channel of open water leading toward the Narrows. "They're a quiet lot," Collingwood said, motioning toward the ship, "usually singing like a choir by now."

"True."

"Maybe they're too young to sing," Cheeseman said sharply. "Clarke couldn't attract any seasoned hands, mostly children by the look of them. See those two on the afterdeck? No more than boys."

"I'm sure they'll be fine," Grieve said.

vi

Clarke was staring blankly at some charts in his cabin when a great thud jolted him forward, almost knocking him out of his chair. The *Southern Cross* had hit the ice on the edge of the stream. By the time he reached the bridge, the barrelman was shouting and making wild gestures.

"Blood of a bitch," Clarke said, "that scunner up there is having a glory fit."

"He's supposed to get us through the channel," James Kelly said, "but he's way off the line. Never even warned the bridgemaster."

The shouting among the sailing crew grew as it became clear that the *Southern Cross* was trapped in the ice. Clarke silenced them with a roar. A pall of silence engulfed the ship. The young boys topside waited to see how their master would handle the situation.

"Goddamn it!" Clarke bellowed from his bridge so everyone could hear. "You'd think this prince of a ship didn't have a rudder."

Several men near the captain smiled.

The scunner started to shout but Clarke silenced him with a raised hand. "No matter the blame," he said, "let's get her loose and be on our way." He turned toward the main deck where the biggest group of sealers had gathered. "After all, lads, we've got seals to kill and money to make. Right?"

In a single voice, the men on deck responded, "Yeah."

"Yes, men," Clarke continued, his voice booming so everyone could hear. "Bloody decks and a bumper trip, that's why we're here."

Another "yeah," this one louder.

"All right then, Mister Kelly, let's see how well these fine men can sally this old ship so we can be on our way." He glanced up at the turret. "Watch this Mr. Grieve," he said under his breath. "I'll show you and your lackey Cheeseman how it's done." He let loose a booming laugh.

James Kelly stowed his pipe and began to shout orders. He commanded the boys on deck to fetch every crew member topside. Once they were assembled, he ordered them to move to the port side of the ship. "Stretch out so there's one of you for every foot of rail. Get as much weight to the gunwale as you can," he hollered. The men obeyed, stringing out along the rails and bulwark. Some leaned out over the ice as far as they could. Excited talk grew as the boys settled into their places. The old ship pitched perceptibly onto her left side with the weight of the men. "When I give the word," Kelly shouted, "every man run to the starboard. We'll rock her free. Ready? Now." The whole crew sprinted across to the starboard side. The deck heaved with the shift of weight and the scraping sound of ice binding on copper-shrouded wood grew louder than the animated talk among crew members.

"Now," Kelly shouted, "back again." The boys obeyed, rushing back to the port rail.

"Again. Again. Again…"

Soon the old ship wigwagged from side to side in concert with the sealers' cross-deck sprints. Waves came from her sides, riffling the now-loose ice along the length of her hull.

"Steady as she goes. Give us some reverse," Kelly shouted into a brass horn in the middle of the bridge. The engines engaged and the ship broke free of the ice, surging backwards.

"Move amidships," Kelly shouted to the youngsters on deck. "Bring her back trim." The boys complied, this time walking leisurely from the rail to the midline of the ship.

"All ahead one-quarter," James bellowed into the horn. The ship lurched forward into the open water.

"Twenty degrees to port, Mister Noseworthy," Kelly shouted toward the stern. With a flourish, the helmsman spun the great wooden wheel. A second ship's wheel, connected to the first with a cylindrical drum around which the rudder cables were wrapped, spun in synch with the other, as though manned by a ghost hand. As the ship began to lug forward, her bow came left and she started to move along the open channel once again, on her way toward the Narrows.

vii

"Jesus," Noah said, puffing from his gunwale-to-gunwale gallops, "that's a lot of work to fix one little mistake."

"That's nothing," John said. "A few weeks back we had to tow her from the ice."

"How did that work?"

166

"We were down there," he said, pointing to the harbour ice, "and had to pull her out of the ice using these fat ropes. Barbarous cold, I'll tell you — didn't stop shivering for two weeks." He stomped his feet. "I reckon Clarke's some clever to get us out so easy."

"Yes, sir. I figure he's a fine master."

"I think so."

John watched the scunner making frantic gestures to the bridgemaster, telling him to steer to the left. "Thirty degrees to port," he hollered.

Once again, the old ship skidded into the ice with a brittle scraping sound that sent shivers up John's back. This time the *Cross* veered before getting wedged and was able to carry on after bouncing against the ice. "Getting the hang of her now," John heard the wheelman say.

viii

Grieve, Cheeseman and Collingwood watched Clarke rescue the *Southern Cross* from the ice.

"What an idiot that Clarke is," Cheeseman said. "He can't steer that ship for Adam, just as bad as when he came into port." He turned toward Grieve, and with a scoff, said, "I guess I wasted all that money on those rudder cables. What a poor excuse for a seaman."

"Give the man credit," Collingwood said with an edge to his voice. "That was clever, the way he wigwagged her out of the ice like that."

"They call it overing," Grieve said, "haven't seen it used for years, but it worked, didn't it?" There was a hint of admiration in his voice.

"Aye," Collingwood said. "That Clarke's no fool."

Cheeseman scowled, looking straight ahead.

ix

John Lundrigan took one last look at the wharf, now barely visible in the fading light. He saw a solitary figure standing at the end of the dock, watching the ship. The man had his hands in the pockets of his blue pea jacket. John's heart sank when he thought he recognized his father. Part of him wanted to show the old man how he had been successful in getting a ticket. But another part of him, by far the greater, was angered by the possibility that his father was trying to stop him. "I just want to chart my own course," John said toward the figure.

"What's that?" Noah asked.

"Oh, nothing, just thinking out loud." He stole one last look at the wharf and saw that the figure had disappeared. "No matter," he said.

x

Grieve refilled the three glasses as they watched the *Southern Cross* work along the stream. "You know, Joshua," he said with a mischievous glint in his eye, "it would be good for you to go out with Clarke next year. You could see what it's like out there on the floes. Maybe that would teach you some respect for these men."

Cheeseman's face flushed and he began to rock on his toes. "Not on your life."

Collingwood chimed in, "William Coaker himself is going to the ice on the *Nascopie* this year. Certainly if he can go, you can."

Cheeseman began to squirm. "The food will be superb on that ship this year," he said. "You can bet your life the *Nascopie* will follow the Sealing Act to the letter with Coaker on board."

"Don't try to change the subject, Joshua," Grieve said. "We were talking about you accompanying Clarke next season, a grand idea. Don't you agree, Thomas?"

"Yes, sir. You can't be a proper man in charge of sealing if you haven't been to the ice. A fine idea, capital. Best thing for the firm." Collingwood laughed.

"You can't be serious," Cheeseman said, his voice rising in alarm.

"I am, Joshua."

The young Scot grew frantic. "No, no, I can't do that. It would be terrible." He shuddered. "No, no, I don't have the constitution. No, no, you can't."

Grieve winked at Collingwood. "There, there now, laddie, we don't have to make the decision today. Buck up. This is supposed to be a celebration."

Cheeseman forced a smile. He took a swig of his sherry, almost choking again.

xi

A sound from forward reached George Clarke's ears. He peered forward to see Herb Butler in the middle of a crowd gathered on the foredeck. They were singing.

> Goodbye, fare ye well
> Goodbye, fare ye well
> We're bound for the Narrows, off swiling me lads
> Hurray my bully boys, homeward bound

In a powerful voice Butler sang out.

> Our captain's George Clarke, a sealer supreme

The skipper smiled. More voices joined in the chorus.

> Goodbye, fare ye well
> Goodbye, fare ye well
> Our captain's George Clarke, a sealer supreme

Over half of the men on the foredeck were singing, voices crackling though the late winter dusk.

Hurray my bully boys, homeward bound

A bayman chimed in with a deep-throated baritone.

Our second's James Kelly, a friend of us all

All of the officers, save Clarke, joined in the chorus.

Goodbye, fare ye well
Goodbye, fare ye well
Our second's James Kelly, a friend of us all
Hurray my bully boys, homeward bound

A short, stout lad sang out.

Our ship's the old Cross, *a trusty old boat*

As the song progressed, the young sealers formed into concentric circles on the foredeck, all singing. Arms raised across the shoulders of neighbours, the whole network of nested circles began to swing back and forth in time with the shanty.

The seals are a whelping, out there in the Gulf

A sense of unity flooded through the ship with each improvised verse. The singing grew more confident with each turn.

We'll come home rich men, with money to burn

Unnoticed, Clarke moved away from his officers and returned to his cabin.

xii

The office at Baine, Johnston was silent as the trio watched the *Southern Cross* pick her way toward the Narrows. She shrunk to an indistinguishable blur as the winter light began to fade. A faint moan of her whistle sounded farewell.

Grieve went over to the cabinet and returned with the sherry bottle. He topped up the others' glasses, noticing Cheeseman's hand was shaking. He filled his own glass and, with ceremony, raised it. "This will be a fine hunt," he said. "To a fine spring on the ice, the finest." The three clinked glasses and drank.

"Aye, the finest kind of spring," Collingwood said.

"And may everyone return safe home," Grieve added. More clinks, more sips.

The room went quiet as they watched the *Southern Cross* steam into the gloom. With her final disappearance, the celebration came to an abrupt halt. Glasses were returned to the cabinet and the daily humdrum returned. Grieve walked to his desk and the other two followed, each taking his usual place. "The only item that remains," he said, "is to tell you both that I will be divesting myself of the day-to-day sealing operation until the ships return. I don't want to hear any updates, no reports, no requests for advice, nothing. I'm leaving everything up to you two. I'm so busy with all of those orders and some other things that I don't have time for anything else. Do you understand?"

"Yes, sir," Collingwood said.

Cheeseman smiled.

"I want you two to work together on this so I'm not distracted one bit. That's your concern now Thomas, and Joshua." He looked intently at each man as he spoke his name.

"Are you sure this is for the best?" Collingwood said. "Something tells me we may need you this year. We might have trouble."

Cheeseman shook his head.

"Nonsense," Grieve said, "you've just got the early trip jitters, that's all."

"I suppose," Collingwood said, gazing out the window at the emerging darkness. Still I wish —" He stopped in mid-sentence. "We understand, sir. We'll look after the sealing, as you ask."

"Thank you, Thomas. You're a good man. And thank you, Joshua."

xiii

At first, John had hesitated to join the men on the foredeck, afraid he did not belong. But within minutes he was swept up in the singing, immediately accepted as a member of this raggle-taggle band of boys off to the ice. He was amazed how quickly the crew became so close. And he was in the thick of it. John added his voice to the shanty.

Goodbye, fare ye well
Goodbye, fare ye well

Now in open water the *Southern Cross* turned south toward Cape Race. She began to roll on a moderate sea. The young Red Islander rocked back and forth, one arm around each of the Rowe brother's shoulders, finally realizing that his long journey was beginning in earnest.

We'll be back in St. John's, with a log-load of seals
Hurray my bully boys, homeward bound

John closed his eyes and smiled. "Yes, my son," he said to Noah with a wide grin. "It will be a wondrous voyage."

TWENTY-FIVE

John had discerned three groups of sealers from the way they dressed, talked and kept to themselves. The largest group was made up of men and boys from Conception Bay. They acted like they were the top of the pecking order, old school, with experience at sea, sons and grandsons of men who had gone to the ice. Second were the townies from St. John's and surrounding villages, not as sea-tested as the others, and easily distinguished by their less seaworthy clothes and flatter accents. The third group, of which John counted himself a member, were the boys from other bays, what some called "bay noddies." This motley crew of leftovers included the Rowes, five or six from St. Vincent's, including four Gibbons brothers, along with others from smaller outports. They were definitely the lowest "class," having neither the numbers nor the experience to stand up to the others.

Once underway, the boys were assigned to watches. The first two work groups were made up of Conception Bay men, the third of St. John's boys, and the last the leftovers. Even though it was the least prestigious group, John was pleased to be assigned to the fourth watch because he felt comfortable with those boys. Besides, it kept him with Noah and Jacob. And, as Peter had said, Herb Butler was going to be his master watch. Immediately upon meeting Butler, John understood Peter's view that Butler was, indeed a good man. His boundless energy and caring concern for his men was infectious. John's watchmates, to a man, were drawn to him. "This will be good," John said.

As the light faded, John went alone to the starboard rail of the foredeck, watching the rocks of the island retreat into black nothingness. He wanted to relish a few moments alone, knowing these would be few and far between once they reached the Gulf. The breeze fluttered the jib sail, which rested, still furled, atop the bowsprit.

The young man clutched the rail and looked at the back of his hands. For the first time he noticed how the blood vessels bulged out under the skin. "Real man's hands," he said. John stared off into the blank void of night, full of hope, picturing himself swiling amid the floes, proving that he was a man.

Pieces of loose ice floated by, bobbing in the wake of the ship, phosphorescent against the black sea. One chunk, close to the hull, bounced against the side, thumping noisily as it tumbled the length of the ship. The ice increased the further they went. Soon the banging of ice against the bow and side of the *Southern Cross* became a regular accompaniment to her passage. When the ice became more frequent the sound shifted to more of a battering, copper-plated wood against nature's ice. Every now and then a collision with a particularly large piece would send shivers the length of the ship. The temperature dropped. "Cold enough to freeze the kerosene in a lit lamp," John said, as he shivered in the nighttime air.

The creak of a windlass aft and hollering interrupted his solitude. He looked up to see four boys manhandling a long steel bucket that had been hoisted up the ventilator above the engine room. With more youthful enthusiasm than skill, they manoeuvred the bucket to the rail with whip lines. Someone tripped the cord. Ashes rained down onto the deck, coating two of the boys with what appeared to be grey snow.

"Jesus Christ," the deck router shouted, "get it full overboard before you tip it. What kind of ash cat gang are you boys anyways?" One worker, covered with soot, looked like a dirty snowman as he flailed his arms.

"Get it back down now. Be nimble about it." They swung the bucket back over the ventilator and dropped it. They missed the shaft and it clattered against the deck. "Careful, we've only got one of them."

They repeated the whole process, this time with less spillage and hollering from the deck router. "Hasten slowly, lads." The rattle of the ash bucket would, like the battering ice, become a regular accompaniment to the days ahead.

After watching the ash cat gang learn its duties, John went below to see where the crew had settled. First, he went to the area known as "'tween decks," underneath the long middle deck of the *Southern Cross*. Haltingly he entered, not knowing what to expect in this inner sanctum. After his eyes adjusted, he was amazed to see how lived-in the place had become. Every square foot of the rough wood floor had been claimed by someone's chest or clothes. Tattered quilts they called midnight glories and straw-filled mattresses known as donkey's breakfasts lay atop the makeshift beds. The few open spaces were already strewn with ashes and coal. The steam pipes, as well as the stanchions, were decorated with hanging oilskins, towropes, sou'westers, jackets and jumpers which swung lazily with the roll of the ship. The lanterns, hung from the roof beams, swayed as well, providing meagre orange light that served more to accentuate the smoke in the room than illuminate it. Boots lay floppily on the floor and gaffs were stowed in every possible corner. Some of the sealers stretched out on the double-tiered bunks that ran in rows along the outside. Others hunkered around cracked bogies that stood in pans of ashes. Smoke from these stoves, and a few flickering pipes and cigarettes, choked the air. "Some stuffy in here," one said after quelling a coughing fit.

"Stand aside," a burly voice said from behind John. "Got my hands full. Clear the deck."

John jumped over a sealer asleep on the floor. The man pushed by, balancing a large pannikin of steaming beans and a kettle as he stepped carefully toward three waiting comrades.

John continued past an older sailor showing a group of townies how to end splice a rope. The boys huddled around their teacher in a tight circle, asking questions as the old hand wove one strand around another. Other groups worked their boots, skinny-woppers they called them, nailing studs in the soles and greasing the seams.

His tour of 'tween decks finished, John headed back to the forepeak. Just as he arrived, he heard the voice of Herb Butler. "Up and at 'em," he said, "we've got work to do before we put you slack-fisted loafers to bed. Shovel brigade for you." Everyone in John's alcove streamed toward the door in response to Butler's command. The shovel brigade, it turned out, was responsible for emptying the latrine buckets, a chore reserved for his watch.

"Smells worse than the shitter out behind Dad's stage," Noah said, wrinkling his nose. "Don't remember eating anything that smelled this bad."

After that, Butler set the boys to cleaning up the mess on deck made by the ash cat gang. "Get it down to the bare wood," he ordered. "The deck will be coated with soot and grease soon enough. No need to give it a head start."

Then the boys moved some coal into the engine room from the hold.

It was well after 2:00 at night before they were allowed to retire. "Better store up on your rest, boys," Butler said. "It'll be in short supply once we reach the floes."

On their way back to the forepeak, John and Noah noticed the sea had changed. There was a kick on the water with waves running every which way. "Look at that," John said, "the sea's gone crazy." The two boys stopped and watched in fascination as the ocean appeared to be crashing into itself. "Somebody told me the sea gets confused when the current swirls around Cape Race." The eerie sound of a foghorn loomed out of the murky darkness and the ship began to change course westward. "Yes, sir, we've already reached the Cape." John smiled. "Been riding the current so far, making good time." He looked forward into the darkness. "This old biddy is more of a ship than she looks. She's doing just fine." He gave the rail an affectionate pat.

Noah nodded and the two boys continued to watch in silence. After half an hour the sea regained its composure. They headed toward their sanctuary in the forepeak, as the *Southern Cross* plunged westward toward Channel.

ii

Joseph Youdon was the oldest man on board the *Southern Cross*. He was Clarke's most trusted hand, taking on the important roles of quartermaster and ship's doctor, among others. Over decades of sealing together, he and the captain had developed a deep respect for each other. Youdon's sixty-two years were clear in his stooped posture and slow, shuffling walk. But his sharp wit and gap-toothed grin made him one of the most popular men on board.

Late on the first night of the voyage, he, along with Josiah Newell, the chief cook, approached Clarke's cabin. "Are you sure we should bother him?" Newell said. "I'm afraid he'll get vexed with us. He seems more crotchety than usual." The cook, still wearing his already stained apron, turned to leave.

"Stay," Youdon said, pulling the cook back by the apron straps. "This is important news and the skipper's got to be told, even if he doesn't like what he hears."

Newell shuddered. "Well, you do the talking. The old man gives me the fright."

"Aye," Youdon said as he knocked on the captain's door. He shoved his hands in his pockets as he waited.

The door opened and George Clarke looked out through bleary eyes. "What's so important you have to disturb a man's sleep?" he demanded in a booming voice.

Youdon and Newell stepped back.

"Well?"

"S-s-sir," the quartermaster said, "we're short two chests of tea."

Alarm rose in Clarke's face. "Is this true?"

"Aye, sir," Youdon said.

"How could this happen, Joseph? You tallied everything against the lists like I told you, didn't you?" He loomed over his quartermaster.

Youdon stood fast. "Aye, sir, I did." He pulled two pieces of paper from his pocket. "What we have on board matches up perfect with the lists, to the letter."

"But you say we're short."

"Y-y-es, sir," Newell said from behind Youdon. "The number's right by the lists, but we haven't got the same number as last year. No, sir." Josiah shook his head. He stepped back into the light flooding out of the captain's cabin. "We're two chests lighter than last year," he said boldly. "I know it says on the list we should have six chests, but I know we had eight last year. I'm sure of it. I count them."

Clarke furrowed his brow. "How can this be?" Anger began to well up in his face.

"We don't know for sure, sir, but we think the food may be short too," Youdon said in a low whisper.

The captain's face reddened as he looked down at the men. "You two do a full count and report back to me, right now." He slammed the door with such force it popped open again, forcing him to return to close it. "Goddamn it to hell."

iii

The news was bad. There was less of everything compared to last year. "Short all around, sir," Newell said. "They must have given us the wrong list, maybe the *Bloodhound*'s."

"No, sir," Youdon replied, "See, it says *Southern Cross* right here on the top." He showed the paper to his partner whose hesitation showed he could not read.

"Let me see those," Clarke ordered. He sat down at his table and examined the two lists side by side. "They're both for the *Southern Cross*, all right, one for last year and one for this. See, it says 1914. Other than that, they're identical. Even written by the same hand. I think I recognize that writing," he said. "It looks like it was done by a woman." Clarke scratched his chin. "I can't see how this could happen. The lists are right, but the supplies are wrong — something is going on here."

iv

Clarke gathered his officers in the common room outside his cabin and told them the news. There was disagreement about what to do. Some wanted to turn back to top up, while others felt it best to forge ahead. "Turning back now," Clarke argued, "would put us late to the ice and cut into our hunt. Can't have that." The "yea's" outnumbered the "no's" around the table.

The captain continued, "Josiah tells me we've got enough food to last until early April." He talked slowly, giving the impression he was thinking out loud. "I say we feed the boys as usual. Better to have a happy crew than risk a mutiny from half-fed men."

The number in favour increased, to a large majority.

"There'll be hell to pay when we run out of food," Herb Butler said in a dark voice. He had become the most outspoken of the master watches, the only one who would speak his mind in Clarke's presence.

"We'll deal with that when the time comes," Clarke said, gaining confidence as he talked. "We'll get to the ice and work as quickly as we can." He stood up, hands on the table, looming over his men. "If all goes well, and you do your jobs, we'll be back in St. John's before we run out of stores. Nobody will know the difference."

A chorus of "yea's" serenaded the captain.

"So now we're under the gun to get to the ice — too long on the floes and we'll all be starved to death. Then we'll have to get home in a flash. Double shifts for sure."

"We could hunt on Sundays," Butler said. "As long as we're alone, killing on the Lord's Day wouldn't do any harm."

Clarke glowered at his master watch. He leaned over, staring directly into Butler's eyes. "Mind your tongue, Mister Butler. The fourth commandment is law aboard this ship. If you were an Orangeman, you'd know that. I'll have no more of this talk about working Sundays aboard my vessel."

"Why don't we try to get to Channel early?" Kelly said. "We could wire Grieve to send more stores on the train."

Clarke sat back down.

"If the good Lord wills it," Kelly continued, "We'll get to Channel in time to get more supplies."

After a long silence, Clarke said, "A fine idea, Mister Kelly. We'll take the inside run to Port aux Basques and get there in jig time. It's risky though. We could get caught in the ice. But, if we do get through, we'll have two days in Channel to stock up. I say it's worth the gamble."

"I hear tell there's a lot of ice in Placentia Bay this year," Butler said, again facing up to the captain. "There's a good probability we'll get jammed. I think we should stay outside and hope we have enough time to wire St. John's once we get in."

Clarke's chair slid along the floor behind him as he stood up. For a moment he scowled at Butler. Then, in a loud, authoritative voice, he said, "I've made up my mind, we're going inside."

Apart from Butler, there was agreement with the captain's decision.

"We'll keep a good hold of the land, and trust to God and James' prayers that the wind doesn't shift and jam us up. Then we'll sneak into Channel through the back door." Clarke stopped, then he laughed. "It'll be priceless to see the look on Bartlett's face when he sails into Port aux Basques and sees we beat him there. Yes, that'll be something." He began to pace back and forth. "Okay, men, time to get a stick on."

TWENTY-SIX

"Up and at 'em," Herb Butler hollered as he kicked the mounds asleep on the floor of the forepeak, "we've got us some trouble." As John collected himself, he noticed there was no scraping or battering. The ship held steady, no rolling or pitching. He struggled out into the foggy morning light to find the *Southern Cross* surrounded by ice. No matter where he looked, all he could see was a grey desert that blended almost seamlessly into the dull fog.

"Jeez," Noah said rubbing his eyes. "Somebody picked us up and dropped us into the middle of nowhere. We're jammed up."

"Get some food in you," Butler said. "We've got work ahead to get out of this and make Channel before the hunt starts."

"What happened?"

"We butted the ice all night and the old lady did really well. We were making fine speed cracking through it. But then the ice closed in on us, like a vice. No hope to beat it now. We're stuck tight." The master watch paused. "I was caught for a fortnight like this one time. Felt like forever."

"What are we going to do?"

"Bombs, boys, bombs. We're going to blow a lead clear through it and tow us with the winches. Now go get yourself fed. You're no good to me weak-kneed and famished."

The ship was a beehive of activity by the time the boys came back topside. On the main deck, three older men hunkered over a powder keg, filling quart cans with high-powered blasting powder. One of them clenched a lighted pipe between his teeth. John watched him insert a waterproof fuse into a hole in the bottom of a can and seal the joint with butter.

"Come on, my sons," Butler shouted at John and his friends. "Get yourselves one of those stabber poles and be ready to push the ice away when we get loose." The boys picked out stout poles from a pile on deck. John's was two inches in diameter, fifteen feet long. The boys straddled the bow rail, ready to push the ice away when the time came.

179

While the men on deck manufactured the bombs, two crews led winch lines out ahead of the ship. Herb Butler led one of the groups searching for pinnacles, large chunks of ice, to which they could secure the lines for when the winches tightened. "Put your back into her, boys," Butler hollered. "We don't want to get frozen solid."

George Clarke stood on the bridge, adding his booming voice to the confusion. He shouted orders with enough anger in his voice to make every hand jump when the captain's attention fell upon him. "You, ice crew down there. Dig a better ring. Make sure she's deep enough so the ice shears when she blows. Your trench has to be a foot down all the way around. James," he bellowed, shifting his attention to the second hand out on the ice forward of the ship, "get a hole dug by that big clumper there. Harry's just about got the bomb ready."

One of the men filling the bombs came forward with a tin can nailed to two stabber poles lashed together. The fuse dangled below. They passed it overboard to waiting hands, who, in turn, delivered the bomb to James Kelly.

"Billy, my son," Clarke bellowed. "Where's that poker?"

A small man came forward carrying a metal bar, white hot on one end. "Got her hotted up, Skipper." He passed the poker overboard to more waiting hands. Kelly touched it to the fuse.

Fzzzzzz!

The second hand thrust the bomb into the hole he had chopped, as deep into the water as the poles would allow. Men piled blocks of ice over the hole and scrambled to a safe distance.

"Stand clear now."

Everyone cringed in anticipation of the blast.

B O O N G!

The *Southern Cross* shivered and groaned. The ice heaved up like a giant fist had ascended from the deeps, creating a huge dome at first, then a tremendous eruption. The splintered bomb pole flew straight up, followed by a rain of ice chunks, some as big as Abel's sealer's chest. Everyone ducked as the fragments crashed down. The tinge of sulphur filled the air. A great hole, full of dirty ice, appeared at the ship's bow.

"Get at it, boys," Clarke ordered John's crew. "Push away that ice with those stabber poles."

The engines groaned as the winches came alive and began to pull the old ship into the newly formed open water. The *Cross*'s propellers churned as the stern broke free and her bow headed for the ridge of ice at the far end of the new pond. Butler's winch line came loose and snapped dangerously back toward the ship. Luckily, no one stood in its path. Her bow hit the ice at the far edge with a ferocious crack and the ship came to a dead stop. Hands looked at each other, stunned that the ship had been stopped dead.

"Sweet Jesus," Clarke said, "is there no luck for us?" He paced back and forth on the bridge. "All right, men, let's do it again. Mister Butler, get that winch line secure this time. That high learning of yours must be good for something."

They replayed the scene, chopping a new ring, finding good places to attach the winch lines, hauling and attaching them, packing another bomb, digging the ring and boring the blast hole. After an hour, they passed the reheated poker overboard and waited for another blast.

B O O N G!

Everyone ducked and the ship pulled herself ahead another fifty yards, only to be stopped dead again.

"Looks like the ice has settled in," John said to his friends.

"Stop that chinwagging and get to work," Clarke ordered. "You don't move ice by yattering. Stand ready now."

In concert with Clarke's growing anger, the crew set and reset bombs through the whole morning. Progress was slow. Every time the ship took a run at the far edge of a newly blasted hole, she was rebuffed, and Clarke hollered louder. The crew's frustration mounted. They knew that the other ships, like the *Erik* and *Terra Nova*, had taken the outside channel and were now far ahead of them.

Clarke was unrelenting. He kept them working through the 'levener, the usual late morning break for tea and toast. Grumbling began in earnest when, after one rather poorly placed bomb, the ship could not even free herself to run the length of the open water. The captain's face became redder and his voice grew louder with every hour they were prisoners of the ice. He was beside himself.

ii

After two days of non-stop work, just after noon, the ship made yet another run for the far edge. Instead of a dead stop, a crack opened up in front of her. John heard the ice snap and watched a jagged seam open up and strike off into the distance, like a watery serpent surging forward. The boys cheered.

Over the din Kelly shouted, "Get her bow into that crack so she doesn't close down on us. We'll spread it. All ahead full," he shouted to the bridge master. The *Southern Cross* throbbed, giving all the power she had. The crack opened wider and the old ship began to make headway along the newly created lead.

"All aboard now," Kelly hollered. The men on the ice scrambled across the floe and clambered up the sides. "Leave those lines drag aft. We'll reel them in with the winches."

"You, with the stabber poles," Clarke shouted at John and his friends. "Get aft and see those winch lines don't get fouled." The boys ran aft, enthusiasm revived. Finally, they were making progress. For the first time in days, Clarke was not screaming, but John noticed he was limping and had stopped shaving.

iii

John was jolted awake by a dream about exploding ice. The snoring put up by the Gibbons boys, Sebastian in particular, ensured he would not get back to sleep, so he slipped out onto the main deck. He was greeted by a dome of stars, despite the bank of fog off to the starboard. The clear sky and intense starlight was a welcome change after three overcast days. John climbed the stairs to the foredeck and went to the rail, taking stock of the pre-dawn sky. He could not find all of the navigation stars, but the expansive starscape was an antidote to the lost feeling that had been dogging him. For half a week all he had seen was endless ice and grey sky. Time had blurred and lost its meaning. Now the brilliant nighttime sky allowed him to locate himself in the featureless ocean and ice.

John smiled when he recollected the scunner screeching that he had spotted an open lead just off shore. "Runs far as the eye can see," the lookout had shouted. Then passage was easy. They would make Channel late, but at least before the other ships left for the hunt.

Herb Butler came up beside John, just as the boy shivered against a frigid gust of wind. "Colder than a merchant's heart, I'd say."

John nodded, continuing to look at the stars. He tried to judge the ship's speed from how the stars moved against the ropes running diagonally from the bowsprit to the fore mast.

Butler looked up. "Nice to see some old friends."

"Yes, sir, they're just as bright out here as they are back home. They help me know where I'm at."

"Aye, that they do."

Both grew silent, looking heavenward.

"And where do you belong, son?" Butler asked.

"I was raised on Red Island in Placentia Bay. I'm sure we passed south of her this week, but don't know when that would have been, too busy to watch. I couldn't have seen her from here anyway."

"Yes, we've been working hard. The skipper gambled by taking the inside route, and lost. Seems the ice is heavy this year."

John nodded. "The *Clyde* was jammed in Placentia this February. That harbour is usually ice free. For sure there's more ice than usual."

Butler nodded.

"Where's your home at, sir?"

"Cupids, my son, just down the road from Brigus, where George Clarke comes from." He paused for a moment, "Always the jowler, that Clarke. This year he's out to prove he can turn things around for this old tub." He slapped the rail to be sure the ship heard him. "Some say he's reckless on the ice. I have no doubt he'll move heaven and hell to have a bumper trip this year."

"He sure hollered enough to get the Lord's attention back there," John said with a laugh.

"That he did."

"Perhaps he's used up all his bad luck and we'll do better now."

Butler seemed unconvinced, but said, "Could be like fishing when a bad start is the sign of a good finish."

John looked forward at the bow wake.

"I'll tell you, my son," Butler said. "When I first saw you, I figured you were a stowaway, so young, so small. Didn't figure you for much of a hand." He paused briefly. "But now, I see you're as much of a man as these other boys, smarter than most. You'll do, boy, you'll do." He smiled. "Got the makings of a top hand." He put his arm around John in a way that caused the boy to step back. Butler blushed. He turned away and moved aft down the stairwell into the officers' quarters.

John was confused. The embrace from his master watch had frightened him, but he felt a deep sense of pride recalling the compliment he had been given. For a fleeting moment the boy wished his father had heard Butler's words, but he quickly realized it no longer mattered what his old man thought. The important thing was to be worthy of respect.

The sky began to lighten astern.

iv

"Land ho," sounded from the barrel. "Tall cliff, off to the nor'nor'west." John looked but could see nothing. He heard increased activity among the hands near the wheel and soon Clarke joined them. The hubbub of activity grew as the ship turned. Almost as if by magic, a dark form loomed out of the early morning fog. After spending so many days seeing nothing but ice and fog, the growing number of men streaming from the innards of the ship grew excited at the sight of the cliff. A concert of animated commentary serenaded the approaching landfall.

"See there," one said, pointing toward a flock of white birds flying from shore. "The gulls are coming to greet us."

John began to make out the coast and a few houses scattered like seeds on the black rock. The white line of seas breaking ashore underlined the growing landmass that was becoming more visible the closer they got. Soon he could make out a church steeple and a row of houses above a cliff.

A thin white line showed above the land as the fog began to lift, revealing the bottoms of huge mountains further inland. "Those are the Table Mountains out behind," an excited sealer said. "Dead flat across the top when you can see them. See how they pop out of the fog." A huge valley showed beneath the lifting blanket of cloud, inviting the eye to look beyond the scattered buildings that peppered the rocky shore. John could feel the excitement grow as the land approached.

An hour later, with the sun breaking behind stubborn fog, they rounded Shoal Point and got their first close-up view of the harbour at Port aux Basques. They were greeted by the masts of five ships at anchor, all of the other Gulf sealers. The *Southern Cross* was the last to arrive. The old ship let go a long, drawn-out whistle to announce her arrival. Activity on the bridge increased as she manoeuvred toward an anchorage. After considerable shouting, John heard the anchor splash and the chain clank out. Slowly the old ship swung to face the breeze, coming to rest parallel to the other ships.

"We're here none too soon," one of the Conception Bay crowd said. "Everybody'll be leaving tomorrow for the ice. A day later and we'd have been left behind. Clarke was lucky to find that open lead. There's nothing worse than being trapped in ice when everyone else is killing seals."

"So maybe our luck is changing," John said quietly.

"What's that?" Noah asked.

"Oh nothing, really. Could be that finding the open lead this morning has changed our luck."

"That'd be good," Noah said with a smile.

The boys watched as a boat was lowered from a davit at the stern. Three officers escorted a small boy overside into the tender.

"Jeez, my son," Jacob said. "That boy looks just like you, John. He's your size, same hair, maybe he's your twin." He laughed.

"Who is he?" John asked.

"A stowaway. They only found him yesterday, nearly starved to death. They're sending him back to St. John's."

"Too bad, he must've wanted to come on the hunt some bad."

"I suppose, but they don't want to pay him a share."

"I guess so," John said with a sigh. He felt sympathy for the boy now sitting beside one of the officers as the other two rowed. And he knew that, save for a few lies, the boy in the boat could be him. What a tragedy to be put ashore, just as the most exciting part of the adventure was about to begin.

TWENTY-SEVEN

The next morning at 3:00 AM, George Clarke, along with five of his officers, crept up on deck. The nearly full moon provided enough light for the men to begin preparations to leave Port aux Basques. Apart from the new smoke billowing from the *Cross's* funnel, the ship remained asleep. "Quiet now," Clarke said in a husky whisper, "and no lights. We've got to be the first to leave." He sent Butler and another master watch forward to work the anchor winches, and two to the wheel on the afterdeck. James Kelly and the captain manned the bridge.

None of the other ships showed signs of life. There were no plumes of new smoke and only the *Erik* had lanterns on deck. The rest appeared to be deserted. In a low whisper, Kelly said to the captain, "It's good to be on our way. The crew's in a foul mood after losing all that time jammed up. Getting underway early should boost their spirits." He struck a match for his pipe, being careful to keep his hands cupped around it so it would not give off any light.

"The wind sure came out of the boys' sails once the going got tough," Clarke said.

"Yes, George, I fear they may be a soft lot this year. They gave up as soon as we smacked the ice."

"Lots of Micks, I suppose. We'll have to keep after them. They should be all right once we get into the whitecoats. The blood gets their hearts thumping."

Kelly blew a long puff of smoke toward the other ships. "It's too bad we didn't get here soon enough to wire St. John's. Poor old Joseph was right nettled he couldn't find any supplies ashore. We'll just have to hit the patch early and head home quick before we run out."

"We will," Clarke said, looking off into the darkness.

The first engineer, scrambled up onto the bridge. "Steam's up, sir," he whispered.

Clarke waved forward and the anchor winches engaged. The donkeys groaned and almost stalled. But they caught a second wind and the cables began to wrap on the huge spools. Despite the rusty creaking of the winches, the other ships remained quiet.

Once the anchors broke the surface, a different groan came from the bowels of the ship. The *Southern Cross* began to lug forward, knifing the calm, black sea with her heavy bow. They were underway once again, having stopped in Channel barely long enough to catch their breath.

New smoke emerged from the stacks of two ships in the harbour. The *Terra Nova* let go a long whistle to tattletale on the *Southern Cross's* clandestine departure. Laughter erupted from the *Southern Cross*. "That's more like it," Clarke said as they turned their stern on the resting ships. "Now we'll show those buggers how to hunt seals."

Once out of the bay, Clarke ordered Kelly to steer northwest, straight for the pack ice rather than following the open water south-southwest. "You must know something I don't," Kelly said between sucks on his pipe, "heading away from that open water."

"You know what they say, James. I've got the nose for the seals. I'm sniffing out those whitecoats, sure as you're born." The captain broke off and went down to the main deck. He began to climb the ratline on the main mast.

"Nimble as a moose," Herb Butler said as he watched Clarke scramble upwards. But by the time the skipper reached the lookout barrel, having adroitly swung onto a loose rope ladder from the end of the ratline up to the barrel, Butler had changed his tune. "He's done that a few times before."

Once in the barrel, Clarke leaned against its sides for steadiness, concentrating. He peered off into the distance through his binoculars, scanning in every direction. The ship entered the ice and the chorus of battering began once again. The sky lightened.

The *Cross* came to life with more men streaming on deck, many dressed for the hunt, gaffs in hand, towropes coiled crosswise on their chests, sheath knives on their belts.

"They're getting serious now," Butler said.

ii

The day passed slowly. The *Southern Cross* continued to batter the fields of grey with the crash of ice against hull the only sound. The temperature dropped in response to a freshening north wind. Everyone was wound up, poised and ready. But no seals were sighted.

More and more men left the deck as the day limped on. By mid-afternoon topside was nearly deserted. Clarke stayed in the barrel the whole day, probing the horizon for signs of the harp seal.

iii

Despite the growing cold, John and Noah spent the day topside, hoping to see some sign of life. "Not so much as the whisker of a seal," John said. "Hard to believe anything could live out there."

Noah nodded. "It'd be a miracle if we saw anything but ice in this place."

The boys grew quieter, discouraged by their poor luck finding seals, but persistent in their hope. They kept pacing the length of the ship, up and down the deck stairs, mostly to keep warm. "This ice is different from before, not as solid," John said. "But it sure is slowing us up. We're not making a mile in a long hour, by the feel of it." He sighed.

Noah looked out over the relentless grey carpet of ice and shook his head.

Once more, the crew began to complain, doubting their master's decisions. The grumbles of the few on deck grew louder when Clarke gave up at dusk and climbed down.

iv

John stood at the after rail early next morning, joined by many others whose eagerness had been rekindled by the dawn of a new day. He found himself among a group of Conception Baymen, older than the rest on board, some in their twenties. They were dressed in their warmest jackets. None had their gaffs or towropes. John listened into their talk.

"Paddy's Batch missed us this year," one said, "no snow for a week now."

"Cold enough to freeze the ice candles on your liver, though," another chimed in, flailing his arms to keep warm.

John heard a faint sound in the distance. He cocked his ear in its direction, but it was gone. All he could hear was ice bouncing off the hull.

"Can't figure why the skipper decided to bash the ice like this, lots of open water south."

"The old man always does it the hard way. Not like his brother John who always had it right." The sealer put his hands under his armpits and stomped his feet for warmth.

John heard the sound again, this time louder and more definite. "Ma-ma-ma-a-a-a." It reminded him of the kittens in Ryan's stage back home. Then the sound came again, louder.

"What's that?" John said out loud.

"What's what?" one of the sealers said.

John waited. After an excruciating silence the near ghostly sound came again. "That."

The sealers near John craned to hear. An ephemeral "ma-ma-ma-a-a-a" drifted across the ice towards them. "Yes, b'y," one said. "You're right." His eyes opened wide with excitement. "Yes, my son, that's a whitecoat. I'm sure of it." He shouted for the men at the rail to be quiet and listen.

The quivering mew occurred again, this time from further north. The sound swelled and then vanished into nothingness. A shuffle circulated through the crowd as the pulsing sound came and went on the wind, never from the same place. "Saints be praised, the old man has found us some seals," one of the men on deck said, pointing in the direction of the last cry.

"Sure sounds sad," a sealer near John said.

John nodded as he strained to get a glimpse of the animals making this strange noise, but all he could see was ice.

As the morning slipped away, the seals' bawling remained distant, sometimes close, sometimes barely audible. They saw nothing. "Not so much as a single flipper," one said. The experienced hands pronounced there were not enough to warrant stopping, "But we're getting close."

The sound of life in the midst of this icy wilderness was both strange and wondrous. After a week of nothing but empty ice and water, the quivering call of the newborn seals filled John with excitement. He ached to see the beasts making these noises.

Herb Butler and the other master watches stood around the ship's compass by the wheel, the binnacle. They fiddled with objects in their hands. "See over there," John's neighbour said. "They're setting their pocket compasses to get ready for the ice."

"Won't be long now," another said with a wide grin.

The ship began to pass through huge lakes of open water, punctuated by long lines of fresh ice. One of the more experienced hands said, "That slob ice is a good sign. Things are looking good now. Clarke's got us headed proper."

"Wonderful hummocky ice, that," someone said. "Not too hard. See how she closes up when we pass through her, good whelping ice. There's signs everywhere we're handy to young fat. Let's pray the weather holds."

A tall sealer beside John said, "Not on your life, we've got to get further north to find the main patch. We're just dancing around the good ice now, best to head straight into her."

"Jesus," another said, "we'd get jammed again if we did that. Haven't we had enough bombs for one trip? I say it's proper to keep on this tack. The skipper's doing fine, just a matter of time now."

"You're too easy," the tall sealer said. "It'll be summer before we see a patch worth the effort. The skipper's in some tear, he isn't stopping to look for the good fat. I never sailed with a master who passes by mewing pups."

"The old man doesn't want a few laggards. He's looking for the main patch, so we can hunt without chasing them all over hell." The sealer looked forward. "Be a waste of time to stop and look for such slim pickings."

"No sir," the tall one said, stepping forward aggressively, "a bird in the hand I say. Take them while you can. You never know when they'll disappear. A man should never pass by fat. It's a bad sign."

"You and your signs. If we heeded all your damned tokens, we'd never get out of the harbour. Why don't you batten up and let the men who know sealing do their job."

The two men came toward each other.

Herb Butler appeared. "Easy, boys," he said, slipping between them. "Save your energy for killing seals. We're close." He turned to the smaller of the two. "Better the ice be red with seals' blood than yours."

The men stood down, turned away, and sulked off in different directions.

As the day passed, enthusiasm waned yet again. The number of men on deck dwindled to a stubborn few. The continual sense of being close, yet far away, played havoc with everyone's nerves. After hearing a few more bawls, John retreated to the forepeak.

"Seems we're all dressed up with nowhere to go," Noah said when John came in.

"This waiting plays on the mind," John said. "I wonder if Clarke will ever find a patch."

v

That night the officers gathered around the table in the common room. Cigarette and pipe smoke hovered around the hanging lamps as the men talked about the day's events.

"Yes, my boys," Kelly said, his voice louder than usual, "it was good to see all those other ships follow the open water. None of them had the gall to strike into the ice like us. What a bunch of hangashores." The men laughed.

"A crowd of slow comes," Joseph Youdon said, to a chorus of laughter.

Kelly continued. "Those other captains just tag along, trying to live off our luck. So George headed us nor'west to discourage them, straight into that hungry-looking ice. And it worked, too. Some glad to see that smoke disappear."

"Proper thing," Youdon said with a grin.

Clarke was strangely quiet, sitting in his chair back from the table. Contrary to his usual habit, he had not changed his clothes for several days and the stubble of his beard, white in some places, was pronounced even in the scant light.

"I'll tell you," Kelly said, "it was music to my ears to hear those seals mewing after we crashed through that barrier of ice." He sucked on his pipe several times. "We did the right thing, not stopping to look for them, better to find the main patch." He sat back and relit his pipe.

"I heard the men arguing that a harp in the boat is worth two on the ice," Herb Butler said. "They figured we ought to have looked for them right then and there. The boys are desperate for killing and we may not hear any more."

Clarke finally spoke, silencing all of the men. "When I was younger, Mister Butler," he said gruffly, "I might have agreed with you. But now, I know we'd be wasting our time to stop for four or five sculps. We've got bigger fish to fry." He scratched his stubbled beard as he glared at his master watch.

"You sure?"

"Sure as there's shit in a dead goat," he said. " I have no intention to stop for a few sculps when the main patch lies ahead. I won't make the same mistake my brother would. No sir, we're pushing deeper into the ice, no matter what you say, Mister Butler." Clarke thumped the table.

"Yes, sir," Kelly said.

Butler turned in his chair, avoiding Clarke's angry stare.

There was an awkward silence.

"How about you tell us one of your yarns, George," Kelly said. "You know, one of those funny cuffers."

Clarke looked over at his second hand and began to shake his head. "No, boy," he said, "my heart's not into it. Too much on my mind."

Kelly began to protest. However, the scowl on his captain's face was enough to stop him.

Then Kelly called on Butler to sing. "Come on, Herb, fetch your accordion and let's hear some of those old songs, the good ones that tell about swiling — none of those treason songs."

"No, my son, I can hardly glutch," Butler protested. "I don't sing good enough, my sonny boys, no better than a fooley. I'll word out a piece for you, but no singing."

"No, Herb, you've got to sing. Come on now."

Kelly fetched Butler's accordion and reluctantly the master watch cleared his throat. "I'm not handy with words," he said.

"Yes you are, I've heard you before."

Finally, Butler squeezed off a few chords and began, his voice a bit wobbly.

Four hundred sail of shipping fine
Could then be seen at anchor,
Awaiting time to fall in line
And for a sou'west spanker.

He took a deep breath, and his voice began to strengthen

With topsails set, yea, every sail,
And brave men, stout and jolly,
To face a strong, bold northern gale
With Terry and John Holley

"Yes, my son," Kelly said. The men began to sway with the rhythm of the song.

Six hundred thousand seals were caught
'Midst northern fields of slaughter,
The greatest number ever got
And brought safe o'er the water

The men let the song sweep over them.

But that was fifty years or more
And half that catch today

Is not bought safely back to shore
With hearts not half so gay.

All the officers, except Clarke, laughed and cheered when Butler finished.

"I'll tell you, boys," Kelly said, "we'll find more of that good spirit when we hit the patch of all patches tomorrow. Those gamblers in town will make some money off of us this spring."

More songs followed. A feeling of togetherness flooded over the officers, genuine friendship and closeness. "Men," Kelly said, "we're in for a time of it. No doubt, this is the big one. We've done it right. Sure as the sun will rise tomorrow, we'll be in a patch with more seals than you'd ever hope to see." He raised his glass. "Tomorrow, my friends, the decks will run red with the blood of the harp seal."

Mugs were raised in answer. "Yes, sir."

"To the finest kind of spring," Kelly said, "the finest kind. Tomorrow we'll be burned down in the fat."

Clarke returned the toast and drained his mug. He put it down on the table and limped to his cabin, closing the door behind him. Several of the men exchanged concerned looks, but then the jovial mood returned and the singing resumed.

TWENTY-EIGHT

John was on his way below, an empty latrine bucket in each hand, when he heard the lookout bellow, "Whitecoats off the starboard quarter!" The barrelman's voice broke with excitement.

Everyone rushed to see. "Blessed God," the lookout hollered, "there's millions of them. They're everywhere. Look at them."

A loud rumble passed through the sealers. Many pointed toward the distant ice, black with seals. "Thick as a gallon of shit in a quart jug," one of the men said. The pups looked like fat pin cushions, some pure white, some with a yellow tinge. They did not move and most were nursing. The males, bigger and greyer, were interspersed throughout the feeding pairs. The bawling got louder as they approached. The reek of living seals wafted through the air toward the ship. John could not believe their numbers and how closely packed they were. "Jesus," he said out loud.

George Clarke came topside and limped to the bridge, facing the growing crowd on the main deck.

"Well, my buckos," he shouted, "we're into the main patch. The good Lord has seen fit to bless us. I want three watches on the ice as soon as we kiss that floe. Mister Butler's watch will stay on board and get the ship ready to receive the sculps."

Anger flashed across Butler's face. He began to speak up, but stopped himself.

"This is it, the mother lode, get yourselves ready." The captain paused and then stomped his foot. "I want these decks running red with blood and coated with grease."

The men let out a loud "Hurrah!" Those who did not have their equipment with them ran below to get it, while the others crowded closer to the rail. The air crackled with excitement as the deck space filled with men, gaffs upright, towropes across their chests.

John was devastated that his watch had been assigned to ship duty. All of his dreams were built around going to the ice and proving his worth. Now they were dashed. All he could do was watch, as the others got ready. Nonetheless, his heart drummed and his temperature rose as the *Cross* neared the seals. Spiked boots ground into the ship's decks and streams of hunters surged toward the gunwale. When the ship neared the ice, shouts, cheers and laughter filled the air. Then an expectant silence overcame the men. Anticipation welled up.

The crunch of the *Southern Cross's* side against the ice was the cue for Clarke to holler in a huge voice, "Over the side, my boys. Let's show these little buggers what we're made of." With a shout the men streamed onto the floe. Boots hit the ice. Sealers sprinted toward the waiting seals.

The master watches shouted orders, trying to keep this first rally at least somewhat organized, but to no avail. Confusion and chaos reigned. Over a hundred men and boys poured over the rails, a free-for-all.

As the hunters approached, the seals raised their heads, more curious than fearful. Some humped away toward their bobbing holes with an awkward S-like motion, pulling on the ice with their flippers, arching their backs, and then lunging forward. Large males, the dogs, left first. The edges of open water thrashed with departing adult seals. Just off the ice, seal heads bobbed up and down, looking startled, and perhaps a bit anxious.

"They're some sleek," John said to Noah beside him.

"Look at that," he said pointing, "most of the mothers are going, too. They're leaving their pups alone. See how they wave goodbye with their scutters. Not too motherly are they? Some of the bitches are staying, though."

"That's not too smart," John said. "The ones that stay are as good as dead."

The first wave of men arrived at the seals. One, two, three whitecoats were dispatched with gaff strokes to the head. One fat male remained. He faced his attacker, raised his head and showed sharp teeth. A raspy "Rrrrr-r-r-r-r" came deep from within its throat. There was a momentary standoff.

"Those teeth could do some harm," John said. Both boys nodded.

The hunter raised his gaff and brought it down with all the force he could muster. "Whack," and the old dog's head dropped. "Whack," and he fell over. "Whack," and the seal was still. The hunter rammed his gaff into the ice, flung off his coiled towrope and pulled out his sculping knife. He stood, legs apart, over his trophy, sharpening his knife with a stone pulled from his pocket. "Fwitt-fwitt-fwitt." Then, with considerable effort, he rolled the seal over and did the cutthroat, the full length of its body, all the way to the scutters. Vibrant crimson blood flooded out from the slash and began to paint the ice. Steam rose from the gash.

Everywhere on the ice, gaffs rose and fell, knives were whetted, seals were skinned. They removed the pelt with the fat still attached, leaving surprisingly small masses of muscle and bone on the ice.

"My son," John said, "they sure are brave when they face death. They might run away, but when they're up against it, they turn and show good fight." He paused to watch another sealer do his job. "The big ones look awful fierce when they rear up like that."

"They do, but they haven't got a chance against that gaff, do they?"

The hunters worked their way through the herd, progress marked by a spreading wave of red on the white ice. Whack-whack, shouting, fwitt-fwitt, officers hollering, all melded into a cacophony of death. Chaos dominated, but their singularity of purpose drove the disorganized band forward like a ruthless army routing a weaker foe.

John and Noah watched from the foredeck as the experienced hunters shucked seals out of their skins deftly, quickly. Some of the newcomers got skinning lessons from watch mates, while others, under a killing spell, worked through the patch, batting seals and leaving them to return later for the less exciting job of pelting them.

"Bloody hell," Clarke bellowed, "only kill what you can skin and drag. Don't get too far ahead of yourselves now." The lack of urgency in his voice showed he understood their frenzy.

One hunter stood up and wiped a dripping knife on his sleeve. He looked to be wearing crimson gloves as he knelt down to attach his towrope through a flipper hole in the sculp.

The pelts, lying in pools of deep red, steamed in the crisp March air.

Butler's watch cheered the hunters on. Some climbed the ratlines, many crammed against the rails of the upper decks. Gibes, catcalls and laughter filled the cold air. Many of the hunters worked their way out of sight behind pinnacles and clumpers. The sounds of the kill slowly receded as the front moved away from the ship.

Soon men began to trudge back to the *Cross*, towropes slung across their shoulders. They leaned against the weight of their tows of five or six pelts which they dragged fur side down, converging on the ship from several directions. Their progress painted red pathways across the grey ice. When they reached the ship, the hunters untied their towropes, unloosed the sculps, recoiled and restowed the lines across their chests, turned and headed back for more.

ii

"All right, boys, the show's over. Time to get to work," Herb Butler said. He assigned men to all manner of chores loading their rich cargo. "You, Lundrigan," he said, "go below and help store the sculps when they arrive. You can stay topside and gawk until we start dropping them into the hold."

Noah and the Gibbons boys went overside to collect ice to "salt" down the sculps in the hold. "They say spreading ice between the layers of skins helps keep the fat from going to gurry," Noah said to John as he left. "Doesn't make sense to have all that good oil drain into the bilge and be pumped away." He slung an axe over his shoulder and jumped.

Others were assigned to crews lifting the sculps aboard. The ends of the winch cables were fitted with straps that were run through the tow holes in the skins to lift seven or eight sculps onto the deck at a time.

"Out with those straps now," Clarke shouted from his pulpit on the bridge. "Look alive there, get them aboard. Ready on that whip line now." They tied the whip line to the load to pull it away from the ship and prevent painting her sides with grease and blood.

But the boys manning the whip line were not ready when the winch engaged. The pan slid across the ice dragging the custodians of the whip line with it. The skins slithered up the side of the old ship and flopped over the rail, leaving a trail of slippery red in its wake.

"Heavy on those whip lines, you idiots. Get four of you on them," Clarke bellowed. "Keep those pans off the sides and bulk those sculps up proper, in good piles."

Once topside, another crew unstrapped the sculps and released the winch for another load. The skins made a slithery pile on deck. John watched another crew haul them over to the hatch, his cue to get to work.

iii

Down in the hold, John and his crew had to move smartly to avoid being hit by the skins raining down from above. He touched the seal fat on one sculp. It looked like Elsie's currant jelly. The fat felt greasy to the touch. He rubbed his fingers together, amazed at how slippery they became on just one touch.

Butler told them to pile the pelts in the hold and salt them down with Noah's chipped ice that arrived in big baskets. Then they were to repeat the process, over and over again. Within minutes, John was covered in grease and had a difficult time holding on to the skins. The smell of seal fat grew stronger with each downpour of sculps from above.

They stored the skins in pounds; planked rooms that reminded John of the stalls in Dunphy's barn back home. They consisted of heavy boards slotted into vertical grooves in the hold wall. He did his best to fit the old boards so the pounds would be steady, but many of the planks were either too short or rotted at the ends. Despite John's best efforts, the pounds ended up being floating walls held up by the sculps.

The shower of sculps from above became a thunderstorm, a torrent of pelts that soon overwhelmed the crew of eight working as hard as they could. In the mid-afternoon Butler came by, "You boys been sleeping down there?"

John looked up, covered from head to foot in grease and blood. "We're doing the best we can. A few more hands wouldn't go astray, sir."

"There's nobody left," Butler replied. "Everybody's busy." He paused and looked around. "I see a few hunters coming aboard. I'll send them down after they eat." In a flash, he vanished.

But relief never came. John's crew fell further and further behind as more and more sculps poured down. Even though they worked at a frenzied pace, they could not keep up.

Later in the afternoon Herb Butler stuck his head over the hatch. "Just took number twenty five hundred aboard. The best day this old girl's ever had. And there's still more coming. Keep at it, boys."

iv

A pitch black sky met John and his gang when they finally emerged from the hold. Their tea had a rusty taste, but it hit the spot. The lobscouse, a rich stew made of salt beef, biscuit, potatoes and onions, was outstanding. "A fine celebration," John said with grease dripping down his chin.

"Yes, my son," the cook said. "We made nearly four thousand today. I've been on trips when we never got that many all told. Never seen the likes before." He grinned a toothless grin. "They were so thick the boys could kill four or five without taking a step, just had to turn around." He spun on his heel imitating a sealer gaffing in every direction. Then he roared with laughter.

"That's true," John said with a chuckle, "and I had to stack every single one of them. Boys, my back aches and, look, I can hardly hold on to my mug."

A spirit of celebration overtook the Southern Cross. Everyone talked with renewed energy and stepped lively. Laughter filled the old ship. John got swept up, too. Before long his back and hands stopped hurting. The ship had never been so alive.

v

The next day, George Clarke stood on the bridge with his second hand. He looked even more bedraggled with a six-day beard and rumpled clothes. Three watches on the ice dragged back enough sculps to keep the tail counters over-whelmed. The winches screeched in protest as they hauled the pelts aboard. The air reeked of seal blood and the deck overflowed with pelts. "Acres of fat, a beautiful sight," Kelly said with a smile. Everywhere, surrounding every hummock, the ice teemed with seals, as far as the eye could see. "I've never seen so many in one place, never. And they're prime, plump and healthy, not a single cat or nog-head in the lot. And big, they'll bring the good money." He slapped the rail and pointed toward another line of sealers with their tows emerging from behind a huge pinnacle. "This is the greatest patch these old eyes have seen."

Clarke was silent for a moment. "Yesterday, a few boys got into a killing craze," he said. "I tried to call them off, telling them that everyone had to sculp what they killed. Most of them listened, but a few didn't. I told the master watches to make sure everyone skinned their own kills, even if they had to stay on the ice all night. We've got to have discipline." His speech was clipped.

"Yep," Kelly said. "I saw one boy still working when I came topside at one o'clock last night." His eyes narrowed as he nodded his head. "He'll be more heedful the next time."

Herb Butler climbed up to the bridge and came up to Clarke and Kelly. "You wanted to see me, sir?"

"Yes, Mister Butler," Clarke said. "I want to talk to you about your watch. The men on the ice are doing fine, but I can't say the same for your boys on the ship."

Butler looked down.

Clarke continued. "They were complete fools with the whip lines. Have you seen those red swaths up our sides?"

"Give them a chance, sir. They're just learning. They're improving."

Clarke looked at Butler, clearly disagreeing. "And your loading crew is too slow. See how the sculps are backing up." He pointed toward the deck covered with piles of pelts. "What are they doing, sleeping down there?"

"That's not fair, sir. The boys are doing their best. We've never had so many come aboard at one time. They're doing a good job," Butler said.

Clarke stepped back. His stubbled face reddened. "Doing a good job, you say?"

"Yes, sir, a fine job, sir."

"You really think so?" Clarke said even louder.

"Yes, sir," Butler replied in kind.

"Well, if that's the case," Clarke said with an air of finality, "your watch can stay on board from now on. No hunting for them." Clarke motioned to dismiss his master watch.

"You can't do that," Butler said. "My boys have as much right to hunt as the others."

Clarke's face darkened as anger began to well up. "Not on my ship, they don't. They do what I say." He thumped Butler's chest with an outstretched finger. "And so do you. Do you understand?"

Butler stepped back, looking toward the second hand for support.

Kelly shrugged.

"Training another watch would be a waste of time," Clarke said. "With a proper ship watch we can let the hunters do what they do best. Your job, Mister Butler, is to get your boys working. They've got to get better." He loomed over his master watch.

"But, sir…"

"No buts, Mister Butler." Clarke was in a fury. He stepped forward, forcing the smaller man to step back. "Now, off with you," he said with a wave of his hand. "Get those boys working."

Butler began to protest, but thought better of it. He turned and left the bridge.

"A hard ticket, that man," Clarke said to Kelly after Butler left. "I can't abide his high and mighty talk. Too cocky, needs to be taken down a peg or two." Clarke paused, looking across the ice. "We'd better watch him, could be trouble. The men like him too much."

Kelly nodded.

A long line of hunters, each with tows, approached the ship. "Look at that," Clarke said. "A richer prize than even I imagined. I can't wait to see the look on Cheeseman's face when he sees this river of wealth. Then he'll have to take back those things he said."

"Four thousand aboard yesterday, and it looks like at least three today," Kelly said.

"Seven thousand in two days!" Clarke whistled. "Got to be a record."

"Aye, aye, sir, and it'll be the same tomorrow and the next day. There's no end in sight. You found the big one George, the main patch in a good year."

Clarke did not smile. He just squinted out over the ice.

vi

"Goddamn it," Sebastian Gibbons said, "I came to hunt, not to be a ship granny. This isn't fair." His face reddened and then he punched a stanchion with such force that one of the slickers hung on it tumbled to the floor. The forepeak grumbled with the anger of boys denied the opportunity to hunt.

"It's that Clarke," Jacob said, echoing Sebastian's ire. "Butler tried to get us onto the ice, but the captain would have none of it. The Skipper's got a broomstick up his arse about our master watch."

"Seems so," Noah said. "There's no love lost between those two, like a couple of tomcats. And now we've got to pay for it by being shipbound. It isn't fair."

"A more reasonable man, like John Clarke, would make sure everyone got to hunt," the older Rowe said. "But our skipper says, 'oh no, they've got to stay on board.' Damn it." He flopped down onto his blanket.

John shared their anger, not because he minded the work in the hold, but because Clarke's orders made it impossible to fulfil the images he had of proving himself on the ice. "I suppose there's not a lot we can do, just have to put up with what we've got," he said.

All of the Gibbons boys shook their heads.

"It isn't right," Sebastian said, rubbing his hands together angrily, "especially with so many seals on the ice."

A dark silence settled over the forepeak.

vii

"This has been the hardest week of my life," Noah said, as John entered their cramped quarters. "I'm licked out."

"Can you believe it? It's been seven days since we hit the patch and the seals are still coming aboard like capelin rolling ashore in June." Jacob added.

"You don't have to tell me that," John said, fatigue clear in his voice. "I stacked every last one of them. Oh, my bones," he said, as he fell stiffly onto his midnight glory. "They say we're over thirteen thousand already!" He rolled over. "Jesus, I wish I could get on to the ice, just for a change."

"Serves you right," Jacob said. "If you weren't doing such a bang-up job in the hold, Butler might let you go with our ice crew."

"I suppose, but somebody's got to look after things down there. Most of the boys would be happy just to throw the pelts into a corner. I'm proud I found a place where I can help, even though I haven't been to the ice."

"I hear Butler put you in charge down there. Not bad for a rawny hagdown."

"I can't really understand why the boys do what I tell them to down there, but they do."

"Must be your Western man's charm."

"Morning, boys, time to get back to work," Herb Butler said, standing over John.

"Where'd you come from?" John asked in a daze. "You weren't here a minute ago…" Then he realized he had fallen asleep in the middle of his chat with the Rowes and had not moved a muscle all night.

"Well come on, buckos. We haven't got all day. Sculps are already coming in. You've just got time for breakfast. Show a leg now."

John struggled up and made an unsteady way toward the galley, still groggy. "This switchel will get you moving," the cook said, passing him a steaming mug of tea. "You look like you could use it." The brew warmed him up from the inside, and the toast, slathered in butter, helped to wake him up.

John stepped out on deck and noticed a change in the weather. A bank of grey clouds loomed to the west and the wind had shifted north. Despite the sky, there was an unexpected springlike softness to the air.

Nothing had changed on deck, though. The winches puffed and groaned. Men huffed and wheezed. A few hands waved to John as he waded through the pile of sculps on deck, heading toward the hold. He stopped and looked out over the sea of carnage spread out on the ice in front of him.

In the hold John found his crew lounging on a stack of pelts. They jumped up when he came in. John laughed. "Well, men, I guess it's time to get back at it." A bucket of ice clattering down into the hold served as a cue to begin the next layer of packing. They walked on a carpet of seal with the skins halfway up the stanchions. John wondered where they would store the rest, once the hold was full.

"Don't fill her full," Butler said from behind him, as though he had read John's mind. "Leave enough room so some of the boys can creep in. We'll start stowing them 'tween decks when they reach this high," Butler said, as he marked a spot on the stanchion that would allow just short of five feet headroom. "Some of the men will have to bunk down here."

John began to shovel ice onto the piles on the port side. Butler was gone by the time he came back for a second load. The day settled into the same humdrum cycle of spreading, salting and stacking sculps.

TWENTY-NINE

Early in the afternoon of March 23, Herb Butler stood on the foredeck enjoying the springlike sun on his face. He smiled to see some of his boys clowning around as they chopped ice to salt the pelts in the hold. Off by the stern he saw a lone figure sprinting away from the ship. With no gaff or towrope, the runner was out of place moving across the grey ice. "Hey, you," he hollered, "where do you think you're going?" Lithe movements suggested a seasoned hand, despite the seeming youth of the runner. "Hey, come back," Butler shouted out even louder. The runaway kept going. The master watch squinted into the sun, placing his hand atop his eyes as a visor. "No, it can't be," he muttered. "Not my best hand." He shook his head. "Lundrigan, you get back here," Butler hollered, cupping his hands in an improvised megaphone. The boy did not even look back. He just kept running. "You'll be sorry when you get back," Butler shouted, his voice dropping off as the boy disappeared behind a needle-shaped pinnacle. "You just can't trust these bay noddies," he said under his breath, "even when you treat them the best." He sighed. "And he didn't even take a gaff."

ii

At first, John simply had felt something was wrong, a faint twinge of concern. But the feeling grew. Soon, the sense of alarm from his visions had overcome him. Jacob Newtry's advice echoed through his head, "Never ignore those hunches, my son." Without a word, he left the hold, went topside, and climbed down one of the side sticks to the ice. He struck off across the floe running as fast as he could. When the ship was out of view, he slowed to a quick walk. The light bounced off the pinnacles, sparkling in the afternoon sun. Moving across the floe was like walking on the skin of a massive animal, undulating up and down as if alive. Yet John felt safe. He detoured around open lakes and scrambled over pressure ridges. The crimson spots marking seal deaths got fresher the further he got from the ship. The silence became absolute as he left the other hunters, and struck off on his own, toward a destination he could only feel.

A strange hummock, shaped like a sugar loaf, appeared in the distance. John knew this was where he should go. He began to run. A slatch of open water lay in his path. Frantically, the boy copied across, skipping on loose chunks of ice. He reached the far side and sprinted to the hill. Nothing. He ran around to the other side, breathless, and saw a dark object at the base. A sealer, one of the Conception Bay boys, lay in a pool of blood at the foot of the ice mountain. He was dead still, with terrible gashes to his arms and legs, his left shoulder bare, jacket ripped. Muscles were visible where the skin had been torn away. A skinned whitecoat lay by the man's feet and, ten feet away, a gaff rested on the ice. A serpentine trail of blood led from the body to an open rifter.

John went over to the sealer, not sure what to do. "You alive?" he asked. No response. The sealer did not appear to be breathing. "Maybe I'm too late." He reached down. The man's face was warm and he felt a faint pulse on his neck. "Yes, b'y, you're still with us. Hang on, I'll get you home."

He did his best to bandage the sealer's wounds, using both sleeves from his own shirt. Then he removed the towrope from the man's chest as gently as he could. He attached it to the whitecoat sculp, using the knot he had learned from one of the older hands. It took all of his strength to roll the sealer onto the pelt. Then he put the rope over his shoulder and towed his load across the ice. He slipped a number of times before getting the balance right. Slowly, John headed back toward the *Southern Cross*.

He had to detour around the slatch he had copied over. This took three hours. Four times he had to drag the sealer by his jacket over raftered barriers and then replace him on the sculp sled. John's strength began to wane.

The temperature fell as the sun dropped. John trudged on. His knees throbbed and his feet ached. Doubts flooded through him. Could he make the ship? Was the sealer still alive? Was he going in the right direction? Had the ship moved? As night conquered the late winter day, turning it creak-cold, he was overcome by a desperate sense of abandonment.

iii

At first, John thought he was having another vision, orange flecks of monstrous eyes. But soon, he recognized the light of torches reflecting off the ice. "Over here!" he tried to shout. No response. "Over here!" this time louder, expending the last of his energy. John fell to the ice.

iv

When he opened his eyes, John was next to a fire, crackly warm, on the ice. Three men knelt over him, concern on their faces.

"Ah, there you are my good man," Herb Butler said. "You can get yourself all nice and warm by this fire. We thought we might have lost you. How are you feeling?"

John shook his head, uncertain. The fire warmed his face. Dumbly, he smiled and nodded.

"That's good. Your friend here is one lucky fellow." The master watch pointed to the injured sealer lying on the other side of the fire. "You came along just in time to get him home. That's one fortunate sealer," Butler said, looking over at the unconscious man on the other side of the fire.

"Is he going to be all right?"

"I believe so. We've sent back to the ship for Joseph Youdon. If anybody can fix him, it's Joseph. Not much longer and he would have died, no doubt about that."

John smiled and closed his eyes.

"It is a fine thing you've done, young man. You rest now and we'll look after you."

v

The next two days were the best of the trip for John. Not so much because they treated him like a hero, but because he began to feel a new sense of fulfilment.

Upon return from the ice, they took him to the officers' quarters and put him in one of the bunks. Joseph Youdon attended to his frostbitten feet. While not a trained doctor, he had been treating sealers' injuries for over fifteen years. The old hand buzzed around John, doing his best to make the young man comfortable and to get circulation back. "Proper thing," Youdon said as he fussed, "we have to look after our top hands."

John looked away, embarrassed.

Youdon continued. "Your feet aren't too bad off. You just take it easy now and we'll have you walking in two or three days. You're a lot better off than Isaac James."

"Who?"

"Isaac James, the boy you pulled off the ice."

"Oh."

"He's getting better, but it'll be a long time before he gets back onto his feet."

John found himself alone in the quarters shared by the master watches. This area suffered from the same leaking and griminess as the crew's lodgings, but not to the same extreme. With double the space per man, not only in the cabin itself, but also in the bunks, this space was pure luxury. All four master watches and the second hand shared this cabin, each with his own bed. John had been stowed in Herb Butler's bunk.

The master watch's cabin, along with a number of others, led off the common room that served as a general meeting and eating area for the officers. A large table sat in the middle, surrounded by wooden benches and ramshackle chairs at the heads. Men, including Butler and Kelly, sat around the table eating their breakfast and swilling tea.

The door of the captain's cabin swung open and Clarke limped out, sliding into his chair at the head of the table. "Goddamned gout," he said as he swung his left foot under the table. The captain's beard, while still scruffy, was beginning to take shape. The room grew silent.

"Yes, my son," Kelly finally said, "I've been to the floes for twenty-four years and never seen the likes of this. I swear this patch is bigger than the whole of Conception Bay."

"More seals than we know what to do with," Herb Butler said.

"No, Mr. Butler, I know exactly what to do with them." Clarke scowled, causing every man to look over at him. "We'll jam them into every nook and cranny. You can count on that."

Kelly nodded and added, "By the time we're done you won't be able to fart on board without hitting a sculp."

The conversation continued with eventually Clarke withdrawing entirely. Dark circles under his eyes and his slovenly appearance gave the impression he was exhausted. Without a word, Clarke got up and retreated to his cabin.

vi

Herb Butler came into John's room. "How're the feet?" he asked as he sat on the bed.

"They're throbbing some, but don't hurt too bad."

"That's good. You'll be back to work soon, then? Sure could use you." He looked intensely at the young man. "I'll tell you John, I was some angry when I saw you streaking off across the ice. I can't abide a hand deserting his post. 'There goes my best man,' I said. 'You just can't count on any of the boys these days. They're all the Devil's pelts, they are.' I cursed you up and down all day." He scratched his chin. "When I heard you saved that sealer, I felt some foolish. I should have known you had a cause." The master watch looked at John warmly.

John shuffled uncomfortably, moving under the covers to keep a distance between himself and Butler. He braced himself for being asked how he knew where Isaac was. "Yes, my son, you're a natural born sealer," the master watch said. "You've got the feel for it. A few more years and you'll be a top hand. You rest up now and we'll have you back on your feet in no time."

"At last," John thought, "I've found a place in this man's world, where I belong, where they take me for who I am." He smiled. "Do you have the hold full yet?" he asked his master watch.

"Yep, we got thirteen thousand down there, just barely. We started 'tween decks now. Should be able to jam four or five thousand in there. After that, who knows? They're saying there's more out there than we can stow." During the embarrassing silence that followed, John refused to look at the master watch. "Well," Butler said as he stood up, "time to get back to work." He patted John on the shoulder. "You get well now. Let me know when you're ready to get back to work."

vii

Several hours later, John awoke from a nap to find James Kelly standing by his bunk. "So tell me the story," the second hand said, his head wreathed in pipe smoke. His eyes twinkled as John recounted his adventure. "Yes, my son," he said when the story was finished, "must have been the hand of God took you out to that clumper." He began to laugh. "You tell a fine yarn, my boy. Almost as good as the time Charlie Murphy had his pants tore clean off by an old hood. He was so cold when he come aboard, his balls were clean pulled up." He laughed again. "How you feeling?"

"Oh, fine. I should be out of your hair any time now."

"Is my memory wrong, or did you work on the ship getting her ready back in St. John's? Below decks wasn't it?"

"Yes, sir. Us boys from Placentia Bay had to come early to get a ticket."

Kelly nodded. "Do you know what became of that boy from Red Island, Peter Lamb I think his name was? I gave him a ticket, but he never showed up."

John looked away. Lying never came easy. "I heard he got a ticket on the *Newfoundland* at the last minute. He said he'd do better at the Front."

"Hmmm," Kelly said.

After a time, John added, "But the way things are going, I'd say he made the wrong choice."

"Yes, his loss, I suppose." They chatted for a while about the time in St. John's. Kelly seemed especially interested when John told him how Tommy found the loading took less time this year, compared to last.

By the time John was ready to leave the luxury of the officers' quarters, he had spoken to most of the men who bunked there. Everyone had been fine company, except Clarke who only mumbled a few words at him. John was impressed by the seriousness of purpose of these veteran sealers. And to make matters even better, he had been accepted as one of them. "Yes, sir," he said to himself as he returned to the forepeak, "the *Cross* is my home now."

viii

While John learned a lot in the officers' rooms, he had been a guest, never completely comfortable in someone else's bunk. He was happy to return to the forepeak where he felt more at home on his own little piece of floor. However, when he arrived he found that things had changed. Many more sealers were crowded into the already cramped space, refugees from 'tween decks. Noah, Jacob and the others had been able to hold onto their spot, but not without Jacob's having to face down one particularly belligerent Conception Bayman. The argument had been won because the space belonged to the hand who rescued the injured Conception Bay sealer.

"Well, well, look who's come down from heaven to join us plain folk," Noah said as John came in.

The Red Islander grinned.

"Thought we lost you there when Butler came after us to find out where you were off to. He was some furious, I'll tell you. We figured you'd be keelhauled when you got back. Never seen a man so vexed."

"And then he goes and gets mad at us because we didn't know where you were," Jacob added.

"Sorry," John said.

"We knew all along you were doing a good thing. Butler wasn't that hard on us." He exchanged an argumentative look with his brother. "So tell us what happened now, all about it."

ix

As John got back to work, the hunt continued to go well. "We're over eighteen thousand now," Butler said.

After his second hard day back on the job, John fell onto his quilt, exhausted. "I'm some knackered," he said. His feet hurt, his back was sore and his hands ached from handling pelted seals. He retrieved his bottle of Radway's Ready Relief, upon whose healing powers he had been drawing all day, and drained it. The smatchy taste lingered as he felt the potion slip down his throat and begin to spread its curative numbness. "Could use a bit more of that," he said. The young sealer rifled around in his chest for the second bottle. After a good swig he corked the bottle and lay down to let the tonic do its magic.

"That stuff's more rum than medicine," Noah said.

John nodded, praying that the morning call did not come too soon.

"You Lundrigan?" a deep voice asked. A huge man loomed over him. He had an ominous scowl on his face.

"Yes," John said.

"You have to come with me."

"Huh?"

"There's someone wants to see you."

"Who? And who are you?"

"I'm Elias James. My brother is Isaac, the one you pulled off the ice. It's him wants to see you." The way the giant moved made it clear this was not a request.

John struggled up, doing his best to fight off the effects of the Radways. "Well, pleased to know you, Elias." He extended his hand and looked the stranger straight in the eye.

The huge man shook John's hand and a smile broke across his face. He laughed. The once-sombre giant became childlike, his reticence overcome by John's openness. "My brother's on the mend," the big man said. "He's finished for the season, but he'll be back next year, thanks to you." He looked down at the floor and scuffed his feet. "It's a wonderful thing you've done, sir, saving him like you did."

"Sir?"

"Yes, sir. We're all beholden to you. That'd be me, Isaac and my two older brothers, Herb and William."

"You're from Conception Bay?"

"Yes, sir, Harbour Grace. My father and his father were sealers. It's in our blood. We figure it must be in yours, too." Elias turned, gesturing John to follow. "Let's go see Isaac now."

John followed the gentle giant, flattered to be called 'sir,' though not at all sure he deserved it. They slipped between sleeping men on the floor of the fore-peak, onto the main deck, and through a door that led to a steep stairway. Down at the level of the hold they followed a narrow hall, crammed with barrels and crates. Elias turned and opened a door leading into a dark room. Were it not for a lighted sconce on the stanchion, the space would have been pitch black.

"This is the sick bay," Elias said, motioning for John to enter.

Three beds were crammed into the small space, with the middle one occupied. Joseph Youdon sat on one of the side cots. "Well, I see you're up and around," he said to John. "How're your feet?"

"Healthier than the cure, sir," John said, "thanks to your good work."

Youdon nodded. "Good. This is Isaac," he said, touching the arm of the man in the bed. "He's doing well, too. Got the heart of a dog, he has."

John looked down and saw his former charge covered with more bandages than clothes. His right arm was in a sling. His face was pale. John drew a deep breath, relieved to see a twinkle of blue shoot from the patient's now open eyes. A grin came across the patient's face. Clearly in pain, Isaac sat up with Joseph's help.

"So you're the one who saved me. I figured you'd be some giant like Elias. You must be a strong little bugger, and so young, too. I'm honoured to meet you, John Lundrigan." He held out his left hand, which John shook awkwardly.

Isaac began to struggle against his pain. "I can't put words to what I want to say." He looked away, paused to regain his strength, and then pushed on. "We're all grateful, and hope we can repay your kindness."

John looked down, embarrassed. "Never you mind that, you just get yourself mended up."

"That'll be a few weeks," Youdon said. "He's got a lot of healing to do."

"So where do you belong?" Isaac asked.

"Red Island, Placentia Bay."

"How does a covey feller like you get to be such a top hand?"

John smiled. "I'm not sure. My father went to the floes, and I've always wanted to, for as long as I can remember."

"Well, I'm one greasy jacket who's happy you did." He grinned, trying to hide his pain.

"Can you remember what happened?"

Isaac closed his eyes and gritted his teeth. He began slowly. "I just skinned a whitecoat when this big dog hit me from behind. He came around that sugar loaf and I never knew he was there. He knocked me on my face and was on my back before I knew it. I could feel his teeth in my shoulder."

John grimaced.

"I was more surprised than hurt," Isaac said, speaking slowly. "I was able to roll over and get my knife into him, but I couldn't get it out. The old dog clawed away at my arms and legs." His talk sped up and his manner became more animated. "Jesus, I kicked like hell to try and get him off me. Finally the bugger scravelled off to that rifter. Took my knife with him." His face saddened. "It was a gift from my father." Isaac paused, closed his eyes, and drew a deep breath. "I didn't know how bad off I was until I tried to stand up. The next thing I know, I'm here, shivering like a dog shitting herring bones." He managed a weak smile. "The shivers broke this morning." He stopped, looking a bit lost. "Then I heard about how you pulled me safe." His face blanched. Joseph helped him to lie back down. John saw tears well up in the sealer's eyes.

"I'd best be off," John said quietly to Youdon.

The old healer nodded.

John turned to leave. "Tell him for me," he said to Elias, "that I know he'd do the same if it was me out there." The big man patted his shoulder as he left.

THIRTY

George Clarke and James Kelly stood at the aft rail of the *Southern Cross*. Clouds lifting after the end of a short-lived winter storm had allowed the sun's warmth to creep over the deck of the old sealing ship. They watched as men trudged back and forth, dragging tows to the winches and then turning around to fetch another load.

"Praise the Lord," Kelly said, "these boys have turned into fine workers."

"They have," Clarke said. "But I'm worried, James, really worried. We've got less than a week of stores left."

"I talked to some of the boys who worked on the *Southern Cross* in St. John's," James said. "They told me they saw wagons full of food and tea leaving the wharf. And I heard it took less time to load the ship compared to last year. I reckon our missing stores were skimmed off and sold."

"That couldn't be. I checked and double checked the lists. Everything's in order." Anger began to build in the captain's voice.

"But maybe the lists are wrong. They were both written by the same hand and the old list is no more worn out than the new one, no more wrinkles, or stains. What are the chances of that?" He paused and began to fiddle with his pipe. "I think both lists are short."

Clarke stared off across the ice. He began to limp back and forth, scratching his bristly chin.

Kelly pulled out his tobacco flap and began to load his pipe. "I say there was a mock list for last year, light on everything. When we checked against that list, our stores seemed to be in order." With a flourish, he struck a match against the rail and began to suck to get his pipe going.

"No. Grieve would never allow that," Clarke said, trying to control his welling rage.

"He probably didn't know," Kelly said between puffs.

Clarke turned to his second hand, face flushed. "You could be right, James." He looked out toward the ice. Suddenly he straightened up. "I remember whose handwriting that was on the lists." His eyes narrowed. "It was Cheeseman. I saw the invoice he did for the rudder cables, it was exactly the same. Cheeseman did those lists." He began to pace faster. "I'll bet it was him who stole our stores, that thieving little bastard."

"You may be right. No matter what, it's definitely the Devil's work."

"How underhanded can you get?" Clarke said. "I'll bet even my brother would have been fooled by that." A steely look came over the captain. "Now we've got another reason to get home as fast as we can. The sooner we get to St. John's, the sooner we can give that Cheeseman what he deserves."

Kelly pointed the stem of his pipe toward the sculps piled on deck. "Yes, sir, we should hurry. We'll lose a lot of oil down the bilges if we stay out too much longer. Perhaps we should leave now."

Clarke paused and looked out over the ice. "Not so fast, James. Don't forget why we came out here in the first place." He pointed to the sculps. "We'll stay on the ice and keep hunting — remember Grieve's speech about all those orders? When we're full we'll get home as quick as we can."

Kelly nodded.

"We'll hunt on Sunday, though," Clarke said.

Kelly's mouth dropped open.

"Yes, I've been giving it a lot of thought. That's the only way we can be full and get home before we run out of stores."

"But remember what you told Butler about the fourth commandment?"

"Butler be damned," the captain said, anger spreading across his face. "There are times when the Lord's rules are meant to be broken." He glared across at his second hand. "And right now is one of these. It's the only way we can get out of this mess." Clarke shuddered. "We're between the Devil and the deep blue sea here, James. Leave when we have to and we won't be full. Wait, and we'll starve." For a moment he looked like a helpless child. Then he scowled and slammed the rail with his huge fist. "I'll be damned if those bastards will get the best of me. I'll move heaven and earth to get us home early and full, just to show Grieve and Cheeseman and that bloody brother of mine how good I am. Yes, James, that's how we'll do it. We'll send the boys out on Sunday." Despite his unkempt appearance the captain gave off a kind of regal authority. He was clearly a man on a mission, prepared to do whatever it took to get the largest possible cargo back to St. John's as quickly as possible.

ii

"Smoke off the starboard quarter," the scunner hollered from the high, main mast barrel. Clarke, who had been supervising the winches, raised the binoculars that always dangled around his neck. He could not identify the ship, so scrambled up the ratline to get a better view. After five minutes he came down with a disgusted look on his face. "It's that goddamned Martin on the *Erik*, snooping around to see if he can steal our sculps." The captain looked back and forth between the men on the ice, still dragging in fat tows, and the plume in the distance.

"Ernest," he shouted to a master watch on the ice, "hold your pelts there. I'm leaving off. That thief Martin is on his way. We'll be back for the tows soon as I can be rid of him." Clarke turned and issued orders to heave off the ice anchors and steam toward the unwelcome intruder. "We can't let him see this patch," he said, amid the flurry of orders to get the *Cross* as far away from the seals as he could. "He'd pull up broadside and help himself. Can't have that."

The two ships drew within hailing distance an hour later. Daniel Martin, one of the older captains, walked across the ice with his second hand. They were better dressed than the *Cross*'s officers. Martin's beard was newly trimmed. He was wearing a clean jacket. The visitors scrambled up the side sticks put out by the *Southern Cross*.

"Well, Captain Clarke," Martin said, looking around the main deck for clues regarding his success, "how're you doing?" He extended his hand.

Clarke received the handshake with warmth. "I'm well, Captain Martin, but the hunt hasn't been too good."

"Really?" Martin said, scanning a pile of sculps on deck. "You're already working on the coal bins. You must have a good load."

"No, skipper, we just started the bins this morning. We're not close to full below. I'm trying to keep her in trim."

Martin scratched his chin, unconvinced.

Clarke continued. "I suppose we hail at twelve thousand. We hit a small patch east of here, nothing to get too excited about. But then they disappeared. Now my men are scattered all over the ice, picking up a few here and there."

Martin continued to scan the ship. "You look heavier than that."

"No, b'y, twelve's all we've got. This old ship always looks low in the water when she's in the ice." Clarke stared directly at his visitor, daring him to disagree.

"As you say," Martin said. "We hit a good patch south and are just shy of nineteen thousand." The visitor smiled. "Too bad you weren't with us."

"Aye, too bad."

Martin nodded, still scanning the *Cross*.

"Will you join me for some tea, or grog?"

"Thanks, Captain Clarke, but I should head back south. Those are storm signs," he said, pointing to a bank of black clouds in the west. "Bound for a blow, I fear."

"Yes, you'd best get to the open water before that blunk catches you," Clarke said with a grin. "Don't want to get weatherbound."

Clarke watched the stern of the *Erik* beat south out of the ice.

"She's moving slower than a slug," Kelly said, pointing to the stern of the visitors' ship.

"That *Erik*'s so underpowered she'd stop dead in the water if Martin blew her whistle," Clarke said with a laugh. "You, boy," he said motioning to a youngster on deck, "go aloft and make sure that weasel doesn't double back."

"Aye, aye, sir."

After an hour Clarke ordered the *Southern Cross* to return to the men on the ice. In the middle of loading the masses of sculps that had arrived since they left, the barrelman sung out, "The ice is clear, no smoke in any direction."

Clarke laughed and slapped James Kelly on the shoulder. "We fooled that Martin, didn't we?"

The second hand smiled. "That we did, George, that we did."

iii

After two more days of hunting, Clarke and his officers were touring the ship looking for every possible cranny in which to stow their rich cargo. The holds were bursting, likewise 'tween decks. Even the coal bins were jammed full.

"Let's have a look now," Clarke said as they entered the storage holds that still held coal. "If we toss the coal in this bin overboard, we can fit another five hundred down here, maybe a few more." He smiled. "I'd love to see the look on Cheeseman's face if he saw us throwing coal overboard."

Herb Butler scowled. "Are you sure we have enough coal to get home?"

"Yes, Mister Butler," Clarke said with more than a hint of annoyance. "See over there, in that pound." He pointed to the bin on the starboard side. "There's enough right there to get us to St. John's from here."

"I can't abide that kind of waste," Butler said.

"Well, you can abide all you want, Mister Butler," Clarke said, anger growing. "Those sculps are worth a hell of a lot more than this soft coke." He stepped on a lump of coal on the floor, crushing it into a mush. "You'd think Cheeseman could at least give us some decent fuel."

Butler stared at the floor and said nothing.

"Mister Butler, have your boys clear this bin and start stacking the pelts. There's a huge pile on deck, so get at it."

"Yes, sir."

"Find a few more hands to help down here. This crowd looks like the good's all played out of them."

"Yes, sir, we'll get started right away." He paused. "Captain," Butler said, "isn't it time to call the boys off the ice? We're full and it doesn't make sense to leave pelts on the floes."

"Not on your life," Clarke said, his voice getting louder, "I'll drown them before I'll leave them on the ice for those others."

"But don't you think we've already killed enough?"

"No, I do not," Clarke said, "so long as there are whitecoats on the ice, we go killing. I'm not going to let those other captains live off our good fortune. You hear me? I'd rather drown every single pup than leave one here for Martin or Bartlett to clean up." His voice had risen to a shout. "You seem to have forgotten, Mister Butler, about that pile of orders on Grieve's desk. He needs every scrap of seal we can find. Do you want to let him down?"

Butler shook his head. "But they're nearly all gone. Most of the whitecoats have turned raggedy, and they'll be taking to the water any minute now."

"If that's the case then, we won't have any to kill, will we?" Clarke was shaking, his face beet red. "We'll hunt until there's no pups left on the ice. Do you understand me?"

"Yes, sir."

iv

"Rise and shine my lovelies," Butler said, as he kicked the feet of each of the sleeping bundles curled up in their midnight glories. "Time to look the sun in the eye."

Noah Rowe rolled over. "Jesus Christ, today's Sunday. Don't we get any rest?"

"No, sir, not today," Butler said. "We ought to, according to the Sunday law, but Clarke's got other plans. He's not one to let us sleep when there's whitecoats on the ice." Butler paused to make sure all of the lumps on the floor were stirring. "He's already got hunters on the floes."

Jacob groaned and rolled over. "I figured we were heading home yesterday. That's what we all thought."

"And we're full, nearly twenty thousand," John added, sitting up and stretching.

"Yes, my boys, that's true," Butler said. "But Clarke says there's more on the ice. We aren't done yet. Right now we're cruising to find a bigger patch that's still white. So let's get at it."

"Where'll we put all these sculps?" John asked.

"The captain says we'll stack them on deck. You can get a good pile against those bulwarks. Should be able to load at least a thousand more, maybe two. So hop to it. Can't be sleeping your day off away." He grinned.

"Lord above. There's no rest for the wicked," Jacob said as he stood up and stretched.

Lawrence Gibbons, now on his feet said, "That Clarke. Just because there aren't any other ships around, he figures he can do as he pleases. No respect for the Lord, none at all." He clenched his fists. "I've got a mind to complain about having to work Sunday when we get back. That would be proper. We deserve fairity."

"That would make you a tattle-tongue. You want that?"

"I can handle it," Lawrence said, puffing out his chest.

"You can talk to the Fishermen's Protective Union when we get back," Butler said. "Their boss, William Coaker, would be the man to tell, if you've a mind to."

"That's it, then," Lawrence said. "You point out this Coaker to me when we get back. I'll do the rest. Yes, sir." He smiled. "I'll set things right."

"I wager you will," Butler said.

213

John got to his feet and began planning how he might stow the pelts on deck. He could not put his finger on anything, but recognized old feelings of fear beginning to stir.

v

When they arrived on deck, the fog was being burned off by the early morning sun. Despite the bright air, the cold wind signalled that winter was still lurking. They watched the slob ice pass by, hoping against hope the seals were gone and that Clarke would finally have the good sense to head home. But it was not to be.

"Whitecoats!" the scunner hollered. Machinery and men alike jumped into action.

"So much for the Lord's Day," John said, shrugging his shoulders.

"Yes, b'y. It's a grievous thing to be as greedy as our skipper," Noah said. "Gives me a bad feeling."

John nodded his agreement, but he knew that more than Clarke's greed was at play. He began to sense that things were changing for the worse. "If everything stays on this course," he said to himself, "we'll be in real trouble." He shuddered as old feelings from his visions began to recur.

THIRTY-ONE

At first, the sculps arrived at a frantic pace. John began by trying to keep the scuppers clear, so any water trapped on deck could drain off. However, this left gaps in the wall, making the piles likely to tumble over. He was puzzling over what to do when Herb Butler came up to him.

"Looks like a row of bad teeth the way you've got them stacked there, my son," the master watch said with a glint in his eye.

"Aye, sir," John said. "Seems proper to keep the scuppers open. You never know what kind of seas we'll meet on the way home."

Butler nodded. Pointing toward the captain's cabin, he said, "By the look of things though, he's not going to give us any choice." He motioned toward the heaps of sculps accumulating mid-deck. "That madman is set on jamming as many on deck as he possibly can."

"Should we stack them solid then?"

"I believe so, right to the rails." Butler looked toward the bridge and said quietly, "Try to keep the aft and forward scuppers clear if you can. Lash the stacks in, too."

Butler turned and walked away.

John now knew for certain that the ship's troubles had begun for real. He looked up at the steel blue sky. The sun warmed his face and an unexpectedly soft breeze, springlike, seemed to say that his worries were needless.

"All right, boys," John shouted to his crew. "Fill in those gaps there. Let's make this a real wall."

ii

By late morning the stream of freshly killed sculps dwindled. Gangs of hunters returned empty-handed.

"Jesus," one said as he scrambled aboard. "Every single harp is gone. Now you see them, now you don't, bloody magicians."

"Yes, my son," another added. "The young ones have all taken to the water now, not a whitecoat in the lot. They're all raggedy." He looked at the bridge. "I suppose the old man will want to start shooting them now."

"God, I hope not," John said looking at the pile of sculps on deck.

By noon there was no more room against the bulwarks. John had managed to keep the fore and aft scuppers clear, but a pile of unstacked pelts still remained on the deck. He decided to search out Herb Butler for advice about where to put the remainder.

Just then, George Clarke came on deck. His ruffled clothes and scruffy beard gave him a particularly menacing look as he shuffled over toward John. He towered over the young sealer.

"Well, my boy," Clarke said, "finished?"

John started to ask about the remaining sculps, but Clarke interjected.

"Sloppy work there. You haven't run the stack all the way to the end. She'll shift in a heavy sea."

"But the scuppers, sir. They should be clear."

"Who says?"

"I just thought it would be a good idea. We could meet some heavy seas on the way home. She'd never drain."

Clarke bristled. "So you thought, did you? And exactly who told you to do the thinking around here?" He stared at John for an answer.

John looked down at the grease-encrusted deck. "It's only wise, sir," he mumbled.

"What did you say?" Clarke shouted. "Speak up, man."

John tried to speak, but could not. He wanted to turn and run. Taking a deep breath, he gathered all his strength and met Clarke's eyes straight on. "It's only wise, sir, I said."

"Wise, you say. How can a young snip like you talk about wise? I've been on the ice for twenty-six years, boy, since before you were born, and you're telling me what's wise." The captain raised his huge hand in the air.

John readied himself for the blows, but none came.

"Listen here," Clarke said, "there's only one version of wise on this ship, and it's mine." His face reddened as he thumped his huge chest. "It's mine. Do you hear me? Mine." He was shouting.

John nodded, continuing to look at the deck.

"It was me told him to leave the deck drains clear," Herb Butler said from behind John. He was puffing, having run from somewhere. "Lundrigan here was following my orders. Leave him be."

Clarke looked right through John toward his master watch, who was trying to regain his wind. "You?"

"Yes, me. I told him to leave the fore and aft scuppers open."

"And what about those?" Clarke said, pointing to the pile of sculps on deck. He raised himself on tiptoes, glaring down at Butler. "I suppose you want to give them to Davy Jones."

John turned to see Butler stand erect and, with an insolent shrug, suggest that would be better than the decks not draining properly.

Clarke erupted. His jaw hardened as he strode over, nose-to-nose with Butler, almost knocking John over as he passed. The captain thumped his finger on Butler's chest. "You listen here, Mister Butler," he shouted, "and you listen good. Those sculps are going in those spaces." He jerked his finger toward the gaps John had left, "There, there, there and there." He thumped Butler's chest even harder, causing the master watch to stagger backwards. "And any you can't get in there are going in your bunk. Do you hear me?"

A pall came over the men on deck who stood in shock as their favourite officer was dressed down in public by their captain, who seemed to have lost control. They kept their eyes to the deck, lest Clarke's ire settle on them.

"You put those sculps in those open spaces right now," the captain bellowed.

"No, sir, I will not, sir," Butler said.

Clarke's face turned even redder. He paused to collect himself. "Mister Butler," he said in a menacing voice, "are you refusing to obey an order from your captain?"

Butler stood erect, looking straight at Clarke. "Yes, sir, I am, when the order poses a clear danger to the ship."

The captain stepped toward Butler, fists clenched.

Butler stepped back.

Clarke managed to restrain himself. In a very quiet but ominous voice, he said, "Mister Butler, you can rest assured that this is the last trip you will be taking with me. I'll have none of this mutiny from my officers, you hear? Now you do as I bid."

"I will not," Butler replied. He turned his back and began to walk toward his quarters. "I will not be party to this insanity."

"You come back, Mister Butler!" the captain shouted.

Butler kept on walking.

"You go to your cabin, then. Be sure you stay there until we get home."

Without looking back, Butler walked directly to the officers' quarters and slammed the door, leaving Clarke to sputter at the weatherworn wood.

"Consider yourself put on the log, Mister Butler. I'll make sure you never get work on a sealer again." The captain was trembling. He turned around and looked at the men, all standing with their heads down. "Well?" he bellowed. "Is there no man here with the courage to obey a simple order?" A shuffle passed through the men "Well?"

James Kelly pushed forward. "I will," he said. He approached Clarke and whispered, "You go to your cabin, George. I'll take care of this." A bewildered look passed across Clarke's face. He surveyed the men once more, looking like a lost schoolboy. An eerie silence engulfed the ship as he turned and limped toward his cabin.

After the captain was gone, Kelly went over to the rail and looked over the ice for a long time. Finally, he turned and walked over to the stack of pelts mid-deck. "Well, let's get at it. If that's what he wants, that's what he'll get." He pulled a sculp off the pile, dragged it over to a gap, adroitly sliding it into the open space. "Let's do the man's bidding and plug up those holes."

A whole wave of men flooded forward to help. Kelly kept working too, like a common deckhand. Within fifteen minutes the wall of pelts was filled in and lashed. The sculps spanned the full length of both the port and starboard bulwarks. Like a massive jigsaw puzzle, all of the sealskins had been fitted into place. The wall had displaced the *Cross's* lifeboats so the men stowed them atop the piles.

When the men left, the main deck was deserted, save for John and Noah who stood side by side, surveying the massive stockade of pelts. "Now, that's a wall of wealth," Noah said. "Lord Jesus, we're so overloaded that if an ice bird shit on us now we'd go down like a stone." Noah retreated to the forepeak.

John was positive they were in for it now. Without doubt, the ship was in grave danger. He saw Clarke's wall of wealth was a wall of death, certain to trap any water that came over the side. If there was even a hint of bad weather on the way home, the ship was doomed. And somehow he knew weather was on its way.

iii

John headed below to his little corner of the forepeak. Since the other sealers had moved in, his refuge, formerly full of goodwill and humour, had become a hard place. Everyone seemed to be angry since they were crowded and less comfortable. No one smiled. Even the corners of the rough-hewn stanchions looked sharp and harsh now.

The boys stopped talking when John entered.

Jacob broke the awkward silence. "I thought the old man was going to knock your block off out there."

John nodded. "Me, too."

"You should never have done what you did, getting Butler in trouble like that. See what happened because of you?"

John ignored this. "The skipper's losing his keel. He's not thinking straight. Boys," John said, "we're in for it. I know for certain the ship is going to sink." He paused to be sure everyone was listening. "She's overloaded. If the copper didn't cover the load line, you'd see we're down way past the safe point. She's top-heavy too, with those sculps on deck. We're going to sink, sure as the sun will rise." He looked over at his friends.

"Don't talk so bad," Lawrence Gibbons said.

After a stony silence, Sebastian, the biggest and meanest of the Gibbons, spoke. "We ought to be happy. We're loaded heavy, the best hunt this old boat has ever had. You're just a jinker, talking like that. We should be celebrating, not worrying. Leave us be. Take your frets somewhere else. We don't want to hear them." He looked at the other boys, urging them to agree. Several "yeas" confirmed his position. "Off with you now." He gestured at John as he would a scolded dog.

"No," John said defiantly, "our success will be our undoing. The extra seals on deck will sink us."

"Don't be such a maid."

"Butler was right, you know, to refuse to block off the scuppers. She won't drain properly."

"Why should we listen to that turncoat? He won't follow a simple order."

"No, no," John pleaded, "he was right."

"What foolishness," Sebastian said, "you're just sorry you lost your position now we're full."

"What?"

"You been all chuffed up like a bandy rooster every since Butler put you in charge of loading. You've been acting too proud."

More "yeas."

From the corner Lawrence Gibbons added, "The only reason Butler put you in charge of the loading crew is because you're too small to do anything else."

John looked over at him, mouth open.

"And he's got a thing for you, too. Don't think we haven't seen it. You've gotten pure beside yourself with notions," Sebastian said. A vicious glint issued from the corner of his eye. "Now, little John, you're just one of us ordinary sealers."

John was thunderstruck. By refusing to meet his gaze, Noah agreed; Jacob too. "But you don't understand," he pleaded. "We're in grave danger."

Sebastian took a step toward him. "Shut your mouth," he said through clenched teeth. "No cause to stir up a lop in a piggin."

John never saw it coming, a roundhouse right that landed square on his jaw. A golden light flashed and then everything went black.

THIRTY-TWO

James Kelly was on his way topside when Herb Butler motioned to him from his quarters. The second hand began to pass by, but Butler's urgency made him stop. He turned back to the master watch who mouthed the words, "Please, it's important," while motioning Kelly to enter. The second hand hesitated, checked to be sure no one was watching, and then entered the cramped room. Butler was the only person there.

"Shhh," Butler hissed, "don't want the old man to know we're talking." Kelly nodded and went over to a bunk. He sat down and Butler moved in beside him. "There's something wrong with the captain," Butler whispered. "He's lost his way, crazy with his anger."

"You didn't help that any, standing up to him like you did. You embarrassed the poor man — made things a lot worse."

"He left me no choice," Butler said.

Kelly shook his head. "You've certainly got yourself in a jam now."

"I don't care for myself, my concerns are the men and the ship."

Kelly shook his head and began to get up. Butler grabbed his arm and pulled him back down. "Haven't you noticed? He's gotten so pigheaded he can't think straight."

Kelly moved away. "I've seen him worse," he said, with a hint of defensiveness. "You've got to understand the burdens he's carrying."

"Burdens?"

"Yes. He's all caught up in his obligation to Grieve. It weighs on him like a millstone. Add to that, he has to show everyone, like his brother and Cheeseman, he's the top swiler. The captain wants the silk flag worse than anything in the world. Wants to do well for the men too." He paused and then moved away. "He's got to have a good load so he can build his captain's house when he gets home. And this business about running out of food has only made it worse."

"That's no excuse. He's still not thinking straight."

"I'm not making excuses, just trying to show how it is for him." There was an awkward pause. "He's doing the best he can," he said somewhat unconvincingly.

"You must agree with me that blocking off the scuppers is foolhardy." Butler moved closer to the second hand, who, for the first time, showed doubt. "Well?"

Kelly shuffled uncomfortably on the bunk. "The scuppers may be a bad choice, but that doesn't matter now."

Butler was puzzled.

"He's just ordered us to leave the ice for home. There's nothing to worry about." Kelly regained his confidence and managed to stand up and move away before Butler could pull him back down. "Just a quiet cruise home now. All we have to do is get to St. John's. Come on, Herb, we've got the best load this old ship has ever seen. Why should we worry?" Kelly began to leave.

"Why should we worry?" Butler said getting up to block the door. "Why should we worry?" His face began to redden. "Haven't you seen the way he's changed? Hunting on Sunday after he almost knocked my block off for suggesting it — fourth commandment, my arse. He's not shaving or looking after himself, and limping around like a cripple. And, my Lord, James, the amount of time he spends alone in his cabin — shocking." He moved toward the second hand. "I tell you, he's not right. He's not the same man that left St. John's."

"You just don't know him like I do," Kelly said, trying to step around the master watch. "He's always been moody."

"You have to do something, James, something to make him see reason. The way he is now, we can't trust him to make the right decision. The ship is in danger." He grabbed Kelly by the shoulders. "Please, for the sake of the men."

Kelly broke away from Butler's grasp and turned away. "There's no way I could stop him now, even if I wanted to."

Butler groaned. "Well maybe you should be a man and step up to do the right thing then — relieve him of command."

Kelly turned back toward Butler, mouth open. "You don't mean that do you? Mutiny!"

"Yes, I do," Butler said, his jaw firmly set. "Captain Clarke has lost his way. He's put the ship at risk and should be replaced."

Kelly began to shake his head. "Just the thought of it scares me."

"According to the Book of Maritime Law—"

"Never mind your books," Kelly interrupted, "they're no use here. Taking over command is simply out of the question. I'd never do that to my old friend, never. Anyway, things are nowhere near serious enough for that." He looked perplexed, then his expression hardened. "There's nothing to worry about. We'll be home before anyone knows there's a problem. The weather's fine and we're making good progress." He brushed past Butler and moved toward the door. Turning back he stopped and whispered, "I'll forget we had this conversation. George would go mad if he knew we were talking." He began to leave.

Butler scowled. "You mark my words, James Kelly," he said, "you haven't seen the end of this." He lowered his voice. "The old man has lost his anchor. That bugger will be the death of us all."

Kelly was watching Butler's face as he slipped out the door. He failed to notice that the door to the captain's cabin was open a crack.

ii

When John regained consciousness, he found himself in a corner of the main area 'tween decks, his sealer's chest and gaff beside him, midnight glory tossed over it. His head pounded. His jaw ached. From what he could tell, it was after midday. Groups of St. John's men sat in small circles nearby. Occasionally, one glowered at him. John had been expelled from the forepeak and thrown in among the St. John's men. He tried to sit up, winced, lay down again, and pulled the quilt over himself.

Later in the afternoon he rose and made his way topside. The *Southern Cross* had been flagged out for the trip home. A string of multicoloured pennants running from the tip of the bowsprit, over the tops of the masts, led all the way to the end of the aft gaff boom. The gaiety of the flags snapping in the warm spring breeze helped to create a carnival atmosphere, as if to say all was well. More than anything, John wanted to believe that. Maybe Clarke was right about the scuppers. Maybe the weather would hold and there was no cause for concern. Maybe they would simply slip quietly into St. John's Harbour, safe and sound, and that would be that. But he could not shake the consuming feeling of dread that plagued him. His whole being screamed that they were in grave danger. Over and over in his head, he heard old Jacob say, "Whatever you do, don't ignore those feelings." Yet Clarke could still be right. John didn't know what to do.

From the foredeck, he watched a few loose pieces of ice glide by. After a while he grew so agitated he could not stand still. He had to tell others about what was going to happen, but there was no one who would listen. He went back to his sealer's chest and dug out a paper and pencil. Ignoring the hostile looks from the townies, he knelt down and began to write in a slow, laboured hand.

I know were in for it. The ship is overloaded over 20,000 on board. The main deck is plugged off with pelts. The ship is moving like a slug. The boys are happy we are on our way home and wont hear of any danger. We hunted Sunday. Hope the weather holds. If it doesnt were done.

JL, Southern Cross

John read his note over and then folded it, slipping it into one of his empty Radway's bottles. He jammed the cork back in and slipped the bottle into the pocket of his jacket.

A sealer, face blackened from soot dissolved in seal grease, burst into the room. "Boys," he shouted, "we're passing Channel. I just saw Table Mountain."

The men cheered.

"We must have been some far east to reach Channel already," a sealer near John said.

"It's only half six."

"At this rate, we'll be standing on the wharf in St. John's on Tuesday afternoon," the first sealer said, unable to hide his excitement. "Three cheers for Captain Clarke," he shouted.

"Hip-hip-hurrah! Hip-hip-hurrah! Hip-hip-hurrah!" reverberated through the room.

"Yes, boys. He's as fine a skipper as there is. We're loaded and headed home." More cheers.

John watched the celebration from his isolated corner. He found it strange that these men were so happy in the face of the real danger the ship was in. It was as though no one wanted to know the truth of their dire situation. John half expected someone to break out into a come home shanty, but no one did. All he heard was the hubbub of townies chattering in small groups.

iii

The next day, John spent most of the afternoon on the foredeck. He watched the diminishing ice bob by and tried to identify the landforms visible off the port side. Previously, this deck had been a hub of activity, a place where you could meet others and watch the world pass by. But now it was forlorn and isolated. John drank in the warm air with a deep breath. The softness reminded him of Red Island.

Black and white birds escorted the *Southern Cross*. They skimmed over the water, sometimes veering off, only to return again, portside sentinels marking the passing minutes with their wingbeats. Then, like the harp seals on Sunday, the birds were gone, leaving John to pine for the return of some sign of life in the relentless expanse before him.

The plodding slowness lent a kind of uneasy elegance to the voyage. Waves crashed below the dark cliffs of the south coast, scribing a white line that separated ocean from land. Occasional groups of sealers passed by on deck, but most lounged below. The clear sky and the ocean disturbed only by a lazy groundswell lulled everyone into a sense of security. The usually vigilant men had let down their guard in the excitement of heading home. But John's fear only grew as did his frustration that no one wanted to listen. He was trapped in a nightmare where only he knew what was going to happen and the world was unwilling to listen.

Early in the afternoon the humps of St. Pierre showed below a hanging fog bank. The brownness of the islands and their sandy-coloured cliffs were a welcome change from the dismal, nearly black land John had been watching. He could see houses and stages, signs of a life he had almost forgotten.

As dusk approached, the wind freshened and shifted to quarter off the ship's starboard bow. This new wind had a winter's edge to it. Yet, as if to say John's fears were needless, the temperature remained warm in between the gusts cresting across the grey sea.

The sun disappeared behind a bank of black clouds, blazing orange. From behind, brilliant rays reached for the sea like the fingers of a great hand. Within minutes it was gone, with only a metallic grey afterlight remaining.

John waited for the moon to rise. For the whole trip, he had followed her progress like a navigator as it waned from being full when they struck the main patch. The diminishing size of the crescent had mapped the amount of room left in the *Southern Cross* for sculps. Perfectly on schedule, the moon had turned new the day the whitecoats disappeared.

The sky darkened and the stars popped through the gloom. He used the Lode Star to imagine a pathway northward, through the heart of Red Island. This brought thoughts of his father and how the old man had driven him so hard. He remembered his father's constant calls to "be a man" and the way he had never given him a chance to prove himself, the frustration, the hurt. He remembered the beatings and how his father had cut him down and refused to talk with him at the hour of his greatest need. An image of Abel's seaworn face came to him. First, he saw the hateful glare and huge hands raised in anger. He cringed. But then the old man's face softened. John saw tears in the creased corners of his father's eyes. He felt the old man reach toward him. For the first time since he had left, John wanted to see his father, hear his cuffers, and to be part of that world again. He understood how, by leaving home, he had found it. From away, Red Island was no longer the prison he had thought it was. Now he knew he could truly say that he "belonged" to Red Island. The people and the place were his anchor, the things that made him who he was. He peered northward from the foredeck of the *Southern Cross*, knowing that his home was hovering beyond the horizon.

He went below and picked up his father's gaff, unbloodied and untested. He whipped it through the air. He could feel his father's hands in how it lived in his grip. He caressed the metal hook with his fingertips. Slowly, with respect, he put it down and covered it with his blanket. John looked around at the men in the room most of whom were sleeping. Then he returned topside.

When he came back on deck, the moon had finally risen off the stern. The entire circle was visible, huge against the black sky. Only a fingernail was actually lit, but he could see the whole moon as a dark, shadowy presence, the Earth Light. The brightened portion lay nearly on its back, inscribing a U-shape in the late March sky. The lighted part shone with such a deep orange and so brightly that it appeared to be disconnected from the darker part of the disc. John had never seen a moon like this before. "A token?" His fear for the ship continued to grow.

The moon rose in the western sky, getting smaller the higher it went. A fox-eye appeared around her, a perfect halo that retraced the full moon's shape. John had never seen a circle as tight and distinct, particularly around a new moon like this. He remembered Joe Skinner saying this kind of moon meant bad weather.

iv

After half an hour watching the sky John felt the wind pick up and the temperature drop. The low lazy lop of the sea started to grow edgy, its earlier tranquillity about to be shattered. John caught some movement out of the corner of his eye, off to the southeast. He looked as hard as he could but nothing changed save for the wind growing colder. The young man pulled his jacket tight and stomped his feet. Then he saw it, a line against the sea, slowly moving upwards. Now he recognized the same premonition he had experienced on Stoney Point. His heart raced as he watched the cloudbank move high enough to vanquish the moon. The wind increased and within minutes the waves had grown to three feet. Sea caps exploded atop the crests as a particularly strong gust caught the *Southern Cross*. John held on to the rail as the old ship began to pitch in response to the growing sea.

A commotion on the bridge caught John's attention. James Kelly was pointing toward the approaching cloudbank, barking orders to several men. He sent a man aft to join the one at the wheel. Then the second hand scrambled up one of the ratlines and glassed the oncoming clouds. He came down and sent another man to lash down the boats atop the seal pelts at the rail. Back on the bridge Kelly paced back and forth watching the weather as it approached, constantly consulting the instruments.

Stronger winds, which felt even colder, began to agitate the sea, turning it into an ominous black with the occasional white sea cap.

John closed his eyes. He did not want to see any more. The boy knew exactly what was going to happen. And despite this certainty, there was absolutely nothing he could do but wait for the end.

A powerful gust of wind almost knocked him over, cutting through his jacket like a knife. Slowly he made his way back to his spot 'tween decks. Some of the men now had worried looks as they huddled in circles, talking in low whispers.

THIRTY-THREE

"Who's there?" George Clarke said on hearing a weak knock at the door of his cabin. He was staring at maps unrolled on his table, his back to the door. "Off with you, I want to be alone."

"James Kelly, sir. I have news." Timidly, the second hand pushed the door open. "The weather is changing."

"The weather's always changing," Clarke said gruffly, not turning to acknowledge the opening door. "Be gone."

"But she's worsening. The swell is growing. The wind's up and baffling to the sou'east."

"No matter. Off with you now," Clarke said.

Kelly did not leave, but continued to stand in the doorway, fidgeting with his pipe. "Sir, the most prudent course would be to shelter up in St. Mary's Bay before the swell grows so big we can't cross it." He inched deeper into the cabin.

"Shelter up, and lose precious time?" Clarke said.

"Aye, sir. Everyone knows a wind like this leads to four times the nor'wester."

The captain turned around and glared at his second hand. "Turn tail and run, you say? Grovel like a coward before a whiff of wind. That's your advice?"

"Yes, sir." Kelly began to twist his pipe between nervous fingers.

Clarke's eyes narrowed as he turned to face Kelly. "You know as well as I do that we have to get home and claim our prize." His voice broke. "You'd think a man of God like yourself would understand that." His face hardened. "We must be home at once." The cabin grew silent. Clarke stared blankly at the back of his huge fist. It was shaking.

"Please, George, shelter up," Kelly said softly.

Clarke puffed out his chest. "Let me tell you Mister Kelly," he said, so loudly it startled the second hand, "I have no intention of giving up the head start we've worked so hard to win." His voice grew stronger and louder. "The Bartletts and Martin are just behind." He gestured toward the stern with a vicious shake of his head. "I'm not going to let them beat me, not this time. Come hell or high water, I'm going to win that silk flag — no hiding from this so-called weather of yours."

Kelly began calmly. "Think for a moment, George, common sense says we should turn for St. Mary's Bay to wait out the storm." He paused as Clarke sat forward and glared at him. Kelly's voice rose, betraying his growing anxiety. "Surely, it does."

Clarke's jaw hardened as he placed his palms on the table. Through clenched teeth he said, "I don't give a damn about your so-called common sense, it's of no consequence, no consequence whatever. We're pushing toward home, and that's that." He said the last word with such force that Kelly winced.

Again the second hand mustered all the persuasiveness he could. "Isn't sheltering up what the owner would want? Remember what he said about all those orders on his desk? We've got to get these seals home," he said.

"That's exactly what I have in mind. And Grieve can go to hell as far as I'm concerned," Clarke stood up. His face contorted even more as his weight came down onto his left foot. "I've lost all respect for any man who'd hire a crook like Cheeseman." His face began to redden. "For all I care, Grieve can stand on Signal Hill and piss into the wind. You're always prattling on about that miser as if he was my conscience. The only owner of anything aboard this ship is me." He thumped his great barrel chest as he shouted. "My conscience is the *Southern Cross's* keelson, not some fancy desk in that old man's office." He stomped his good foot on the floor. "Now you leave me be."

"Wouldn't it be best to shelter up, just until the storm vents, and then speed our way home? We'd still beat the others through the Narrows."

"We can't," Clarke said, "there's not enough coal. We'd end up dead in the water while all those others passed us."

Kelly stepped forward. "Please, George, we must head for shelter?"

"And what do you propose I do about having no food left?" Clarke said, his voice getting louder. "Do you want to get everyone so riled up that Butler and his friends can lead a mutiny?" He stopped, eyes narrowing. "Or maybe that's what you're up to ... trying to slow me down enough so you can have time to turn the men against me."

Kelly looked shocked.

"Don't you try and fool me, Mr. Kelly," Clarke said, menace clear in his tone, "I know about your secret meeting with Butler. I saw you."

"But—"

"Don't you but me, Kelly. I know what you're up to." Clarke placed his hands on the table.

"No, no, George," Kelly said. "You've got it all wrong. I told Butler to stop undermining you, that's all. You have to believe me." He began to fidget with his pipe, unable to look his old friend in the eye. "Please, George, please, my only concern is this weather." He motioned upwards. "I'm not sure we can manage. That's all, George, that's all." Kelly's pipe snapped in his hands. He looked at the pieces and then slid them into his pocket.

Clarke sat down.

"Captain Clarke," Kelly said moving deeper into the cabin, "I beg you, for the love of God, please reconsider. The glass is down and the wind is growing by the minute."

"The Devil have you, Kelly. Are you questioning me?"

"No sir, never." After an uncertain pause, he continued. "Haven't I always stood by you?"

"Aye, you have, but now you're acting like a regular Judas."

"Doesn't that say how important this is? Please, for God's sake," Kelly said, his voice rising.

Clarke stood up, sending his chair tumbling backwards. He hobbled over to the gun rack and pulled down a rifle. He held it at his hip, and aimed it at his second hand. "There is one God that is Lord over this Earth, Mr. Kelly," he bellowed, "and one captain who is lord over the *Southern Cross*." He paused to catch his breath. "I've spoken my piece. Now leave me." He directed Kelly toward the door with the rifle.

The second hand stepped back.

Clarke's rage grew. A long finger wrapped itself around the trigger as he raised the gun to his shoulder and aimed it square at his second hand's face.

Kelly backed out of the cabin. "You're scaring me, George, but you haven't changed my mind." He continued to back off. Looking into the captain's eyes, he said. "Beware, old friend, beware. The Devil has you in his grip. It's his evil I'm hearing."

"I never trusted you, Kelly," Clarke shouted. "Everybody calls you this religious man, but I know better." His face was beet red. "It's no secret your family turned. Your people were once goddamned Micks. I always knew in my heart you were one of them. This proves it." A sneer came across his face. "Be gone, you Papist turncoat." He gestured forward with the gun.

Kelly stepped back even further into the deserted Common Room. The captain continued to aim the gun at Kelly, who, after a moment of indecision, turned on his heel and left.

Clarke slammed the door.

ii

As the grey light of early morning crept through the scuttles, 'tween decks came to life. The sound of talking grew, along with the increased smoke from bogies being lit for warmth and to boil tea.

"Boys," one sealer said as he came in from outside. "She's turned some coarse out there. The sky's grey as a ghost, and it's a stepmother's wind now." He wrapped his arms around himself and shivered. "There's sleet, too."

"Where're we at?"

"Can't say. We're still pushing east."

John peered out from his cover and looked around. Oil from the sculps stored on deck had begun to soak through the boards above him, sketching a form that reminded him of the ferocious black bird from his visions. He could feel the old ship rising and falling on much larger waves than he remembered from earlier. The *Cross* felt like she was labouring hard, but handling the larger seas well.

Then the ship crested a particularly big wave. John felt a shudder through the floor. At first it seemed as though nothing had happened. But within minutes the ship began to labour, like she'd lost her trim. John sat up and placed the tapered cork from his Radway's bottle on the floor. It rolled back and forth with the pitch of the ship, sketching semicircles. But the cork always gravitated toward the port side. "The sculps have shifted," John said to himself, "we're listing to port. Those pound boards were too rotten to hold the pelts in place." He shuddered as his fear heightened. John restowed the bottle in his pocket and then struggled up. He headed for the doorway to the main deck, picking his way through the crowds of sealers huddled around their small stoves.

"Lord Jesus, kid," someone hollered as he slipped out. "Close the damned door before I get the shivers."

He jerked the door shut. The howl and bluster of the growing storm replaced the noise in the hold. A brutal wind lashed his face.

John stepped out into seawater sloshing on the main deck, four inches deep. The green brine trapped on deck made its own waves, cascading in concert with the pitching of the ship, waves within waves, a storm within a storm.

He looked up and saw the scunner's barrel midway up the foremast. It looked like an inviting refuge as well as place from which he could get a better feel for how the ship was doing. John made his way to the rail and clambered over a lifeboat atop the stack of seal pelts. As he passed over the sculps his hands got coated with the seal grease he had been living with for weeks. That smell of death assaulted his nostrils again. He swung around on the ratline ladder and climbed upwards. Through the scud, he saw two men at the wheel, one in black oilskins, the other in yellow. They made frantic gestures at him, shouting, but nothing, save the howl of the wind, reached his ears. He continued up, breaking the ice coating the ratlines as he went. At the ladder top the young sealer pushed the trap door up and pulled himself up. It was unexpectedly quiet hunkered down there in the barrel; warmer too.

After a time, he got the feel of how the ship moved through the heavy seas. Up high, it was even clearer that the *Southern Cross* listed to port. After sliding down a trough and plunging her bow into the next wave, the old wooden ship never made it back up plumb.

John braced his hands on the barrel top and rode with the ship as she climbed the next wave. Closing his eyes, he embraced the wild ride as she plunged forward into the scud. For a moment he was distracted by the movement, so high up, so powerful. He remembered the photograph of a roller coaster he had seen in a copy of *Boys' Life* at Elsie's and wondered if this was how it would feel. His body danced with the pitch and weave of the boat. He shouted into the wind, drinking in the violence of the gale and the motion of the barrel, gusts whipping through his black hair. But when a large wave broke over the bow scattering spray so high it caught him in the face, John crashed back to the present. The inevitability of what was going to happen gripped him like a vice. He screamed as loudly as he could. "Goddamn you all. It serves you right. Every last one of you." The only reply was the screeching wind.

Another man joined those at the wheel, helping to hold her against the kick of the growing waves. All three hands leaned into the wind, holding onto the wheel for dear life. They squinted into the sleet, now showing flecks of snow. The storm whipped the skirts of their slickers out behind.

The *Southern Cross* continued to battle the heavy seas that battered her relentlessly. Never quite trim, she did her best to fight through the increasingly large grey mountains of water that coursed toward her. From his perch high up, John saw it coming before it struck the ship, a huge wave, twice the height of those they had been riding so far. He braced himself. The old ship dove into the wall of water. Spray exploded as she buried herself at the comber's base. Slowly she began to rise. Then the *Southern Cross* shuddered like an old dog and, after what seemed an eternity, rose to the top of the huge wave and tottered at the top. Decks awash, she crested the wave and began to slide down the back side. There was another explosion of spray, this time less violent than the last. A welcome steadiness returned to the ship. After three more waves the ship regained her composure.

"The old girl's doing well," John thought. "I hope that was just a single wave and not an outrider."

One of the men at the wheel had fallen. He pulled himself up, doused in brine. All three tied themselves in with lifelines.

Water trapped on the main deck was a foot deeper. The lifeboat over which John had just scrambled was gone, as were the others. The flags were in tatters.

iii

In the forepeak, the Rowe brothers and Gibbons boys were silent. The pitching of the ship had become so severe that getting up and walking was out of the question. They were forced to sit with their backs against whatever support they could find. Noah hunkered beside Jacob, both with their hands wrapped around their shins, foreheads resting on their knees.

iv

In the sick bay, Elias James did his best to keep his injured brother, Isaac, from rolling out of his cot.

231

v

Herb Butler lay on his bunk facing the wall. He paid no attention to the talk of the others which grew louder with each rise up a wave and suspenseful descent into the trough.

James Kelly sat on his bunk, back turned toward the others. His hands were clasped together at his chest, head down. "Please, oh Lord, deliver us from evil," he said over and over. The second hand began to rock back and forth. He closed his eyes. "Please, oh Lord, deliver us from evil."

vi

George Clarke arose from his bunk. He staggered over to the coat rack and struggled into his oilskins, almost falling three times as the ship pitched. He looked for his sou'wester but could not find it. "To hell with it," he said, lurching out toward the gangway. The captain clung to the wall in an effort to keep his balance. As he climbed the stairs to the upper deck he bellowed, "I'll show those bastards."

vii

From his position in the barrel, John could see that the sea had turned to a menacing black. The wind whisked sheets of grey spray off the top of each wave, making them appear even more ominous. Each wave beat down on the *Cross* with such force that he was not at all certain she would rise. Nonetheless, she did. The old girl was handling the seas better than he had expected.

John was startled to hear the sound of a ship's whistle pierce the wind's scream. A coastal steamer loomed out of the abyss, just off the *Cross's* bow. She ran with the wind, decks awash. The ship crested a wave and slid down, making brisk progress. The whistle of the *Southern Cross* moaned in reply, but the sound was overwhelmed by the howling wind. As she vanished into the scud, the steamer's stern rose on a swell. SS *Portia* was painted across her tail. As abruptly as the ship had come, she disappeared. The *Southern Cross* was alone again, shrouded by the merciless pounding of the North Atlantic and the frenzied snow.

Everything grew more intense. The pounding waves now erupted over the deck with every swell. Yet the ship was doing well.

Then the seas subsided. Several waves failed to rattle the ship. The North Atlantic grew calmer. The *Cross* pitched on the swell, but not with the same desperation. The waves changed, becoming confused and arriving at the ship from several directions at once. They rose in sea caps when they collided. The old ship handled these lesser waves more easily, but John could feel she was riding deeper in the water.

The snow cleared. John could see the entire deck of the ship below. Black smoke bellowed out of the funnel. The wind grabbed it the moment it left the stack, sending a flat column hurtling toward the stern. Water ran on deck, but not as deeply as before. She was settling down. "Maybe we've made it," John thought.

A hatless man emerged from the officers' quarters. With a limp, he made his way, hand-over-hand, toward the wheel. He nearly fell when the ship heeled over in the face of a strong gust. He slipped on his way to the wheel, grabbing it at the last minute to prevent himself from falling. John watched him dismiss the wheelmen who slithered to safety below deck. The man took his position at the wheel, legs apart, leaning into the gale. His hair was slicked wet as he stood up to the fierce storm with cocky defiance. He spun the wheel erratically to keep the *Cross* heading into the swell, no easy task in the confused sea that surrounded them.

The man at the wheel spotted John watching him. In the brief moment before the boy ducked down, he recognized George Clarke. The captain was taking matters into his own hands to show he was not only master of the *Southern Cross*, but of the North Atlantic as well.

Then the huge seas returned. Even bigger than before, the waves began to pummel the old ship with such force John could feel her shudder with each assault. He slid down into the barrel. After the *Cross* managed to survive a particularly large swell, John peeked out. He saw the deck space filled with water two-thirds up the sculps on deck. He watched, more curious than concerned, as the trapped water began to disappear. Before the next wave hit, the water level had dropped by half. Another comber came over the stacked pelts. Again, he watched the water trapped on deck disappear. The last wave had taken away most of the aft hatch cover.

The black smoke coming out of the ship's funnel began to change. Only slightly noticeable at first, it shifted to a dirty grey. Bit by bit the smoke lightened, then, as if by magic, it became pure white. The smoke had become steam. John's heart sank, "The engines have been doused. That's where all the water was going." The *Southern Cross* was dead in the water. John could feel the old ship slowly being pushed broadside by the powerful seas. Before long she was parallel to the waves. Her masts were swinging back and forth in the swell with such force that John had to hang on with all the strength he had. The sea began to push the ship around like a stick in river rapids. Water washed over the stacked seal pelts. The sea in the fully flooded main deck jammed the doors shut, trapping the crew inside. Within minutes, the upper decks ran with water.

Clarke's efforts to control the ship were now futile. Nonetheless, he kept spinning the wheel, trying to keep the *Cross* facing into the swell.

John watched as another huge wave swept up over the bridge. The water took Clarke's feet from beneath him. The big man tried desperately to hold onto the wheel but it broke and he was swept overboard. All John could see was Clarke's hatless head bobbing in the giant wave. The captain raised a fist upward toward the black sky as the distance between him and the ship grew. He was shouting something, but the only thing the boy could hear was the rush of the gale. Clarke disappeared into the scud.

The lower deck vanished beneath the sea, followed surprisingly quickly by the two higher decks. Gaffs, pound boards and stabber poles, everything not nailed down was being whisked away. John took his Radway's bottle from his pocket. He checked the cork, and then threw it as far as he could toward the dross on the water. He watched the bottle splash beside a piece of hatch cover and then pop up.

The ship was strangely steady as she submerged. The masts no longer swung crazily as she continued her descent. Soon the bridge vanished beneath the sea.

Three masts and the funnel, now without steam, was all he could see. John watched the black water consume the old sealer and creep up the mast. He hunkered down into the barrel and closed his eyes. A montage of images captured his mind, swirling, each melding seamlessly in to the next...

The terra cotta cliffs off Red Island with the impending peril of the summer storm. The smell of sulphur and a great explosion of ice. Tommy's face, red hair, freckles and silly grin. Ice covered with seals as far as he can see. Men, in concentric circles, singing as the Cross leaves the Narrows. The peaceful look on Issac's face. The rancid smell of St. John's. In a shivery voice, old Daniel tells about his rescue from Sand Pond. The slippery sensation of seal fat on his hands. Peter, smiles with kindness — he reaches toward him. Clarke, bristling with anger, screams at Herb Butler. The pong of evergreens on the rail line. His father's voice tells of the Devil on Red Island and slowly transforms into a scream of violence. Then Abel's face, windworn and wrinkled, smiles and invites him to be part of his world. He hears old Jacob's voice telling one of his tales. Then the old man reaches out to him as if calling him to a new world. A woman comes toward him and holds him to her breast. He knows it's his mother.

Then the ship was gone. The great shroud of the North Atlantic surged on as though nothing had happened. The *Southern Cross* had vanished forever.

THIRTY-FOUR

Eight months later, a small, dignified woman, dressed in black, entered the crowded courtroom gallery. She walked up and down the aisle searching for a seat. A tall, redheaded man stood up and motioned to a vacant chair beside him — the last in the room. The woman nodded and began to work along the row of chairs in front of people. After stumbling over several pairs of feet, she arrived at the man who stood to let her pass and then helped her with her overcoat. He draped it carefully over the back of the chair. "Thank you, young man," she said as they both sat down.

The oak woodwork in the courtroom gleamed, the brass shone, all doing their best to impart a sense of importance to this inquiry into the sinking of the SS *Southern Cross.*

"I wonder if we'll hear anything new," the man said.

"So do I," the woman replied. "I've been here for every session so far and can't say as I've learned much, just opinions, not many real facts. The only interesting part was when George's brother, John, told us how difficult a ship the *Southern Cross* was. He said she'd go over on her side if she was heavily loaded." She paused and looked over at the young man. "What brings you here?"

He hesitated. "My best friend shipped on the *Southern Cross.* I hoped I might find out what happened to him." He paused. "My other best friend was lost on the *Newfoundland.*"

"Oh, dear," the woman said as she looked down at the floor. "I'm so sorry." After a moment, she straightened up and offered her hand. "My name is Lucy Clarke."

He shook her outstretched hand, holding it gently like he thought it might break. "I'm Tommy Dunphy. I come from Red Island." He pivoted in his chair to face Lucy. "Did you say Clarke?"

She nodded.

"Are you related to the skipper?"

She nodded. "His wife."

Tommy looked away. "Oh." After a moment, he said, "It must have been a terrible time for you, waiting all that time to hear about your husband."

Lucy nodded. "Yes," she said. "It's particularly hard now because there's nothing left. George and his ship have simply vanished. There's nothing to hold on to, not a thing."

"Nothing?"

"The only things that tell the *Southern Cross* ever existed are a few photographs and an old ensign. That's it. She's gone, as if she never was." Lucy wiped a welling tear from her cheek.

"Aye, ma'am."

Tommy pulled out a crucifix that was hanging around his neck. He began to fiddle with it.

Lucy was watching and, after a moment, she sat back with a start. Under her breath she said, "Was it retribution?"

"Beg your pardon ma'am," Tommy said.

Lucy sat up, embarrassed. "Oh, nothing really. I just saw your cross there and it reminded me of something George said he'd do to that big white cross on the hill when he got home. It's nothing." She turned away.

After a few minutes Lucy asked, "What will you do now, Tommy?"

He looked over at her. "I'm not sure. After my time on the *Bloodhound* and losing my friends I wasn't happy back home — not the same anymore." He paused, looking out the window. "There's been so much happening I don't feel like I belong anywhere. I hear they're forming up a new company for the Regiment, seems this war is taking longer than they expected. I think I'll sign on — see the world. Maybe that'll help." His face flushed.

Lucy reached across and touched his shoulder. "I'm so sorry, young man. I hope you find what you're looking for."

"Thank you, ma'am."

A clerk, dressed in a black gown, entered, silencing the courtroom. He turned to the gallery and raised his hand. "All rise." The room filled with the sound of shuffling feet. "Hear ye, hear ye," the clerk said in a booming voice. "This Marine Court of Inquiry into the sinking of the SS *Southern Cross* is now reopened, on this 28th day of November, in the year of our Lord nineteen hundred and fourteen, the right honourable A. W. Knight presiding."

A portly man, also in a black gown, came in through a side door. He sported an ill-fitting white wig and wire-rimmed spectacles down over his nose. The judge tottered up to the dais and moved behind the pulpit-like desk that commanded a view of the entire room. With considerable stiffness he sat down, letting out a loud wheeze. "Be seated," he said in a voice with a British accent. He rapped his gavel. "Ladies and gentlemen," he said to the now silent room, "we are concerned here with the tragedy of the SS *Southern Cross*, being charged with the responsibility of assembling the facts that led to the loss of a fine sealing ship with its cargo of seals, as well as the drowning of one hundred and seventy-three men." He paused to catch his breath, looking at the gallery over the tops of his spectacles. "I've heard all kinds of accounts about wives being visited by fetches of their drowned husbands, flotsam from the ship being found as far away as Ireland, tales of men seeing the *Cross* as a ghost ship, all manner of stories trying to explain what happened. The challenge for us here is to get past these fictions, and down to the truth of the matter."

An awkward shuffle passed through the gallery.

The judge looked out over his spectacles. His voice softened. "I realize how difficult this has been for all of you, indeed for all the people of Newfoundland, not knowing what happened. I pray we will be able to make determinations here to ease, at least in small measure, the grief being felt by you all." He paused, struggling for words. "Today is the final day of our deliberations. I have every expectation that I will deliver my findings in a few days." He looked over to his clerk. "Is the final witness ready?"

The clerk nodded. "I call Walter Baine Grieve."

A rustle at the back of the court was followed by the footsteps of Grieve walking forward. The old merchant moved slowly, stooped over. He had black rings under his eyes.

The clerk guided him to a chair beside the judge's dais. "Your name and occupation."

"Walter Baine Grieve, merchant of St. John's."

"Thank you, please be seated."

Grieve lowered himself into the chair, eventually taking an uncomfortable position on the edge.

The judge took off his glasses. "Please, Mr. Grieve, tell this inquiry about your relation the *Southern Cross*."

The merchant began slowly, "I am a member of the firm of Baine, Johnston of St. John's. That firm has been responsible for the SS *Southern Cross* ever since 1901 when it was first engaged in the seal fishery of Newfoundland." He went on to give a brief history of the ship's successes up to 1913, his manner strangely distant and flat.

"Tell us about the trip this year."

In a monotone Grieve delivered a well-rehearsed summary of what was known about the *Cross*'s voyage. When he was finished, the judge asked the merchant if he had any opinion about what had happened.

Grieve nodded. "When the ship failed to arrive within a reasonable time after the storm, I concluded that she may have gone back to the ice in the Gulf. She had some St. Mary's men on board, so it also occurred to me that he might have gone to St. Mary's Bay for shelter." The merchant stopped talking and looked up at the judge.

"Go on."

"The other possibility was that Captain Clarke had tried to put his ship to sea with the result that she foundered." He stopped, looking down at the floor.

In a quiet voice, he said, "That appears to be what happened." Then he turned and spoke directly to the gallery. "The *Southern Cross* had a very high poop and forecastle with uncommonly high bulwarks. If she shipped a large quantity of water, she might have foundered before freeing herself of the water."

Excited talk burst out in the gallery.

"Silence," the judge said, punctuating his order with several raps of his gavel. Calm returned. "What can you tell us about the condition of the ship, Mr. Grieve?"

"This spring she was in first-class order. Mr. Black, the ship inspector from Lloyd's, reported that the ship was perfectly equipped for the seal fishery. Between 1902 and 1914 we spent a sum of over $20,000 upon the *Southern Cross* for up-keep and improvements."

The resulting buzz from the gallery was silenced by the judge's gavel.

Grieve continued. "I ordered the *Southern Cross* be well outfitted for the hunt, with adequate stores. Unfortunately, I cannot confirm this was achieved because Mister Cheeseman, the clerk I placed in charge, left the Island before I could contact him." The old merchant closed his eyes and stared at the floor. "I have no idea where he's gone." There was a long silence and then he looked up at the judge. "I've heard speculation that some of the *Southern Cross's* stores may have been skimmed off, but I can't be certain. To be sure, my other ship, the *Bloodhound*, was undersupplied, despite my orders that she not be." Grieve hesitated. "The good Lord only knows if the *Cross* was undersupplied, too. That may have prompted Captain Clarke to strike for home in the face of that storm." Grieve grew restless. Finally he said, "I just don't know, I just don't know."

"Thank you Mr. Grieve," the judge said, "is there anything you would like to add?"

Grieve was quiet for a moment and then looked out toward the gallery. Colour returned to his face. "I know how all you must feel about this dreadful tragedy. I've lived the same kind of hell you all have, praying to God that the *Southern Cross* would miraculously show up in the Narrows with her crew safe and sound. But, as we now know, that is not to be." He stopped to regain his composure. "If there is one thing we must do, it is to be certain we never forget those gallant men on the *Southern Cross*. When ships go down with no survivors, like the *Cross*, it is too easy to forget. There are no mementos, no stories from survivors, like there were with the *Newfoundland*. People remember the more sensational wrecks and pass over the others. We must not let that happen."

Again he stopped, but slowly resumed. "Compared to the *Newfoundland*, almost a hundred more men were lost on the *Cross*, making her the greatest tragedy ever on the floes. Yet the *Newfoundland* seems to be all they talk about. I'm afraid the *Southern Cross* may be doomed to vanish from memory, just like she did from the North Atlantic." Grieve stopped a third time, seemingly finished, but then added. "That would be another tragedy." The room was completely silent.

"Thank you, Mr. Grieve."

The merchant stood up. Every eye was on him as he plodded toward the back of the room.

The clerk stood and announced: "Today's proceedings are now concluded. All rise."

The old judge eased himself out of his chair and waited for the room to become quiet. He turned to the gallery, looking over his spectacles, and said, "We have found no direct evidence as to the cause of the tragedy of the *Southern Cross*. In my report I will state my view that she foundered and went down with all hands in the heavy gale and snowstorm of March 31st. From all accounts, this occurred in the vicinity of Cape Pine."

The gallery was dead silent as the judge began to leave. He stopped himself and turned back. "There are times when words fail," he said in a much less formal voice. "Try as I might, I cannot shake from my mind the image of those brave men struggling through that fierce storm." He hesitated, taking off his spectacles to rub his eyes. "I pray those gallant lads reached heaven safe and sound." He smiled. "No doubt, they're living the wonderful lives denied them here on this hard Island. I can see them laughing and clowning around in my mind's eye — somehow that makes it a bit easier to bear." He looked out at the gallery struggling to find the right words. Finally he turned and tottered off toward his chambers.

"That wasn't much," Tommy said to Lucy. "Sounded more like Grieve was trying to protect his precious investments than tell us what happened."

"He did the best he could. He probably doesn't know any more than we do."

ii

The train began to slow down and screeched to halt at Whitbourne. Abel Lundrigan disembarked. He looked much older and stooped over than he had a year ago. The fisherman began walking toward the Placentia train which was waiting on a siding. The rain had let up a bit.

In a crowd of young men on the platform, he saw someone he recognized. "Tommy, Tommy Dunphy," he called out as he approached.

The redhead stopped talking, squinted, and upon recognizing the old fisherman, left his friends and came over toward Abel. "Hello, Mr. Lundrigan," he said, "What are you doing here?"

"Been in St. John's waiting for John to come home."

Tommy's face fell, seeing that the old man did not seem to know what had happened to his son. "How're you feeling, sir?" He asked cautiously.

"Best kind, son, best kind," the old fisherman said. He stood back and inspected the young man. "You look good boy, like a real sealer. You heading home?"

Tommy smiled. "Yep. I'm going home to see the parents. Where you off to?"

"I'm going home, too. I have to be there for when John gets back. Got to get the business growing so there's room for him when he arrives." Abel smiled, oblivious to the concerned look on the boy's face.

"But, sir," Tommy sputtered, "John's dead. He drowned on the *Southern Cross*."

"No, boy," Abel said. "They put him ashore in Channel and he went over to Canada. He'll be back as soon as he gets that travel bug out of his blood."

Tommy's eyes opened wide. "Is that true? Have you heard from him?"

"No, not yet, but four men now have told me that John was the stowaway they landed in Port aux Basques. Figure he headed west once they let him go in Channel. 'Twas a happy day, I'll tell you, when I heard that." A lopsided grin spread across his face.

"But he had a ticket. He wasn't a stowaway."

Abel paid no attention. He spoke fervently. "Isn't it grand he's still alive?"

Tommy grimaced. Slowly, as one might speak to a child, the young man said, "Yes, Mr. Lundrigan, it's grand he's still with us." They grew quiet. Finally Abel said, "Tell me, Tommy. Can you remember anything else that might help me find John? Anything?" He grabbed Tommy's arm.

"I can't think of anything. As far as I know he signed onto the *Cross* using a false name. The last I saw he was heading down to Baine, Johnston's with that blue chest and his gaff, happy as a clam. That's all I know." Tommy freed his arm from Abel's grip. After an awkward pause, he added, "Come to think of it though, we did see some wreckage on the water on our way home from sealing, near Cape Ballard."

"Really? What was it like?"

"Gaffs, pound boards, a Radway's bottle, even a sealer's cap. We didn't know the *Cross* was overdue then, but it was from a sealer. I wonder if that was her?"

"Did you pick up any of that wreckage on the water?"

"No, sir, the seas were too heavy. The *Kyle* followed us back to port and I hear she never found any sign of it when she went back out to look for it." Tommy's face darkened as he turned away from Abel. "You know," he said in a whisper, "I saw a chest on the water that looked a lot like that blue one John had, metal corners." He fell silent.

The old fisherman put his hand on Tommy's shoulder. "Don't give up boy," he said with unexpected softness. "I know John is still alive. I can feel it in my bones."

The whistle blew on the Placentia train.

"We better get over there before she pulls out," Abel said.

"No, sir," Tommy said. "I'm walking from here."

"But it's raining. Why would you walk?"

Tommy blushed. "Oh, I just like to walk this time of year. Hardly a stain of weather in the sky," he said with a wink. "And she's some warm. Walking's good for what ails you."

"I can buy a ticket for you if you want, Tommy." He reached into his pocket.

"No, sir. Thank you very much, sir," the boy said. "I want to walk—need time to think. Now you go get on your train before she leaves."

Abel turned and began to walk away. He didn't look back.

Tommy waited for the train to leave and then began to walk the rail line. His stride was awkward at first, but soon he slipped into a brisk rhythm. As he got deeper into the woods he began to think more and more about John. He re-lived his friend's journey along the rail line when he went to see Doc Newtry. He remembered many of the wonderful times they'd had in their great adventure in St. John's. While sad at first, the more he reflected on their time together, the lighter his heart became. Somehow he knew John's spirit was doing well. Hap-piness, unknown for months, began to surge up from within. He ambled through the endless cavern in the trees, passing section man shacks, waving at children. Tommy rounded a corner and saw a long trestle over a rock-strewn river. He began to sing.

> Oooooh, the Block House flag is up today
> To welcome home the stranger
> Annnnnd Stewart's House is looking out
> For Barbour and the Ranger

Louder singing filled the empty landscape.

> But Job's are wishing Blandford first
> Who never missed the patches
> He struck them on the twenty-third
> And filled her to the hatches

Tommy came to at turn in the railbed, atop a hill. He looked down at the grand view of a tree-covered land spread out before him. The sun exploded from behind the clouds, bathing the land like a giant floodlight. A rainbow, faintly shimmering at first, then intensely vivid, spread across the sky in front of him. The red on top was as radiant as any he had seen. The stripe on the bottom glis-tened in saturated purple. A huge flock of birds flew south. Whisked by a warm wind, the scraggly black clouds retreated before the strengthening sun. The whole landscape throbbed with life — a new beginning.

EPILOGUE

One hundred seventy-three men perished when the *Southern Cross* went down on March 31, 1914, the greatest tragedy ever to befall the sealing industry. Drawn from towns across the Avalon Peninsula, as well as St. John's, her crew was the "flower of Newfoundland youth." The following list of crew, arranged by hometown, hints at the enormity of these losses.

HARBOUR GRACE
Arthur Benson
John Bradbury
Herbert Bray
James Bray
John Callahan
William Coombes
George French
John Griffin
Elias James
Issac James
Thomas James
William James
W. C. Janes
Ronald Knight
James Lynch
Arthur Martin
M. Morrissey
Norman Noel
Ernest Noseworthy
James Noseworthy
Lorenzo Parsons
Wilfred Parsons
Herb Pynn
William Webber
Mark Yetman

ST. JOHN'S
John Boland
Gregory Bremnan, Fireman
Walter Clarke
Thomas Connell, 2nd Engineer
John Ebbs
John Field
W. Hammond, 3rd Engineer
Allan Lindsay
John Mansfield
James Martin
David Parsons, Chief Engineer
Charles Quetel
James Robertson
M. Scammell, Fireman
Fred Squires
Patrick Stepleton, Fireman
W. Walsh, Fireman
John Whalen, Fireman
Lawrence Yeo

SPANIARD'S BAY
Thomas Barrett
George Chapman
Nathan Chetman
Art Clarke
Robert Clarke
William Clarke
Ed. Crane
Robert Goss
George Smith
George Vokey
Isaac Vokey
William Vokey
Joseph Yetman

CARBONEAR
Hy Clarke
Oscar Forward
Robert Gillett
John P. Hiscock
William J. Howe
George Murray

Josiah Newel
James F. Patrick
Amos Penney
Norman Penney
Robert Penney
Alfred Pike

FOXTRAP

Joseph Batton
Alfred Bussey
Gordon Bussey
Noah Bussey
Thomas Bussey
Henry Butler
W. C. Butler
George Patten
Ambrose Taylor

KELLIGREWS

John Bishop
Joseph Bussey
Samuel Butler
William Butler
William J. Butler
Uriah Button
Henry Leary
James Maley
Samuel Ridout

BRIGUS

George Clarke, Master
John Clarke
James Kelly, 2nd hand
Noah Sparkes
Thomas Sparkes
B. Watts
Angus Winsor
Joseph Youdon

COLLIERS
Patrick Burke
Ed. Cole
John Cole
John Conway
M. Conway
George Hall
John Walsh

ST. VINCENT'S, PLACENTIA BAY
Cornelius Fleming
Edward Gibbons
Lawrence Gibbons
Sebastian Gibbons
Thomas Gibbons
James Walsh

PARADISE
Albert Clarke
John W. Clarke
Walter Lynch
Ambrose Sharp
William Sharp

CONCEPTION HARBOUR
John Costello
Thomas Costello
John Mansfield
James Walsh

ISLAND COVE
John Coombes
John Mercer
James Neil
John Robbins

LONG POND, MANUELS
James Porter
Henry Smith
John J. Stanley
William Stanley

SEAL COVE
William Kearney
Samuel Kennedy
Alex Morgan
Joseph Morgan

CATALINA
Elias Mason
Charles Norman
Walter Pierce

CUPIDS
Herb Butler
William Norman
Kenneth Taylor

TOPSAIL
George Hiscock
Alex Squires
Ed Squires

TORBAY
John Evens
Alex Field
Thomas Manning

BROAD COVE
Fred Follett
James Squires

CHANCE COVE
Jacob Rowe
Noah Rowe

CLARKE'S BEACH
Joseph Corbett
Eleazar Morris

LOW POINT
James Blundon
John Hannon

NEW CHELSEA
John Landry
Ambrose Matthews

OUTER COVE
Walter Carroll
Walter O'Rourke

UPPER ISLAND COVE
Fred Newell
Martin Newell

ADEYTOWN
Abner Harris

ARNOLD'S COVE
James W. Hollett

BREEN'S COVE
Thomas Bright

FERMEUSE
Edward Kenney

GOULDS
Patrick Hearn

GREY ISLANDS
James Foley

HOLYROOD
Thomas Hickey

HORSE COVE
James Quilty

LITTLE BAY
William Gosse

LOGY BAY
Pat Dyer

LOWER ISLAND COVE
Ben Robbins

NEWMAN'S COVE
Leonard Skiffington

NORTHERN BAY
William Walsh

PETTY HARBOUR
Hy. J. Chafe

RED ISLAND
John Lundrigan

ST. MARY'S
William White

TILTON
Edward Barrett

TOR'S COVE
James Dunphy

TURK'S GUT
Thomas Bartlett

Shortly after the inquiry, official memory of the *Southern Cross* began to fade. Other events, such as the outbreak of the First World War just months later, began to fill the newspapers. Their pages contained equally devastating lists of Newfoundlanders lost in battles such as Beaumont Hamel, July 1, 1916. Nearly a whole generation of young men and future leaders was lost to the sealing disasters and the First World War, leaving a terrible vacuum in the fabric of the Colony, one that took years to overcome.

ii

This book is fiction, a story created within the framework of the calamitous events of the spring of 1914. The narrative dances between the lines of official history, in an effort to honour what happened and those involved.

Background information was garnered from many sources, especially Shannon Ryan's *Ice Hunters*, George Allan England's *The Greatest Hunt in the World*,

Levi Chafe's *Sealing Book*, Cassie Brown's *Death on the Ice*, the pages of the *Evening Telegram*, and Paul O'Neill's *Oldest City*. Specific sources include:

Abel's story about the Devil on Red Island in Chapter Two is based on a tale in Alice Lannon and Michael McCarthy's *Fables, Fairies & Folklore of Newfoundland*. St. John's, NL: Jesperson Press, 1991, pp. 43-46.

The lyric for Tommy's song in Chapter Nine ("With bat and gaff...") is excerpted from a song entitled "Seal Hunting Song" in James Murphy's pamphlet *Songs sung by old-time sealers many years ago*. St. John's, NL: James Murphy, 1925.

The song that John sang while walking the rail line in Chapter Eleven and that Tommy reprised in Chapter Thirty-Four is a slightly modified version of "The Sealers' Song" from Gerald S. Doyle's *Old-time songs of Newfoundland* (3rd edition). St. John's, NL: Gerald S. Doyle, 1955, p. 52. You can hear this song sung by Jim Payne and Fergus O'Byrne on the enclosed CD.

The heave-up shanty, sung as the boys were pulling the *Bloodhound* out of the ice in Chapter Nineteen, is entitled "Heave Away," from Jim Payne and Fergus O'Byrne's CD *Wave Over Wave* (St. John's, NL: Singsong Records, 1995). A recorded version is available for download at www.singsonginc.ca.

The farewell shanty, sung by the crew as the *Southern Cross* was leaving St. John's in Chapter Twenty-Four, is based on "Homeward Bound," in Gerald S. Doyle's *Old-time songs and poetry of Newfoundland* (5th edition). St. John's NL: Gerald S. Doyle, 1979, p. 25. A recorded version is available for download as "Bound for St. Peters" on Jim Payne and Fergus O'Byrne's album *Wave Over Wave* at www.singsonginc.ca.

The song Herb Butler sang in the officer's quarters in Chapter Twenty-Seven is based on "Sealing Fifty Years Ago" in Shannon Ryan and Larry Small's *Hauling Rope and Gaff*. St. John's NL: Breakwater, 1978, p. 63.

Parts of the dialogue in Chapter Thirty-Four are based on the transcript entitled "*Inquiry into the Sinking of the* Southern Cross," kindly made available by the Newfoundland Public Archives.

The *Southern Cross* crew list in the Epilogue is from the *Evening Telegram*, April 4, 1914, p. 4.

iii

I first encountered the *Southern Cross* when I heard Omar Blondahl sing a ballad about the tragedy. That was in 1961. When I had a chance to do some research during a sabbatical fellowship at Memorial University of Newfoundland in 1979, I began to chase down details of this story that had captured my imagination. I received invaluable help and encouragement from Ted Rowe, Graham Skanes, Hank Williams, Martin Labba, Tom Burke, to mention only a few. I chatted to many intriguing people like Grace Roberts, Clarke's niece; Joe Prim, Angelina Burke and Kitch Moore, discovering all sorts of details that fed into this great tale.

The academic articles I wrote about the *Cross* were not up to the task of telling the story. The human dimensions of this tragedy could not survive the passive, distancing prose demanded by the academy. Over the years, the untold aspects of this great tale festered in my unconscious, finally bursting forth when Fred Stenson encouraged me to "go for it" and write it as a fictional novel. The lack of detail about what really happened made doing a non-fiction piece impossible, so a fictional account was all that remained.

Deciding to go ahead with a novel put me face to face with the challenge of learning a different style of writing, one that would allow me to address the unbelievable human dimensions of this tale. The list of people who helped me as I tried to shuck off forty years of academic writing is very long. I would especially like to thank Betty Jane Hegeret, Bruce Porter, Rona Altrows and Audrey Thomas for their insight and helpful nudges and prods as I worked toward trying to learn the craft of fiction writing. In addition, the critiques of many friends and colleagues were invaluable. Included here are Patty Rogers, Liann Bobechko, John Leeder, Fran Keevil, Linden Rogers and my colleagues at the Alexandra Centre in Calgary and Banff Centre's "Writing with Style" Program.

The image of the SS *Southern Cross* on the front cover is used with the permission of The Rooms Provincial Archives Division, St. John's, NL. The photo on the back cover is used with permission of the Maritime History Archive, Memorial University of Newfoundland, St. John's, NL.

Sincere thanks go to the late Cliff Kadatz who designed the map, Todd Manning who designed the cover, Joanne Snook-Hann who did the layout and inside page design and Bill Hanna for his help navigating the publication seas. Thanks to the Double Paradox Image Consortium for the photo of me. Joan Sullivan's editorial wisdom was most helpful and Donna Francis's help during all stages of getting the book ready was most appreciated.

I also want to express my heartfelt appreciation to Jim Payne who not only provided advice on song selection for the text, but who also, along with Fergus O'Byrne, did such a marvellous job on the CD. Jim was also exceeding helpful in providing information on the songs on the recording.

Thank you all.

Through all of this, one person's constant support and insightful commentary was critical. Indeed, the book would not have happened were it not for Ted Rowe, whom I met in graduate school, and who is now a dear friend. Ted was a beacon of encouragement and an unending font of information and contacts as I went through the various stages of preparing this book. I cannot possibly thank him enough for the countless hours he spent working through various drafts, giving suggestions for framing the story, and helping to minimize my CFA gaffes (those that survived are purely of my doing). I thank him most profoundly for his generosity, wisdom and understanding.

THE CD

One of the goals of this book is to animate the lives and times of sealers in the early nineteenth century—to bring to life the humour, the hard work, the seriousness of purpose, the pain and the joy that was so much part of how they and their families lived. While the written word is critical to this, music adds another dimension, one that sometimes escapes even the most valiant attempts to write it. There's something about a well-sung song that tells us more than we might otherwise understand from words alone. We are fortunate that some of the music composed and sung during these times has survived, providing us with a unique snapshot of the sealing industry and its people during that period. We are doubly fortunate that some very talented performers have dedicated themselves to presenting this music in a way that honours these brave men and their families. The CD included with "The Mystery of the SS *Southern Cross*" is a very special presentation of this vibrant music and offers us a rich insight into the times. Whether it is rollicking song celebrating the seal hunt, a tragic ballad written by a grieved relative, or a poem that helps provide closure, the CD paints an intimate portrait of these troubled, yet very special times. Two of the very best Newfoundland traditional singers, Jim Payne and Fergus O'Byrne, have poured their creative energies into this project and the result is a stunning recreation of music that was part-and-parcel of the lives lived by the kinds of people we met in the novel.

THE SONGS

The *Southern Cross*: The first track on the CD is one of two songs entitled "The *Southern Cross*". This one is by far the less common and more rarely heard of the two. It takes the position of someone trying to fathom the uncertainty of the *Cross*'s fate. Written in what might be considered an "old school" poetic style, the writer looks to the wind over the waves to reveal what may have happened.

Collected in 1976 by Genevieve Lehr and Anita Best from the late Carrie Brennan of Ship Cove, Placentia Bay, it appeared in the song collection *Come and I Will Sing You*, edited by Genevieve Lehr, and published by University of Toronto Press in 1985.

The Sealers' Song: This rollicking ditty about a sealing voyage forced to seek shelter in Trinity Bay, and the ensuing hijinks, is sung to the tune of a well-known Newfoundland melody, "The Girl I Left Behind Me". There are several other short songs in the Newfoundland sealing tradition also sung to this melody. This version appears in *Old-Time Songs of Newfoundland: Songs of the People from the Days of Our Forefathers*, 3rd edition, 1955, published by Gerald S. Doyle Ltd.

of St. John's, Newfoundland. Incidentally, Brenmer's store, as mentioned in the song, was in Catalina, Trinity Bay.

In Chapter Eleven, John Lundrigan sings a slightly modified version of this song as he walks along the rail line on his trek to Little Harbour. It is also reprised in Chapter Thirty-Four, this time sung by Tommy Dunphy.

Elegy for Lost Sealers: This poem was written by well-known Newfoundland historian and poet, the late Paul O'Neill. It is a poignant tribute to the countless men who went to the ice. The words are copyright to The Estate of Paul O'Neill, and used by permission from Irene O'Neil and the Estate of Paul O'Neill. The poem was published in *Doryloads*, an anthology of Newfoundland literature, edited by Kevin Major and published by Breakwater Books of St. John's in 1974. Fergus O'Byrne composed the music.

Ice in the Harbour/Uncle Bern's Jig: In telling of his adventures aboard the *Bloodhound* in Chapter Nine, Tommy Dunphy raved about "the accordion player from Keels who could play the notes off a banker." This track of the CD gives a sense of what Tommy would have heard back then, and throughout the sealing fleet of the times.

The lively tunes on this track are a fitting counterpoint to the songs telling the tragic side of the story with ships and men lost to the ice. They were composed by Jim Payne and are representative of the kind of dance music popular in Newfoundland and Labrador, then and now. The tunes are played on the king of instruments, the 4-stop button accordion.

Lines Written on the Missing SS *Erna*: In Chapter Four of the novel we met the SS *Erna*. She was a steel-hulled steamer that Greive's firm had refitted as a sealer. As we learned in subsequent chapters, the *Erna* was the reason why George Clarke became a captain. The SS *Bloodound*'s former captain was sent to Scotland to bring the *Erna* back to Newfoundland in the spring of 1912, leaving the *Hound* to be Clarke's first ship. Sadly, the *Erna* never made it to St. John's, foundering with all hands somewhere in the North Atlantic. These were the very seas that claimed the HMS *Titanic* the same spring.

The *Erna*, previously named *Prins Hendrik*, was a steel screw steamer built in 1890 by Messrs. Caird & Co. Ltd, Greenock, Scotland, for the Stoomvaart Maatsehappij, Nederland. She was purchased from them by Messrs. Murray & Crawford in September, 1911, for the purpose of converting her into a sealer.

Fergus O'Byrne created this moving tribute by putting a poem written at the time to music.

Sally Brown: In Chapter Nineteen, John and the boys became part of a crew pulling two ships out of the ice in St. John's Harbour. While hauling away, a shanty broke out to help coordinate the work and help time pass. This track is one of a number of such shanties from Newfoundland tradition and gives a flavour of what the young Lundrigan would have heard. "Sally Brown," is a capstan or windlass shanty popular on sailing ships the world over. This version was widely sung by Newfoundland seamen in the early part of the 20th century. Also found in Gerald S. Doyle Ltd. *Old-Time Songs of Newfoundland: Songs of the People from the Days of Our Forefathers,* it originally appeared in *Ballads and Sea Songs of Newfoundland,* collected by Elisabeth Bristol Greenleaf and Grace Yarrow Mansfield, published in 1933 by Harvard University Press. They got it from the singing of Captain John Gullage and members of his crew aboard the SS *Sagona* in 1929.

"Heave Away" is the shanty John helped to sing in Chapter Nineteen. You can download this song, performed by Jim Payne and Fergus O'Byrne on their album *Wave Over Wave,* at www.singsonginc.ca.

A Noble Fleet of Sealers: In the wonderful tradition of local songwriting, this sprightly number provides a portrait of sealing around 1914. Many local personages and ships are mentioned as we're transported into the bravado of the times with a nod to the hard work and trials experienced by the men.

This another song from *Old-Time Songs of Newfoundland: Songs of the People from the Days of Our Forefathers,* 3rd edition, 1955, published by Gerald S. Doyle Ltd. The melody was also used in another well-known Newfoundland song "The Old *Polina*", which is itself a variant of a widely sung Scottish whaling song, "The Old *Baleena*".

The *Southern Cross*: This ballad reads almost like a newspaper account of the events surrounding the *Southern Cross.* It tells of various sightings of the ship and things that occurred, sometimes using verbatim quotes from newspaper articles. The concluding verse sums up what must have been one of the few hopeful sentiments that could have emerged during those dreadful times when the fate of the *Cross* was becoming clear.

This song about the *Southern Cross* is widely known, having been performed by numerous other singers over the years. It was collected by Greenleaf and Mansfield for their *Ballads and Sea Songs of Newfoundland,* Harvard University Press, 1933. They learned the song from the singing of Philip Major of Sally's Cove, Great Northern Peninsula. "The *Southern Cross*" was also published in the 1955 Gerald S. Doyle Ltd. collection as remembered by Lizzie Rose of Fox Harbour (now St. Lewis) Labrador.

The CD was produced by Jim Payne and Fergus O'Byrne for SingSong Inc. Recorded at SingSong Studios, St. John's, NL. Mixed by Jim Payne and Kevin Pinhorn at Record Time Productions, 55 Bond St., St. John's NL. March, 2014.

THE PERFORMERS

Jim Payne, a native of Notre Dame Bay, Newfoundland, is one of the province's most prolific songwriters, as well as being a singer of traditional songs, a multi-instrumentalist, storyteller, writer, actor, and instructor and caller of traditional Newfoundland set and square dances.

Jim owns and operates his own recording label, SingSong Inc., which has released twenty-nine titles, and produces special event programming for conferences, conventions, festivals and other celebrations, and educational and historical events featuring traditional and contemporary music, song, story and dance that reflect the Newfoundland experience.

Jim is also an adventurer who has sailed through the North West Passage on several occasions, travelled extensively by sea through the Canadian and Scandinavian Arctic, and participated in numerous expeditions in the Southern Ocean to Antarctica, South Georgia and the Falkland Islands.

Jim has also appeared in most of Rising Tide Theatre's annual Revues and is a past recipient of the NL Arts Council's Arts in Education and Outstanding Cultural Achievement Awards, a Cultural Tourism Award from the provincial Dept. of Tourism and the federal Dept. of Canadian Heritage, and a Queen's Diamond Jubilee Medal. He has developed and teaches a course in traditional Newfoundland accordion music at Memorial University's School of Music, and in 2011, he was one of five world musicians, and the only one from North America, invited to Kagoshima, Japan to participate in a symposium on musicians whose original songs have become part of local traditions.

Fergus O'Byrne was born in Dublin, Ireland and emigrated to Canada in 1967, where he became a founding member of the Irish folk band, Ryan's Fancy. The band recorded fourteen albums and was featured on the CBC network series, *Ryan's Fancy*, for five years, and on the *Tommy Makem/Ryan's Fancy* show, which was syndicated throughout Canada and the world.

In 1987, Fergus graduated from Memorial University of Newfoundland with a degree in Education. Since then he has been bringing folk music to children both as a classroom teacher and a performer. He has developed a program of songs, stories and slides related to his native Ireland for use in schools and leads a series of initiatives around the province through the auspices of the St. John's Folk Arts Society called *Young Folk at the Hall*, designed to get young people playing traditional music.

Fergus has been a member of the award-winning band Tickle Harbour, and is a past recipient of the NL Arts Council's Arts in Education Award, as well as

Music NL's Music Educator of the Year Award. In 2004, Ryan's Fancy received the East Coast Music Award's Dr. Helen Creighton Award, in recognition of three individuals who had "a profound and lasting effect on the Atlantic Canadian music industry".

Together, Jim Payne and Fergus O'Byrne have brought Newfoundland music to the world, performing extensively throughout Canada, the United States, Europe, Japan and Australia. They are two thirds of the popular musical comedy trio, Wicked Altogether, with Pete Soucy (Snook) and half of the traditional music band, A Crowd of Bold Sharemen. They have recorded several CDs with a heavy emphasis on maritime and seafaring music, produced radio programs around specific historical themes, and performed in a variety of unusual settings including an annual tour of offshore oil installations on the Grand Banks of Newfoundland. As solo acts and members of various local ensembles, they have contributed to several anthologies of Newfoundland music, and performed on recordings by a variety of Newfoundland artists.

You can find music by Jim and Fergus, along with several other folk and traditional Newfoundland and Labrador artists at www.singsonginc.ca.

Tim B. Rogers

Tim Rogers's job as a professor at the University of Calgary was interfering with his writing, so he quit. That was six years ago. Since then, he's been picking up the pieces of a writerly career that was emerging, albeit in fits and starts, during the few peaceful intervals of his day job.

In 1979, as part of a longstanding interest in people's music, Tim spent a sabbatical in Newfoundland. He took courses in folklore and folk music. When he researched a ballad about the *Southern Cross*, he found himself drawn into the mystery of that immense tragedy. As the story began to bubble in his unconscious (some might say fester), he wrote several academic articles about the event. But these failed to quell the growing need to tell the human side of this great story.

As his academic career progressed, he developed an increasing interest in story telling. He wrote several major textbooks adopting narrative to teach complex topics like psychological testing and research methodology. This, combined with his fascination with the *Southern Cross*, led to increasingly frequent trips to Newfoundland where he began to pull together the pieces of "The Mystery of the SS *Southern Cross*." At the same time he began to work at the difficult job of shucking off forty years of academic writing to enable writing this grand story as a novel.

Tim presently lives in Victoria, but retreats to his small farm in the Purcell Mountains as frequently as he can manage. In addition to treasured writing time, flyfishing and legendary campfires, at which songs about cowboys, railways and the *Southern Cross* come to life, are mainstays of these wilderness retreats which nourish his passion to tell stories of the people.